WING COMMANDER:
PILGRIM STARS

Also available from HarperEntertainment

Wing Commander Novelization

Wing Commander Junior Novelization

Wing Commander Confederation Handbook

WING COMMANDER:
PILGRIM STARS

by Peter Telep

HarperEntertainment
A Division of HarperCollinsPublishers

■ HarperEntertainment

A Division of HarperCollins*Publishers*

10 East 53rd Street, New York, N.Y. 10022-5299

ISBN 0-06-105986-2

First printing: September 1999

Printed in the United States of America

Visit HarperEntertainment on the World Wide Web at
http://www.harpercollins.com

❖ 10 9 8 7 6 5 4 3 2 1

FOR KENDALL ANNE

ACKNOWLEDGMENTS

Warm thanks as always to the folks at HarperCollins: John Douglas, Caitlin Blasdell, Rich Miller, and John Silbersack for their continued commitment to my writing.

Chris McCubbin and David Ladyman at Incan Monkey God Studios gave their much-needed advice and criticism during the early stages of this work. Moreover, the *Wing Commander Confederation Handbook*, produced by Chris and the other talented people at IMGS, allowed me to create a strong sense of continuity within this new *Wing Commander* film-based universe. I'm deeply indebted to their fine work. Those familiar with the handbook will notice my many allusions to it in this text.

I'd be remiss if I did not salute Mr. Ben Lesnick and the other passionate and articulate members of the Wing Commander Combat Information Center website. They provided me with timely information on film-related news, answered my pesky questions, and even helped to promote my work.

Finally, I'm overjoyed to note that my wife delivered our second daughter during the writing of this novel. Any woman who can do that and put up with a workaholic geek like me should either be committed or get a medal. Actually, she had expensive jewelry in mind . . .

VEGA SECTOR,
DOWNING QUADRANT

NEAR THE KILRATHI
BORDER

2654.079

1100 HOURS
IMPERIAL STANDARD
TIME

Flight Captain Torshk nar Caxki drew in a long breath of nutrient gas, felt his whiskers brush annoyingly against the inside of his helmet, then shifted his head to fix tawny eyes on the void that enveloped his Dralthi fighter. Four plastisteel talons extended from the wings of his craft like burnished spikes threatening to impale any ship or sentient who dared venture into Kilrathi territory. For the moment, though, there were no trespassers, and Torshk predicted that he and the rest of Gold and Black Claw Squadrons would not engage in battle any time soon. Their task force of two Ralari-class destroyers and a Thrakhra-class ConCom ship had been ordered to break off from the *Shak'Ar'Roc* battle group to perform a routine border patrol. If Torshk had his way, they would be penetrating Confederation space and attacking Confederation ships, not sniveling like lowborns on their side of the fence. But Torshk knew he must obey his orders without question, focus on the strongest threat if one miraculously presented itself, and respond to any challenge. Yes, he understood the Kilrathi social constructs that dictated his behavior, but a blood frenzy simmered within, one that would soon reach a boil.

Reports had come in of Kalralahr Bokoth's death, and Torshk

found it difficult to believe that the emperor had not ordered a retaliatory strike on the Confederation. Bokoth had been one of the empire's most revered admirals and a member of the imperial house. He had taken the famed super-dreadnought KIS *Grist'Ar'Roc* into Vega Sector, had destroyed the Confederation's Pegasus Naval Station, and had managed to steal the station's Navcom AI, a computational system that would guide the Kilrathi through the Charybdis Quasar and directly to Earth. According to spy satellite reports, Bokoth's ship had reached the Sol system but had been brutally ambushed by a Confederation battle group. The hairless apes had taken Bokoth's life with, it now seemed, impunity. Though Torshk did not belong to Bokoth's clan, he felt the blow just as painfully. The emperor had already begun uniting the major noble clans of Kilrah, and Torshk's clan, the Caxki, had been one of the first to join the new imperial alliance. Before scrambling for the patrol, Torshk had discussed his frustration with the rest of his squadron. They understood his rage and had tried to quell it by reminding him of the rumors that Bokoth's ship may have been destroyed by a gravity well and that the admiral's plan to attack Earth relied upon his trust in a human traitor, a human who belonged to an ancient and strange clan of humans called Pilgrims. Torshk refused to believe that one as highborn as Bokoth could make such an error. He shook his pale head and bared fangs as a hiss rose from his gut. *No, Bokoth. You did not dishonor the imperial house. You died a warrior's death and your soul shall find solace in Sivar's hand.*

Swallowing a bitter tang, Torshk toggled on his tactical display as a diversion from his introspection. A schematic of the task force appeared on the screen. The two destroyers glided directly overhead, their cylindrical hulls and stubby prows affirming their battering power. Rotating sensor dishes and an array of imperial satellite link antennae crowned T-shaped super-structures whose viewports appeared as silhouettes since the ships operated in stealth mode. Above the destroyers hung the ConCom ship, a command and communications vessel with a hull design that reminded Torshk of his own Dralthi. Shoots of sharp-edged plastisteel extended amidships, curved forward, and reached well past the bow like *Koractu* swords. A lone portside wing jutted out and supported two hardpoints for six ship-to-planet missiles that should have been replaced by ship-to-ship missiles, but departure orders had allowed no time for that. The ConCom probed the area of operations with powerful, long-range sensors, searching for electromagnetic emissions and for sudden releases of photons and neutrinos—part of any invading ship's post-jump residuum. Torshk doubted they would pick up anything. "Gold Claw Leader to Dark Eye. Report on contacts."

The ConCom's communications officer, Sh'ahte nar Caxki, peeled back his gray lips, and the thick fold of skin on his brow lowered in fury. "Gold Claw Leader, you have disobeyed the order for silence."

Torshk narrowed his eyes and took several long breaths. "There are no contacts, are there?"

"Break transmission now."

Extending a serrated nail through a slot in his gauntlet, Torshk flicked a toggle and broke the signal. *We cower here like boryangee!* He summoned an image of the frail, hairy creature that often raided the garbage heaps on Kilrah, then glanced sidelong at Covum nar Caxki, a cousin two years his junior who flew the Dralthi at his wing. Covum bowed his head, but Torshk could sense that the younger warrior did not approve of his public display of frustration.

How could so many of Torshk's clan deny who they were? Descended from predators, from pack hunters, the Kilrathi people were not prone to lying in wait without a plan to attack. Were his clansmen able to suppress their instincts? He doubted that. Did they know something that he did not? He would challenge all who concealed information from him. His growl confirmed that thought.

"Dark Eye to Gold Claw leader," the comm officer began excitedly, his wide, flat nose and bulbous eyes filling a monitor. "Photon and neutrino emissions detected. Uploading coordinates now."

Torshk recoiled in a wave of surprise as quickly overcome by his tingling blood frenzy.

A Confederation attack.

It had to be.

Now he would make the hairless apes pay for Bokoth's death. His laser cannons would light the path of revenge. He studied the coordinates scrolling down his navigation display, and the grooves in his cheeks deepened. A ship had jumped into the quadrant, but it had not followed any known jump path. In fact, the coordinates placed it within striking range of the K 'n' Rek system. He looked to his cousin. "Leader to Gold Claw Two. Break off from escort."

Covum throttled up and swept under the destroyers, toward the anitgraviton flux some twelve hundred grid points ahead. Twin thrusters dimmed into the void as Torshk watched his cousin advance.

Young Covum had twice proven his bravery. He had saved Torshk's life by destroying a Confederation Rapier fighter that Torshk had been unable to outmaneuver because of thruster damage. And he had accepted a challenge from J'talc of the Kur'u'tak clan. J'talc's jealousy had flared when Covum had received the Banner of Fa'orc'al, given by the emperor himself to the most courageous pilots. J'talc had felt that he deserved the banner. The killing rage had consumed both warriors, *vorshaki* dueling blades had flashed, and in minutes J'talc's blood had warmed the cold flight deck. Covum regretted the incident, but he had behaved honorably.

Torshk now felt apprehensive over sending out his cousin as decoy, despite the honor Covum would garner. The strategy of using a decoy had been born of instinct, born of ancient times when Kilrathi would dispatch one warrior to lure a pack of opposing clansmen. The pack would chase the lone warrior into a designated area, where they would fall prey to an ambush. Torshk stiffened in anticipation of Covum's rapid and safe return with the enemy in his wake. He considered opening a channel but thought better of it. *Patience.* There seemed little honor in that act. He squinted through the canopy and remained in that position for several minutes—

Until impatience overwhelmed him. He accelerated ahead of the destroyers, along Covum's vector.

A pinpoint of reflected light birthed in the distance. Even as Torshk noted the speck, a proximity beacon wailed. The tactical display showed Covum's Dralthi headed toward him. Something huge trailed his cousin, and the targeting system had trouble identifying the contact. Fluctuating geometric patterns glowed and intertwined across the Heads Up Display. The image finally coalesced into the crimson schematic of a vessel shaped like a spearhead—a Concordia-class supercruiser. Six of its thirty point-defense missile stations had already launched ordnance in Covum's direction, while two of its tubes had opened to fire torpedoes at the ConCom ship two hundred meters above.

Torshk stared at the oncoming supercruiser, rapt by the view, by the startling fact that it bore no insignia and traveled without escorts. Standard Confederation protocol called for supercruisers to be escorted by at least two destroyers and a cruiser or larger battleship. Transports, ship tenders, and resupply operators frequently accompanied the convoy.

"Gold Claw Leader? The prey comes!" Covum cried.

The tactical report showed the destroyers adjusting tack. They would make a series of intercept approaches, feinting until the last moment when they would increase thrust and spring on their catch.

But Torshk could not ignore the oddity of a supercrusier traveling alone through Kilrathi-held space. Had the ape in command lost his senses? If so, weren't there other apes aboard who knew better? Or was the rest of its battle group preparing to jump in behind it? A chill coiled up Torshk's spine as his gaze wandered over the cap ship's immense hull, past a few of the many torpedo tubes and the colossal antimatter guns mounted on the upper deck. His display reported the battleship's length at 855 meters, but he swore she was bigger. He stole a final look at her superstructure, rising several dozen meters from the deck like a durasteel volcano, then cocked his head as Covum's fighter darted by with a pair of missiles chewing through his thruster wash.

Torshk seized his control yoke and yawed to port, heading at full throttle toward his cousin, the supercrusier now rushing in behind him. "I will assist!"

The missiles tightened their gap on Covum's Dralthi as Torshk plowed through exhaust trails, activated his targeting computer, and centered his reticle over the starboard rocket. Meson fire leapt from his blasters, struck the rocket with accelerated subatomic particles that instantly decayed inside the missile and heaved a terrific internal explosion. Torshk roared through the fireball to glimpse the second missile—even as it tore into Covum's Dralthi.

"For my *hrai*! For my—" Covum released a strangled cry as his fighter blossomed into fire-licked wreckage.

Torshk's howl rose from the core of his being and rang piercingly through his helmet. Every sense registered the throbbing agony of his cousin's loss. Panting, he increased velocity and soared above the destroyers—just in time to watch the ConCom ship explode in a coppery mushroom of smoke and fleeting fire. Howling again, Torshk steered toward the five remaining Dralthi in his squadron. "Gold Claw Squadron! Standby to attack!"

Even as the destroyers shifted to port and fired a quartet of torpedoes at the supercruiser, Torshk reached the others and flew as the poisonous tip of a tight wedge formation. They swooped down toward the cap ship's bow. Torshk toggled off his missile safety and surveyed the targeting report in his HUD. The computer automatically selected the ship's most lethal points and prioritized the attack while simultaneously receiving data from Black Claw squadron's targeting computers. Torshk noted that the seven Dralthi fighters of Black Claw planned to concentrate fire on the ship's stern in an attempt to knock out ion engine control. Since they would take out propulsion, his warriors would focus on weapons. "Claws Three and Four. You will target the forward guns. Claws Five, Six, and Seven will concentrate fire on torpedo stations."

"She has not launched fighters, Gold Leader!" That from Gold Claw Three, whose voice bore an icy astonishment.

"And where are her escorts?" Gold Claw Four added.

Two of the ship's antimatter guns pivoted toward them, barrels lifting.

With widening eyes, Torshk gave the final order: "Break and attack!"

Two Dralthi rolled away, dropping sharply in sixty-degree dives toward the guns. The other three cut hard to starboard and would skim along the hull, targeting torpedo stations and dispatching missiles at point-blank range. Human blood would spill. Sivar would smile.

As Torshk eased his control stick forward and the targeting computer locked on to the cap ship's bridge, a beeping alarm diverted his attention to his tactical display. His gaze barely met the screen when the voice of Flight Leader Norj'ach of Black Claw squadron burst through the channel. "Torshk! Look at our destroyers!"

Squinting at his display, Torshk could not find the glimmering representations of the destroyers. He noted the tiny dots flitting about the supercruiser and the sudden appearance of an odd, circular distortion positioned about eight hundred meters ahead of the cap ship. The thing's diameter measured nearly five hundred meters, though it fluctuated by several dozen meters along its perimeter. The report showed concentric yellow rings forming horizontal to the supercruiser and funneling down nearly three hundred meters to a solid point. A sidebar displayed something about "gravitic warping in progress." Torshk jerked back the stick, pulling into a high-G climb. He rolled to port and leveled off, taking in the view with his own eyes.

The two destroyers' bows had dropped ninety degrees, and both were being dragged into a whirlpool of wavering gloom. Torshk switched to their comm channel and suddenly wished he hadn't. Once bold warriors now squealed in horror as their battleships slowly broke into meter-sized fragments that hurtled toward the darkness amid tendrils of jettisoned gases and streamers of multicolored liquids. A powerful blow rocked Torshk's Dralthi and drowned out the comm channel. Thrown forward, he suddenly found himself barreling toward the abyss. He reversed thrust, and the engines whined against an overwhelming force. Reports from his comrades echoed distantly in his headset, voices smearing into each other:

"Gold Leader? Praise it has to Sivar me! Can home now come to see honor by for clan be so the Lord and this die for blood to can for truth Sivar and know what heart is me in for . . ."

The supercruiser passed swiftly below Torshk's fighter. He braced his control stick with both paws and watched the ship draw close to the gravity well's perimeter. *We embrace in death! Sivar grants justice this day!*

But the cap ship did not descend into the whirlpool. A veil of shimmering light fell over the vessel as five hundred meters ahead, on the opposite side of the well, an identical flash lifted into space. *It jumped . . . it jumped the well.*

Enraged by their escape and by the certainty of his fate, Torshk reversed thrust once more, charging at full tilt toward a cave of filmy night. No, he would never die by their hand. He still had that much control.

As the seconds burned away, he thought about how it would feel to die, if there would be pain, if he could take that pain with honor and not shame himself by crying out. The control stick suddenly shook free of his grip. His seat restraints snapped, and he floated out of the chair, feeling himself shake independently of the ship, teeth chattering, joints grinding, spittle dappling his helmet. He listened to the sound of his labored breathing, saw only a blur of gray, and sniffed at the smoke from damaged instruments that wafted in his nutrient gas line. His bones pushed against his skin.

He gasped.

Gasped again.

Knew it had come.

Fought for the glory of silence.

And won.

VEGA SECTOR,
DOWNING QUADRANT

CS TIGER CLAW

EN ROUTE TO NYLON
SYSTEM JUMP POINT
2654.079

1340 HOURS
CONFEDERATION
STANDARD TIME

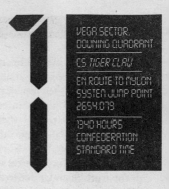

Lieutenant Christopher Blair sat in the *Tiger Claw*'s flight wing briefing room, arms folded over his chest, a definite smirk forming on his clean-shaven face as he listened to Lieutenant Todd "Maniac" Marshall wax evangelic about his piloting prowess to Elise "Zarya" Rolitov, a slim dove recently assigned to the 88th Fighter Wing, First Squadron. "And we didn't just come in hot, honey. We came in hot *and* inverted."

Blair lifted his smirk in Maniac's direction, but the blonde braggadocio's gaze held tight on Zarya, who made matters worse by returning an expression of awe, tugging fingers through her short, auburn hair, and fidgeting in her seat. That kind of body language would propel Maniac to newfound heights of lust and conceit. Blair bolted to his feet and crossed a few chairs down to face Zarya. He raised his voice over the other five pilots jabchatting around them. "What he won't tell you is that he nearly mowed down the deck boss while pulling that stunt. Take it from me, Lieutenant. If you want to keep out of trouble, keep away from this guy."

Zarya cocked a slender brow. "Trouble is what we're about, Lieutenant"—she read his nametag—"Blair."

He could live with the retort, but they had already met, and she had not remembered his name. "Maniac here deals in a particular brand of trouble that will get you booted off this ship before you've finished checking in."

She nodded. "I'll take my chances."

Maniac smiled tightly, eyes aglow in the fire of a new ally with whom he intended to bump uglies. "Lady's got taste. Can't fault her there, Ace."

"Ten-hut!" someone shouted.

Lieutenant Commander Jeanette "Angel" Deveraux hustled into the room, stepped onto the dais, then moved behind the holograph control podium. "At ease. Give us another moment, people." She flipped nervously through pages on a clipboard and frowned.

Blair remained at attention, noting how Angel's long, wavy mane had been pulled into a bun and how the overhead lights cast her in a sheen that suggested her call sign. He imagined himself close to her and reminisced on the moment he had nearly kissed her pouty lips. He felt the sudden urge to damn social convention and military regulations to hell, march up there, and take her. If nothing else, that would leave Maniac speechless. He sighed inwardly and continued to stare.

Yes, she looked well for a woman still recovering from frostbite and hypothermia. She had saved the *Tiger Claw* by destroying a Kilrathi Skipper missile, but her Rapier had been wrecked by the blast wave and she had ejected in her pod. Blair knew very well what it felt like to float powerless and adrift in space, waiting for the cold to take you.

A blow to the shoulder broke his thought. "Hey, lover," Maniac cooed, leaning in front of Zarya. "I see our squadron commander's up. Shouldn't you get her back into bed?"

Blair found his black look.

Maniac draped an arm over Zarya's shoulders. "He talks about me getting into trouble. Well, what if I told you that he and our dear squadron commander—"

"Ten-hut!" Blair shouted as acting Captain Paul Gerald arrived, offered a curt nod, then headed for the dais.

Though Gerald's promotion remained unofficial until the

paperwork came in, most officers had already taken to calling him by his new rank. Blair wouldn't go that far. Not yet. He called Gerald "sir." After all, the guy still hated Pilgrims, half-breeds, and Pilgrim sympathizers since fighting in the war against them. Blair's mother Devi Soulsong had been a Pilgrim. Blair couldn't change that. He didn't want to. Pilgrims might have originated as religious fanatics who saw themselves as the "elect," as the only humans destined for the stars, but the war had ended over twenty years ago, and most Pilgrims had peacefully rejoined Confederation society. Gerald simply had to get over the past. Admittedly, the man had confessed that he needed Blair, that he did respect Blair's skill as a pilot and had made him a command-approved wing commander, but that was as far as it went. There would never be any love lost between them. That was a shame. Blair could learn a lot from the man, but if Gerald continued to treat him indifferently, he would return the same.

"Have a seat," the captain said, wearing a new haircut to complement his new command. Gone were the dark curls in favor of a low maintenance flat top. He self-consciously patted his hair, then pursed his lips as the squadron settled in. "Our scheduled space dock has been delayed again." This to a chorus of moans as an opportunity for shore leave—once so close they could taste it—withered before the pilots' eyes. Even Blair, usually silent during such collective complaints, added his voice to the discord.

"All right," Angel snapped.

"Our own Damage Control Crews will continue as scheduled," Gerald went on. "Yes, we're still licking our wounds from our last engagement with the Kilrathi, but this war won't wait for us, and I wanted to brief you myself because matters have grown, in a word, delicate. Admiral Tolwyn has ordered us to Mylon Three." He tapped a control on the podium, and a holograph of the Mylon system shimmered into view. Four planets orbited a medium-sized star that a data strip indicated was slightly more massive than Sol. The aforementioned third planet tossed up a verdant glow with jagged continents splayed like leather patches over its watery backdrop. "You can consult your data readers for more detailed information on Confed settlements there. According to a drone intercepted by the CS *Rigaria*, on zero-seven-seven at nineteen hundred hours local time an unmarked Confederation supercruiser launched a planet-wide attack."

Murmurs erupted.

Lieutenant Adam "Bishop" Polanski, who sat to Blair's left, leaned forward, his expression of incredulity buckling the ragged scar on his cheek. "Sir, was the ship captured by the Kilrathi?"

"Maybe there was a mutiny," Zarya chipped in.

"Mutiny?" Polanski snickered. "No way."

"Intelligence is still gathering data," Gerald said. "As it stands, we're the principal element of a Space Warning and Control Mission. Our Marine detachment will deploy to MyGov, the primary settlement's capital, while Black Lion Squadron will recon the area of operations, eliminating any unfriendliness or mines and searching for survivors."

"Sir. Just one squadron to recon the entire zone?" Blair asked. "With short-range sensors that could take hours, maybe days."

"I'm aware of that, Lieutenant. We'll be entering the system in stealth mode. Those people were just attacked by—for the sake of argument—a *Confederation* ship. The arrival of another Confed ship will alarm them. And there's a strike base on planet. If it hasn't been taken out, we could encounter SAM fire and elements of the nineteenth fighter wing."

"We'll run three patrols on this one, Ladies," Angel said. "Bishop, Hunter, and Cheddarboy got point. Sinatra and Gangsta? You're with me. Maniac, Blair, and Zarya? You got reserve."

Maniac snorted.

Angel's gaze locked on. "Problem, Lieutenant Marshall?"

"No, ma'am."

"I take it you'd rather fly point."

"Absolutely, ma'am."

"Which is exactly why you will remain close to the ship, in ready status. Showboaters call too much attention to themselves."

"Yes, ma'am." Maniac bit his lower lip, and Blair read the curse balanced there.

"If we do encounter resistance, you will *not* engage," Gerald said. "We're going there to bandage the wound—not rub salt in it."

"Sir? How many people are we talking about?" Zarya asked.

"Five major settlements. As Confed colonies go, it's a small one. Five, maybe six million. Most of them reside on the northern continent."

"And supercruisers routinely carry strategic munitions," she said gravely.

"Yes, they do. We'll hope for the best." He regarded the group. "Other questions? No? Dismissed."

Blair stood and headed for the door.

"Lieutenant Blair? Can I see you for a moment?"

As he moved back toward Angel, Maniac passed him and whispered, "Can I spank you for a moment?"

Hiding his reaction, Blair forged on. "Yes, ma'am?"

"You're in command of your patrol. Keep a close eye on your people. I don't want the past to repeat itself. Understood?"

"Yes, ma'am."

The past to which she referred involved Maniac and Lieutenant Rosie Forbes, best pilot in the squadron and Angel's best friend. Horseplay and reckless courage had resulted in Forbes's death. Before Maniac had come aboard the *Tiger Claw*, Forbes had been a textbook flyer, much like Blair. But Maniac had lured her into his bed and into his flying style. He would do the same with Zarya. At least Blair wasn't the only one who saw that coming.

Angel eyed him suspiciously. "What's wrong, Lieutenant? I've never seen *that* look before."

Blair surveyed the room to be sure everyone had left. "Permission to speak freely?"

"Granted."

"How are you?"

She averted her gaze. "Better."

"Why no visitors?"

She hesitated. "I don't know."

"You almost died out there. You come back and lie in sickbay for two days and won't let anyone see you. Did they tell you I came by five or six times?"

"I just needed to be alone."

"I thought—"

"Don't think too much."

"Okay. Sorry." He groped for something more, saw that she still wouldn't face him, then elected to leave. He prayed she would call after him.

She didn't.

Twenty minutes later, the ship reached the Ymir system and the jump point to Mylon. Blair and the others would ride out the jump in their Rapiers and launch within the first minute of their arrival. Having already completed his pre-flight checklist, Blair waited for a fuel Bowser to pass, then crossed the busy flight deck to where Maniac stood beside his Rapier, being chewed out by Deck Boss Peterson. The boss's furor probably had something to do with the sandwich in Maniac's hand.

"What's it gonna take?" Peterson asked, his face flushed. "A suspension? I blink. It's done. You want that?"

Maniac's face paled. "No, sir."

"Then get that food off my flight deck. Now!"

"'kay." Maniac took a huge bite and jogged away toward the hatch leading to the galley.

"I'm running a flight deck—not a day care," Peterson shouted. "Come back when you can read the rules." He faced Blair. "You illiterate, too, Lieutenant?"

Blair jolted.

"No loitering on the deck. If you're not working, get out!" He spun on a heel, ripped off his headset, and stormed toward Weapons System Chief Mackey, who had launched into a tirade of his own while shaking a finger at two frightened ordnance specialists standing before the nose of a Broadsword bomber.

"This is the most uptight ship I've ever seen."

Zarya had drawn up to Blair's side. He glanced at her and

sighed. "It'll get tighter because we keep turning over so many pilots. We lost Knight and Forbes, then Spirit got transferred and Sinatra got transferred in, along with Cheddarboy and Gangsta. And now you've joined the party. We haven't flown enough with each other. That's dangerous. And we're still the smallest squadron in the wing. They're calling us 'The Chihuahuas.'"

"Hey, kids." Maniac rushed over to stand between them. "You believe that guy? I think that bastard is gunning for me."

"Maybe he's still mad about you nearly killing him," Zarya said. "Yeah, maybe that's it."

A series of beeps filtered through the ship-wide intercom, then Gerald's voice boomed: "Attention all personnel. On jump point vector. Sixty seconds. Assume jump stations."

"Whoopeedo," Maniac groaned. "We'll be sitting on our hands for this one anyway."

"Just do your job," Blair said, then jogged back toward his Rapier.

"Hey, Blair? What's your problem now?"

He ignored Maniac, gave a passing nod to his flight crew, then mounted his cockpit ladder.

It felt comforting to be back in his fighter after a three day absence, the pit like a nest of power and technology with the magic to make him forget about rejection, about the troubles his half-breed heritage brought on, about the war, about everything. He slid on his headset and helmet, buckled on the O_2 mask, then attached the power and oxygen lines to his flight suit. Routine preparations performed thousands of times now took on a peculiar reverence. He sensed a certain nobility about being a pilot, and delusion or not, he enjoyed the moment. But it was time to get down to business. He switched a toggle, and the canopy lowered into place.

Now in the muffled quiet, he surveyed his instruments, noting a few differences between his present fighter, the CF–117b Rapier, and the old F44-A he had flown only three days prior. The new model had increased missile capacity to ten guided or dumbfire missiles and packed a second generation nose-mounted rotary-barrel neutron gun that allowed for longer continuous neutron fire than the old F44's first generation cannon. A switch on his stick allowed for alternate or synchronous fire, and standard laser cannons mounted to the 117's short, upturned wings provided longer-range support. The standard Tempest targeting and navigational AI remained the same, as did the jump-capable drive array and twin thruster/afterburner package. Monitors and control panels seemed slightly smaller, but that could be an illusion. The seat felt a hell of a lot better though, with the welcome addition of lumbar support. Even as Blair brought up main power and engaged the pre-flight sequence, the Rapiers on either side of him did likewise. He glanced left to Hunter. The Aussie had not attached his mask yet; he would, of course, wait until the last minute so that he could chomp on his unlit cigar, the stogie as much a permanent fixture as his shaggy hair. Though Blair and Hunter had gotten off to an exceedingly shaky start, with Hunter threatening Blair's life because he did not trust Pilgrim half-breeds, Blair's actions during their last mission had apparently won Hunter's trust. During the past three days, Hunter had treated Blair as an equal, had invited him to the rec several times, and had even asked if he could buy Blair a drink. Despite all of that, Blair still sensed that the man was watching him, probing for the first sign of waning loyalty.

The pilot to his right, one Sachin "Cheddarboy" Rapalski hailed from an amazingly long line of Wisconsin dairy farmers who had weathered the twenty-third century's ecocatastrophe with the zeal and perseverance of ancient American pioneers. Cheddarboy's call sign had been chosen for him by his flight school instructor, who had used it as chide so often that it stuck. Of course the pale, baby-faced jock with the body of a fence picket hated cheddar cheese; in fact, he hated all cheese except the mozzarella on a well-done pepperoni pizza and had, in fact, split one with Blair only the night before. Now strapped into his cockpit, Cheddarboy gave Blair a terse nod, his face shielded by his mask, large blue eyes radiating with the nervous electricity of a new pilot flying his first real mission off his first real strike carrier.

Angel's voice abruptly sounded through his headset. "All

right, Ladies. I take it we're all in tight. Pre-flight checklists have been logged and looking good—except for yours, Maniac."

"Excuse me, ma'am?" Maniac responded quickly.

"That's right. You've overlooked targeting and navigation systems."

"My chief did 'em for me. Guess he forgot to log 'em in."

"You're responsible for your own checklist. You don't sub-contract it to your chief. Understood?"

"Yes, ma'am."

Blair's left Visual Display Unit flashed the words INCOMING COMMUNICATION ON SECURE CHANNEL. Blair dialed up the channel, already knowing who had called. "No, she's not just being a bitch, Maniac. She's right. And you know that."

"No, I *was* being a bitch," Angel said, then her face showed on the display, or at least what wasn't rudely hidden by her helmet and mask.

"I'm sorry, I—"

"Save it. I just recommended you for some chicken guts, the Bronze Star to be exact, for exceptional bravery under fire. I'm sure it'll get approved."

"Thank you, ma'am. But I'm not sure if bravery had anything to do with it."

"I don't know any other pilot who would navigate his way through a quasar without NAVCOM coordinates. If it wasn't bravery, than it was insanity. But we don't have a medal for that."

He smiled behind his mask. "We should."

"Jump in ten seconds. Launch in thirty. Stand by." The VDU went blank.

However, a fountain of light appeared before it and gathered into the shape of Merlin, the holographic interface generated by Blair's Portable Personal Computer. As was the bantam's wont, Merlin brushed off his tan tunic and breeches, slid up the rubber band that bound his long, gray hair into a ponytail, then fixed Blair with a severe frown. "It may seem ridiculous to you, but forcing me into standby mode for long periods is like stuffing me into a little box. Never mind what it does to my appearance, it's my attitude that's really suffering. I'm depressed again, Christopher. I'm feeling unneeded. I thought you should know that. I think you should do something about it."

"Merlin, don't lay this crap on me now. How would you feel if you thought your holographic assistant needed a shrink? The guy's supposed to be helping you, and you wind up counseling *him*. Sometimes I feel like ripping your processor out of my wrist. My Dad programmed you because he thought he was doing me a favor. If only he could see you now."

"That's not fair. I shouldn't be feeling guilty about how I feel." His gaze turned up to probe the overhead. "Oh, dear. We're jumping again." He vanished.

"Fusion engines engaged," Gerald said over the intercom.

Despite his own idling thrusters, Blair felt the characteristic rumble pulse through the entire carrier as the ship's powerful ion engines came online. Then a jolt tore through his Rapier as the *Tiger Claw* paused to get a precise bearing on the jump point that accounted for the gravity well's drift rate.

"This is the part my stomach hates," Bishop said.

"Don't think about it, Mate," Hunter instructed. "Put it all in your breath and let it out."

Another jolt told Blair that the jump-drive had been engaged. Now the *Tiger Claw's* high thrust propelled it toward the exact coordinates along the rift in space. An antigraviton field surrounded the ship, and Blair felt his senses shut down.

He knew she would come. He had tried to bury the thought of her, to bury his fear of jumping, but at the very last second, he panicked, and during the perfect moment that joined him to the space-time continuum, he saw her once more, haloed by the void—

His mother. Dark hair spilling like wine over her shoulders, eyes sometimes soft with understanding, sometimes narrowed in disappointment. "Christopher. I wish I could help you. At least you don't bear the pain of knowing."

"Knowing what?"

"Your path."

"Another warning? You said I shouldn't come here, that this isn't my continuum. Why? Tell me."

"You believe you have power over this, but you have nothing. You can't do what you feel."

"What am I? A Pilgrim? What does that really mean? Am I just a freak? A human with a sixth sense for direction? Or is there more? I want there to be more. I want to know who I am."

"If you learn who you are, you will fall. Like the others. You're too young, and the pain of knowing is too great."

"I can take the pain!"

"Who is that? That you, Blair?"

A blurry view of the flight deck snapped out of the darkness, along with the steady hiss of his oxygen flow, the reverberation of his thrusters, and the nagging ache of his shoulder harness that he had fastened too tightly.

"Hey, Blair? You with the living?" Maniac asked.

"Yeah, yeah. I'm just . . . that one hit hard."

"Attention all personnel. Battle Stations! Battle Stations! This is not an exercise," Gerald said. "Standard orbit of Mylon Three in ninety seconds. Deploy ground force."

Blair watched as Deck Boss Peterson waved on the wedge-shaped CF–337d Marine Corps troopship, armed to the teeth with ten missile hardpoints each packing a trio of rockets. Two turreted rotary-barrel neutron guns, not unlike his Rapier's primary weapon, jutted out on port and starboard sides. The troopship's nose bore the vivid likeness of a snarling Doberman pinsher, drool dripping from gleaming incisors. Once lined up on the runway, the vessel ignited thrusters and swept toward the environmental maintenance field's fluctuating curtain of energy. It shot through the barrier and climbed away, out of sight.

"Show time, ladies," Angel said.

Hunter floated into position first, followed by Bishop and Cheddarboy. One by one, first patrol received launch confirmation from the flight boss, got the green light, then thundered across the runway. Second patrol hovered into position. Gangsta took off first, her launch a perfect demonstration of textbook maneuvering. Sinatra followed, jumped the throttle before the deck boss gave him the final signal, then got out there, the deck boss's scolding ringing in his ears. Sinatra was a damned good pilot with more experience than even Angel. His problems with authority had gotten him busted down from captain to lieutenant. Based on his years in and his age (twenty-nine), he should be a major or colonel. From what Blair could gather from his limited experience with the man, he didn't hotdog like Maniac; he simply told people exactly what he thought of them and their skills. Many of the younger pilots marveled over his political incorrectness, but Blair chose to avoid the guy, taking the same advice he had offered Zarya about Maniac.

Angel rammed her throttle forward and streaked away, gone through the energy curtain in a pair of blinks.

"Reserve patrol? You're up," Flight Boss Raznick said from Blair's VDU. The boss's shaven head glimmered like an egg under a spotlight. "Zarya, Maniac, and—you figure out a call sign yet, Blair?"

"Pilgrim."

"You're kidding."

"No, sir."

Raznick snorted. "Can't say I like it better than Maverick, but it's your choice, young man."

For the past couple of days, Blair had been contemplating a new call sign. "Maverick" had suited him well during academy training, an ironic moniker since Blair had established a reputation of flying by the book. But he felt he had outgrown the name, and since he had lost his Pilgrim cross—an obvious means of identifying himself as a Pilgrim—he figured the call sign would serve as the next best thing. He didn't want to ram his heritage down his comrades' throats, but he felt strongly about people knowing who he was. And if they had a problem with that, so be it.

Zarya took her cue from the deck boss and launched. Maniac's Rapier glided in ahead of Blair's, pivoted ninety degrees, and aimed for the energy field. Surprisingly, he took off sans his usual over-thrusting flourish and verbal high jinks.

Blair slid over the Heads Up Display viewer attached to his helmet. The viewer covered his right eye and supplied a series of data bar readouts of each of the Rapier's major systems. During combat, the targeting system would seize control of the viewer, and smart targeting reticles would replace the clutter of data. At the moment, all systems were nominal. Pressure gauges stood in the green. The nav system had already been preprogrammed with coordinates uploaded directly from flight control.

Wearing his patented sinister stare, Deck Boss Peterson flashed Blair the signal for launch. Blair hesitated just enough to widen the boss's eyes, then slapped the throttle and burst forward.

Acceleration struck like a wrestler's beefy forearm. The tall columns on either side of the deck flashed by, along with the dozens of Rapiers and Broadswords moored beneath a lattice-work of connecting beams. The energy draped over his canopy and suddenly sloughed off to expose the exterior runway walled in by the two great halves of the cylinder that made up the *Claw*'s fuselage. Blair waited a few seconds more for his velocity to increase before pulling up toward a sheet of darkness. Chatter clogged the squadron's general frequency as the point and second patrols gave assessments of the planet.

Mylon Three finally scrolled into view, its sun partially eclipsed and burning with a significant glare in the distance. The polarization unit kicked in, tinting the canopy so that Blair now had a clear view of the bluish green world and the black clouds blanketing nearly all of its northern hemisphere. Specks of reflected light flashed like unwelcome fireworks, some in the upper atmosphere, some in low and high orbit.

"This place is dead," Maniac said, not bothering to temper his astonishment.

"It's like a holo," Zarya added. "And hey, there go the Marines. They won't find much. Looks like MyGov has been leveled."

"Advance to escort coordinates," Blair ordered, taking his Rapier between their fighters. Nearly in unison, they banked right and followed a vector that took them lateral of the *Claw*. The nav computer beeped, and the circular radar screen showed a flashing white cross, indicating they had reached their assigned position: waiting on the bench, as Maniac understood it. They lined up and throttled down. Blair had trouble removing his gaze from the planet, had trouble removing his thoughts from the millions who had died under an onslaught of planetary torpedoes. No doubt about it. The Kilrathi had to be responsible. They had somehow captured a supercruiser and intended to incite a civil war with it.

"I'm running a short-range scan, and I'm already picking up a lot of debris. I'm talking *a lot* of debris," Zarya said.

Blair switched to Angel. "Reserve leader to second patrol, copy?"

Her face lit his display. "Copy, Lieutenant."

"We're at station. No sign of hostile contacts, roger."

"None on this end either. Picking up wreckage from, I don't know, could be hundreds of ships, mostly private and commercial transports. No military craft IDed yet."

"They were probably trying to get offworld." Blair snorted in disbelief. "Bastards just shot them down."

"I've seen holos of the Peron Massacre, but that pales in comparison to this," Angel remarked. "We're looking at the total annihilation of a Confederation world. This place won't be habitable for a century, and that's with terraformers rebuilding around the clock."

"I don't get it. Why Mylon Three? It's along the Kilrathi border, but there aren't any jump points from here into their space. And from what I've read, it is—or was—your basic agricultural world. I don't understand what they're gaining from this, besides sending a message."

"Maybe that's all they wanted to do. And Mylon was simply a target of opportunity since at the time of the attack, no Confed cap ships were in the immediate vicinity."

"Angel?" Gangsta called. "Found a small shuttle, civilian registry. Or at least what's left of it. Life support still functioning. Got two live ones inside."

VEGA SECTOR,
DOWNING QUADRANT

CS TIGER CLAW

HIGH ORBIT NYLON
THREE

2654.079

1500 HOURS
CONFEDERATION
STANDARD TIME

Second patrol moved in on the civilian shuttle, and Angel and Gangsta activated retrieval tractors to tow the ship back to the *Tiger Claw*. They tried to contact the survivors inside, but shipboard communications had been destroyed. One survivor, a frazzled teenage girl, waved to them from a porthole. First patrol continued probing the wreckage, and Blair listened in as they encountered another tattered vessel with more survivors on board.

About an hour into the operation, Angel declared the area secured, and for the next four hours Blair sat in his cockpit and watched as more patrols launched, scoured the wreckage, and discovered still more survivors. Deveraux continued to hold Blair's patrol on reserve, despite his best arguments. True, a hostile vessel could return to thwart their rescue efforts, but Blair considered that more unlikely as the hours passed.

"Man, how much longer are we going to sit on our asses?" Maniac had unclipped his mask, and his expression hung so low that it promised to fall off.

Blair shook his head at the VDU. "We're sitting tight until we're ordered or forced back."

"Well, we ain't draining systems in this hover. Oxygen's rated for seven hours, but I'm good for another five, dammit. If the order doesn't come in, I say we lie about our status. I didn't get to finish my lunch, and we're already heading into supper."

"You hearing this, Zarya?" Blair asked. "Pay attention to the way Lieutenant Marshall operates."

"Hey, I just ain't for wasting us out here. The whole wing is involved in this effort, and there's only one other reserve patrol. They haven't been out here as long as us."

"Sometimes it ain't all guts and glory," Blair said. "And sometimes it ain't fair. You know that."

"Lumberjack to, uh, Pilgrim, copy? That you, Blair?"

"Copy, Lumberjack. New call sign. What's up?"

"We're your relief. Be there in a ninety seconds."

"You don't know what a pleasure it is," Maniac said. "Hey, L.J.? When we get back, I owe you a tongue kiss."

Lumberjack, a burly twenty-six-year old man fond of wearing flannel during off-duty hours, grunted and said, "That tongue comes within a meter of me, and I'll tear it off and bloodpin it to your chest."

"You'll never see it coming. They never do."

The big Lumberjack sniggered. "Get out of here, you idiot."

"Reserve patrol? Throttle up," Blair ordered, then engaged his own thrusters and wheeled back for the carrier, gratified to escape Mylon Three's oppressive gloom.

The second Blair penetrated the flight deck's energy curtain, a Dantean scene of chaos assaulted his gaze. Fighters and bombers had been shifted back, some doubled up in repair bays to accommodate the fifty or more scorched and shattered fuselages of commercial and civilian shuttles that lay in ragged rows parallel to the runway. Civilians were being helped or carried out of the wrecks, with, it appeared, all twenty-five medics assigned to the *Claw* addressing wounds or rushing the incapacitated to sick bay. Two dazed civvies wandered dangerously close to the runway as Blair took his main thrusters offline and braked frantically with maneuvering jets. "Boss! Get 'em out of the way!"

Peterson sprinted across the runway, extended both arms, wrapped them around the civvies' necks, then dragged them back toward the shoulder. Blair cocked his head as his starboard wingtip drew within a meter of Peterson's back. A flash of light ahead made him realize that he came up too hard on Zarya's tail, her jets emitting bursts of thrust as she only now turned off the runway, aiming for her starboard berth. Blair leaned on the throttle, increasing reverse thrust.

"Give me another second, Pilgrim. I have like a meter clearance on each side."

She hadn't exaggerated. The fighters in their section of berths appeared freshly squeezed from concentrate. Her Rapier's portside wing glanced off Maniac's neutron gun as she lowered the fighter onto its skids. Techs from both crews began hollering their protests as Maniac's canopy lifted back and the man himself stood, ripped off his helmet, and shouted, "People! Chill! Just a love tap. Check it out. No harm done."

Blair's crew chief, Rina Temples, guided him to his berth, a slot no bigger than Zarya's. Three Rapiers would now be moored where only one had stood.

"Don't worry, Lieutenant," Rina said over the channel, headgear and goggles protecting her from the wash, "we'll have this mess cleaned up soon. Once we get the civvies out, we'll plow away this junkyard."

"I hope so. Can you imagine if the entire wing had to scramble now?"

"Can't think about that," she groaned. "Okay. Five meters. Little more . . . little more . . . that's it."

He thumbed down on his high-hat control, and the Rapier descended. A trio of thuds from the landing skids triggered a mild sigh. Blair engaged the automatic powerdown system, then sent off the data from his flight recorder to the Shipboard Information Datanet so that it could be automatically assessed and delivered to Angel, who would debrief them in the pilots' ready room.

By the time he had his gear off and the canopy open, Rina had already rolled up a ladder and had vanished beneath the Rapier, probably inspecting a coolant conduit that had been giving her people some trouble. Maniac and Zarya waited for him, and Blair heard Maniac muttering something about a steel-beach picnic and a bottle of champagne he had been saving for a special occasion. Blair hit the flight deck, legs stiff and sore. Yes, Maniac and Zarya had waited, but now they failed to acknowledge him. Maniac was too busy looking surprised, while she eyed him with utter incredulity.

"How can you talk about our fun after what we've just seen?"

"What? Am I supposed to feel guilty or responsible for this? Hey, I'm real sorry about what happened to these people. But my life's too short to be depressed for them. This is a war. Remember?"

Zarya started to say something, puffed air, then strode away. Her helmet slipped from the crook of her arm and rolled across the deck. Maniac darted to retrieve it. She beat him to it with a snarl.

"C'mon. You know I didn't mean that. I'm just tired."

"And just an asshole." She shot him a potent scowl, a remarkable expression for a woman so attractive.

Maniac watched her go, then resignedly faced Blair. "Goddamned bitches, man."

"That's your problem right there. They're all objects to you, objects to be conquered. It's never about them. It's always about you."

"This from a guy who can't even get a woman *who already likes him* into bed."

"Who said I wanted to bed her?"

"Last time I looked you were a man."

"I want to say grow up. But then you'd be boring."

A grin slowly flickered across Maniac's lips. "I would."

They started for the hatch to flight control as more civvies continued to emerge from the shuttles. At the hatch, Blair paused a second to gaze across the hangar. "How many you think we saved?"

Maniac shrugged. "Couple hundred, maybe."

"Couple hundred from five or six mill. And you want to have a picnic?"

Captain Paul Gerald leaned on a gurney in sick bay, staring at the mother and daughter who had been aboard the shuttle brought in by Angel's patrol. The survivors had been floating for nearly three days, and once aboard they had showered, changed, devoured the sandwiches the medics had brought them, and had each downed nearly a half gallon of water. Gerald had been at their bedsides for nearly fifteen minutes now, attempting to subtly interrogate them. But a puzzling fact regarding the attack wore down his diplomacy, and he repeatedly directed them back to it.

"Are we done yet, Captain?" the mother asked. She had introduced herself as Iridessa Long, president of Mylon's largest hydroponics co-op, president of nothing now. Her combative demeanor reminded Gerald of his estranged ex-wife. The fact that she resembled Brenna made it all the more difficult for Gerald to control his temper.

"No, we are not done yet," he told her. "I need you to think hard about them. Are you absolutely certain they were Confederation Naval officers?"

She rolled her eyes. "Let's see now. I've told you that, what? Four times? I've heard that military minds are dense, but I assumed that was just a stereotype. I guess you'll be wanting me to draw you a picture now, eh? I can't believe that my hard-earned tax money pays for people like you."

"Ma'am, we're just trying to learn what happened."

"What happened is that some of your people launched an unprovoked attack and massacred civilians."

"Mom, please . . ." the daughter said from the next bed. Only fourteen, Janey Long seemed more upset with her mother's embarrassing behavior than with what had just happened to her homeworld. Gerald understood her reaction, at least a little. When he saw his daughter Sandy during R&Rs, the thirteen-year-old continually warned him not to humiliate her in front of her peers, which meant that Gerald could only smile when greeting them and dare not mouth a word of criticism. Yes, he knew that drill all too well.

"My daughter seems to think I'm being too harsh with you, Captain Gerald. She fails to remember how harsh the Confederation military has been with us!"

"Mom!"

Gerald raised a palm in truce. "I know this is rough, and I know that I've been asking the same questions, but we have to know every detail. Is there anything else you can remember? Anything?"

Iridessa bit her lower lip and whispered a curse. "You got our story. All of it. Now why don't you go figure out why these people attacked, why they took some of us prisoner while murdering others, and where the hell they are?"

"I assure you, ma'am. We're already on that. Now the CS *Scrimshaw* will arrive shortly to ferry you and the other survivors to Ymir. I hate to say this, but you'll probably have to repeat your story to authorities there."

"And the news just keeps getting better." Iridessa exhaled loudly in disgust. "Tell you what. When we survivors get done suing you, the Confederation will be bankrupt. Count on that."

We have insurance, Gerald thought, though he wouldn't dare stoke her fire by uttering that. He nodded, spun, and hightailed out of there.

Angel waited for him by the hatch. "Captain. Just launched three patrols to continue the search, and I've finished debriefing my squadron. I know you've been busy here, so I thought I'd come and tell you myself."

"That report hardly warrants your presence." Gerald stepped past her and into the passageway."

"Permission to speak candidly, sir?"

"Go ahead."

"What's going on? Are we on a need-to-know here?"

"Yes, we are."

"Raznick's people just broke up a riot on the flight deck. Some of those survivors attacked our medics. Why don't you put an end to the rumors before they get out of hand."

"I'm not at liberty to do that."

"The survivors are saying Confed troops attacked. They took prisoners. I don't understand."

"To be frank, neither do I. But I'm sure we will." He nodded. "Commander." Quickening his pace, he hoped to evade any more of her questions.

"Captain?"

He gritted his teeth, paused, faced her. "Yes, Commander?"

"How many Pilgrims do you think are aboard that super-cruiser?"

"Pilgrims?" He shook his head and abandoned her scrutiny.

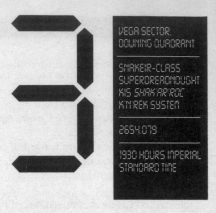

VEGA SECTOR,
DOWNING QUADRANT

SNAKEIR-CLASS
SUPERDREADNOUGHT
KIS *SHAK'AR'ROC*
K'N'REK SYSTEM

2654.078

1930 HOURS IMPERIAL
STANDARD TIME

Admiral Vukar nar Caxki rose from his command chair as Flight Leader Norj'ach of Black Claw Squadron limped his way from the lift, his bad leg the result of an old challenge. His narrow escape from the supercruiser had actually taken little toll. His color held a perfect sallow, and his eyes radiated with the fire of Sivar. "Kalralahr. I submit myself for punishment."

Vukar gave a solemn nod as nutrient gas jetted from his flaring nostrils. "I have reviewed your flight record. But before I permit you the honor of *zu'kara*, tell me in your own words what you saw."

"I saw our ConCom explode, then two of our battle group's destroyers were pulled into a gravity well, along with Torshk and Gold Claw Squadron. I barely escaped the well. The rest of my squadron met their fates. They fought bravely. Every name must be added to the temples of our ancestors. Every name but mine."

"And from what I have gathered from your flight record, this well was *created* by an unmarked Confederation supercruiser. Is that correct?"

"It is, my Kalralahr."

"Impossible. The Terrans' jump-drive requires the presence of natural rifts in the space-time continuum."

Norj'ach's gaze lowered to the deck. "I tell you only what I saw."

Tactical officer Makorshk nar Caxki crossed the *Shak'Ar'Roc's* bridge to arrive at Vukar's side. "Kalralahr, if I may speak?"

Vukar regarded the subordinate with mild disdain. Makorshk had a reputation for voicing his opinion despite his meager rank of second fang. But on more than one occasion, Vukar had found useful truth in the young warrior's thoughts. If only Makorshk would come to him in private instead of forcing Vukar to favor him before the others. "Speak."

"The Terrans do possess another drive system."

"Of course they do. Sub-light impulse drives. But those do not create gravity wells."

"My studies of their history will prove valuable now, my Kalralahr. The hopper drive, developed late in their twenty-second century, produced a localized matter-antimatter reaction that resulted in a temporary space-time well in its immediate area. I believe *that* is what our task force encountered."

"I, too, have studied the apes. Hopper drives were extremely dangerous. The Terrans could not engage them near gravity-generating objects, and they were slow, requiring eighteen of their hours between jumps. The distances traversed were less than half a light year. They would be foolhardy to rely on such volatile devices."

"But it seems they've discovered a way to control the matter-antimatter reaction and a way to neutralize the gravitic interference created by nearby systems or ships." He raised his voice over the hum of instruments. "They could jump into our space, fly close to one of our worlds, generate their gravity well, then jump out while the well consumes the planet the same way it consumed our task force."

Vukar felt a blade of ice impale his gut as the six other bridge officers seated at their stations murmured over Makorshk's alarm. "That is an interesting assessment, admittedly speculative, but I am impressed with it nonetheless."

Makorshk's upper lip quivered in self-satisfaction.

Communications officer Ta'kar'ki spun in his chair. "Kalralahr? Incoming transmission from the emperor."

"The emperor?"

"Yes. Direct transmission. The signal originates from K'n'Rek."

"Route it to my ready room." Vukar turned to Norj'ach, who absently stroked his whiskers. "You may now join your clansmen in seeking Sivar's forgiveness."

"Thank you, my Kalralahr." Norj'ach withdrew his *zu'kara* knife from the sheath buckled to his thigh. The blade's ornate handle, made of the rare wood from the sacred forest of Kovokum, had been carved to fit Norj'ach's paw. The flight leader bared his fangs, dragged the blade across his neck, and his life's liquid jetted down his dull armor. He dropped to his knees as the bridge officers rose, faced him, and bowed respectfully. Vukar offered Norj'ach a terse nod, then hurried to his ready room.

Inside the cramped quarters, Vukar sat in his meditation chair and pivoted to face his private comm display. He tapped the control panel with a thick knuckle, and the emperor abruptly stared at him, framed by the dozens of banners that hung from the bulkhead of his suite aboard the imperial shuttle. The old Kilrathi looked tired, his robes ruffled. "Vukar, we received your drone. Have you learned more about this Terran supercruiser?"

"No more, yet. But with your permission, I will see to this personally. You need not have traveled here, my emperor."

"Yes, the clan leaders feel as you do. But I want to be close, to direct actions myself if necessary. Something is happening in this quadrant, something very unusual. According to our spy satellites, the planet Mylon Three has been rendered lifeless by the same supercruiser that your destroyers encountered."

"Mylon Three is a Confederation world. Why would they annihilate their own people, unless—"

"I've ordered battle groups to the Ymir and Nephele systems. The Terrans will believe we are attacking in retaliation for the death of Kalralahr Bokoth, the loss of his battle group, and the loss of your two destroyers. The attack will satisfy the pressure I have been receiving from the clan leaders, though I'm unsure we can afford the expense. In truth, we will also gather as much intelligence as we can about this supercruiser and the destruction of Mylon."

"One of my flight leaders escaped. Did you—"

"Yes, I reviewed his report. And it troubles me. If the Confederation has learned to create gravity wells, then the time has come to launch a massive assault. But I suspect the Confederation is not responsible."

Vukar stiffened. "Pilgrims?"

"Perhaps. That would explain a lot."

"Then we can sit back and watch them destroy each other."

The emperor extended a finger. "If the Pilgrims are building a force, then we have a new and more powerful enemy. And if they succeed in destroying the Confederation, they will move on to our empire. They are descendants of Terrans, but Terrans nonetheless. Bokoth attempted to bargain with them. He died. There will be no more bargains." The emperor lowered his hand, narrowed his gaze. "Vukar, I charge you with the task of finding that supercruiser and, if possible, recovering its drive system. Analysis of your pilot's data indicates that the gravitic field has a unique and frequently traceable signature. We have already made a course projection." He leaned forward and touched a button on the panel before him. "I'm uploading the data now. Our best estimates put that ship somewhere in the Tartarus system."

Vukar raised a fist. "By the blood of Sivar, that ship will be ours."

A sullen atmosphere pervaded the *Tiger Claw*'s bridge and would not lift any time soon, or at least Gerald thought so. Shuttles continued to ferry survivors out to the CS *Scrimshaw*, a Drayman-class transport that had made orbit thirty minutes ago. The survivor count stood firmly at two hundred and twenty-seven. Another one hundred and twenty-two bodies had been recovered

semi-intact from the debris, while remaining recovery teams estimated that at least two or three hundred others had been killed,
but their remains were too fragmentary to provide an accurate
number yet. Thirteen injured had died in sick bay, but Gerald
had been assured that all other civilians would live to sue the
Confederation—if Iridessa Long had her way. No, Gerald was in
no way saddened by her departure. In the meantime, the Marines
had reported of massive devastation across the northern continent. No sign of survivors. They would move on to the remote
regions of the southern continent, where Gerald expected they
would encounter six or seven thousand settlers dying of radiation poisoning. Durasteel bomb shelters were a luxury on agricultural worlds, and even if any had been built, Gerald doubted
the farmers had reached them in time.

"Sir?" hailed Lieutenant Falk.

Gerald faced the young officer, who stood behind the radar
station's Plexi tactical screen, one hand pressing his headset's
speaker deeper into his ear. "What do you have, Mr. Falk?"

"Another ship just came through the jump point. Merchant-
man-class errant. ID coming in now." He regarded a thin monitor to his right. "It's the *Diligent*, sir."

Doing a poor job of repressing his disgust, Gerald bolted from
his command chair and looked to Lieutenant Commander
Obutu, whose dark face registered an equal measure of loathing.
"Mr. Obutu? You have the con."

"Aye-aye, sir. And sir? If it is him, well—"

"Of course it's him, Commander. And he's just the person we
need to inspire morale."

Obutu grinned crookedly, then rose as Gerald swore under his
breath and trudged toward the lift.

Commodore James "Paladin" Taggart entered the Flight Control
Room, wearing the brown slacks and casual tunic of a colonist
on holiday. His coal-black hair had been gelled neatly back, but
his face bore the mottled shadow of a drunk. Thick hair on his
chest wandered past his V-neck, and Gerald spotted a silver chain

that he knew held a Pilgrim cross hidden beneath Paladin's shirt. It seemed an effort for the commodore to nod his acknowledgment, which Gerald declined to return. He simply stood there, staring at the man who worked for Confederation Naval Intelligence, the man whose ancestors had been Pilgrims, the man who was supposed to be on a covert mission to uncover and eliminate Kilrathi espionage activities in Vega.

Paladin removed a minidisk from his pocket. "Hello, Mr. Gerald. Message from the admiral."

"Thought you were a commodore—not a courier."

Paladin handed him the disk. "Good to see you, too. We'll need a secure terminal to play that. We don't have much time."

Gerald turned back toward the exit and cursed inwardly. "Yes, Commodore. We'll go to my quarters."

They rode the lift in silence, and despite the fact that he stood beside Admiral Tolwyn's right-hand man, Gerald had no intention of trying to win points with the commodore. He respected Paladin's ability to command under fire, otherwise he felt zero affection for the man whose presence meant that the admiral did not trust Gerald to handle the Mylon situation on his own. Gerald did not need Paladin's help, and his feelings on the matter would inevitably surface.

Once inside the modest captain's quarters, Gerald made a point of *not* offering the commodore a drink. Trouble was, Paladin crossed directly into the small kitchen, opened the cooling unit, and fetched a glass of orange juice for himself. He took a long swig as Gerald scowled and moved to a terminal set into the bulkhead. He inserted the minidisk, and a moment later the admiral appeared on the screen; his shock of gray hair and somber countenance loaned him the semblance of a troubled king from a Shakespearean play. "Hello, Mr. Gerald. I wish I could've provided you with more details before sending you out there blind and without an XO, but now we've managed to piece together some of this puzzle, and I've sent Paladin to assist. Four days ago we lost contact with the *Olympus*. She's been positively identified as the supercruiser that launched the attack on Mylon."

Gerald shifted to the sofa, retrieved the terminal's remote, and hit pause. "The *Olympus*?" he asked Paladin. "She's commanded by Amity Aristee. I know her. Amazing record. What happened?"

Paladin gestured with his glass toward the monitor. "Listen . . ."

"I sent out a small task force, including the destroyer *Chippewa*, to investigate," Tolwyn continued. "They have yet to report and may have been taken out by the *Olympus*. Mr. Gerald, it is the joint chiefs' consensus that Amity Aristee has committed acts of treason against the Confederation. We've dug deeply through her records, and despite her extreme efforts to conceal her ancestry, we've discovered that she is, in fact, a Pilgrim. It's clear to us now that Bill Wilson's betrayal was just the beginning of a resurgence of Pilgrim theology and aggression."

Gerald stopped the message once more. "You're telling me she's a Pilgrim and that she gained control over her entire ship—with over seven hundred personnel on board? That's ridiculous. The crew would mutiny."

Paladin cocked a brow. "Unless, of course, many of them were already Pilgrims. Wilson's failure to have the Kilrathi destroy Earth triggered her into action. She's been waiting a long time for this."

"Maybe so. But there's no way she could replace her ship's complement without—"

"Mr. Gerald, we're not saying Aristee did this overnight. Oh, no. She started over four years ago, the day she assumed command of the *Olympus*. One by one she replaced her entire command staff with officers who are either Pilgrims or Pilgrim sympathizers. Then she moved on to the enlisted. She couldn't replace them all, but enough to serve her purpose. We have the names and the transfer orders to prove it."

"If this is true, how many other cap ships are Pilgrim time bombs waiting to go off?"

"Intell's already looking into that."

"What you ought to do is round up every goddamned citizen of Pilgrim ancestry and place them in protective custody."

"Don't you mean under arrest? Consider the logistics involved, not to mention the human rights issues."

"Seems to me that Pilgrims lost their rights when they decided to murder six million people."

"We can't blame every citizen of Pilgrim ancestry for what a few zealous individuals have done."

"I wouldn't call three, four, maybe five hundred a few. And what about the *Olympus's* escorts? Survivors here reported that the ship operated alone."

Paladin pursed his lips. "We're not sure. She couldn't replace the officers aboard those ships since escorts rotate so frequently, and that kind of breach in protocol would call too much attention to herself. She may have destroyed them."

"What does she hope to gain? She's got control of one supercruiser. Does she think she can bring down the Confederation with it? Does she think she can get near Earth?"

"She's on a crusade, a jihad to win back the holy land, Mr. Gerald. And she's recruiting individuals as she goes—that's why some citizens on Mylon Three were taken prisoner. They were part of the elect: people of Pilgrim ancestry whom she intends to sway back to the cause. She's especially looking for Confed Naval officers of Pilgrim descent. I don't believe she'll attack Earth with just one supercruiser, but she *is* building a force."

"How long does she think she can evade us? We have enough ships to post at every known jump point in this entire sector. She comes through, we got her."

"Maybe she'll leave the sector. And don't forget that she doesn't need known jump points. She can jump pulsars and other uncharted wells without NAVCOM coordinates. She's a Pilgrim."

Gerald snickered. "Like you." He thumbed the remote, and the admiral continued:

"Long range reconnaissance reports that Aristee is now at Lethe in the Tartarus system, waging the same war she waged on Mylon Three. You are hereby ordered to Lethe and instructed to use any means necessary to disable that ship. We want her back intact, Mr. Gerald. The destroyers *Mitchell Hammock* and *Oregon* will rendezvous with you there. Good hunting. Tolwyn out."

"Tartarus is on the border between Downing and Day quadrants, four jump points from here," Gerald reminded the commodore. "Aristee will be long gone by the time we get there."

"I'll get us there in a single jump," Paladin said, then started for the hatch.

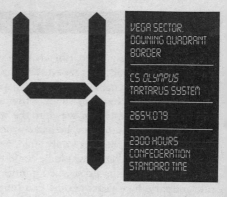

4

VEGA SECTOR,
DOWNING QUADRANT
BORDER

CS OLYMPUS
TARTARUS SYSTEM

2654.079

2300 HOURS
CONFEDERATION
STANDARD TIME

"Remember Peron! Remember Peron! Remember Peron!"

William Santyana stood on a catwalk that overlooked the *Olympus*'s flight deck. He tugged at his ill-fitting Confederation utilities and stared down at the twenty-four pilots who, standing at attention, continued to shout their battle cry. Captain Amity Aristee paraded before the two squadrons, having just delivered a speech laced with enough anti-Confederation sentiments to upset even a politically apathetic person's stomach. "Go now!" she ordered. "Deliver our message."

The pilots scattered toward their waiting Rapier starfighters, some still shouting about Peron, an agricultural colony in the Luyten system that represented the Pilgrim's last stand in the old war. For seven months Pilgrims had held fast against brutal sorties and counter-offensives. More Pilgrims died defending Peron than in any other engagement, an engagement eventually known as a massacre, an engagement they had clearly not forgotten. Santyana's parents, both Pilgrims who had actively fought in the war, had thankfully not been anywhere near Peron during the attack. After the Pilgrim Alliance's surrender, they had resignedly moved to Divinity, a Pilgrim enclave in the Tamayo system, where Santyana had been raised. By fifteen, he had grown weary of their fanatical teachings and had run away. He had worked for three years as a longshoreman, offloading cargo cruisers. By eighteen, he had tested his way into the Space Naval Academy on Hilthros. And by nineteen, he had learned of his parents' deaths in a freak shuttle crash. An only child, Santyana often wished he had a family member to whom he could turn for support. But his surviving relatives had disowned him for joining the Confederation military. Five years ago he had found Pris, a blonde vision who had somehow been born with the missing piece of his soul. When they had met, he had only two years of Confederation service left, opting to discharge after two five-year tours. He had wanted to settle down, farm the land, escape the rigidity of military life.

"You got business up here?"

Santyana faced the wiry, baggy-eyed deck boss who had addressed him. The man's Pilgrim cross dangled from a chain around his neck and seemed wholly out of place against his bright green uniform.

"I said, you got business up here?"

"I don't know. Couple Marines dragged me out of my quarters and left me here. Told me to wait for her." He tipped his head toward Amity Aristee, who climbed a steep staircase leading to the catwalk.

"You Santyana?"

"That's right."

"Heard a lot about you. Test-piloted the first B model Rapiers. You were the leading war ace for, what was it? Two consecutive years?"

"Three. But that was a while ago."

"I read they gave you quite a send-off."

"Yeah, they did. And I'm still retired."

"So you think. And what the hell were you doing on a farm anyway? Good thing we saved you from playing with dirt. Now you can put your skills to work for the elect."

"I don't plan on flying for anyone right now, whether they be divinely or militarily inspired."

"And why is that?" Aristee asked, pulling her plum-black hair into a ponytail and fastening it with a small band. Like the deck boss, she wore a Pilgrim cross that hung between the gold buttons of her dark-blue uniform, and the juxtaposition—the contradiction—awed Santyana.

"You invaded my home. Scared the hell out of my wife and daughter. We agreed to come with you. But that's it. If you think I'm going to fly for you people. . . ."

She furrowed her brow. "You people? You're one of us, William. Your parents were both compasses, your father a visionary with the ability to find systems suitable for Pilgrim expansion, your mother an explorer with the gift to navigate through unknown environments. You, I suspect, are an explorer—just like your mother. Your record shows an unexplained jump in Douglas Quadrant about seven years ago. You found your way through a previously undiscovered gravity well. Care to comment on that?"

"No, I don't."

"I also know you've done some research on theories of parallel tonality and other scientific explanations on Pilgrim abilities. That a hobby of yours?"

"What do you care?"

"Actually, I do care. A lot. You can't deny your blood." She took a step closer, eyes widening. "I chose Mylon Three for our first attack because there's only one jump point in the system, making for a slow Confed counterassault. And I chose it because it had once been a Pilgrim settlement before MyGov sold out to the Confederation. Pilgrim descendants lived there. But what first turned my attention to Mylon was you. Captains don't leave their ships during assaults. But I went down there especially for you. You're the best Pilgrim pilot I have."

"I don't believe this. You kidnap me and my family, keep us locked up in officers quarters for days, then you drag me down here and expect me to just say, yeah, I'll fly for you? Lady, I think you've spent a little too much time communicating with the divine."

"I've just made you squadron commander, One Hundred and Twenty-first Fighter Wing, Eighth Squadron," she said, unfazed by his jibe. "And FYI: we'll preserve the Confederation chain of command and wear Confederation uniforms to avoid confusion here *and* create some with our enemies. But that'll change after this assault. I suggest you suit up, review your mission log, and begin your preflight checklist." She winked at the deck boss. "Mr. Towers, will you escort Brotur William to his Rapier?"

"Yes, ma'am." The boss seized Santyana's elbow.

"You can't force me to fly," he said, grinning over the absurdity. "I'll just sit there. I won't touch the controls."

"I want you to do this because your heart tells you it's right," she said. "The stars were meant for Pilgrims—not humans. They invaded our space, stole from us, murdered us. We're taking back what was once ours, and *ours* is a just cause."

"Conscription has nothing to do with justice."

"This isn't conscription. It's all part of the settling-in process. I don't expect you to suddenly swear your allegiance to us. That will take time and a deeper understanding of who you are."

"So what makes you think I'll fly?"

She reached up, about to stroke his cheek. He snatched her wrist. "Easy, William. You'll fly because the first time you refuse me, I'll kill your wife. And the second time, I'll torture your daughter. I won't kill the little one; she is, after all, part Pilgrim."

He cursed her through gritted teeth.

"There, now." She looked on him with transparent sympathy and spoke like a mother consoling a son with a scuffed knee. "I know it hurts. I know you hate me. That's okay. But don't doubt me. Six million souls will testify that I keep my word. And historians will record the same."

"There's already a place for you in history. See: mass murderers."

She smirked, then spun and headed for the staircase. "Good luck, William. I'm counting on you, as are Pris and Lacey. Don't let them down."

He glowered. The names of his wife and daughter had no place on her lips.

And behind all of her Pilgrim posing lay nothing but blackmail.

"Come on," the deck boss said. "Let's get you suited up."

Commodore Richard Bellegarde stared through the porthole as the troopship made its final approach toward the *Concordia*'s aft flight deck. He would never tire of staring at the majestic supercruiser and often found it difficult to believe that he had been assigned to her as naval operations adjunct. The largest battleship in the Confed's fleet, the *Concordia* was named the Confed flagship in 2654 and presently served as mobile command center for naval operations. If you closed your eyes and swept yourself back to Earth, circa World War II, you could easily place the *Concordia* among the old seagoing battleships of that day, her pointed bow suggesting that she could cut through salt water as easily as vacuum. And like her ancient predecessors, she had been fitted with a magnificent, cone-shaped superstructure that rose in three tiers to a bridge crowned by a complex sensor array. A quartet of immense antimatter guns sat at equidistant positions along her upper deck and attested to her staggering firepower. Presently, she traveled in the company of four supply ships, two Exeter-class destroyers, and a Bengal-class cruiser. Bellegarde noted how the destroyer *Talmud* had been replaced by the CS *Carraway* during his brief visit to Scotland.

Yes, he had gone back to Glasgow, had visited the stomping ground of his forefathers, and had thought he could rekindle his connection to the place. He had argued with Admiral Tolwyn that he was a native of the Eddings system, that Earth was not his homeworld. He did not place as much emphasis on its survival as those who had been born there, those who still had families there, those who deemed the planet the sacred birthplace of humanity. Bellegarde had wanted to forget the place and consequently forget his past. Earth's destruction would hardly strike a blow. And he had finally confessed to Tolwyn why he wanted to

forget. His forefathers had systematically wiped out an entire
family and had assumed their identities. Brilliant criminals one
and all, they had forged a future for themselves among the stars,
a future founded on bloodshed. Bellegarde was not Richard's
true surname. When, at sixteen, he had learned of his family's
murderous rise to prestige from an uncle whose lips had loosened
from alcohol, Richard had confronted his father, but the man
would neither confirm nor deny the story. And he had never
revealed the family's true name. Since then, Richard had searched
the databases on over a dozen worlds but had come up empty.
And back at Glasgow, he had done the same and once more had
found nothing.

But there had been something in the air of the old city, something that made him feel like he belonged as he stared across the
tranquil waters of the Clyde River and imagined the ancient shipbuilding yards that had once thrived along its banks. He had felt
a sense of why people fought so desperately to preserve the planet,
that something natural, something innate, something one could
never deny dwelled in both the land and the people. The link
could never be broken. Tolwyn had said that he would discover
a lot more in Glasgow that he had expected. While Bellegarde
had not found complete reconciliation with his past, he had
reached a plateau of understanding that might now put the war
into perspective. It was no longer "Us versus Them" but a war
to preserve the blooming of a flower, the flight of a dove, the
smile of a small boy reeling in his first fish. It had nothing to do
with politics and everything to do with a small place in the universe from which we could share our lives with others and never
forget who we were, who we are.

Bellegarde turned away from the porthole and leaned back in
his seat. He closed his eyes as the troopship fired maneuvering
jets and swept into the flight deck. He thought of the vidcall to
Trish, how he had broken off their three-year affair. Her tears
had awakened a tearing sensation in his chest. She had to have
known that having an affair with a married man, a Confederation officer no less, would be complicated and lead to

either heartbreak or scandal. He had known the same, but Trish had given him all of those things that Melissa had either refused to give or had been incapable of giving. Trish had made him feel whole after twenty-one years of living with a woman who despised his career, who despised everything he believed in. Melissa had talked him out of wanting children, and now, at forty-six, it seemed too late. Though he often found himself feeling uncomfortable around children, he figured that she had taught him that feeling, and he would never forgive her for that. But he stayed married to her, more out of pity than anything else, and had numbed his sorrow with alcohol.

He suppressed a sudden chill as he considered whether he had made a terrible mistake in saying good-bye to Trish. But the admiral had advised him to end the affair, and Bellegarde had complied, both because he had great respect for Tolwyn and because Tolwyn controlled his destiny. Bellegarde wanted a promotion to rear admiral and a fleet to command. Adulterers and sloppy drunks rarely ascended to that particular throne. *Keep your nose clean and do what they tell you* had been Bellegarde's motto for his entire Confederation career, though he only partially lived up to the ideal. Tolwyn had somehow learned of his failings and had at least given him the chance to redeem himself. Bellegarde had not passed up that opportunity, painful though it was. He opened his eyes as landing skids thudded to the deck.

After the usual check-in and greetings from a few of the pilots who continually invited him to their nightly poker game, Bellegarde accessed the shipboard data net and learned that the admiral was in his quarters. He caught a lift and rode impatiently with two ordnance specialists who stood at attention and would not speak in his presence.

In the corridor outside Tolwyn's hatch, Bellegarde touched the intercom and identified himself. The admiral's distracted greeting piped through the speaker. Bellegarde moved inside and found Tolwyn seated at his comm terminal in the narrow living room, staring at a large flat screen mounted on the bulkhead.

The words ACCESSING INTER-SHIP COMMUNICATIONS CHANNEL glowed on the screen. Tolwyn whirled in his chair. "Good to have you back, Richard. Welcome to the Lafayette system. Have a seat."

Bellegarde crossed to a leather sofa. "Good to be back, sir. I came as soon as I heard."

"Yes, I hated cutting short your leave, but the situation has grown markedly worse."

"I read the briefing you sent along. Where is she now?"

"At Tartarus, launching an attack on Lethe. I sent the *Tiger Claw*, the *Mitchell Hammock*, and the *Oregon* to intercept. Paladin's already on board the *Claw*."

"Excellent. But couldn't we spare more ships?"

"No. In fact we still haven't received word from the *Chippewa* and the *Olympus*'s escorts. We're down seven capital ships in just three days. Recent intell indicates that the cats are mobilizing in the K'n'Rek system. Seems two of their destroyers and a ConCom were taken out by a Confederation supercruiser. The details are still sketchy, but it seems Aristee left Mylon and traveled through Kilrathi space."

"That seems foolish."

"Yes, it does." Tolwyn paused, and Bellegarde sensed he was holding something back.

"Communications established," came a cool computer voice from the admiral's terminal.

Tolwyn swung back to face the screen. "Excuse me for a moment."

Space Marshal Sandra Gregarov appeared and gave a quick nod of acknowledgment. Her double-breasted uniform with ornate lapels, her curly blonde hair brushed with gray and deftly styled, and her probing hazel eyes afforded her a presence that radiated grace and command. And for as long as Bellegarde had known her, he had never witnessed a single word escape her lips that had not been carefully measured. A supreme diplomat, politician, and an enormously successful line captain during the Pilgrim war, Gregarov had been the joint chiefs' first pick for the

Confederation Navy's highest ranking post. She had served in that position for two years now and had earned a large measure of respect for the freedom she gave and the trust she placed in her subordinates. She had even won the hearts of the Senate, a feat Admiral Tolwyn himself had yet to accomplish. Then again, Tolwyn wasn't in the business of making friends, and his impatience and short temper underscored that. Just as well. Bellegarde would hate to serve a man whose agenda leaned more heavily on pleasing senators than winning wars.

"Ma'am, I assume you've read my latest report," Tolwyn began steadily.

"I have. And frankly, Geoff, I'm worried. My staff has been swamped by Terran News people. Seems a shuttle of survivors from Mylon Three escaped the attack and jumped to Ymir before the *Tiger Claw* arrived on scene. They sought out the press and gave some unfavorable interviews. I've had to evade the accusations that Confederation forces wiped out Mylon."

"But you didn't—"

"Of course not. We can't afford a public witch hunt for Pilgrims. Not yet, anyway. The press believes we're still investigating the incident. But I can't feed that cock-and-bull story to the Senate. They demand and deserve answers. Bill Wilson's betrayal has already made their faith in us wane. I'll be jumping back to Earth within the hour."

"Then you know what you have to do."

She learned toward the camera, her gaze growing more intent. "Yes, I need to assure them that this mess will be cleaned up swiftly and decisively and that, as previously ordered, any technology valuable to the Confederation will be recovered. Can I do that?"

"With certainty."

"Thank you, Geoff. I'll keep you informed." She broke the link.

"Well, there it is, Richard." As Tolwyn swiveled back, he drew in a deep breath and suddenly appeared much older than his sixty-two years. His watchphone beeped. "Yes?"

"Admiral? Intelligence drone from K'n'Rek just came in," Radar Officer Abrams said. "Data is being uploaded to your terminal, sir."

"Very well. Come have a look, Richard."

Bellegarde rose and stood over Tolwyn's shoulder as the admiral accessed the report. Long-range reconnaissance video showed a thin, tube-shaped haze slowly dissipating in space. Data columns identified the object as the remains of a ship or ships. The officer who had made the report noted in his comments that the haze's composition included elements found in Kilrathi plastisteel and that he suspected that a gravity well had been responsible for the devastation, though no known well existed in the region. The report also indicated that two Kilrathi battle groups had jumped out of the system, their suspected destinations Ymir and Nephele. A third battle group had jumped, its course still unknown.

Tolwyn bolted from his chair. "Mr. Bellegarde. Let's get to the bridge. We need to get the hell out of here ASAP. And we need ships in Ymir and Nephele even sooner."

"Yes, sir." Bellegarde rose and followed Tolwyn to the hatch. "And sir? Regarding that report. How could a gravity well be responsible for destroying those Kilrathi ships? My physics tells me that wells don't suddenly appear and vanish."

"You heard the space marshal, Richard. 'Recover any technology valuable to the Confederation.' Gravity wells *do* suddenly appear if they're being generated by a Pilgrim hopper drive, one that can be operated within planetary systems, one with an amazingly powerful range."

"There's no such technology."

Tolwyn reached for the hatch control panel, then froze. He stared gravely at Bellegarde. "Welcome to the new war, Richard."

VEGA SECTOR,
DOWNING QUADRANT
BORDER

CS *TIGER CLAW*

ENTERING TARTARUS
SYSTEM

2654.080

0600 HOURS
CONFEDERATION
STANDARD TIME

"Mr. Obutu? Stealth mode," Gerald ordered.

"Stealth mode, aye-aye, sir." From his forward station, Obutu tapped a series of commands on his touchpad, and standard lighting dimmed to stain the bridge crimson.

"Sir?" Radar Officer Falk called. "The *Mitchell Hammock* and *Oregon* arrived at oh-four-thirty and are in position behind Lethe's moon. They report no signs of planetary torpedoes."

Gerald nodded. "Our ETA to Lethe?"

"Seven point three-one minutes, full impulse."

"Very well." He looked to Mr. Obutu. "Engage telescopic imaging."

"Telescopic imaging, aye-aye, sir."

Leaning over Obutu's shoulder, Gerald studied the image piping in from the *Claw's* laser-guided reflecting telescope. The scope might be able to detect coruscation generated by the super-cruiser, but as it was, only the spectacularly blue orb of Lethe dominated the readout. Eighty-five percent of the world lay beneath oceans, with just a cluster of three continents rising a few thousand meters above sea level. The planet's available land remained slightly larger than the continent of Australia, at about eight million square kilometers distributed mainly between the two larger land masses. Some nineteen million people jammed those continents, nineteen million souls who now weighed heavily on Gerald's shoulders. "Keep scanning, Mr. Obutu."

"Aye-aye, sir."

Gerald crossed back to his command chair, noting with curiosity that Paladin had left the bridge. Strange. Gerald accessed the comm terminal on his armrest and keyed in the code for the commodore's quarters.

"Yes, Mr. Gerald?"

"Thought you'd want to be up here for the attack."

"I'll monitor from my quarters, thank you."

"I see."

"Don't worry, Captain. I haven't stopped loving you."

Gerald jerked in his seat, eyeing the bridge to see if any of the fourteen officers in command and control had heard; if they had, they weren't letting on. "Well, uh, thanks for your assistance in the jump. Seven hours. That's outstanding."

"Thank the Pilgrims. They charted that well in the first place."

"You'll understand if I don't do that just now."

Paladin did not respond.

And Gerald simply ended the link. "Mr. Obutu? Do you have a visual of the *Olympus*?"

"I believe so, sir. Waiting to positively identify and triangulate position. And . . . got her, sir. Looks like seven troopships breaking through the upper atmosphere, headed toward her. Squadron of Broadswords a quarter klick behind. Two squadrons of Rapiers running defense. Her ion engines coming on line. They know we've tagged her, sir."

Gerald stood and squinted through the viewport. In the distance, Lethe's medium star burned brilliantly, and to starboard, the planet hung like an ornament whose radiance wavered as the supercruiser shifted position. He whirled to his newly assigned helmsman, a hard-faced blonde named Veronica Schultz, a loner more interested in a promotion than in socializing. Gerald had approved of her the moment they had met. "Ms. Schultz? Maneuvering burst. Adjust course to intercept."

Schultz repeated the order and added a cool, "Aye-aye, sir." She tapped her touchpad, and the *Claw* suddenly leapt forward, maneuvering jets adding their thrust to the main engines. Though unconventional, the trick pried a little more velocity out of the old carrier, and Gerald felt a pang as he remembered the day the *Claw*'s former captain, the late Jay Sansky, had taught him the technique. Sansky had been part brother, part father, and an excellent mentor—until he had decided to expose his Pilgrim ancestry and help Bill Wilson. The two had conspired with the Kilrathi to launch a devastating assault on Earth. While Sansky's participation had been ancillary, the Confederation did not recognize degrees of treachery. Any help to a traitor condemned one's career, reputation, and life. Sansky knew that, and he had chosen suicide to spare himself further disgrace. Less than a week had passed since the man's death, and Gerald still felt the brutal stab of his mentor's betrayal.

"Mr. Obutu? Shields up. Sound general quarters. Launch fighters."

"Aye-aye, sir. Shields up. Sound the general alarm. Launch fighters."

As klaxons reverberated, Gerald regarded Communications Officer James Zabrowsky, a slightly built redhead who sat at his starboard station before a bank of monitors. "Mr. Z? Open a channel to our destroyers."

Zabrowsky touched a key and squinted as he listened to the series of encryption beeps sounding in his headset. "Channel open."

"Fitzmorris? Shanney? Break from cover and attack!"

The two destroyer captains responded tersely.

"The *Olympus* is pulling out of orbit, sir," Obutu reported. "But she's crawling. Troopships have safely docked. Broadswords returning to base. Rapiers turning to engage."

"Sir?" Falk cried. "The *Olympus*'s tube doors are opening. First salvo will be out in twenty seconds."

"Mr. Z? Get me Commander Deveraux."

"Aye, sir."

Gerald hustled to the starboard side observation station, and, taking the cue, Comm Officer Zabrowsky transferred Angel's signal there. The screen erupted in static, then she nodded. "Captain?"

"The *Olympus* has opened her tubes. I want you to get in tight and intercept that ordnance."

Blair tensed in his cockpit and focused on the glistening dot breaking away from Lethe, then his gaze lifted to the squadron. Angel and Hunter flew point a hundred meters ahead, with Gangsta and Cheddarboy positioned a hundred meters back at three o'clock and Bishop and Zarya holding steady at nine. Maniac and Blair formed the bottom of the iron-cross formation, and, once again, Maniac had complained over being held back. At least he was flying. Sinatra had come down with a case of post-jump vomiting that had left him too weak to fly, but rumor had it that he had spent too much time with his lips wrapped around a bottle of vodka.

"Standby, ladies. Let's light 'em and fight 'em!" Angel hollered.

Three pairs of afterburners lit in synch, and Blair watched the forward fighters rocket toward the supercruiser. He punched his burners, as did Maniac, and they thundered to join the others. His radar scope beeped as twenty or thirty crimson blips suddenly freckled the display. It seemed odd that the unit would identify Rapiers as hostiles, but the system had now been programmed to alert him of all vehicles not registered to the *Claw*.

"Tallyho," Maniac said. "Multiple bandits inbound."

"Ignore them," Angel snapped. "Second and Third Squadrons will engage enemy fighters."

"Enemy fighters?" Maniac asked. "They're Rapiers. You'd better tell me they're being flown by Kilrathi, Commander."

The briefing Angel had given them had been, in a word, clandestine. She would neither confirm nor deny the pilots' speculation that the Kilrathi or the Pilgrims had seized control of the supercruiser. And when Blair had pulled her aside to ask for her own opinion, she had cut him off.

"They're enemy fighters," she told Maniac. "Period. Got visual confirmation of starboard side tubes. Hunter? You got the first one. I'll take the second. Zarya and Bishop? You got third and fourth. The rest of you will remain defensive and keep those fighters off our backs."

Like any decent and correct furball, it all happened in a gasp and surge of adrenaline:

Ten enemy Rapiers flew head on, their neutron cannons spewing a fusillade that tore through Black Lion Squadron.

Two planetary torpedoes burst from the *Olympus*'s forward tubes and dragged their vaporous tails toward Lethe.

Angel and Hunter dropped into eighty-five degree dives, barreled through the onslaught, then swept up on the supercruiser's stern. Even as they came abreast of the ship, they fired guided missiles toward the pair of torpedoes.

Gangsta and Cheddarboy flew high above the supercruiser, then pulled maximum yaws to starboard and targeted a second pair of torpedoes that streaked away. As they fired their guided missiles, one of the *Olympus*'s antimatter guns pivoted toward them, cannon lifting. White-hot rods began punching holes in their vapor trails.

Bishop and Zarya chose an attack vector that placed them one hundred meters out, at the cruiser's six o'clock low. They climbed toward the ship, slaloming through antimatter fire to dump off their contribution to the counterassault.

"My missile's locked on," Angel announced.

"Ditto here," Hunter said.

Twin flashes turned a region of Lethe's blue aura into a sheet of blinding light as the first two torpedoes detonated harmlessly in the planet's exosphere.

Before the light cleared, two more bursts lifted their shoulders, and Gangsta and Cheddarboy shouted their victory cries.

Alternating his gaze between the radar scope and the planet,

Blair noted that "The Mongrels" of Second Squadron, led by a highly decorated pilot named Achilles, had engaged a squadron of enemy Rapiers. Third Squadron's "Screamin' Shepherds" had launched to take on the other group. In the meantime, he and Maniac would continue wheeling over the cap ship, dodging antimatter fire, keeping eyes bugged for Rapiers that escaped the net.

Another magnesium-bright burst from the planet stole Blair's attention.

"Bishop takes bomb," Bishop quipped.

"Aw, shit!" Zarya moaned. "Mine missed. Guidance system malfunction."

"I got the torpedo on my scope," Maniac said. "Locked on. I'm going down to take the shot!"

"Negative. Stay on my wing," ordered Blair.

"And let like a million people die?"

"Stay on his wing," Angel repeated.

"Second and Third got this ball sewed up," Maniac argued. "I ain't got time for this. Court martial my ass, but I won't let those people die. See ya, Blair."

With that, Maniac broke from the circle and arrowed toward the planet.

"Got that torpedo on my scope, too," Blair said. "It's already too far. You can't get in close enough for a lock."

"Maniac, get back here," Angel shouted. "Know what? *I* don't have time for this."

"That's right, Commander," Hunter said. "Got two more torpedoes in the air!"

He's going to get too low, Blair thought. *The Rapier's not capable of sustained atmospheric operations. He'll lose control and burn up. Even if he manages to eject, there'll be no one there to tractor in his pod. I'm not going to do it. I'm not going to do it.*

Swearing aloud, Blair cut the stick hard right and traced Maniac's path toward Lethe. The expected shouting from Angel never came; she and Hunter were too busy tracking the torpedoes. As he plummeted toward the fluctuating blue expanse broken only by the fiery dot of the torpedo's engine and the glowing eyes of Maniac's thrusters, Blair frowned as he considered his wingman's motivation for violating orders. Was Maniac really the noble pilot who wanted to save millions? Or did he only intend to bail out and impress Zarya? The latter seemed more shallow, much more like Maniac. The fact that he would save lives in the interim only further enticed him.

"I'm on your six," Blair said, his signal broadcast on Maniac's private channel. "About a K out and closing."

"Get out of here, Blair."

"Too late. We're both committed. Just get the lock and take the shot. Got mild chop already. Clock's ticking."

"Just need a few more meters," Maniac said distractedly. "Come on, you son of a bitch. Come on. Come on. Yeah! Got the lock! And firing!"

Close enough now so that he could see the sharp-angled outline of Maniac's fighter, Blair watched the guided missile drop a meter from the Rapier's short wing then burst off toward the distant torpedo. "Rocket's away. Now pull out."

"Thanks for the tip, Ace." Maniac pitched up ninety degrees.

Meanwhile, Blair rolled to port, electing to retreat more slowly and give himself more time to adjust to possible fluctuations in the exosphere. His radar scope showed Maniac's fighter about fifty meters to port and gaining fast. The guided missile stood at the scope's edge, hauling ass toward the torpedo.

"Impact in three, two, one. Bang!" Maniac cried.

The missile and torpedo scattered themselves in a fleeting conflagration that might very well have marked the end or the rise of Lieutenant Todd Marshall's naval career. Fitting possibility for a man of extremes.

As though cued, Angel broke into their private channel. "Maniac? Blair?"

Blair could see why she had called. Two torpedoes charged toward them, with guided missiles in pursuit. ETA: twenty seconds. "I see 'em, Angel. Setting evasion course."

"And I'm in his wash," Maniac added.

"Oh, shit," Blair said through a shiver as he stared at the quartet of incoming ordnance backdropped by the supercruiser and the spectacular firefight raging around it.

"I'm locked on to one of 'em," Maniac said.

"But we're still too close."

"Get ready. Firing!"

Maniac's missile lanced out at the starboard torpedo, the one closer to Blair. Even as he jerked the stick toward him, pulling into a high-G climb, the missile struck the torpedo and sent up an explosion that rose over their Rapiers. Hundreds of torpedo and missile fragments slashed against Blair's shields as he fought for control. The Rapier shimmied and suddenly propelled free of the blast. He craned his neck and saw Maniac's fighter emerge from billowing black clouds, climbing in a high-speed flat spin with attitude thrusters firing ineffectually.

"Maniac!"

"Give me a sec," the jock said, cockpit alarms nearly over-powering his voice. He swung out of the flat spin, banked hard, and lined up quickly on Blair's vector. "Damn. You want to talk recoveries? Check the recorder on that one."

"You two are still in the cone," Angel observed. "Move out to cover."

"Roger that," Blair said. He increased thrust, aiming for his original position directly over the supercruiser as the ship seemed to lose momentum.

"Fighters bugging out," Hunter said. "I don't get it. They're leaving the ship undefended. They can't be that low on fuel. And now look. She's slowing down even more and taking missile fire from the destroyers and the *Claw*. She surrendering or what?"

Blair saw it, too. Enemy Rapiers abruptly ducked out of their dogfights and bounded for the supercruiser, whose meson shields flickered with the azure talons of a missile barrage. First, Second, and Third squadrons would now add their fire to the cap ship bombardment. Clearly, the cruiser had surrendered. Her velocity measured just a few meters per second.

"Guess they *are* Pilgrims," Maniac said. "They're on their knees, but prayer ain't' gonna help 'em now."

As Blair neared the ship, a strange feeling seized him, a feeling that began as a cold wind blasting through his helmet and flight suit. The wind suddenly grew warm and concentrated on his face. He squinted against its force and trembled as he wondered if he was suffering from G-induced spacesickness or something worse. He gasped as the hot wind felt like fingers stroking his cheek and a woman's voice—not his mother's—repeatedly called him by his first name. He gazed out past the supercruiser, to the disk of wavering darkness that devoured the surrounding light. Then, as quickly as they had come, the voice and the caress were gone.

Dazed, Blair blinked hard and found Merlin pacing over a bridge of air, tugging nervously on his ponytail. The holograph occasionally self-activated during times of crisis, and his expression indicated no less. "Christopher, my sensors are reading a massive, localized disturbance being generated by the supercruiser. Analysis confirms that a gravitic warp has formed approximately eight hundred meters ahead of the ship. I'm reading a matter-antimatter reaction, but it's remarkably controlled. I can't explain this, but the warp contains a peripheral field of indeterminate particles that are apparently neutralizing the gravitic interference created by nearby objects, most notably the planet."

He heard Merlin, but the words hardly registered. "What?"

"Forget what I said. Just hit the brakes!"

Even as Blair frantically throttled down, the comm channel erupted with the stricken voices of his squadron:

"What the hell is that?" Maniac asked.

"Don't know, but it's got me!" Gangsta said. "I'm fully lit and can't break free."

"Commander? Commander?" Cheddarboy cried. "I'm being pulled in with her."

"Oh my god," Bishop muttered. "Look at The Mongrels. They're breaking up! Oh, man. Now it has me."

Blair riveted his gaze on the disk, his mouth opening as the

Rapiers from Second Squadron spun, barrel rolled, or tumbled bow over stern, shedding pieces until they finally disintegrated. Radii of debris zippered back toward the disk's center, wiping the universe clean of the destruction, save for vines of lingering haze.

"Jinxman? Get your people back to the *Claw*," Angel told Third Squadron's commander.

"We were already falling back. That well has an antigraviton cloak that extends for about five hundred meters. Lost two in the fight, but the rest are accounted for. And we IDed those enemy pilots as Confederation officers. What the hell is going on here?"

"Never mind that, just—" She broke off.

Blair stiffened. "Angel?" He spotted her Rapier caught on the well's rim.

"You're still in the clear, Blair. Hook up with Third Squadron. Don't . . . come . . . any . . ." Exertion robbed her words.

"Wish you would've told us that sooner," Maniac interjected. "Thing's reeling me in."

Now hovering high and behind the *Olympus*, Blair counted all seven of his comrades battling against the well's unfailing pull. Had it not been for Merlin's warning, he would be with them, though he would still experience the distinct horror of watching them die.

"I'm gonna run out of fuel in a minute," Gangsta said.

"I'm right behind you," Cheddarboy added, his voice cracking.

"Tell you what? If this is it, then I'm going out like an officer," Maniac announced. "We all should. Set self-destruct for ten seconds."

"Maybe he's right," Zarya said. "My afterburners are in the red, turbines starting to overheat."

"Yeah, and if this well doesn't finish us first, the cruiser will mow us down anyway," Bishop said. "It's coming right at us."

Blair closed his eyes and rocked in his seat, groping for a solution. He couldn't let them die. He couldn't let *her* die.

It's coming right at us. Bishop had said that. The *Olympus* would not create and fly toward a gravity well unless it intended—

"What are you doing?" Merlin asked as Blair advanced the throttle, ignited afterburners, and swooped down at the murky lake of darkness.

"The *Olympus* is going to jump that well," Blair answered. "And so are we."

"Even if we jump the well, they'll capture us on the other side."

"No, they won't. You'll see. But first we have to pick up the others."

"The others? It's too late for them."

"Wrong again."

"I can't watch," Merlin said, then blinked out.

Two-handing the stick, Blair wrestled against the well and brought his fighter within ten meters of Angel's.

His VDU crackled to life. "You're a fool," she said.

Ignoring her, he engaged the retrieval tractor system and fired a beam at her Rapier. "You're locked on. Now listen up, people!" Blair regarded his radar scope, taking mental note of each Rapier's position relative to each other and to the well. "Gangsta? Fire a tractor at Cheddarboy, and Cheddarboy you latch on to Bishop."

"Interesting plan, mate," Hunter said. "We'll embrace in death."

"Do what he says," Angel shot back. "All of you. Link up. And Blair, can you do it?"

He swallowed. "I think so."

"What's he going to do?" Bishop asked. "And how the hell will linking help? We'll buy it anyway."

Angel huffed. "Everyone *except* Bishop link up."

"Uh, that's okay," Bishop said shakily. "I'm with you."

Blair stared out across the string of jets, all facing away from the gravity well, every thruster burning brightly. Though he couldn't see the beams that joined their crafts, his tactical display revealed the emission lines. The chain looked good. "Okay. On my mark you will engage emergency flameout systems, bringing thrust down to zero."

"At which time we get sucked in," Maniac said.

"That's the plan," Blair retorted. "And if anyone wants to bail, do it now." He waited a moment, listening to the grinding of his thrusters as they began to superheat. "Okay. Ready now? Here it comes. Mark!"

Like a string of holiday lights winking out, the squadron's thruster cones darkened—

And Blair cut into a hard, starboard roll at ten degrees per second, dragging the other Rapiers behind his. The afterburner gauge rolled even higher into the red as he now faced a whirlpool of swirling haze traversed by hunks of rubble. The radar scope showed the supercruiser just one hundred and fifty meters behind them, but with an abrupt flash that fell over Blair's canopy, the *Olympus*'s jump-drive engaged, and it blurred over-head to dematerialize into the well.

"It jumped," Zarya said. "It created its own well and jumped it."

"But we ain't going to be so lucky," Bishop predicted. "They probably had NAVCOM coordinates to negotiate this thing. We only got Blair's good intentions and his one-and-oh record."

The well tightened its grip, and Blair anxiously reached out with his mind into the gravitic eddies. He had jumped the gravity well known as Scylla and had jumped the Charybdis Quasar, relying only on his Pilgrim senses to navigate. The well in front of him shouldn't be any different—

But it was. As he drew closer, the Rapier shaking violently, he expected to see his mother since she, or more precisely, her essence, resided across the universe and passing through gravitic warps enabled him to experience her for a fleeting moment. He reached deeper into the well, squinting into his mind's eye, prob-ing with every sense, with all he was, fighting for a glimpse of her face, a whisper, a warning, anything. He saw only a curved cor-ridor representing a safe passage that looped through the well. *Where are you, Mother? Have you left me forever?*

"Ten seconds to the well's Point of No Return," Merlin shouted as he reappeared with a shimmer and peeked through fingers covering his eyes.

"Thought you couldn't watch this," Blair said, thumbing a button to engage the Rapier's jump drive.

"Thought you could use some help."

Blair closed his eyes and called off the first set of coordinates to his navigation computer.

"Coordinates plotted," the computer responded.

He rattled off the second set and heard the response, followed by the computer's warning about reaching .7 light speed, the well's PNR velocity.

"I'd tell you that you're off course for the jump, but I know the reply," said Merlin. "I still do not understand how or why this distortion affects my CPU."

"Save the mystery for another time," Blair shot back.

An alarm blared rapidly, indicating an aft hull breach. Thankfully, the cockpit had not been compromised. Yet. He shut down the alarm, then checked the jump drive clock. Four seconds to jump. Three, two—

The gravity well shucked itself off into a tableau so white that it seemed to absorb the Rapier, absorb Blair, absorb the others and lift them all into its silky arms. For an instant, the frailties of being human seemed meaningless. Blair felt as though he could be anyone and anywhere, do anything, join with every bit of matter down to the quantum level.

Then it was dark, over, and he was just Blair, seated in his cockpit, enveloped by the familiar void tinged blue by Lethe's reflected light.

"We're back?" Merlin asked.

Blair heaved a sigh. "Wasn't sure that was possible. Now we know it is." He brought up Angel's private channel. "Commander?"

"Blair," she acknowledged, gathering her breath. "You know, I was supposed to jump Charybdis with you, and I was kind of upset that I missed that. This puts it all into perspective. Question. Why aren't we on the other side of the well with the *Olympus*?"

"We could've jumped there, but I figured they would just

launch fighters and overtake us. So I looped us through the well and back onto our original vector."

"But now we've lost them."

"No. I marked their coordinates. I'll read them to my nav computer and upload to the data net."

"Nice work, Blair."

"It's Pilgrim."

"Choose another call sign."

"I won't. And I wish everyone would use it."

"All right, I'll give that order, but you deal with the harassment—because you're asking for it." She resumed the steely tone of squadron commander. "Ladies? Disengage retrieval systems and sound off."

VEGA SECTOR,
DOWNING QUADRANT
BORDER

CS TIGER CLAW

TARTARUS SYSTEM,
PLANET LETHE

2654.080

0730 HOURS
CONFEDERATION
STANDARD TIME

Gerald shifted past the hatch and stormed into Paladin's quarters. He cocked his head, searching the dark living area, then found his target in a corner meagerly lit by a desk light.

The commodore sat back in a chair, boots kicked up onto the work surface of his terminal.

His gaze remained on the hard copy dossier resting on his lap, and Gerald spotted an old picture of Amity Aristee printed in the corner of the first page. "Good morning, Mr. Gerald. I expected you sooner."

Gerald showed his teeth. "I was a little busy going over the casualty report. With all due respect, sir, I want answers. And I want them now."

"The folks at Intell still have a bit more corroborating evidence to consider before I can deliver any definitive information."

"That, sir, is horseshit, the same horseshit I had to feed my people during the first briefing."

He finally had Paladin's attention.

"Go ahead—classify and compartmentalize this," Gerald continued. "But my people have a right to know who killed their comrades. Morale is low. Rumors are running rampant—even among my command staff."

"All right, then. I'll conduct a briefing for you and your department heads."

Gerald recoiled a bit in surprise. "We'll need specifics, like exactly how that ship created and jumped a gravity well. We need to know what we're up against."

"I'll tell you what we know so far," Paladin said resignedly.

"One more request. For some odd reason I've been locked out of the satellite link to the Confed network. My shipboard records don't indicate which of my people are of Pilgrim ancestry. I assume you have access. I'd like that information uploaded to my personal account."

Paladin smiled—or was it a sneer? "So the witch hunt begins . . ."

"I have a right to any information that may compromise the safety of this ship and her crew. And it sounds to me that your department has already begun that hunt."

"Not exactly. And for the record, there are only two people aboard of Pilgrim ancestry: myself and Lieutenant Christopher Blair."

"Are you certain?"

"I examined the records myself while en route. But there may still be Pilgrims aboard who have evaded our detection."

"Has Admiral Tolwyn alerted the other line captains?"

"No. Any Confederation officer or enlisted person is still protected under Confederation law. If we alerted the captains, I'm certain that the rights of those Pilgrims would be violated. At the least, those people would be rounded up and tossed in the brig. At the most, they'd be shot. Check your history. Read up on the plight of Japanese Americans during World War Two."

"Permission to speak freely, sir?"

"I thought you already were," Paladin said acidly. "But granted."

"Sorry, sir, but my boots are firmly planted in the present. I can't trust you. Not until this is over. You may know this group and their tactics better than anyone aboard, but as far as I'm concerned, you're more dangerous than valuable."

"I know you have an especial hatred for Pilgrims since your

father's passing. And I'm sure that experience tells you that you can't let those feelings influence your judgment."

"My father wasn't just killed by you people. He was tortured first, dismembered until he bled to death. My mother found him in the backyard. Not much left. Just a pile of meat. You won't find that in my psyche ops profile or the fact that there aren't any pictures of him in my mother's apartment. My sister and I can't even mention his name. So when you say I have an especial hatred for Pilgrims, you have no idea."

"No, I guess I don't. But as I told you once before, we can't blame every citizen of Pilgrim ancestry for what a few individuals have done. Admittedly, it's fanatics like these that made me reject Pilgrim theology. You lost your father to them. So did I. Now, alert your people. We'll assemble in thirty minutes. And I'd like Lieutenant Blair there. We may need to address his heredity . . . and my own."

Sitting on his bunk, rubbing his eyes with the heels of his hands, Blair thought about how he felt and realized that for once he was at a loss. Sure, he felt worn out from the jump and its accompanying adrenaline rush, and deeply saddened over the loss of Second Squadron, but something else gnawed at him. His spirit glided over a black expanse, and from that expanse rose a figure in a white robe whose face he could not see, but whose arms reached out to him. He had no idea what the feeling or vision—or whatever it was—meant. He only knew that it had come on suddenly during landing and persisted.

He looked over at Maniac, clad in Skivvies and lying on his own rack. If Zarya could hear the music produced by Maniac's nostrils, her interest in him would definitely dwindle. Knowing Blair's luck, she probably had a fetish for men who snored loudly. He sighed, rose, then padded over to the latrine and stared at himself in the scored mirror. "You are one ugly bastard."

"Though I hesitate to agree since I am, in fact, a part of you, I would ultimately have to endorse that assessment." Merlin stood on the shelf above Blair's bunk, hands folded over his chest, shoulders hidden by steel-gray hair that he had unloosed from its band.

"Look who's talking. That a new hairstyle or a bug in your system?"

"I remind you that my appearance was molded after one of your father's favorite teachers, a man named Jebiah Omans who taught a class that linked particle physics to Shakespeare. Now there's a blending of art and atoms—"

"You never told me he taught that."

"Oh, yes. Particles play a vital role in human behavior, and Shakespeare was an expert in that area. Some even acknowledge him as the first particle physicist."

Blair gave the holograph a penetrating stare.

Merlin's lips finally curled. "All right, Jebiah Omans was, in fact, one of your father's teachers and the inspiration for me, but he only taught physics."

After a nod, Blair moved back to his bunk and plopped down. "No offense, but sometimes I wish my father had programmed you in his likeness. You've been with me since I was five, Merlin. But it just isn't the same."

"Your father never told me why, but he insisted against an interface that resembled him. Maybe he thought it would be too painful for you or that I could never replace him. Maybe he wanted that separation. I'm your guardian, your advisor, and my chips contain your father's protein, but he was and will always be your father. Now I suggest you get dressed."

"Why?"

"Because Lieutenant Commander Deveraux is about—"

The hatch bell sounded, and Merlin disappeared.

"I'm not waiting, Lieutenant. Be at the wardroom in ten min-utes for a briefing. Tell Maniac that I'll brief him and the rest of the squadron afterward."

As he fumbled with his trousers, Blair glanced at Maniac, who remained dead to the world. "Ma'am, if you can wait another second, I'll head down with you."

"Sorry, Christopher. She's already gone," Merlin said.

He looked to the holograph. "Yeah, and I know why."

"If you'd like my advice—"

Blair lifted a finger. "We both know what happened the last time I took your advice on women."

"But Christopher, I could have hardly known that she would be allergic to Italian food."

"Yeah, but she ate it anyway to be polite. Thought maybe it wouldn't bother her for once. Wound up spending the whole night in the hospital because *you* went off on that Italian spiel, talking about the whole romance language thing, the food, and *you* talked me into it. Never again. I think of that date, and all I see is this poor girl with hives all over her face."

"Fine. I won't help. I've made some observations of Lieutenant Commander Deveraux, but I'll keep them to myself." He tipped up his nose, snapped off.

"Merlin? Wait. What observations?"

The holograph would not activate. Blair checked his watch. Just as well. He had to get dressed.

"Commander," Blair said as he approached Angel. She stood beside the wardroom's open hatch, her uniform crisp, makeup sparingly applied. It didn't take much to enhance her beauty; the gifts were already there.

"You saved our lives today," she said softly. "I might just recommend you for more chicken guts."

His cheeks warmed, and he nervously shifted his gaze to the wardroom, where he spotted a knot of five department heads arguing bitterly. "What's with them? And what am I doing here? This looks like a briefing for senior-level officers."

"Commodore Taggart asked that you be present."

"Paladin? He's here? Whey didn't he tell me?"

"He's been busy. C'mon."

As they entered, the department heads fell silent and gave Blair the once-over, their expressions betraying no prejudice but no thrill to see him either. He took a seat next to Angel in the front row of folding chairs, then glanced back at the familiar faces. Flight Boss Raznick and Deck Boss Peterson sat in the back row, muttering to each other. Representatives from ordnance, maintenance, technical, and damage control sat on the far left. The other five squadron commanders had taken seats directly behind Blair and Angel, and two of those men, Jinxman of the Third and Lightning of the Fourth, returned somber nods and kept silent. Jinxman had draped a blue beret over the empty seat next to his, the name ACHILLES emblazoned on a patch.

During the next few minutes, Marine Corps Lieutenant Tori Andover and Sergeant Gulliver Cogan arrived with expressions that asked, *Why are we here and not out kicking ass?* Then the rest of the command staff filed into the room, including Lieutenant Commander Obutu. Blair liked the man and hoped that Gerald had recommend Obutu for a promotion to XO. Obutu had gone out of his way to make Blair feel comfortable during his first visit to the *Claw*'s rec. He had even beaten Blair in a game of virtual dogfighting. When queried about his obvious piloting skills, Obutu responded that he "had a little experience." The mystery intrigued Blair.

Paladin finally entered with a data slate in one hand while he used the other to tug at the color of his black Naval Intelligence uniform. The chatter died, and everyone snapped to their feet.

"As you were." The commodore crossed to where Gerald stood before the assembled personnel.

"Place your bets," Jinxman sang, leaning forward to whisper in Angel's ear. "I say we get five percent truth, ninety-five percent bullshit."

Angel looked back, eyes brimming with reproof.

"A few announcements before we begin," Gerald said. "At seventeen hundred hours there will be a memorial service in the chapel for Second Squadron and the others KIA. Tell your people to see Lieutenant Palladino in personnel if they'd like to make donations to the families. Replacements won't come any time soon, so I suggest that you make immediate recommendations for promotions and adjust your duty rosters to compensate. We've been here before, people. I'll expect those recommendations ASAP." He eyed Paladin. "I think most of us know the commodore, but for those who do not, this is Commodore James Taggart of Naval Intelligence, call sign Paladin. Admiral Tolwyn sent him to assist us. Commodore?" Gerald retreated a few steps, and Blair guessed that he was not the only officer who detected the bitterness in Gerald's tone.

Paladin pulled once more at his collar, tightened his lips, then seemed to sum up the officers, deciding what he would and would not say. "Ladies and gentlemen, we're presently en route to coordinates that will place us between the Lafayette and Tamayo systems. We believe this is the jump target of the CS *Olympus*. Unfortunately, it will take us three days to get there, and she may be gone by the time we arrive. We can analyze gravitic residuum to approximate her next position, but that will only provide an estimate. I assure you, though, that we haven't lost her yet."

"Commodore, are they Pilgrims?" Jinxman asked.

He nodded. "They're being led by one of the most skilled line captains in the fleet." He went on to explain how Captain Amity Aristee had managed to take over the *Olympus* and how Admiral Tolwyn had sent out a task force to investigate. Then he added, "I've just learned that the remains, or more precisely, the remaining haze of that task force was discovered approximately twenty hours ago in the Enyo system. Those ships were destroyed by a gravity well. Eighteen hours ago, another haze was encountered near Vega, and we believe that it represents the remains of the *Olympus*'s original battle group. We also suspect that at these coordinates she jettisoned remaining non-Pilgrim personnel, creating a limited but pure Pilgrim complement."

"She's a fanatic and a mass murderer who's creating gravity wells and using them as weapons and jump points," Gerald chipped in, then cocked a brow at Paladin. "Would you elaborate on exactly how she's doing this?"

"We believe she's in possession of a new generation of hopper drive that allows her to create space-time wells with a controlled matter-antimatter reaction. The well has a limited gravitic cloak verified by the pilots of this wing. But she can still manipulate the well's position and take out ships within five hundred meters."

"How did she obtain this technology? Better yet, how did she hide it from Confederation Intelligence?" Gerald asked.

"This isn't something that happens in a day, or a week, or a year. The Confederation legally recognizes three Pilgrim systems and five colonial enclaves. We routinely inspect them to be sure they're not developing technology or engaging in renewed military activity that could threaten us. For years we've had no trouble with them because those most devoted obey the edict that Pilgrims should no longer travel through space or engage in any other activities reliant on technology. They do this as penance for their loss in the war. In fact, when the Kilrathi war began, they insisted on remaining neutral and presently maintain that status."

"That's an informative history lesson," Gerald said impatiently. "But I'm not sure it answers the question, sir."

"Indulge me," Paladin said, more a threat than a request. "You see, it's not those Pilgrims who pose the threat but a more radical sect whose ancestors assimilated back into Confederation society. These Pilgrims are members of our own military. They've abandoned their edicts in favor of a new order: destroy Earth, dismantle the Confederation, reclaim what is theirs. Irony is, the Confederation taught them how to do it. We believe that research and development of this new hopper drive has been going on for ten, possibly twenty years, with construction occurring within the last four. Alarmists call it a Pilgrim conspiracy, and maybe that's what it is, but these radicals have taken advantage of those neutral systems and enclaves. We've already discovered evidence of their research in all of them. Seems they threatened those Pilgrims with force, bribed Confederation inspectors or had them replaced with Pilgrims or others sympathetic to their cause, and operated without our knowledge. The Kilrathi war still provides them with a convenient diversion and a possible ally. Admiral Bill Wilson managed to conspire with the cats."

"Sir, you said that Aristee hopes to destroy Earth, dismantle the Confederation, and take back what belongs to the Pilgrims," Angel said. "How does she intend to do that with just one super-cruiser? Why isn't she building a fleet?"

"We don't know. On the outset, her plan seems reckless. But she's a brilliant woman, not be underestimated. She's choosing her targets carefully in order to recruit Confed Navy personnel of Pilgrim ancestry. Maybe she'll begin building a fleet—or maybe the Kilrathi already have one waiting for her."

"I find it highly unlikely that she has access to shipbuilding facilities, unless you're about to tell me that the Trojan Yards and others now belong to the Pilgrims," Gerald said. "She may be working with the Kilrathi. That seems more reasonable."

"And now she's gathering people to crew those Kilrathi ships?" Angel asked. "Why doesn't she simply defect to the Kilrathi, strike a deal, and have the cats do her dirty work the same way Admiral Wilson did?"

"Yeah, but his deal with the Kilrathi went south," Jinxman reminded. "Maybe the cats won't bargain anymore."

Paladin nodded in understanding. "We should continue to speculate on her plans, and I encourage your input on the matter in person or through the data net. But our mission now is to stop her and recover that ship, and we've been authorized to use whatever means necessary to accomplish those goals. Questions?"

"Sir, we're talking about a possible Pilgrim conspiracy," Marine Lieutenant Andover asked. "How will security handle this?"

"I'll post details of what's being done on the fleet level as soon as I'm notified. As far as the *Claw* is concerned, it's business as usual."

Even Blair had to frown at that.

"But there could be Pilgrim saboteurs aboard this ship," Andover challenged. "And no offense, sir, but rumor has it that you're a Pilgrim yourself."

"You're out of line," Gerald said, glowering at the Marine.

"No, she's just curious," Paladin corrected. "Yes, I descend from

Pilgrims. In fact, I could be a saboteur. If it makes you feel more comfortable to place me under guard, then by all means do so. However, I should mention that your skipper's had people watching me since the moment I hit the flight deck." He shot Gerald a black smile. "I won't attempt to prove my loyalty in this room. But let's get out there, then I'll show you whose side I'm on. Deal?"

"Yes, sir."

"I'm also a Pilgrim," Blair said, launching to his feet. He turned to face the others. "You can place me under guard as well."

"Sit down, Lieutenant," Gerald ordered. "Most of us are already aware of your heritage."

Blair complied as Angel quickly added, "Lieutenant Blair single-handedly saved our entire squadron today. I respectfully suggest that anyone who needs more proof should first submit to a psyche ops evaluation."

"All right, enough," snapped Gerald. "The last thing we want to do is create an atmosphere of paranoia. Just keep your people informed and do your jobs. Dismissed."

As the group dispersed, Blair sensed that no one had really been satisfied by the briefing, that it had probably created more questions than it had answered. However, one question remained that Paladin could answer. Blair hurried to catch the commodore, who had exchanged a few words with Gerald and now moved to the hatch. "Sir?"

"Hello again, Lieutenant. We seem to keep running into each other during times of crisis. Who's got the bad luck? You or me?"

Blair flashed a smile. "As a junior officer, I assume responsibility for the bad luck, sir."

"As you should," he said with mock seriousness. "And we should make this brief to avoid more rumors."

"I can deal with that. Guess if I wasn't a Pilgrim, I'd be suspicious, too. Admiral Tolwyn told me that the wounds of civil war run deep. He was right."

"He usually is. Well, you look good, Mr. Blair. And it's a pleasure to see you again. Now, if you'll excuse me—"

"Sir, I have to ask. Do they know about you and Amity?"

He paused, his eyes growing reflective. "The admiral does. Probably why he wants me on this. Sometimes you can fall in love with someone and never really know them. But her? I really thought I knew her."

Blair watched him go, taking with him memories so vivid that he probably lived more in them now than anywhere else. Those memories had taken up residence in his shadow, in his heart, in his dreams. Blair worried for the man and wished there was more he could do.

"Are you going to stand there all morning? Or are you going to have breakfast with me?"

He turned, his heart missing a beat as he stared at Angel, alone and beaming at him. "Yes, ma'am."

"That's very good, Lieutenant. You're learning."

"I'm a quick study," he said, raising his brows.

She shuffled past him. "There's a lot to learn."

VEGA SECTOR,
DAY QUADRANT

CS OLYMPUS

MIDPOINT: LAFAYETTE
AND TAMAYO SYSTEMS

2654.082

1430 HOURS
CONFEDERATION
STANDARD TIME

William Santyana swore at the two Pilgrim Marine guards who had escorted him from the flight deck to his quarters, then he slammed the hatch in their faces. He entered the main living area and threw his helmet at the viewport. It bounced off the Plexi and hit the floor with a clang that sent Lacey running into the room. "Daddy?" The three-year-old looked at the helmet. "Why'd you throw that?"

"Daddy's just mad, honey. That's all."

"Will?" Pris appeared in the narrow corridor that led to the bedroom. She wore a white robe made of a fabric that resembled silk, though it lacked the luster. Pictorial symbols Santyana recognized as Pilgrim "storicals" had been stitched into the hem, sleeves, and collar of the robe, forming an ornate, multicolored border. The storicals told stories about the first Pilgrims and had been modeled after Egyptian hieroglyphs. "Well, they finally got us some clothes," Pris said.

Only then did he realize that Lacey wore an identical robe that perfectly fit her tiny frame. He hunkered down to the little girl. "Do you like that robe?"

She nodded. "The nice lady gave it to me."

"Well, you'll have to take it off." He looked to Pris. "And you, too."

"But we don't have any other clean clothes. Unless you'd like your daughter to run around naked. They gave us these robes, we'll wear them. You will, too. Besides, the woman who dropped them off said they're made of *ko'a'ka*; it's supposed to have a calming effect on the central nervous system. I do feel more at peace now."

"That's funny, considering the war this bitch is waging."

Pris tipped her head toward Lacey. "Watch your language."

He exhaled loudly, stood, and massaged his temples. "She made me fly against Confederation fighters. They lost an entire squadron when we jumped."

"You told me."

"And now she's got me flying patrols."

"You told me that, too." She came to him, buried her head in his shoulder. "Stop thinking about it. Just do what she says. Please, Will. For Lacey's sake. We can deal with this. We can. I'm starting to understand these people."

He gripped her shoulders, shifted her back. "How?"

"They took us to a meeting today."

Chills fanned across his shoulders. "What kind of meeting?"

"They called it a con-crit session. Five or six of them were there. I think they were civilians; I'm not sure. It wasn't weird or cultic or anything. Just a distorted history class, biased to be sure, but interesting in that they really go to extremes to illustrate Confederation atrocities. They put on this little play. Actually, they're really good actors. Told the story of the Peron Massacre, the exodus to McDaniel's World, and their exile after the alliance fell. They said today is the Holy Day of Acclivity. And did you know that some of their ancestors used to live on ring stations? The ones who lived closest to the hull had trouble having children. The embryos had mutated and weren't allowed to come to term. They called it Space Syndrome Mutation. Did you know that it was from those mutations that their powers of navigation emerged?"

"I know all about the reports and the book of Ivar Chu McDaniel," he answered disgustedly. "He's the fanatic who started all of this. Probably bought it in some gravity well, but now he's a deity. My parents made me memorize the story. He headed out to the Sirius system with twelve hundred followers and was translated directly to a higher plane of existence. He directs us from there. What a crock."

"It's not any more far-fetched than some of the stories you'll find in the Bible."

"You're defending them?"

"No, I just think that if we're stuck here, we might as well get to know our enemy. And maybe they're not really the enemy. They're just misguided. And, when it comes down to it, they're who you are."

He crossed to the narrow, thinly padded sofa and collapsed on it. "They kill six million people—and they're just *misguided*? Wait a minute. I get it now. You want to know more about them because you think you'll learn more about me. Well, you won't. I'm not them. I'm a retired Confederation officer who just happened to be born into the wrong family."

She stood over him, lip twisted in anger. "Maybe I wouldn't be so curious if you talked about it. But you won't. We've been together for more than five years and I hardly know anything about your past. It's not fair."

"Mommy? Can you play with me?"

Pris's expression softened as she regarded Lacey. "Okay, honey. We'll play that game on the terminal." She took Lacey's hand and led her toward the bedroom, their robes fluttering behind them.

Santyana closed his eyes. His imagination swept him into visions of Pris and Lacey being drugged or cerebrally altered by the Pilgrims, being turned into stereotypical cultists blind to the injustices and atrocities committed by their "broturs" and "sosturs." Yes, they would become Sostur Pris, Sostur Lacey, and Brotur William, and they would subscribe to the notion that Terrans had plundered known space and needed to be eradicated.

They would pad around in their robes, drink and eat the Pilgrims' "sanctified" offerings, and fall blithely to their deaths in an act of spiritual servitude. He shivered off the thought, then imagined himself taking his Rapier head on toward the *Olympus's* bridge. Amity Aristee would stone up in horror as his neutron cannon belched out a lethal spray a second before he tore through the command and control center. His funeral pyre would consume them all. But even if Aristee died, she might have standing orders to have Pris and Lacey killed. There had to be another way out. But they kept him so closely guarded. He needed a plan to smuggle his family off of the ship.

If he only had an ally. There had to be someone aboard whose loyalty faltered. Yes, that was it. Instead of ignoring the rest of his squadron, he would talk to them, probe for weakness, exploit it, and win a soul or two to his side. They were Pilgrims, but they suffered the same frailties as humans. He would play on their guilt, on their instinct toward self-preservation, and even on their egos. How many others had families they might never see again? How many others questioned Aristee's actions? How many others were motivated by fear instead of duty? How many others saw no future in serving a renegade? Santyana swore he would find out.

"Talk to me, Brotur Hawthorne," Aristee said, staring at the comm monitor.

Hawthorne, the *Olympus's* forty-five-year-old hopper drive control officer, gazed back at her, his woolly hair gone awry, his unshaven face drawn up in a look of sheer frustration. "We're still having containment problems, ma'am."

"How much longer?"

"We've been working on it around the clock. I can't give you an accurate estimate."

Her jaw stiffened. "Let me spell it out for you. If we don't jump by oh-seven-thirty tomorrow, the *Tiger Claw, Oregon,* and *Mitchell Hammock* will arrive. Don't underestimate their ability to track us."

"I'm not. We're doing everything we can. At least modifications to the drive are proceeding as scheduled. We should be able to extend the gravitic cloak from five hundred meters to at least thirteen kilometers, as you ordered. However, a cloak that size will pull in many more objects than usual, and I'm not sure how well the drive's AI will compensate for the increased number of distortions. We'll have to test it, and we'll need Frotur McDaniel's help."

"As long as we keep moving, we'll have time for that. Continue updating me hourly."

"Yes, ma'am."

"Was that my name I heard?"

Aristee turned away from the starboard observation station to meet gazes with Frotur Johan McDaniel, the last living descendant of Ivar Chu McDaniel. The frotur's hazel eyes seemed to light up his surroundings, and they took no exception with the bridge. Attired now in his *ko'a'ka* robe and sandals, he resembled a pool-bound vacationer who had taken a very wrong turn. But when the next hour chimed, every soul aboard would shed the old Confederation skins of slavery and don the ceremonial garments of a new age. And the timing could not be better: this was the Pilgrim Holy Day of Acclivity, the day that marked Ivar Chu's rise to become one with the space-time continuum. Some argued that he resided on an even higher plane incomprehensible to mortal minds. Aristee had always leaned more toward pragmatic explanations, toward theology born of science, toward a blurring of those lines. She smiled now at the frotur with a deep, heartfelt reverence, with a love that transcended anything she had ever felt for her parents—both traitors to the Pilgrim cause. "Brotur Hawthorne says he might need your assistance with the hopper drive."

"I'm a visionary, a navigator, and a compass—but I'm still eighty-one years old. I wish these youngsters would remember that. I feel as though everyone aboard needs my help. But I'm not bitter. Just tired. I'm not used to this kind of excitement."

"These are exciting days. I'm not sure if they'll ever live up to my dreams, but if nothing else, we *will* make a statement that humanity will never forget."

"We won't survive this."

"Of course not. And we'll never be able to spare every Pilgrim life. This new rebellion requires our sacrifice. I'm not resigned to that. I welcome it."

"Destroying Earth won't bring an end to the Confederation," he pointed out somberly.

"No, but it will demonstrate our power and renew our people. They won't hide anymore behind post-war edicts that are no longer valid. We'll head to McDaniel's World, continue staffing this ship, and take aboard as many as we can. Then we'll head to Aloysius. I have friends waiting for us there with supplies and more personnel."

"We shouldn't go to McDaniel. It's not safe."

She took his hand in her own. "Frotur, what's wrong?"

He lowered his gaze, thought a moment, then nodded. "I've grown quite fond of you. I don't want to lose you just yet. It's in your nature to listen to the crackling of that flame that burns so hotly inside you. I did the same. But if you want to bring our people home to a free universe, you have to live long enough to create that symbol of our power. I know why you want to go to McDaniel. You want the protur's blessing for what you're doing so that when you make the ultimate sacrifice, you'll assure your place in the continuum."

Amity had known the frotur all of her life. Her parents had been friends with him until they had turned their backs during the war. When they had been killed for their treason against the alliance, the frotur had made sure that Amity was placed in the loving care of foster parents who had raised her under Confederation colors and had attempted to instill in her Confederation ideals. But frequent visits from the frotur had kept her Pilgrim roots thriving. Even when she had first joined the Confederation Navy, she had done so with the dream of one day liberating her people. And all of these years later, the dream was finally unfolding. She had not hidden her dream from the frotur, nor could she hide anything else. He always saw what lay in her heart.

"I'll ask for his blessing," she told him. "And he'll give it."

"Or what? He'll die?"

She huffed and turned toward the viewport. Starlines wove baroque patterns as the supercruiser cut through space, but she barely saw them. She saw the protur come down from his altar, lower his hood, and condemn everything for which she stood. "I'll ask for his blessing. I need it. It'll be another symbol for our people."

"I don't believe he'll give it. He's been influenced by too many who fought in the old war. That blood is still fresh on their hands. They don't want another." He approached from behind, slid an arm over her shoulders. "Dear Amity, I wish my blessing could be enough. But I've always been a rebel, and despite my name, my blessing hardly constitutes a symbol. I'm the trouble-making McDaniel. The blasphemer. The last. Hallelujah."

He had drawn her smile, though she still felt very young, very vulnerable, and charged with the desire to get that blessing— though there existed more than one way to get it. "I'm sorry, fro-tur. As dangerous as it may be, I have to go to McDaniel. I have to try. I should've gone there first and gotten his blessing before any of this began. But Wilson's failure came so quickly. And we desperately needed those people from Mylon and Lethe. There just wasn't time."

"In this existence, there never is enough time. Oh, how I look forward to life in the continuum. It'll be my revenge for all of those lost hours. Come now. Let's get something to eat. The Sos-turs of Promise have prepared a feast in the officer's dining room."

"I'm not hungry," Amity said. "But I'll come anyway."

Commodore Richard Bellegarde bit his lower lip as he watched four squadrons of the *Concordia*'s fighters and a squadron of Broadsword bombers soar away from the ship, vectoring toward the Sivar-class dreadnought and three Fralthi-class cruisers at coordinates just two kilometers ahead. The *Concordia* had jumped into the Ymir system forty minutes ago to assist the CS *Beacontree*, a Bengal-class strike carrier that had been closest to the trouble zone. Tolwyn had sent the *Beacontree* to Ymir with orders to simply stall the Kilrathi until the *Concordia* and her battle group jumped in. Odd thing was, the *Beacontree* had arrived nearly twenty-four hours ago, and the Kilrathi had yet to make a move. They hovered between the third and fourth planets of the system, on the periphery of an asteroid belt. And they had remained there since their own arrival, over thirty-six hours ago.

"Now we blow them back to Sivar," Tolwyn said, beating a fist into a palm. He stood, gave a cursory glance of the wide bridge, then joined Bellegarde near the viewport. "They ought to bloody well know the penalty for trespassing."

"Either way, we'll teach it to them," Bellegarde added.

"Any news from Nephele?"

"Not since the last report. The *Bedford Falls* and the *Tricaliber* should be able to hold their own. But like these cats, the Kilrathi in that system are just sniffing around."

"Here's what I think, Richard. The emperor learned of the attack on Mylon. Of course he also lost a couple of destroyers out near K'n'Rek to the *Olympus*. So now he's thinking that Pilgrims are responsible, since Mylon is Confederation territory. He sends out two battle groups to attack Ymir and Nephele, but then he realizes that if he starts these two battles, he'll have to finish them. And I think he lacks the resources to do that. So he gets cold feet. Sends them in here anyway to gather what intelligence they can and deploy cloaked spy satellites. Now, if you mark my words, reports will come in from our fighters that the Kilrathi are in retreat, headed toward the jump point." Tolwyn craned his neck and looked to the radar station. "Mr. Abrams?"

"Our fighters are still pursuing the battle group, sir. The Kilrathi have altered course. Looks they're headed to the jump point."

Bellegarde shook his head in mild astonishment. "When will you teach me that trick?"

"It's no trick. Just think like a pack hunter. Now if our squadrons continue to pursue, they could be ambushed by one, perhaps two destroyers that broke off from the main battle group. Mr. Wilks? Give the order for recall."

The comm officer nodded. "All fighters return to base, aye-aye, sir."

"You see, Richard, despite the emperor's cold feet, he wants us to know that he has these battle groups within jump range. Call it posturing, but it does humble the more keen strategist."

"Do you think he knows about the *Olympus*?"

"Yes, and if I know the Kilrathi, the battle group commander whose ships were lost has sworn an oath to find her—"

"Which makes this even more precarious."

Tolwyn gave a sober nod. "If the Kilrathi find the *Olympus* before we do, then pray that they annihilate her. If they recover that hopper drive, well. . . ."

"This new war against the Pilgrims is more about that drive than about ideology. I'd like to know more about this drive and our knowledge of its inception."

"Sorry, Richard. This one's compartmentalized. Orders came down directly from the space marshal. I've told you all that I can. But I am working on something of my own. When I can tell you more, I will."

"Admiral? Data relay coming in from a drone dispatched in the Tartarus system," Comm Officer Wilks reported. "It's from the *Tiger Claw*."

"Decrypt and transfer to my station," Tolwyn said, then hurried to his command chair.

Bellegarde swung the admiral's small data screen up and into place, then shifted for a look himself. The text-only report detailed the *Claw*'s encounter with the *Olympus* at Lethe. Bellegarde muttered a "whoa" as he scanned the casualty list. Then, in the final summary, a familiar name jumped out at him, and even the admiral tapped his finger on the letters.

"Well, well, well. Young Lieutenant Blair is back at it again," Tolwyn said. "I'd almost forgotten there was another Pilgrim on board the *Claw*. It seems that young man saved his squadron and discovered the *Olympus*'s jump target."

"I know how you feel about him, sir. And about his father. But we are talking about Pilgrims here."

"Honestly, Richard, he's not the one I'm worried about . . ."

8

VEGA SECTOR,
DOWNING QUADRANT
BORDER

KIS SHAK'AR'ROC
BATTLE GROUP

TARTARUS SYSTEM

2654.082

2200 HOURS IMPERIAL
STANDARD TIME

After making four jumps and traveling for three standard days, Admiral Vukar nar Caxki's patience had worn as thin as the *kaschee* ceremonial scarf coiled around his neck. He emitted a steady growl as he contemplated the image pouring in through the forward viewport. The Confederation world known as Lethe shimmered like the great blue eye on the Caxki clan's temple. Scanners had already detected clouds of debris from Rapier starfighters, clearly indicating that a battle had occurred in the system not too long ago—but a battle between that supercruiser and who? Probably Confederation forces trying to stop it, and Vukar prayed to Sivar that they had not succeeded in capturing or destroying her.

"Kalralahr, we're picking up more debris at coordinates five-six-two by eight-two-one," Tactical Officer Makorshk said, sitting at his station directly behind Vukar's command chair. "The debris is particulate—evidence of another gravity well. Analysis in progress. As expected, it's the remains of more Confederation Rapiers. It appears that no ships larger than their standard utility fighters were destroyed here. I believe the supercruiser made another jump. Gravitic residuum analysis in progress, but it will take some time, my Kalralahr."

"What about ion emissions?" Vukar asked.

Makorshk studied data on a convex display, his snout cast in an emerald flicker. "Sivar smiles on us. Another day or so, and all traces would have vanished. A strike carrier and two destroyers operated here within the last fifty imperial hours, though that is the computer's best estimate. Scan also detects emissions from a supercruiser. Identification positive. Emissions match the ship our destroyers encountered near K'n'Rek."

"Alert me as soon as you have its jump target plotted. I'll be in my ready room."

Makorshk grunted his acknowledgment.

Once inside his small sanctuary, Vukar advanced to the tiny shrine at the rear bulkhead. The six *sivistian* candles that burned in a circle around the meter-high statue of Sivar were now little more than stumps, their light shying off into reflective puddles of wax. Sivar's coppery countenance held a permanent glower, and Vukar closed his eyes and knelt before the war god. "The honor is always yours, Sivar. I find my strength in you. But I am tired now. And my quest seems foolhardy. The blood frenzy throbs within me, but I sense it will all be for naught. I sense I'm but a lowborn in a universe that cares little for me, for us, for our people's actions. Will we really be remembered? Or are we merely victims of the petty games between clans, empires, species? Show me the way, Sivar, and I will follow. I pledge my bones and blood to you. Make me worthy to accept your blessing, to receive your strength, to act according to your wisdom." Vukar stood, went to his meditation chair, and collapsed into it. He swiveled to the comm terminal, touched a key, and replayed the conversation he had had with Satorshck nar Caxki. Before leaving for the K'n'Rek system, Vukar had contacted the leader of Caxki clan to report the emperor's wishes.

"That's very interesting, Vukar. Very interesting indeed," Satorshck had said upon learning of the emperor's plan to send battle groups to Ymir and Nephele. "He's simply placating the clan leaders but failing to truly act, as we suspected. The Caxki may have been the first of the noble clans to join the emperor's new imperial alliance, but we may also be the first to secede. If you find and capture that supercruiser and its new drive system, understand that it will be the property of the Caxki clan. You will not, under any circumstances, turn it over to the emperor. Do this for the *hrai*, Vukar, and you will reap the rewards."

"I understand, but if I fail to obey the emperor's orders, the prince will make a challenge."

"And you will accept that challenge," Satorshck said vehemently. "And if so, you will die for the *hrai*, for the greatest noble clan Kilrah has ever seen."

"As you wish."

Vukar switched off the recording, then leaned back and stroked his whiskers in thought. Better to toil over what to do with the hopper drive *after* he had it. For now, he would patch the tear in his loyalty with a newfound desire to recover that ship—not for the emperor or his clan, but for the courageous warriors who had lost their lives under his command.

The terminal beeped. "Kalralahr?"

"You have the coordinates?" Vukar asked as he hit the vid display and Makorshk appeared on the screen.

"We do. Estimates, of course. They put the supercruiser between the Lafayette and Tamayo systems."

Vukar stood. "Sound the pre-jump alarm. Plot best course to those coordinates."

"Course already plotted, my Kalralahr. I'm afraid it will take two-point-seven-five standard days to get there, providing we do not meet any resistance at the jump points. We'll have to jump at Montrose and Lafayette, both well-guarded Confederation systems. Also, I should remind you that those coordinates will place us well away from jump points and deep within Day Quadrant. That will be dangerous, but what troubles me even more is why the supercruiser would venture there in the fist place, unless it is rendezvousing with another ship."

"That may be the case. Perhaps they're taking on supplies."

"Or perhaps they require a position well away from gravitic interference. Perhaps they're testing their hopper drive."

Vukar lowered his thick brow. "Testing it? I believe it functions properly. Over two hundred Kilrathi souls will testify to that."

"Yes, but earlier I said that they could use the drive as a planet killer. Since then I've been analyzing the data and discovered that I was wrong. That drive's gravitic cloak extends for about five hundred meters and funnels down about three hundred meters. A gravity well that small would have to be placed within a planet's atmosphere to consume matter, and the supercruiser cannot operate within most atmospheres."

"Then maybe it's not as dangerous as we first thought."

"But Kalralahr, consider this: If the gravity well created by the drive could be made larger, then it could be placed beyond a planet's atmosphere and still pull it in. Imagine that supercruiser jumping into orbit around Kilrah. We surround it. There is no chance it can fire a planetary torpedo and cause damage. But, without warning, it activates its hopper drive, and the resulting gravity well instantaneously pulls in every ship *and* our homeworld. It all happens much more quickly and efficiently than a conventional attack. The supercruiser jumps the well while everything behind it is ripped out of existence."

"All the more reason to find that ship." Vukar pawed off the terminal and left the room, stepping back onto the bridge, where Makorshk regarded him with a quick bow of the head.

"Stations report pre-jump readiness," Comm Officer Ta'kar'-ki said, switching off the gonging alarm. "PNR velocity for Tartarus jump point achieved."

"Engage jump-drive," Vukar said to the helmsman, Yil'schk. "This, I sense, will be a long hunt. . . ."

Blair jerked awake as the high-pitched alarm for general quarters sounded. He stared at the overhead of his quarters for a second, then checked his watch: 0730 hours standard time, eighty-third day of the year. Damn, he'd forgotten what the time and date meant.

"Somebody burned breakfast," Maniac said through a yawn. He rolled over and covered his head with a pillow.

"It's jump day. We're still tailing that supercruiser, remember?"

Maniac didn't answer. Blair rolled quickly out of his cot, and cussed as his bare feet connected with a glacier that looked remarkably like durasteel. "Maniac? Wake up."

"Maniac who?"

"Five minutes to stations or that'll be two more demerits. I can afford 'em. You can't. You're lucky that you're still on the roster after your little torpedo maneuver."

"I'll always be on the roster," Maniac said, removing the pillow. "It's supply and demand, Ace. And speaking of demand, my sore muscles demand that I stay right here. Tell your sweetheart I'm sick."

Blair hustled to his locker, withdrew a clean uniform and Skivvies. "She's not my sweetheart."

"I know, loser. The reg against fraternizing is the first one I break." Maniac worked himself a little deeper into his mattress, and Blair knew very well why the pilot had so much trouble waking up. Maniac had been up until the wee hours, tripping the light fantastic with Zarya in the rec. She had been teaching him an old-fashioned dance called "swing" that had him literally swinging her through the air as though she were a drum majorette's baton. The music, Blair had to admit, thrummed with an infectious rhythm punctuated by lively saxophone and guitar improvisations. The lyrics focused mainly on the dance itself, with allusions to something called "jive" and references to people as "cats." That seemed ironic to Blair, but Zarya had assured him it was all part of the fun.

After dressing quickly, tossing some warm water over his face, and wetting down his short locks, Blair looked once more at his pathetic bunkmate, then hurried out.

With thirty seconds to spare, Blair made it to the flight wing ready room and strapped into a jumpseat between Hunter and Bishop. Pilots lined the walls, chatting with each other or staring straight ahead, sleeping with their eyes open. The six squadron commanders entered from a hatch that led to the flight control room. They eyed the rows, taking silent attendance. Blair glanced at the empty seat that belonged to Maniac. Zarya sat beside the seat, her gaze focused on the entrance in anticipation of Maniac's arrival.

"Lieutenant Marshall?" Angel asked, inspecting the room to be sure she hadn't missed him.

"Uh, he's sick, ma'am," Blair said. "I think he was going to see a medic and strap in down there."

She managed to restrain most of her sneer and the rage that lay behind it. "I hope you're right," she said, then hastened to the data net terminal beside the main hatch.

Blair looked to Zarya, who mouthed, "Where is he?"

Closing his eyes, Blair tilted his head to one side to show her. When he looked up, he saw Zarya swearing to herself.

After another moment, Angel returned from the terminal, her gaze like a flamethrower. "Lieutenant Marshall is not in sickbay. And if he's in his quarters, he's not answering my call. Any ideas, Lieutenant?"

Blair shrugged.

"I wouldn't find him dancing in the rec, would I?"

He stifled a snort. "I doubt that, ma'am."

Her exaggerated sigh said it all. She turned back to confer with Jinxman and Lightning, and for a moment the ready room's lights caught her at the perfect angle. Why did he keep seeing her in the light like this? Why did she have to be so damned beautiful?

Three days ago they had eaten breakfast together. They had drawn the stares of a few officers stuffing their faces, but she had been unfazed by that. The stares had bothered him more, and for some reason he couldn't get past the notion that he should keep his distance, that when she leaned over her food to say something, bringing her lips so close that it made him dizzy, he should keep his torso rigid. Twice he had even recoiled from her advance. They had chatted about the war, about news from Earth, about a new film showing in one of the vidrooms on Deck C. While her words came out naturally, gracefully, his dialogue felt forced, ragged, shaken by nerves and thoughts of rejection.

Anyone else would have probably asked her to come back to his quarters. Anyone else would have made love to her as though it were his last time. But Blair felt pinned under his insecurities, and when the breakfast was over, she headed back to her quarters and he sat there for an hour, damning his ineptitude. For the next two days he saw her only during training sessions. He had ghosted his way around the flight deck, hoping to bump into her, but instead bumped into Deck Boss Peterson—literally. The man ordered him off the deck. And so it went.

Then, last night, he had spotted her sitting alone in a far corner of the rec, watching Maniac and Zarya dancing. Tentatively, he had approached and had asked if he could join her. Her smile had been a perfect reply, and he had bought her next drink, an expensive beer produced by a boutique brewery on Nephele. She had never tasted it before, had said it was great, and had thanked him with a salacious look that continued flashing through his mind's eye. For the rest of the time they had just sat there, rapping idly about more trivialities until she had finished her glass, bid him good-night, and suddenly left.

Seeing her go, Maniac had looked to Blair, and his mouth had formed a single word: "loser."

Blair blinked off the memory as Maniac now scampered into the ready room, ducked by the squadron commanders, then slammed himself into his jumpseat. Zarya helped him buckle in as Lieutenant Commander Obutu rattled off the final countdown from command and control, each number booming through the ship.

The squadron commanders took their own seats, and Angel set her crosshairs on Maniac. At least the pilot knew better than to find her gaze.

Bulkheads groaned, overheads rattled, and lights flickered as the *Claw*'s jump drive came on line. Blair had grown quite used to the shipboard effects of jumping, especially those associated with jumping known rifts in the space-time continuum. Jumping quasars, pulsars, black holes, and other unpredictable phenomena would always keep him on edge. But this standard jump freed him to focus on other things, other people, most particularly his mother. He hoped she would come to him and explain why she had not appeared during his jump of the supercruiser's gravity well. He would demand that she explain the voice in his ears, the caress on his cheeks, the figure who had risen to beckon him from the plain of darkness.

Even as he turned his thoughts to her, the pilots' murmuring decrescendoed into nothingness. The straps of his jumpseat and the tug of his uniform surrendered to a feeling of numbness. He no longer detected the smell of detergent that lingered on everyone's uniforms, and his mouth lacked the aftertaste of last night's beer. He looked across the room at the other pilots frozen in mid-sentence, then he darted through them and into the cosmos as though strapped to a runaway drive. He orbited Earth several thousand times, slingshotted around Sol, then rocketed out of the Milky Way, heading deeper into the local group, toward Andromeda and its companion galaxies. And as he traveled, he glimpsed his mother for a moment. She looked repeatedly over her shoulder as she ran through a seemingly endless corridor of star clusters.

"Mother!"

"Don't come, Blair." She dissolved into the stars.

He willed himself after her, moved in front, and she came to a jarring halt, out of breath and beaded with sweat. The lines spreading out from her eyes had deepened since the last time he had seen her, and the color of those eyes seemed to fluctuate with the beating of her heart, sometimes green, sometimes blue, sometimes a color he could only describe as sad.

"What's wrong?"

"I want so badly to talk to you, my son. But I can't."

"Why?"

"Because if I change your path, I change the paths of countless others, including my own. I can do nothing for you."

"Just tell me about—"

"The voice? The caress? The figure?"

He took her shoulders into his hands, and he felt her warmth surge up his arms. "Tell me! There's no pain in knowing. The pain is my ignorance."

"Doesn't it bother you that some of us have murdered billions over the years?"

"Of course it does. It makes me question even more who and what I am."

"Don't ask that question. And don't go looking for the answer. Oh, Christopher. I didn't want to leave you—I didn't. Know that, at least."

"What about the voice? The hand I felt on my cheek?"

"Beware them," she said, then repeated the words until they blurred into gibberish, became a tone that rose in pitch until he screamed for it to leave.

It did.

His chin rested on his chest. He panted as though he had just run a dozen kilometers.

"You got to lay off that beer, mate," came a familiar voice. "Hard to really tell what they put in that microbrew. Better you fix yourself right with a nice oil can of Foster's. Over six centuries of tradition. You'll learn."

Blair looked up, saw Hunter unbuckling from his jumpseat harness. Some of the other pilots were already on their feet, and a casually dressed man beamed at him from the hatchway. A harder look revealed him as Paladin, hair still wet from a recent shower, cheeks freshly shaven. For his part, the man made no remark of Blair's particularly rough post-jump appearance and came quickly forward. "Mr. Blair. It seems that the *Olympus* has already jumped. We can get a rough estimate of her destination from the *Claw*'s sensors, but I think you and I can do a more accurate job. Care to take a ride?"

Within five minutes Paladin had the *Diligent* preflighted. The first time Blair had seen the merchantman, he had thought that she resembled a twenty-five-meter-long Ping-Pong paddle. His appraisal had not changed, but his affection for the vessel had deepened. Though no visual thrill, the old girl had, according to Paladin, never failed him. He sat at the portside helm controls while Blair handled navigation. They received clearance from Boss Raznick and rumbled out of the hangar, soaring up into the endless folds of interstellar space. A patrol of Rapiers had already been launched and had fanned out to scan the Area of Operation's perimeter. Blair caught sight of one of the fighters through the starboard viewport and double-checked his course, making sure he would avoid the fighters' vector.

"Initiate residuum scan," ordered Paladin.

Blair shifted to a small touchpad and tapped in the command. One of the nav station's screens mounted to a swivel arm abruptly illuminated with columns of data regarding the composition of the void ahead: mostly hydrogen, with traces of nitrogen, oxygen, and carbon detected by their radio emissions. Then the screen flashed as it picked up a concentration of gravitons and anti-gravitons—the residuum from the supercruiser's jump. "Locked on to her jump point," he informed Paladin.

The commodore looked askance. "Thought you'd be full of questions. You all right?"

"Yeah," Blair answered softly. "And *I am* full of questions. But I'm not sure you can answer them."

"Try me."

"Do you . . . ah, it's ridiculous." Blair pursed his lips, returned his gaze to his instruments.

"You didn't look so well after our jump. Something happen?"

"Sort of. It's about my mother."

"A lovely lady."

"You knew her?"

Paladin thought a moment, a smile slowly curling his lips. "I introduced her to your father."

"Why haven't you told me?"

"When you were ready to know, you'd come asking. I've already told you a little about how the Pilgrims rose to power, then plunged to defeat. But there's so much you don't know."

"That's what my mother tells me."

A curious glint came into Paladin's eyes. "Your mother died on Peron during the attack."

"I know. But sometimes when we jump . . . I don't know. That moment between points, when you don't feel anything, when it seems like—"

"You see her. You talk to her."

"Yeah. I mean, is it really her? Am I talking to somebody else? To a ghost? To God? Am I nuts?"

"Have you done any research on this?"

Blair frowned. "I thought this was only happening to me. Is speaking to the dead common among Pilgrims?"

"You're not talking to the dead. According to one theory, you're tapping into a script that lies in a parallel dimension. It's been suggested that the human brain isn't a device for storing information but a tool for scripting it. This other dimension, they've dubbed it the Tanque Dimension, holds the scripts for every human being that ever lived, but Pilgrims can tap into that information. That's why when you get near a quasar or pulsar or what have you, you can sense a course through it. You're actually tapping into a script written by the first Pilgrims who navigated through."

"So it's nothing mystic. It just has to do with the ability to read that information," Blair concluded.

"Yes, but explain to me how you can interact so intimately with a piece of stored information. There's no advance AI at work. I think that's when it gets mystical."

Blair thought back to his first ride with Paladin. "When we jumped Scylla, you seemed surprised that I was able to navigate through her. And if you're a Pilgrim and you can tap into these scripts like me, then why didn't you jump the well itself?"

"I could have, but I couldn't have done it as easily as you. Why do you think I have all of those Pilgrim maps back in my quarters?"

"I don't know, but you're a Pilgrim."

"We're not all the same, Blair. Some say we evolved from savants. There were 'zappers' who were experts at electrical systems; 'chipheads' able to engineer flawless hardware designs; 'toolkits' who could fix things with whatever happened to be lying around; 'crunchers' who could perform complex mathematical calculations without computers; and 'rabbitfoots' who supposedly brought good luck to missions. From there, other types of abilities emerged, and one in particular is the most interesting to us: the compass. These are the Pilgrims I told you about, those with a flawless sense of direction. They were subcategorized into the visionary, the explorer, and the navigator."

"Which one am I?"

"From what I've seen, you're a navigator. Me, on the other hand, I'm a visionary. I can determine which systems would prove most valuable for human expansion. Visionaries can throw their minds across the galaxy, seek out new systems, and analyze their composition. You don't even need to send a ship out if you have a visionary on your team. I have to admit that my skills are pretty limited, and I've been wrong on more than one occasion. I wish I were a navigator like you."

"What about the explorers?"

"They're able to navigate through uncharted regions. Most of the Pilgrim holocartography we have today was created by explorers. Some argue that of all three subcategories, explorers are the most powerful."

"What do you think?"

"I think there's one Pilgrim who's more powerful than any individual. He's a visionary, an explorer, and a navigator, and his name's Johan McDaniel, the last living descendant of Ivar Chu McDaniel. He's kind of a legend. I met him once. Nice old man— until you cross him. We're out here now because I want you to tap into his script. It's out here somewhere."

"His script? Why would it be—" Blair answered his own question before even asking it. "He's on board the supercruiser."

"Amity knows him as well as I. She's using him as a supplement to her hopper drive. The calculations involved in creating and jumping a gravity well are sometimes too complex for the NAVCOM. McDaniel is handling that for her."

"What is she? A navigator like me?"

"No, she's an explorer." Paladin's hand went reflexively to his chest. The Pilgrim cross that hung hidden beneath his shirt had been given to him by Amity. Blair had once borrowed the cross and had read the inscription on its back. She wanted him to remember love across the cosmos, to remember her. Blair smiled bitterly as he realized that Paladin wasn't the only one who would remember her now.

Blair's nav computer chirped a warning. "We're right in the residuum now," he said, reading his screen.

"Okay, Mr. Blair. Get to work."

He gave his mentor an awkward look.

"Reach out and find that script. Learn where they're headed."

"Okay," Blair said sarcastically. "But I don't even know how to reach. When I jump a well, the feeling is there. I don't have to look for it."

"You learn something new every day. And here's today's lesson. On your feet, mister. Go the viewport. Just look out there. I mean *really* look out there." Paladin's voice came in a breathy lilt.

Blair stood, worked out the kinks in his legs, then went anxiously to the viewport. He tossed Paladin a worried look, earning himself an insistent, wide-eyed stare.

Stars, nothing but. Pinpoints against a void so familiar yet so alien that nothing Blair could do would ever change that. *What am I supposed to see?*

"Me, probably," came a voice from behind.

Whirling, Blair came face-to-face with an old man dressed in a strange white robe and dark sandals. He looked past the man to Paladin, who sat motionless and unaware at the helm.

"So, Brotur Christopher. I take it you'd like to know where we're going." The old man's hazel eyes flashed like light through a prism, and his skin held a ruddy sun glow. He stood quite erect for a man so wizened, his chest bulging like a powerlifter's beneath his robe.

"Are you part of a script? Am I accessing your data?"

He chuckled. "That's a clumsy assessment, don't you think?"

"Then what are you?"

"I'm just me. And you're just you. And here we are."

"You with Captain Aristee? Are you helping her?"

The old man's brow knit as he took offense. "Of course. Where else would I be?"

"I don't know. Where are you now?"

"Why, I'm here, brotur, with you."

"Where is Amity?"

"Oh, were it that easy, young man."

"There's enough residuum here for me to estimate her destination. You can't hide that from me."

"Yes, I can. But her destination should already be quite obvious to you. If she's made a fatal mistake, this is it. Oh, I'm tired of sitting in judgment. We each have a path." He took in a long breath, sighed loudly. "Now, young Pilgrim, let me teach you about who you are, where you belong, and why life among the elect is yours."

VEGA SECTOR, DAY
QUADRANT

MERCHANTMAN
DILIGENT

MIDPOINT: LAFAYETTE
AND TAMAYO SYSTEMS

2654.083

0800 HOURS
CONFEDERATION
STANDARD TIME

"Mr. Blair? Mr. Blair?"

The voice rang through him, and for a moment, Blair did not recognize his own name. He discovered himself staring at Paladin instead of the old man.

"Did you find him?" the commodore asked.

"I think so," Blair replied, straining to remember exactly what had happened. "He never said who he was, but I think it was McDaniel. He said he wanted to teach me about being a Pilgrim. Then someone called. I'm not sure if it was you or maybe even Aristee. And here I am."

"Where are they headed?"

Blair sighed in disappointment. "He wasn't giving that up. I didn't know he could hide the coordinates."

"That's not something the average Pilgrim can do," Paladin said, then added under his breath, "sanctimonious bastard."

"He did say that their destination should be obvious and something about Aristee making a fatal error."

Paladin set his lips together, threw his head back, and studied the conduits crisscrossing the overhead as though they were lines on a star map. All at once he snapped out of the vacant look and activated the comm console. "Mr. Z? Tell the captain to recall all fighters and set course for star number"—he leaned toward one of Blair's nav screens—"ten-two-nine-one."

"Aye-aye, sir," said the *Claw*'s comm officer.

Blair hustled back to his nav station and pulled up data on star 10–2–9–1. White dwarf. Part of the binary system called Blytheheart. He frowned. "Why is she going there, sir? No Confederation colonies. Some mines, refineries, mostly commercial operations. Is she recruiting?"

Paladin waited to answer until he had redirected the *Diligent* on a new vector, back toward the *Tiger Claw*. "Amity's not headed to Blytheheart at all, Lieutenant. We are."

Although Blair deepened his frown, the commodore focused his attention on the helm controls. Ah, yes. Paladin wanted him to figure it out for himself.

Using the nav computer, Blair quickly plotted a course from the *Claw*'s present position to Blytheheart. He studied a three-dimensional map of the surrounding star systems and quickly realized that Blytheheart represented the jump point nearest them. Okay, so Amity wasn't headed there, but they were. *Wait. She doesn't need jump points. We do. So we're going to Blytheheart to jump where?* He tapped in a barrage of commands that would bring up every destination ever achieved by Confederation craft via the Blytheheart jump point. Names of star systems scrolled down the display, and one immediately caught Blair's eye: McDaniel's World, the name of a system and a planet that represented a spiritual headquarters for the Pilgrims. "Sir? I think I know what you're up to. But if she just jumped to McDaniel, then she can probably take care of business and be gone before we arrive. According to my data, it'll take the *Claw* just under five standard days on full impulse to reach the Blytheheart jump point. She can waste that entire planet in five minutes."

"Mr. Blair, Captain Aristee has made a grave error—and we'll take every advantage of it."

"I don't understand."

"She's not going to McDaniel to destroy it. That planet represents everything she stands for. Someday she'd like to see it as the hub and governing force in the universe, much like Earth is today. Yes, if I know her, she's going to McDaniel to see somebody, a man named Protur Carver Tsu the Second."

"Protur . . ." Blair repeated, reaching into his memory. "That's the title of the Pilgrim elect's most powerful leader. Kind of like t he Roman Catholic church's pope or the Vegan Victorists' *kreekson.*"

"That's right. She's going to McDaniel to seek the protur's aid or blessing. If she can win him to her cause, she'll have the entire system behind her. The systems of Faith and Promise will quickly follow. It'll take the enclaves a bit longer, but they'll eventually fold under the pressure."

"All right, so she's there for a chat. Probably already sipping espressos with the guy. Where does that leave us?"

Magic found a home in Paladin's grin. "Yesterday, zero eight two, was the Pilgrim Holy Day of Acclivity. For seven days following the celebration, the protur has to remain in solitude. He goes to a retreat whose location is known only by him. There, he fasts and prays, and seeks communion with Ivar Chu and the others who ascended to the higher plane."

"Today's eight three, so she'll have to wait until eight nine to see the protur."

Paladin nodded. "And we'll be there on eight eight."

"Wait a minute," Blair said. "Why would she hang around there? Why not just come back when the protur returns?"

"She knows exactly what she's doing. Her request to see the protur has to be made as soon as possible. He's a busy guy. And no one leaves McDaniel after making such a request. It's a convention that plays right into our hand. And remember, that blessing is extremely important to her. She'll probably position the *Olympus* behind one of the moons and shuttle down to the planet. We'll dispatch our Marines to pick up her, while the *Claw* and the destroyers disable her ride."

"It won't be that simple."

The commodore grinned knowingly. "Of course not. But

there's always theory before practice. And the shit always hits the fan. . . ."

Within five minutes after their return to the *Tiger Claw*, the strike carrier made way under full impulse for the Blytheheart system.

As Blair and Paladin plodded down the *Diligent*'s loading ramp, Blair said, "Sir? I thought Mr. Gerald would have a problem with rushing off to Blytheheart."

Paladin winked. "Who said he didn't?"

"So that's why you went to your quarters while I landed?"

"Diplomacy is one of my strong suits, but Mr. Gerald taxes me. I didn't want to embarrass you or myself. But don't get me wrong. He'll make a fine captain. He just needs to better recognize his biases. He has softened a little."

They hit the flight deck, and the raised voices, humming thrusters, and aroma from fuel Bowsers tugged on Blair like a drunken friend.

"You know, sometimes I miss this," the commodore said, acknowledging the allure as well. "Then I get smart and wake up." He winked. "We got five days to kill. What are you going to do, Lieutenant?"

"I'll probably do some work in the sim. Catch up on some reading. Pretty boring stuff."

"Were I you," Paladin began, squeezing Blair's shoulder, "I would get that kiss she owes you. Call it intuition, but I suspect she's still in debt."

Blair looked away, digging his hands into his pockets like an embarrassed schoolboy.

"I'm out of line," Paladin said, releasing his grip. "I'm sorry. It's just that I've been in your position before."

"And what did you do?"

"I caught her. Hung on for a while. Then she got away. Don't let that happen to you, son."

Still a bit fatigued from the jump and the conversation with Johan McDaniel, Blair headed back to his quarters. On his way, he stopped at a data net terminal. According to the duty roster, his shift would be over at 1400 hours. All personnel presently worked six hours on, twelve off to keep everyone well-rested and in a state of extreme readiness. The day's schedule seemed pretty loose, with nothing officially on the agenda except a Combat Assessment Meeting at 1300 hours. The meeting would focus on their engagement at Lethe and would be Angel's chance to stomp on Maniac's ego. Though the cocky pilot deserved a scolding, Blair hoped that Angel wouldn't be too hard on him. He had, after all, saved lives.

Blair left the terminal and hustled past three jump-drive specialists in white utilities who appeared exceptionally exhausted. The *Claw* had jumped from Mylon to Lethe to the Lafayette-Tamayo midpoint, and would now jump at Blytheheart. The ship would make more jumps in a week than it had in the past two standard months. Blair empathized with the techs; while everyone else had time to kill, they worked furiously to maintain the drive, an older system infamous for breaking down.

Two corridors later, he slipped into the lift and ascended to the pilots' quarters. This section of the ship took up three decks, began amidships, and stretched back to the environmental control room. Nameplates hung outside each hatch, and Blair's legs grew weak at the sight of Angel's door. As squadron commander, she enjoyed the luxury of private quarters. The rest of the pilots had been paired up to share quarters—not a bad arrangement unless your bunkmate happened to be Maniac. Before the *Claw*'s refitting, twelve or more pilots had been assigned to a single cabin crammed with cots and lockers. Blair's past experiences told him to be thankful for his room and head, despite having to share them with Maniac.

"Lieutenant?"

Blair shuddered as he recognized the voice. He turned to face Gerald. "Yes, sir?"

"I was just coming down to see you."

"You were?" he asked, astounded that the man had not summoned him. Captains, interim or otherwise, didn't go waltzing around the ship in search of junior officers unless that particular junior officer was in a whole lot of trouble.

"Were you headed to your quarters?" Gerald glanced at Angel's hatch. "Or are you here to see Commander Deveraux?"

He stammered. "No, I was headed to my quarters, sir."

"We'll talk on the way."

Blair grimaced inwardly, then joined the man. They walked in silence for several steps, then Blair blurted out, "Sir, if this is about my loyalty—"

"You might be a Pilgrim half-breed, Lieutenant, but you've earned my trust. You killed Admiral Wilson, a traitor to the Confederation. You could have just as easily killed me."

Though barely into his twenties, Blair felt a heart attack coming on, one inspired by Gerald's forthrightness. Wilson had forced Blair and Gerald into a duel, and Blair had chosen to throw his blade at Wilson—not out of any particular love for Gerald, but because it had been the right thing to do, a less bad choice in a flawed universe. "Sir, I was just doing my duty, sir."

"Yes, you were. And now I have a particularly delicate assignment for you that requires your faith in the unified chain of command and what you know your duty should be, what it *always* should be. This assignment will be compartmentalized. You will report only to me."

Ah, yes, Gerald's forthrightness had been born of an ulterior motive. Moreover, Blair thought it odd that the man would brief him on some covert op while walking through a corridor outside the pilots' quarters. Then again, anyone who spotted them might think the captain was just making his daily inspection and had run into Lieutenant Blair. Given recent events and Blair's heritage, the two should have a lot to talk about.

"It's no secret that the commodore and I, well, we have political differences," Gerald continued. "Despite that, I respect his knowledge of Pilgrim tactics and theology. But I've just received some disturbing information."

"Sir, for what it's worth, Commodore Taggart is one of the most skilled and loyal Confederation officers I know. Sure, I'm biased because we're both Pilgrims, but we're as loyal to the Confederation as any pure-blood Terran. Admiral Tolwyn trusts Paladin, sir. Why can't you?"

"Because our esteemed commodore had a five-year relationship with Captain Aristee. According to my sources, she broke it off."

Though difficult, Blair feigned his surprise. Paladin had told him a little about his relationship with Aristee. They had met when she had been temporarily assigned to Intell as part of her XO training. Paladin had described her as "a woman of sinister beauty," and "a siren who made me drunk and silly in love, then flitted off with my broken soul." Blair enjoyed the way the commodore spoke, his taste in reading evident in his speech. But how the hell had Gerald discovered this with the *Tiger Claw* deep in interstellar space? And if Paladin learned that Gerald knew, then Paladin might blame the leak on Blair. Better to go to the commodore and tip him off before word reached him through another channel. But who had told Gerald? Had Paladin told anyone else on board?

"You don't look so surprised," Gerald added.

"I don't think the commodore's personal life is any of my business, sir."

"I figured he told you. And your expression confirms that. I want to believe that Admiral Tolwyn sent him because he had that relationship and might be able to second-guess her. But I think the admiral is taking a great risk with my ship and her crew. It's safe to assume that when push comes to shove, Mr. Taggart will attempt to arrest Captain Aristee rather than kill her. Would you agree with that assumption?"

Blair looked into his mind's eye and saw Paladin's somber expression when he spoke of Aristee. "Sir, I believe that Commodore Taggart would make the right decision." Blair wished he could have said that again; the words sounded half-hearted. In truth, he could not be sure what Paladin would do. And the doubt he felt now was exactly what Gerald wanted him to feel.

They paused a moment as two pilots from Fourth Squadron saluted them, then moved by. Blair looked after the jocks, who returned curious glances.

"It seems that the commodore is the best—and the worst—man for the job," Gerald said. "While I trust his desire to find Captain Aristee, once we do, I need you to act in the best interests of the Confederation. Do you understand what I'm saying, Lieutenant?"

"Sir, you want me to spy on the commodore?"

"I didn't say that."

"I see. Then I assure you, sir, that I *will* act accordingly."

"Very well, then." He muttered a quick, "Lieutenant," then spun on his heel and double-timed back toward the lift.

Blair saluted the man's back, released a loud sigh, then walked the fifteen meters to his hatch. He keyed in the code and stepped inside.

Maniac had returned to bed after the jump, to continue sleeping off his dancing and drinking binge. Blair settled back onto his own cot, closed his eyes, and considered what Gerald had told him. He wanted very badly to believe that Paladin would do the right thing, but when it came to lost love, didn't most people act foolishly? *But he's a mature, seasoned officer,* Blair reminded himself. *He knows how to callous himself when necessary.*

But what would I do if I were in his position? What if Angel and I had a long-standing relationship, then ten years later I discover that she's a traitor to the Confederation and I'm charged with the duty to bring her in? Wouldn't I want to save her somehow? Wouldn't I want to put aside all of the bullshit politics and save her?

Blair jerked as he realized that he would. And maybe it was safer to assume that Paladin had a personal agenda. Sure, he could confront the man, but—

Another thought snared him. He bolted out of the cot, went to the terminal, and dialed up the commodore's quarters. A handful of seconds later, the man leaned toward the camera, shirtless and bleary-eyed. "What can I do for you, Lieutenant?"

"Sir—" Blair choked up as the enormity of what he was about to do hit home. "Gerald is aware of you and Captain Aristee. He says he has sources who informed him."

"And he's recruited you to be a spy. Am I correct, Lieutenant?"

The commodore's quick deduction and ironic tone put Blair at ease. "Yes, sir. I just want to do my duty, sir."

"And so you shall. You may spy all you wish. I have nothing to hide. And I take no offense."

"Thank you, sir. Sorry for bothering you. Oh, just one more thing. Who do you think are Gerald's sources?"

"Don't know. A few people aboard must have been aware and finally came forward. Could have been anyone who knew us back then. Just bad luck. I figured it would eventually get out, but I had no intention of volunteering it."

"Yes, sir. Sorry again." He switched off the terminal.

"You talking to your mystic Pilgrim mentor again?" Maniac asked through a yawn.

"I was talking to Commodore Taggart, who, if he heard you call him that, would tear you a new asshole."

"You're a bit sensitive. Feeling achy and bloated, too?"

Blair returned to his cot. "I feel like a serial killer with a fetish for blond pilots."

"Speaking of fetishes, did you know that Zarya—"

"I don't want to hear it," Blair snapped.

Later that day, at the Combat Assessment Meeting, Angel flung Maniac's ego around the room, bounced it off bulkheads, then shoved it back down his throat for the stunt he had pulled over Lethe. That didn't surprise Blair. But when she turned and gave him a similar tongue-lashing for going after Maniac, embarrassment stole his voice. He finally said, "Ma'am. I didn't want to abandon my wingman."

"Don't twist the situation, Lieutenant. Your wingman had abandoned you. You should have remained in position and continued supplying fire support for us. You failed to do that. And while the captain has made you a command-approved wing commander, I've yet to see any evidence that you deserve the job. You're not on *your* team, Mr. Blair. You're on *ours*. Thought you knew that. Thought wrong."

"Ma'am, if Lieutenant Marshall's fighter became disabled within the atmosphere, there wouldn't have been anyone close enough to retrieve him."

"I wonder if Lieutenant Marshall thought about that before abandoning his position?" She leered at Maniac, who flushed and sprang to his feet.

"I was thinking about all those little kids out playing in their yards. They would look up, see a bright light, then burst into flames. Lots of little bodies running around, turning into crispy critters. I know all about regs and duty, ma'am. And if you want to dismiss me for being insubordinate and put me on report, I'll understand. But when it comes down to it, our job is to save lives. And for one goddamned time I'd like to do that without getting my ass chewed out."

To Blair's surprise, the rest of squadron broke into spontaneous applause. Cheddarboy and Gangsta actually stood, inspiring Bishop and Sinatra to join them. Hunter, no friend of Maniac's, remained seated, as did Blair and Zarya, though Blair expected Zarya to stand. He guessed that she didn't want to thrust her affection for Maniac into Angel's face.

"All right, sit down," Angel ordered. "That's a very moving little rap you got there, Maniac. I can't ignore the fact that you stopped the torpedo and did save lives. And I can't ignore the fact that you disobeyed orders to do so. Which is why I'm confining you to quarters until we reach the Blytheheart jump point. No visitors other than your bunkmate. You'll be allowed out for sim work and briefings. That's it. I think you need the time to consider your future as a Confederation aviator. Any questions?"

"Just one," Maniac said.

Here it comes, Blair thought.

"Have you ever disobeyed a direct order so that you could do what you knew was right?"

"Yes, Lieutenant. More than once. And each time I paid the price. As will you."

"This is bullshit," Maniac mumbled.

"What was that?" Angel asked.

Manic shook his head disgustedly and waved off her question.

After the meeting, Blair remained in his seat while the others filed out. Angel gathered up her files and data disks, then noticed him. "You have a question, Lieutenant?"

"Yes, ma'am. How are you?"

"Haven't we been here before?"

He got to his feet and homed in on her. "You seem tired. Angry, even. Anything I can do?"

She gazed longingly at the exit hatch. "Unless you have something regarding the assessment, Lieutenant, you'll have to cut me loose."

"I'm afraid I can't do that, ma'am. I think something's bothering you, and you're taking it out on me and Maniac." Blair didn't believe that, but he suspected he would get a rise out of her.

And the deep lines of incredulity that mapped out her face confirmed his suspicions. "The only thing bothering me right now is Maniac's attitude. And yours. You seem to think that only end results count, that the chain of command doesn't matter, that protocol doesn't matter. You should've become mercenaries instead of military pilots. I finally got around to reading your flight school evals. They're pretty good, which surprises me given your recent behavior. You might've had them fooled, but you can't fool me. You told me that you had a reputation for being a by-the-book flyer. What happened out there?"

"Maniac's a major pain in the ass, but I still kind of like him. If I had a sister, I wouldn't let him near her, but when it comes to the Kilrathi, he's a pit bull on my wing. Yeah, he's unpredictable and unreliable. But he racks up the kills. And maybe when it comes down to it, surviving *is* the only thing that counts."

"If he doesn't square himself away, he won't survive. Start preparing for that now."

He narrowed his gaze. "Is that what you're doing with me?"

"Are we finished, Lieutenant?" Angel checked her watch-phone. "I have a stack of fire-to-kill ratio reports waiting for me."

"Why do you keep shutting me out?"

"Good day, Lieutenant."

Blair noticed a definite slump to her shoulders as she took off. He thought back to the time he had gone to her quarters and she had told him how she had gotten close to Lieutenant Commander Vince "Bossman" Chen. They hadn't been lovers but the best of friends. Then Bossman had died, and she had lost faith in relationships and distrusted getting close to anyone. She had instituted an unwritten policy that said those who died in combat never existed. If you asked after a fallen comrade, the response would be "Who?" Blair had taken exception to the policy, and when Rosie Forbes had died, he believed that he had penetrated Angel's shield and had made her feel the pain of Forbes's loss. You couldn't just bury your grief. You had to deal with it and use it to make you stronger. No complex psychiatry involved there.

But maybe he hadn't changed Angel at all. Maybe she wouldn't get close because she still feared having to deal with that loss. He understood her response, but he couldn't let her push him away when he believed that behind her mental bulwark lay untapped feelings for him. He wasn't being immodest. He had seen the look in her eyes when they had revived her after she had ejected in her pod. He had moved in for the kiss, and she had been willing to accept it. Then a medic had come between them. Now her own fear created an equally powerful barrier.

"And she escapes once more," Merlin said, sitting a meter away on a recliner of air, his boots propped up on an invisible footrest. "I've quite enjoyed sitting here, watching you stumble around her like an adolescent. Call me an armchair Romeo, but I think you're going about this all wrong. I could fill you in on my observations of Commander Deveraux, but you refuse to take any more advice. So here we are, you with the long face, me with the new pastime."

"All right. You think you've got a clue about women? Tell me." Blair folded his arms over his chest.

The hologram wearily pushed himself up from his recliner, groaning as he massaged the small of his back, then stood. "Begin, well, at the beginning. Jeanette Deveraux became an orphan during the Pilgrim war. She doesn't know what side her parents were on or who killed them. Maybe it's a bit presumptuous of me, but I hacked into the worldcom database before we left for Mylon. I performed a search of the interplanetary genealogy database."

Blair felt a tightness in his gut. "You did?"

"I thought maybe I could gather some information for you. That way you could use it as an excuse to meet with her."

"She told me she had already searched for records of her parents' deaths. Those files were destroyed during the war."

"Ah, according to some sources they were. But I used military access codes programmed by your father to track down travel records for one Pierre Christian Deveraux, her father. He and his wife Marie Sousex Deveraux left Belgium and traveled to Dewey Station Five near Pluto, which subsequently fell under Pilgrim attack. The rest is a bit disturbing, but I think you should know. I think *she* should know." He paused to gather breath, one of the more subtle but interesting features of his program which made him seem all the more human. "The station's south wing succumbed to accidental fire from a strike-carrier trying to target a Pilgrim sloship. Fourteen hundred civilians were killed, including Angel's parents. Angel herself had been there. Her name appears on a survivor list. Her father's will gave instructions for her to be shipped back to Belgium and placed in the care of the Agnus Eve Orphanage."

"I think she was four or five years old when that happened," Blair said. "I guess she doesn't remember it or she blocked it out. Why didn't her parents have her turned over to relatives?"

"I don't know. Her father has a brother living on Mars. And

her mother has two sisters. Couldn't find anything else on them yet. Still checking."

"Stop. This is like digging through her private stuff. She finds out and. . . . Just stop."

"Okay. But you should know that Confederation Naval Command Authority classified and buried the records of her parents' deaths. As in any war, incidents of friendly fire will occur, and responsible parties will often do everything they can to create plausible deniability."

"I don't think she has any particular love for Confederation military brass, and I don't think she'd be surprised by the cover-up."

"Probably not."

All of this talk about Angel's past suddenly made Blair wonder how and why she had become a Confederation pilot. "You know, there are a billion other possibilities for her, but she suffers with us on this aging bucket. She's certainly not in it for the glory."

"Orphan? No real family? C'mon, Christopher."

"If she's looking for a family, she's found one. But she's still a loner. And a mystery."

"She does like Italian food," Merlin said, flapping his brow. "And according to her medical profile, she has no known allergies."

"You know what? Thank you for reminding me where this comes from. I'm not listening to you. In fact, I'm not going to tell her anything. It's not our business."

"But you can pretend you don't know. Just give her the access codes so she can discover it on her own."

"And rip the scabs from her wounds? I don't think so."

"Then just kiss her, you idiot. You'll either get smacked or laid, though both would be—"

"Switch off," Blair ordered with a huff. He stomped into the corridor, chiding himself for entertaining Merlin's suggestion.

By the time Blair reached Angel's hatch, the notion of barging in and taking her into his arms felt so powerful that he lingered outside her door, trembling and listening for sounds from inside. Then he remembered her saying she had reports to make; she was probably in her squadron commander's office. He rolled his eyes and hauled himself toward his quarters.

When the hatch opened, he found Angel stripped down to bra and panties and standing near his bunk. She wrapped an arm around his neck, dragged him inside, then kissed him hard and twirled her tongue around his. The hatch cycled shut, and her fingers fumbled for the buttons of his utilities. Out of the corner of his eye, he saw Maniac's empty bunk and figured that Angel had somehow taken care of that technicality.

"Lieutenant," she moaned after breaking their embrace. "What we're about to do is classified, compartmentalized, and highly erotic."

"Ma'am, are you sure that—"

She put a finger to his lips. "Just get naked."

VEGA SECTOR,
DAY QUADRANT

CS TIGER CLAW

BLYTHEHEART
JUMP POINT

2654.088

0400 HOURS
CONFEDERATION
STANDARD TIME

For once Blair sat through a jump with no intention of reaching out to find his mother. The
secrets of being a Pilgrim no longer seemed
important compared to the events of the past
five days. He shifted in his jump seat and fought
off the shit-eating grin that threatened to burst
across his face.

Making love to Lieutenant Commander Jeanette Deveraux
would stand as one of the most memorable experiences of his life.
They had spent that entire day together, beginning in his quarters, then moving stealthily back to hers. He had explored every
curve of her lithe, well-toned frame, and their bodies felt smooth
and right together. In candlelight, they had swayed as one sil-
houette on the bulkhead, growing more hungry for each other as
the hours wore on. They had kept silent, speaking with their
hands, their eyes. The fire grew, and they had quivered, grimaced
in ecstasy, and had fallen back, exhausted and gratified for their
efforts.

While lying there after the first time, with Angel's head resting
on his shoulder, Blair had half-expected Merlin to suddenly
appear with his appraisal of their lovemaking: "Well, bravo,
Christopher. No performance anxiety this time, eh? And Lieu-

tenant Commander, you're quite flexible, aren't you." He had shaken off the thought, and when Angel had asked him what was wrong, he had told her that he sometimes got the shakes afterward. That much wasn't a lie.

They had set another rendezvous for the following day, knowing that the rumors would begin to circulate but too infected with each other to be apart. Angel had, indeed, ordered Maniac to sim practice that first day, but she could not keep up that diversion. So they would meet in her quarters. Strange, though. During that second day, Blair had asked why she had suddenly changed her mind. She had told him not to ruin what they had by talking it away. After a moment's consideration, he had realized the truth in that, though the unanswered question still troubled him.

By the third day—and the third tryst—Blair had grown frustrated with their silence. They made love repeatedly, working into each other's rhythms like musicians, but the connection between them seemed to weaken instead of strengthen.

On the fourth day, Blair felt as though they were just working out their anxieties on each other's bodies. Tenderness had turned to grunting. Their relationship was all about that final, pulse-pounding moment. Afterward, they would fall back and stare at the overhead, their gazes swimming through the shadows and never once falling on each other.

Out of nowhere, Blair had said, "We're close. But we're not close."

"I know," she had admitted.

"Guess I shouldn't complain. I'm getting what most guys want, right? Sex with no emotional baggage."

"I can't give you any more than that. Not yet."

He had rolled to face her. "But there's hope?"

"You don't know what I'm risking here."

"I think I do."

Blair had closed his eyes and had taken her into arms. She had buried her head in his chest, and he had simply held her there, trying to show that he wouldn't let go, that he would be there for her for as long as fate allowed.

On the early morning of the fifth day, Blair had tiptoed out of his quarters, had keyed himself into hers, and had spooned her for an hour or two before the jump alarm sounded. During that simple moment he had felt more bonded to her than any other time. He had listened to her breathe and had let her silky hair fall in curtains across her face. Her scent, a light blend of perfume and coconut shampoo, had lulled him to sleep.

I always was a dreamer, he reflected, now feeling the ship rumble under his feet. Lieutenant Commander Obutu's voice broke over the intercom: "Jump in five seconds, four, three, two—"

The familiar moment of frozen silence embraced the flight wing ready room, and after a second—or an eternity—a collective groan rose from the pilots. Blair added his own gasp to the racket.

"What the hell was that?" someone asked.

"All hands, this is your captain. We just experienced a minor fluctuation in the jump field, but the jump was successful. Repeat, the jump was successful. Standby to initiate flight operations. Launch reconnaissance patrol." The general quarters alarm punctuated Gerald's report. A second Klaxon announced a flush scramble, and Blair threw off his straps and joined a white water rush of pilots.

Most of the techs who worked on the flight deck had grown accustomed to flush scrambles that had every operational fighter and bomber in the *Claw*'s arsenal launching within the next few minutes. Despite the crew's experience, anxiety painted their faces, and tensions ran expectantly high. A minor fuel spill had Boss Peterson raising hell with two techs near the bomber berths, and two ordnance specialists had the hood raised on their fully loaded missile cart, which had broken down in the middle of the runway. As the techs took heat from their supervisor, the bulky deckdozer was already en route, its driver lowering the broad hydraulic blade affixed to the vehicle's nose. Blair observed a few more verbal entanglements between pilots and maintenance

crews as he picked his way along the port bulkhead, aiming for
his Rapier's berth.

To his mild astonishment, he saw Paladin striding toward him
from the opposite end of the flight deck. The commodore caught
his gaze, then waved him over. Blair leapt twice over fuel lines
that obstacled his path, then reached the man, out of breath.
"Sir?"

"You'll be flying in the *Diligent* with me, Lieutenant."

"Sir?"

"Angel's loaned you to me. Come on." He started up the
deck, in the direction Blair had come.

The *Diligent* sat a short walk ahead, her thrusters already
idling, her disc-shaped forward fuselage auguring missions of
quiet efficiency rather than capital ship battles. In fact, the idea
of him riding with Paladin aboard the merchantman seemed
more than a little odd. Who would take a merchantman out
against a supercruiser when nearly five score of fighters and
bombers were ready to do the job?

"I suppose you'd like to know what's going on," Paladin said
as they reached the ship's gangplank.

"Yes, sir. I assume we've detected the *Olympus*. But you're
qualified to pilot Broadswords and Rapiers. Why are we launching in the *Diligent*?"

"Because, son, we're not going out to fight."

Maniac attached his O_2 mask, then finished his abbreviated pre-
flight checklist. External moorings released. Fuel topped off.
Jump drive, tow system, Tempest targeting and navigational AI,
and life support standing tall in the green. Thrusters growling
like the Dobermans they were. Neutron gun pulse generators
fully charged, with alternate or synchronous fire settings available. Heads Up Display crisp, clear, and alive with data bars that
told him everything but the damned ball score. Comm channel
open. Right Visual Display Unit full of static, left displaying ship
damage in quadrants. The armor and shield indicator, just right
of center, glowed at full strength all around. It would stay that

way. No Pilgrim jock would deliver even a glancing blow if Maniac had anything to say about it. And he'd said it before: They'd meet the best—and die with the rest.

Yet all of the adrenaline-induced bravado failed to extinguish the guilt that had him sweating in his flight suit. Killing Kilrathi had become as routine as stomping on ants; however, killing other people who had once been Confederation pilots seemed like a terrible waste. And besides, he had come to know a Pilgrim, if only a half-breed. His relationship with Blair made him feel even worse now. Thank God Blair had been loaned out to the commodore.

As it had over Lethe, the battle would become more surreal since their opponents flew in identical ships. Were it not for electronic identification systems, friendly fire would become the rule of the day instead of the exception. He almost wished he had been assigned something less personal that would take him out of the killing loop. Most people who knew Maniac would never believe that he had doubts about going out and doing his job. He had once told somebody that if researchers analyzed his DNA, they would discover a new gene—one they would find in only the best pilots. Flying wasn't a learned skill; you were born to it or not. And when you got the target in your sights, you never thought about the children you might be orphaning. You focused on racking up one more for the killboard. *So why don't I feel all gung ho and jingoistic now?*

"Hunter? Bishop? Slot, clock, and burn," Angel said over the comm. "Sinatra? Cheddarboy? On deck. Zarya and Maniac? On their heels. And Gangsta? You're on my wing. Last out and last in. Ladies, while we're waiting for the bombers to launch, I suggest you pull data on the AO. The zone's an ally, not an obstacle."

"Yeah, yeah," Maniac grunted over the old reminder. He had never been one to spend hours analyzing the Area of Operations before heading into combat. Sure, you could learn a lot more about the star system, its planets, its moons, but you might also succumb to a false sense of security because you thought you knew what lay ahead. Maniac's experience had taught him to expect a surprise with every tug on the control stick. But for the hell of it—and to appease Angel, who could tap into his systems at any time to see if he were actually scanning the data—he pulled up the skinny on McDaniel's World.

Well, there's nothing Earth-shattering here to report to the Terran News Channel, he thought as he scanned the info spilling across his display. Star: McDaniel (*Is everything in the system called McDaniel?*). Spectral type: G2 (*Anyone care?*). Absolute magnitude: 4.27 (*Absolutely unimportant.*). Apparent visual magnitude: 0.2 (*Apparently they don't realize how boring this shit is.*). Temperature: 6600 degrees K (*Yeah, like my temper right now.*). Mass: 1.1 times Sol Standard (*My life has new meaning.*). Planets: four terrestrial, two gas giants. Twenty-one known satellites in the system, three in orbit around the third terrestrial planet dubbed McDaniel's World (*My God, what an original name!*).

The right VDU focused on the planet, bringing up a three-dimensional simulacrum rotating imperceptibly in real time. Oxygen worlds were as rare as good pilots in Vega Sector, but even rarer still were worlds with masses nearly equal to Earth's. This rock represented such a place, defying odds and suggesting a sort of cosmic symmetry that allowed for remarkably similar planets to exist billions of kilometers apart. *Easy to see why the Pilgrims quickly claimed the world for their own. Talk about a real estate windfall. . . .* McDaniel emitted a bluish green aura, and her raggedly shaped continents yielded just under half as much habitable land as Earth's. The tides created by her three moons played a lot more havoc with her shorelines than Luna played with Earth's, however.

And there, behind McDaniel's largest moon, a gray, potato-shaped eyesore named Lyatta, hovered the *Olympus.* Maniac tapped in a command, bringing up a nav schematic. A trio of bundled yellow lines that represented the swiftest course to the moon extended from a blue blip marked *Tiger Claw.* He noted that on full afterburners they would be in strike range in one-point-three minutes. Good. Waiting too long to engage would make his itchy trigger finger even itchier.

Hallelujah; Boss Raznick finally sounded over their channel. "Angel, flight control. First pair is clear for launch. ICQ and AO recon reports uploaded. We have confirmation of multiple bandits headed our way. No response to hails."

"Thanks, boss. Okay, ladies. I want a tight box at one K out. You know your positions. Make no mistake, they've been trained the same as us and know all the tricks. Exploit their errors. We'll let them beat themselves. They'll probably jam the *Claw*'s long-range scans, so if anyone catches sight of or reads a tube door opening, inform me ASAP."

"Thought she wouldn't target this planet?" Bishop asked.

"We don't think she will. But if Aristee knows she's going to die, she might want to save her homeworld by destroying it," Angel said, emphasizing the irony.

"So let her," Hunter argued. "My universe could use a few less fanatics."

"The Confed recognizes McDaniel as neutral territory and has agreed to come to the aid of her citizens should the Kilrathi or any other hostile force attack," Angel reminded him. "So everybody stow your bigotry and do your jobs. Hunter? Bishop? Line 'em up."

Maniac let his head fall back on the seat. No, he wouldn't wait long for the battle, but he still had to wait to launch with Zarya. He pulled up her private frequency, flashed her a wink with the eye that wasn't covered by his HUD viewer. "Hey, I just wanted to say that you're the best looking wingman I've ever had."

"What about Rosie Forbes?" she challenged, cocking a brow.

He faltered. "She was beautiful. But in a different way."

"What way?"

"Bad timing for this chat, eh?"

"Not at all," she insisted.

"Look, Rosie got smoked, and I really don't want to talk about it—especially now."

"I'm not Rosie."

"Jeez, you had me fooled."

"Do you know what a soft monkey is?"

"Yeah, it's no fun at all."

"Listen, wiseass, when a mother chimp loses one of her babies, sometimes zookeepers give her a chimp doll to help her deal with the grief. It's a very old remedy, but usually very effective. I think you're still grieving. And I'm your soft monkey."

He snorted, then the laughter came out full and hard. "I've heard some pretty wacky stuff, but—"

"You're beyond reproach." The VDU snapped into darkness. Swearing, Maniac slammed down the reconnect button, and Zarya appeared, gaze averted. "I'm sorry," he said. "I get what you're saying. Call me immature, but the monkey thing sounds funny. Maybe I'm still grieving, on the rebound, whatever. But I like being with you. Can that be enough for now?"

"I guess so. But you won't have me until your head's clear. Until it's right."

His heart sank. A week's worth of fierce wooing to get her into his rack had just gone by the wayside.

"Lieutenants Marshall and Rolitov, flight control. You're clear for launch, copy?" Boss Raznick said, breaking into their private link. Maniac hadn't known the boss could do that; he'd have to be more careful about what he said.

"Copy that, boss," responded Zarya, her tone forceful and all business, ringing quite sexily in Maniac's ears. "Clock stands at ten seconds."

They lined up beside each other, and Maniac flashed her a tentative thumbs up before saluting Deck Boss Peterson. He watched the numbers spin down in his HUD, spotted the green launch light, then slammed the throttles forward. He and Zarya roared through the flight deck and impaled the curtain of sodden energy like the sword whose name their fighters bore. The two Rapiers streaked over the runway that split the *Tiger Claw* in two. Dark gray bulkheads broken by maintenance planes blurred into dull, watery streaks narrowing toward a disk of stars.

"Attack vector set. Switching to auto for five-second burn to regroup and box," Zarya announced.

"Roger, that. In three, two, one." Maniac kicked in his afterburners while simultaneously engaging the autopilot. The fighter climbed sixty degrees away from the *Claw* and toward a tableau dominated by McDaniel's World and the three moons.

Were it not for human intervention, Maniac could've mistaken the view for a painting of celestial serenity by that famous Japanese artist whose name continually escaped him. But Rapiers cut viciously across the canvas, long tails of exhaust drawing straight, even lines in an otherwise curved natural environment. At the moment, McDaniel's smallest moon shied behind the planet, only a crescent still visible. The second moon hung to port, a pale white, perfectly shaped orb with a massive crater near its north pole. The target moon, Lyatta, orbited on a steep incline relative to McDaniel's path around its sun, and the moon's many craters afforded the supercruiser's fighters with excellent cover in which to stage an ambush.

"Burn complete," Maniac told Zarya.

"Copy. Going manual to form up."

Directly ahead, the other Rapiers of Black Lion Squadron had already assumed four of the eight distinct positions that comprised the box formation. Four points represented the top of the box and resembled the corners of a square. Another square would sit about twenty meters back, just beyond the forward square's thruster wash. He and Zarya would assume the base angles of the second square, with Angel and Gangsta taking the top. Angel liked the formation since it gave some of them a millisecond or two to jump once the furball hit. The side of the box closest to the incoming fighters would break first, and the other sides would follow in succession.

Breaking a box formation was much easier than, say, a wedge, which gave you fewer vectors along your three and nine o'clock and more opportunities to crash into your neighbors. Better to be blown out of sky by an opponent than make a stupid course correction and buy it. Maniac had known two cadets who had needlessly lost their lives while breaking from a wedge. He remembered them now as he eased off the throttle and descended into position. He tossed a look at Zarya, but she didn't see him, her gaze sweeping her instruments. He had to hand it to her. When it came to business, she was nothing but.

Two blips lit the bottom of Maniac's radar scope and closed toward the center. The Tempest system immediately IDed them as Angel and Gangsta soaring toward their positions. Maniac glanced up at the belly of Angel's jet as she throttled down to match the squadron's velocity.

"All right, mates. Got some of our spiritual buddies inbound," Hunter reported. "Count nine bandits targeting Lightning's squadron."

"Adjust course to intercept," Angel ordered.

Maniac squinted to his two o'clock, where a bright spattering of thruster lights headed toward the big moon. That would be Lightning's Squadron: twelve Rapiers running escort for the half dozen Broadsword bombers whose blunt noses and boxy wings hinted at their lack of evasion capacity. If Lightning's team could get those bombers in close enough, they could release their massive quartet of over- and underwing antimatter torpedoes. If the *Olympus*'s big guns or fighters failed to intercept just one of those torpedoes, she might suffer a blow serious enough to cost her the entire battle. Captain Amity Aristee obviously knew that, and she would direct most of her fighters to intercept the bomber squadrons, while holding back a squadron or two in reserve for any bombers that penetrated her defenses.

Jinxman's escort team of twenty Rapiers and another six bombers approached the moon from Maniac's five o'clock. They would slip under the satellite and catch the supercruiser from below. But Maniac spotted a pack of thirteen enemy Rapiers buzzing toward them.

The sixteen Rapiers of Sixth Squadron were quick to react and bulleted under Maniac's fighter, in pursuit of the bandits that had tagged Jinxman's people.

Meanwhile, the Exeter-class destroyers *Oregon* and *Mitchell*

Hammock assumed flanking positions of the *Tiger Claw* and lumbered toward the moon on full impulse. At three hundred and sixty meters, they achieved a maximum velocity of one hundred and fifty kilometers per second, respectable for vessels of their size. With bows shaped like narrow isosceles triangles and pairs of short wings that swept back toward their sterns, the destroyers resembled glistening javelins honing themselves on space itself. Their eight turreted meson guns and two dozen torpedo tubes dispelled any rumors of their weakness. At the right moment, they would come in from three and nine o'clock positions and descend upon the supercruiser in an attempt to cut it off, though they had been wisely instructed to remain behind the ship and outside the five-hundred-meter gravitic cloak created by the *Olympus*'s hopper drive.

The *Tiger Claw* would hold back while the destroyers and fighters went about their business. Maniac knew that Gerald wouldn't bring the ship into the fray unless absolutely necessary. The *Claw* sorely needed a dry-docking, and makeshift repairs had been performed throughout the old ship. She would deftly serve her function as a launching platform for fighters, but she couldn't bear another beating like the one she had received near the Charybdis Quasar. Fourteen Rapiers from Fifth Squadron would shadow-hug her hull as escorts, and the thirteen of Seventh Squadron would sit warm and ready on the flight deck.

In all, twelve Broadswords and eighty-four Rapiers participated in the attack, with Second Squadron's loss sorely felt by all. Trouble always was, as pilots died or became incapacitated, they were not summarily replaced. There were often more ships than personnel to fly them, which explained why squadrons had become smaller and why cadets were being pushed through the academies, having to meet only seventy-five percent of the qualifications that Maniac had had to meet just weeks prior. The brass covered it up by renaming programs. It wasn't flight training anymore but "accelerated" flight training, which implied a tougher class that was, in fact, easier. Maniac had heard about the revised training from Zarya, whose sister had just graduated early and had been assigned to the CS *Drayton* as radar officer. Maniac hoped they didn't send any ill-qualified nuggets to the *Claw*. And if they did, he would waste no time pounding them into shape.

"Operation Zeus," AKA "Operation Get Some" in Maniac's engagement book, relied upon simplicity—just the way Maniac preferred it. Enemy Rapiers would go after the *Claw*'s bombers, whose escorts would stick with them and engage only the attackers who broke through the intercepting force. First and Sixth Squadrons served as the first wave of interceptors, which put Maniac and his comrades at the sword's tip to protect Lightning's team.

"Got about eight seconds until primary weapons range," Bishop said.

Without further ado, the order that Maniac lived to hear rattled through his headset:

"Break and attack!" cried Angel.

"Got the tail pair," Hunter said. "Bishop, you bag the one on the far side."

"Got him," the pilot responded.

The high number of fighters in the zone dictated that wingman and wingleaders would stay close and cover each other but were still free to break off when necessary. Maniac repeatedly pushed this unwritten rule to its limits.

As the skipchatter further clogged the general frequency, Maniac glanced to his one o'clock and picked out two Rapiers bound for the lead Broadsword. He skimmed a menu of channels and dialed up the lead bomber pilot's frequency. "Hold course, Pandora. Maniac and Zarya are in to assist." Throttling up, he leaned back on the control stick and fell in behind Zarya as they tore into a forty-five-degree climb. In five seconds they would be within cannon range.

But Zarya had no intention of waiting even another second. Her neutron gun spun and spewed salvos of glittering rounds that strayed wide before drumming along the starboard shields of the fighter nearest them. Now solidly locked on, she held her bead as the enemy Rapier broke off in a sharp, corkscrewing dive and vanished from Maniac's field of view. Zarya stayed with the Rapier, plunging well below Maniac.

The other Rapier maintained course, then suddenly swooped down on the Broadsword to unleash a volley of neutron fire before Maniac could react. He pinned the throttle, lit the burners, and tore into the Pilgrim's exhaust trail. "Got this little problem," he told the enemy pilot, having locked on to the guy's operating frequency. "I'm Pilgrim intolerant. You fanatics upset my stomach and generally ruin my day. I don't like that."

No response from the Pilgrim.

Yes, the bravado had returned, and yes, it remained a weak neutralizer of the guilt. Maniac swore at himself, at his feelings, then tightened every muscle and gave himself to the machine. The smart targeting reticle appeared in his HUD, a green circle that floated just ahead of the enemy Rapier as it wheeled around to make another pass at the Broadsword.

Maniac widened his eyes and jammed down his primary weapons trigger. The rotary barrel hummed and got to work, belching out an unceasing spray that caught the enemy Rapier's canopy. Shields tossed up bursts of azure light as they strained to curtail Maniac's rounds. "Now, listen to a reading from the gospel according to Maniac."

A terrific explosion astern threw a veil of shimmering light over his fighter. Even as he cocked his head to see what the hell had happened, an alluring female whooped and shouted, "Zarya drops one! What's the delay, Lieutenant?"

Not one to have his thunder stolen, Maniac narrowed the enemy Rapier's lead to twenty meters. The other pilot leveled off, cutting through a second furball created by Sixth Squadron. Maniac ceased fire as he wove a hair-raising, torturous course through fighters and bombers crisscrossing about a quarter kilometer away from the pockmarked moon. He scarcely believed that the enemy pilot had navigated through coordinates so densely packed with other starcraft.

Raging aloud, he pulled up and out of the traffic, vowing that before the engagement ended, he would find and smoke that jock who had eluded him.

"Maniac?"

He glanced to his radar scope, speckled now with so many blips that if more popped up, the display might become a solid swirl of red and blue. He threw a toggle, and the scope zoomed in to show his wingman's position. Zarya glided at his four o'clock, about three hundred meters away. "Hold your course," he told her. "Coming down to form on your wing."

As he barreled along the outskirts of the AO, cutting through the paths of dozens of dogfights and plowing through tumbling shards of durasteel and severed pieces of twisted hydraulic line, he jolted as his missile lock alarm woke in a rapid beeping. The computer's automatic announcement chimed in over the alarm: "Warning. Enemy projectile has positive lock. Impact in nine seconds, eight . . ."

Speed is life, Maniac thought as he re-lit his burners and brought the Rapier up to three hundred KPS, three twenty, forty, sixty, ninety—

The right VDU showed the Tempest computer's ID on the missile, a Spiculum Image-Recognition bomb using a computer to memorize Maniac's electronic and visual signature. The damned rocket approached at velocity of 1600 KPS—his evasion would only gain him an extra second or two of life. He thumbed off a cloud of chaff but assumed the superheated fragments of wire and durasteel would do little to fool the missile's advanced guidance system. Were it a Dart Dumbfire missile, he might have a chance.

The computer reached three seconds, two . . .

He reached for the ejection handle.

But a powerful detonation tossed him forward. A second later, roiling flames tongued his canopy before dematerializing into the vacuum. He jerked the stick back, trying to stabilize the Rapier, and shouted, "Computer? Report!"

"Missile detonated. Range, twenty-point-two-five meters. Severe power drain to aft shields. Armor at full strength."

Flabbergasted, he laughed and tried to figure out why the rocket had prematurely detonated.

The answer came quickly as Zarya's face flickered on his right VDU. "Zarya drops missile, saves rocket jock's life. Give me a pen. I'll sign your palm."

"Zarya? Maniac?" Angel called. "We need more fire support. Come around the moon to point three-five-seven by six-two-one. Got a fresh squadron of enemy Rapiers coming in. Lay down suppressing fire and draw Lightning's people another path."

"Roger, ma'am," Maniac said exhaustedly. Be nice if he had a half-second to catch his breath. He eyed his tactical screen and tapped for the right grid. Then he brought the Rapier around in a hard turn to port, shifting the white crosshairs that marked the nav point to the center of the HUD. "En route to coordinates," he assured Angel. Zarya slipped up beside him and tilted her helmeted head quickly from shoulder to shoulder, a dance move and in-joke that alluded to their night of swing.

By now the destroyers had already dropped behind Lyatta, and the moon wore a halo of intermittent light created by the dozens of explosions that occurred behind it.

"Zarya? Maniac? I've IDed a troopship pulling away from McDaniel," Angel informed them. "You got it. Cheddarboy and Sinatra? You take their grid."

Maniac pulled up the vessel on his tactical display, and he didn't need a detailed computer model to project its destination.

"I'm all about the killboard today," Zarya said, lancing out ahead of him.

"Guess you are," he admitted. "But now I'll stop holding back. You think I got this call sign for being shy?"

"No, I assumed that—"

"Whoa, whoa, whoa!" he cried as an enemy Rapier dove in front of his fighter and darted after Zarya. "Got one on your back! Jinx!"

"I'm outta here," said Zarya.

Where had the bastard come from? No warning had flashed on his scope. His gaze sought the tactical display then lifted as a bone-chilling salvo of neutron fire came within a meter of his starboard wing and razored into the distance. Another glance to the scope told him nothing. "They got us jammed up good!"

"I know! I know! And a three-G loop didn't shake this sucker. Gonna try kickstopping him."

Maniac wished he could watch her perform the hard ninety-degree turn to make sure that the enemy Rapier overshot her and that she pulled into the requisite one-eighty to lock on and blow his ass back to that higher plane of existence.

But Maniac had his own problems, namely a Pilgrim pilot who bore down on him with wing-mounted laser cannons blazing and neutron gun spinning like a tornado whose eye blinked white lightning every time it fired.

Sick and tired of these aggressive fanatics, Maniac howled a curse to the heavens, slammed down the throttle, and went ballistic, waving on the Gs like an infuriated boxer waves on his opponent. Acceleration dampeners compensated for some of the force, but he had to focus on his breathing and get his blood back into his extremities. Three Gs. Four. Four-point-five. His vision grew dark around the edges. He knew that in a few seconds he would lose consciousness. He slapped back a toggle, stalling both thrusters, then manuevering jets fired as he rolled onto his back to face the oncoming attacker. The Pilgrim apparently had no qualms about playing an old-fashioned game of chicken. He also had no idea of Maniac's experience with the game, though the Pilgrim could consult a few Kilrathi pilots who would spin him quite a tale.

With reckless abandon coursing through his veins, Maniac snap-fired the thrusters and advanced at full tilt with neutron fire pinging off his canopy shield like droplets of neon blue jelly. He thumbed off the safety cover on his secondary weapons button, then closed his left eye, focusing on the targeting reticle as it swam around the Rapier, then blinked red as he got the lock. Even as he fired the Dumbfire missile, the Pilgrim liberated one of his own.

Holding his breath, Maniac rolled ninety degrees, and the

enemy missile glanced his port wing but failed to detonate.

The Pilgrim plunged into a seventy-five-degree dive and swept under Maniac's Rapier. Though he had evaded Maniac's missile, the Pilgrim had not evaded the man himself. Not yet. Maniac pulled a hard U-turn and pursued the Rapier, gritting his teeth as it took agonizing seconds for him to fall squarely in on the Pilgrim's six o'clock.

"Maniac? Little help here," Zarya said. Static burst through the audio-video transmission coming from her Rapier as she became a cushion for laser strikes.

That was all it took for Maniac to abandon his pursuit of the Rapier and pull up her position on his tactical display. "I'll be right there. Hard brake 'em if you can."

"Roger that. And hey, that troopship's making its final approach. It'll be aboard the *Olympus* in a second or two," she said glumly. "Failed that objective."

"Who cares. Worry about that Rapier on your back."

"Believe me. I'm worrying."

"Five seconds 'till I'm in," he reassured her, stealing glances at his tactical and radar displays. Twin flashes scaled the void above as someone, hopefully an enemy, bought the proverbial one-way ticket.

They had rounded the moon and now drew much closer to the supercruiser. Maniac clearly made out her outline against the ruffled sheet of the moon's surface. Her four primary antimatter guns swiveled to follow targets and dispense humbling clouds of anti-starcraft fire. All thirty of her point-defense missile systems launched Dumbfires at those Rapiers operating along the rim of the five-hundred-meter gravitic cloak zone. The *Oregon* and *Mitchell Hammock* stood about a quarter kilometer off the supercruiser's bow and stern respectively, taking light fire from a few Pilgrim Rapiers that strafed their decks. The destroyers hurled anti-cap ship missiles at the supercruiser, but most of them detonated well short of their targets, cut down by the *Olympus*'s unrelenting antimatter guns. Maniac spotted a few missiles getting through, but the carrier's powerful shields and thick armor could withstand the pummeling, at least for a little while.

Jinxman's squadron had yet to near the supercruiser, and three of the Broadswords in his team's escort had been destroyed. Lightning had fared even worse. His group had been thinned out to nine Rapiers and two Broadswords. Both squadrons had encountered ambushes as they had come around the moon, while First and Sixth Squadrons had been diverted into another fray. Yes, the Pilgrims had taken full advantage of those craters, and no, they weren't better shots—but they sure as hell knew how to navigate through furballs, evidenced by the *Claw*'s blistering losses.

"Maniac? Where are you?"

"Look back," he said coolly as he descended from the heavens like a venom-spitting demon whose every sense focused on the Rapier pursuing Zarya. He engaged his electronic countermeasures system to, in theory, jam the bastard's radar. Relying on a reserve that had taken him his entire academy career to forge, Maniac held his fire and narrowed the Pilgrim's lead, positioning himself just three meters above the fighter. *Looks good*, he told himself, then felt the correct slam as the afterburners kicked in and propelled him directly over the enemy. He thumbed down on his high-hat control and belly-flopped onto the Pilgrim, driving the guy away as his own fighter rocked violently.

And he could have kissed Zarya for taking full advantage of the diversion. She yanked into a one-eighty, pitched down, and got a lock so clean on the Pilgrim that Maniac could almost see the tactical line stretching from her missile station to the Pilgrim's fighter. Her missile flew, curved ever so slightly, then struck the enemy Rapier's rotary neutron gun in a fiery fist of devastation. The starfighter twirled away, leaving behind jagged embers of its cockpit and nose.

"Zarya drops two!"

"With assistance," Maniac quickly added, then began a long, swift turn to port, headed back in her direction. The supercruiser floated below him now, and he spotted the multiple bursts of breaking thrusters.

Another ship boldly violated the five-hundred-meter zone,

and Maniac did a double-take as he realized that he hadn't spotted another Pilgrim troopship, but instead Commodore Taggart's merchantman, the *Diligent*.

"Hey, Maniac? Isn't that the—"

"Yeah. What the hell's going on?" He dialed up Angel's channel. "Ma'am? I'm watching the *Diligent* make her approach toward the *Olympus*. They ain't shooting at her, ma'am."

"No, they're not," Angel observed stoically.

"Is Blair aboard that ship?" asked Maniac.

"I believe he is."

"Well, what is this? We sending over negotiators?"

She didn't answer, her attention stolen by her instruments. "Reading gravitic distortion. All ships clear the zone. Repeat! Clear the zone!"

Somewhere out there, far across the cosmos, a deity with a huge dislike for cocky fighter pilots looked down on Maniac's puny Rapier and thought, *No, it shouldn't be so easy for this one. He's cheated fate one too many times. Now the bill has come due....*

Or at least that's what Maniac thought had happened as one of the Pilgrim Rapiers returning to the supercruiser suddenly blurred by him and fired a missile that struck between his thruster cones and detonated, drop-kicking him down toward the supercruiser amid a shrieking chorus of alarms. "Shit! I just took one up the tailpipe. Got mucho damage. Thruster control is gone. Can't maneuver. I'm falling within the five-hundred-meter zone."

"Pop the top," Zarya cried.

"Lost power to the ejection system," he said, gaze frantically sweeping the right VDU's damage report. "Reactor's offline. Can't even pull the plug on this one."

"I'm coming in to get you," Zarya said.

"Negative. Fall back as ordered."

"No way!"

"Lieutenant Rolitov, you will clear the zone," Angel insisted, cutting into the channel.

"But I can get down there and tractor him in!"

"Don't do it, Zarya," he said softly. "Just go home."

He heard her panting into her headset, then a slight whimper escaped her lips. "Oh, God . . ." The VDU went blank. His radar still operated on emergency reserves, and he watched her break back for the *Claw*'s retreating fighters and bombers.

Once her ship reached them, Maniac looked up.

Bad idea.

The supercruiser's starboard aft quarter rushed toward him.

VEGA SECTOR,
DAY QUADRANT

CS OLYMPUS

MCDANIEL'S WORLD,
MOON LYATTA

2654.088

0510 HOURS
CONFEDERATION
STANDARD TIME

"I'm not dead yet," Maniac whispered as his Rapier advanced into the great shadow drawn by the *Olympus*'s superstructure. In about ten seconds, his fighter would shatter across the supercruiser's hull with all the glory and fanfare of a mosquito spattering on a windshield. He decided to stay alive long enough to remind the deity toying with him that Lieutenant Todd "Maniac" Marshall had chutzpah and flying skills up to here, and did he really want to mess with that?

Who am I kidding? The Maniac-magic is gone, he thought as he tried for the third time to reroute power to his maneuvering jets. The cell lines had probably been severed, despite the onboard computer's failure to report the problem. The computer could at least accurately report how thoroughly screwed he was.

The Rapier's nose suddenly jolted up and to starboard so that Maniac now sat parallel to the *Olympus,* slid sideways toward her, and had a straight view to her bow. The stars ahead had given way to the utter blackness of the *Olympus*'s gravity well. Thousands of pieces of debris flocked toward the gaping maw, on their way to a little town known as Digestion, a town Maniac would soon visit. He laughed ironically as the brightly lit panel of his tractor system drew his eyes. He doubted the beam would be strong enough to hold him to the supercruiser.

Then again, the well had already demonstrated a healthy and forceful appetite for debris but had only slightly affected his trajectory. He now closed in on the well at nearly the same velocity as the *Olympus*, as though he had glided into a neutral field enveloping the ship.

Abandoning any more speculation, he fired up the tractor and launched a beam at the cruiser's hull. The Rapier shook a second, then panels groaned as he began reeling himself toward the cruiser. Twenty meters, ten, five, then a solid thump reverberated through the cockpit as the tip of his port wing bounced once off the hull, then settled onto the durasteel.

Without warning, his stomach greeted his knees and a pinwheel of white light rose out of the well. He reached toward the canopy, feeling numb and disoriented as the pinwheel broadened into a blinding shimmer.

Though he was temporarily resigned to being two steps behind the supercruiser, Admiral Vukar nar Caxki had still clung to the false hope that once his battle group reached the midpoint between the Lafayette and Tamayo systems, they would finally meet up with the elusive Confederation ship.

But they had arrived in the sector three standard days ago and had yet to read any signs of the supercruiser's passage. No gravitic residuum. No ion emissions. Had Tactical Officer Makorshk relied on inaccurate data to calculate their jump? Perhaps, but for the time being Vukar would give the second fang the benefit of the doubt.

The atmosphere on the bridge had long since cooled from the boiling blood frenzy that had clutched everyone's hearts after they had learned of losing so many to the supercruiser. Vukar's officers now stared impassively at their instruments, some seeming lifeless, all wearing the tight lips of the sullen. Too many hours had passed without his warriors seeing combat. As much as they tried, it wasn't in their blood to sit and watch blinking lights and scan schematics. Pack hunters should be more in touch with their instincts, with their environment, if they were to remain strong. Vukar himself felt the tug of ancient desires. Everything his paw touched had been manufactured by Kilrathi hands; nothing natural existed on the bridge. This lack of nature troubled him, gave him no outlet in which to exercise his desires to leap and attack. Where were Kilrah's cliffs and caves? And more importantly, where was the prey?

A hiss rose from the back of his throat as he shifted away from the forward viewport and drifted back to Makorshk's tactical station. "Report?"

"Still nothing, my Kalralahr. We're simply out of emissions range. A little more time. That's all we need."

Vukar hissed more loudly. "I've given you too much time already."

"I have a theory, if you'd like to hear it." Makorshk slowly lifted his head, and the heat of the second fang's glare astonished Vukar.

In a motion so quick that it caught Makorshk completely off guard, Vukar snatched the young warrior's armored collar and wrenched him out of his seat. "Only the dying assume that look with me."

"Then strike," Makorshk said, craning his elliptical head to expose the pale folds of skin protruding from his neck. "But let me speak first."

Every bridge officer glanced nervously at them, most holding their breaths in anticipation of Vukar's next move. Control panels thrummed and beeped, otherwise an icy stillness prevailed.

Nearly tasting the tension and suddenly realizing how it darkened the spirits of his officers, Vukar slowly relaxed his grip and retracted the claws of his free paw. He abruptly thrust Makorshk back into the seat, feeling invigorated and somewhat free of the anxiety that had been coiling around him for days. Yes, the old desires had been quelled for the moment. "What is your theory?"

"That supercruiser has gone from Mylon to Lethe to out here, somewhere. I suspect it has already moved on."

"A priestess could tell me that," Vukar spat.

"Yes, but could she predict that ship's course?"

"You can?"

"A Confederation supercruiser is seized by Pilgrims. The likelihood of such an occurrence is rare, and I believe that such an act could only be carried out by Confederation officers of Pilgrim ancestry. Reconnaissance data on both the Mylon and Lethe attacks confirms that troopships were sent down to both planets. That information intrigues me."

Vukar nodded. "Why send down troopships before annihilating the planet, unless—"

"The Pilgrims planned on saving some of their own first. I don't believe they're attacking randomly. They're selecting planets that have high populations of Pilgrims."

"What are they trying to do? Save all of the Pilgrims before they annihilate the Confederation? And if they plan on doing that, why only one ship?"

Makorshk lifted his chin in the gesture of uncertainty. "Those questions won't be answered until we're aboard that ship. But their course does provide one clue. If they're focusing their attention on systems with high concentrations of Pilgrims, then look at this." The second fang's long, thick fingers worked furiously on a touchpad. His screen glowed with images of insignificant planets clustered around a feeble-looking sun. "McDaniel's World, the so-called homeworld of Pilgrims." The picture zoomed out to reveal McDaniel's position relative to their present one. "You see, my Kalrahalr? We can jump here, at Blytheheart." Makorshk tapped his screen, and another system stitched across the display.

"But we won't reach McDaniel for another five standard days," Vukar said, reading the computer's arrival projection. "We need a plan to narrow that ship's lead."

A screen to Makorshk's left unexpectedly flashed a message. Makorshk excitedly regarded the screen as Vukar leaned over the second fang. "Kalralahr. Ion emissions and gravitic residuum detected. Ion emissions suggest that four, possibly five Confederation cap ships operated within these coordinates."

"Yes, the apes hunt each other," Vukar said restlessly. "That tells us nothing about how we can intercept that ship."

"If we can't catch up with them at McDaniel, we need to discover their next stop."

"If your theory holds true, then they would pick another world with a high population of Pilgrims."

"Yes, perhaps for the specific purpose of recruiting some Pilgrims. A mutiny certainly occurred, and there may not be enough Pilgrim apes aboard to run her efficiently. So they're taking on officers and taking out planets as they go."

"Very well, then, Makorshk. I charge you with plotting their next course. We will attempt to second guess them based on *your* estimates."

Makorshk drew back his head and lifted his shoulders. "Thank you for the honor," he said in a gasp of delight. "We will find that ship. And you, the clan, even the emperor will come to learn that the deadliest warrior hunts with his mind, not with his nose. The old ways will not work here."

"Be wary of such remarks," Vukar said, lifting a finger. "Even highborns cannot change their blood. The ancient stirrings in our hearts that turn rational thought to jabber are what make us who we are and what will bring the Terrans to their knees. Never forget that, lest you become more like a hairless ape than a Kilrathi warrior of the Caxki clan."

"Yes, my Kalralahr," the second fang replied distractedly, his gaze already wandering through star charts flashing on his tactical screen.

Should the young warrior's next set of coordinates fail to place them within striking range of the supercruiser, Vukar decided that he would challenge his tactical officer to a blood duel. That would be the only way to save face after placing so much trust in a subordinate officer.

Breathing a heavy sigh that sent nutrient gas jetting from his nostrils, Vukar turned over command to the ship's pensive first fang, Jatark nar Caxki, then took himself to the lift, guided by pangs of hunger that demanded his immediate attention. He decided that he would never again go so long without food.

Now, if he could only hunt his meal rather than have it handed to him like a weak lowborn or like one of the intellects in Makorshk's favor.

A warrior does not hunt with head or his nose, Vukar thought.

He hunts with his heart.

Stretched out on his sofa, wearing only a wrinkled pair of boxer shorts, Commodore Richard Bellegarde took several long pulls on the bottle of Scotch whiskey he had picked up while in Glasgow. He eyed his Spartan quarters aboard the *Concordia* and came to realize that the empty box aptly represented the empty man. He had left his mistress to satisfy the admiral, but that loss leached away his spirit. While on watch, he pretended to be involved, pretended that he really cared about his career, about his life. But all he really wanted was to take back everything he had said to Trish, to resume their relationship the way it had been, to damn to hell Tolwyn's concern for his career. He took another swig of Scotch, then balanced the bottle on his bare chest and stared at a world blurred by the glass.

His door hatch chimed. Too numb and too lazy to stand, he simply shouted, "Yeah?"

"Richard? It's Geoff. May I come in?"

He bolted up, spilling the whiskey down his legs. "Uh, sir, I'm not feeling so, uh . . . can you give me a little time, say thirty minutes, and I'll meet you in the wardroom?"

"This can't wait."

Bellegarde threw his head back and chuckled. Screw getting a fleet. Screw it all. He would open the door and let the truth pour out. He got to his feet, but the deck rose and fell as though he stood on a seafaring vessel. He reached out to brace himself with the hand that gripped the whiskey bottle. He struck air once, twice, a third time before he lost his grip on the bottle and sent it crashing to the floor. At least it hadn't broken.

"Richard, are you all right?"

"I'm perfect," he said, then stumbled to the hatch and beat a fist on the control panel.

Admiral Tolwyn marched in, looking neither surprised nor disgusted by Bellegarde's swagger and stench. His inspection took all of two seconds, then he crossed to Bellegarde's desk, slid out the chair, and took a seat. As usual, the admiral carried himself with an unyielding enthusiasm that seemed hot-wired to a reactor. In fact, Bellegarde had never seen the man in off-duty utilities. Even now, on his own time, Tolwyn wore his operations uniform, the large buttons running down his breasts reminding Bellegarde of what Confederation Naval officers were supposed to look like. He glanced down at his own bare, Scotch-covered form, then mustered a wan smile. "You caught me."

The admiral shook his head. "These are your quarters, and you're free to do as you please while off duty, providing that it doesn't affect your performance. To this day, your drinking has had no bearing on your work. But take it from a man who's been there—you can't go on like this for much longer."

"I know that. I keep telling myself that. And I keep discovering that nothing's real anymore."

"The Navy's real. And she'll rarely let you down."

"Why don't I believe that?"

"Because you're still in the throes of your pity party. Forget your personal tragedy. We're all bitched from the start. So said Hemingway. I'd add that we all have our moments, and we all must make our sacrifices. But right now I need your strategist's mind."

"You don't want to talk to me," Bellegarde said, then failed to suppress a belch. "Unless you feel comfortable taking advice from a drunk." He returned to the sofa and sat just a little too hard. The room rose brutally, then settled down.

"We don't have time for you to sober up," Tolwyn explained. "I trust that you're in control enough to be useful."

Bellegarde shrugged. "Very well."

"We just received word that the *Tiger Claw* and the two

destroyers I assigned to her engaged the *Olympus* at McDaniel's World four standard days ago. We're en route there now. Aristee got out pretty quickly while still inflicting significant losses on the *Claw*'s bombers and fighters. She's obviously assembled an outstanding fighter wing."

Tolwyn's admiration sounded a bit too healthy for Bellegarde's liking. "Where's she headed now?" he asked.

"The *Claw* analyzed the hopper drive's gravitic residuum. Best estimates put her somewhere between Enyo and Vega."

"Jesus, she crossed half the sector in a single jump?"

"That hasn't been confirmed, but yes, I think she did. That hopper drive is a remarkable innovation."

"Yeah, a little too remarkable." Bellegarde rubbed his eyes, imagining the carnage Aristee had already wreaked. Then he thought about ways to capture a ship with such capability when a puzzling fact hit him. "How the hell did the *Claw* catch up with her in the first place?"

"I suspect that was Paladin's doing. He somehow guessed or knew she would go to McDaniel."

"Well, can he guess her next destination?"

Tolwyn cocked a brow. "Maybe. He's aboard the *Olympus* right now."

"He's where?" Bellegarde sat up and shifted to the edge of the sofa.

"According to Gerald, Commodore Taggart headed down to McDaniel to find Aristee. While en route, he communicated with some Pilgrims on planet, maybe even Aristee herself, and was instructed to return to the *Olympus* and given clearance to land. The cruiser jumped with him and Lieutenant Blair on board."

"Blair? If Paladin went there to negotiate, why'd he take the kid?"

"I'm not sure. I assume there's another reason besides Mr. Blair being half Pilgrim." Tolwyn stared into a thought, then abruptly said, "I have a feeling that something's gone terribly wrong."

"Well, then, it's all about our swift reaction."

"Which is why I'm here, seeking the advice of a drunk." Tolwyn's grin defused the blow to Bellegarde's ego.

"Sir, given Aristee's jump capability, pursuing her now without Paladin's help is a waste of time and resources. We have to do something to bring her to us."

Tolwyn's eyes lit, the glimmer lasting but a second. "I just spoke with the space marshal this morning. She said the press is having its proverbial field day with this, and that senators from nearly all Confed worlds are advising their constituents of Pilgrim ancestry to seek shelter at designated sites. This, I'm told, is being done for their safety."

"Those reporters and politicians are adding kindling to a fire that doesn't need it. And I'd like to see one of those 'designated sites.' Why don't they call them what they are—interment camps?"

"They don't have to. Anyway, it's clear that the situation back home is becoming more tenuous. We have to put down Aristee *now*. If she causes any more deaths, this witch hunt will reach a fever pitch. We can't afford that. And we can't afford to tarnish our image any further. Our budget requests are already in jeopardy."

"It all comes down to policy and perception," Bellegarde said acidly. "I shouldn't be surprised. I should be happy. I joined the Confederation with my fancy Ivy League degrees, but I just missed the first Pilgrim war. Now I'm getting my shot. But this . . . I have a feeling Aristee knows something about the Confederation, about all of this, that we don't. What she's doing . . . it might be bigger than all of us."

"Don't get paranoid and melodramatic on me, Richard. What she's doing is remaining true to herself and her cause. Few of us are so lucky." He sighed deeply. "I've had doubts about military service all of my life. My family thought I was a fool for not pursuing a career in business. I've often thought about that life, but more lives seem to be ruined rather than saved by money. Then again, war has a similar effect." Tolwyn thought a moment more, then straightened. "So how do you propose we bring Captain Aristee to us?"

"That, sir, will involve risking both of our careers."

Tolwyn beamed at the challenge.

Angel exited the lift and moved onto the *Tiger Claw*'s bridge. She fought to secure her gloomy expression, but judging from the worried looks of the command and control staff, she was failing miserably. Lieutenant Commander Obutu wore the deepest look of concern. The sturdy black man rose from his station to greet her at the railing along the bridge's aft section. "Commander, we don't know each other well, but—"

"Call me Angel," she muttered quickly.

"Yes, ma'am. I was just wondering if you'd like to join a few of us tonight. We've got a mean card game going on. Mostly command staff. You'd fit right in. We meet in the wardroom at twenty-one-hundred."

She returned a weak grin. "I'll think about it. Thanks for the invite."

As Obutu stepped back to his station, Angel lowered her gaze and crossed to Captain Gerald, who sat in his command chair, absently stroking his chin in thought. "Captain, I received your request, but at this time I cannot recommend anyone in my squadron for a promotion."

"You don't have much of a squadron left," Gerald said soberly. "Lieutenant Blair is now aboard the *Olympus*. And Lieutenant Marshall, well, I've added his name to those we will honor at the memorial service. Despite his frequent and often blatant insubordination, he was one hell of a pilot. I'll miss that much about him."

"Sir, may we speak in private?"

His brows rose, then he pushed himself out of the chair. She followed him through a hatch and into the shadowy confines of the map room, a rectangular cabin dimly illumined by holo projectors and data screens on standby.

Gerald found a control console on which to lean and regarded her with piercing eyes. "Commander?"

"Sir, I was just curious if you knew why the commodore requested Lieutenant Blair's company."

"Interesting question, considering the scuttlebutt regarding you and Mr. Blair. He was twice seen slipping into your quarters."

She whirled toward the hatch. "Sorry to have bothered you."

"Right there, Commander. We need to have this conversation."

Slowly, she turned back, faced him, but remained rigid, part of her still traveling toward the hatch.

"I've never enforced the standing reg against fraternization. It goes on. It's a necessary evil. I'm okay with it. But if it compromises my ship or her crew, then I will brig the participants. Now then, Admiral Tolwyn has ordered us to break off from our pursuit of the *Olympus*, which, I might add, works in your favor. I wouldn't feel comfortable sending you out against her with Blair and Paladin still aboard."

The news came as a cold wind that chilled Angel to the marrow. "Sir, has Paladin already convinced Aristee to stand down?"

"I don't think so."

"Then why are we breaking off?"

"The admiral has given us new orders. We're going to Hell's Kitchen. We're to assume a high orbit of the third planet, Netheranya, and await instructions."

"There's a Pilgrim enclave there. I think it's called Triune."

Gerald nodded. "I'm sure the admiral is positioning the rest of the fleet near the other Pilgrim enclaves. He's taking the *Concordia* battle group to McDaniel, and sending two others to Faith and Promise."

"Why would Aristee go back to McDaniel or the other systems?"

"I'm no mind reader, and even if I were, I doubt that I could make sense of a mind as complex as the admiral's," Gerald confessed. "I wish we were better informed, but that's the admiral's style. When we need to know, we'll know."

"Is that also the commodore's style?"

"He never told me why he took Lieutenant Blair along. And to be frank, I never questioned him. He said you had already approved, and it seemed like an excellent idea to me."

"Sir?"

"Let's just say that Lieutenant Blair will provide a counter-weight to the commodore's mission."

"Which is . . ."

"I'm not sure if even the admiral knows."

"Well, I owe that man my life," Angel said, remembering how Paladin had saved her when she had ejected in her life pod. "Still, I understand your feelings, and I did find it rather odd that Aristee gave him clearance to land so quickly."

"It didn't surprise me at all." He read the question on her face, but instead of answering, he pushed himself off the console and checked his watchphone. "We'll be jumping in about five hours. I've scheduled another briefing for the department heads at sixteen-thirty. Is there anything else I can do for you, Commander?"

"No, sir."

Fifteen minutes later, Angel sat at her desk and rested her head on an arm. She couldn't believe that Christopher Blair had so quickly vanished from her life. She could easily cling to the pathetic hope that he would return, keep those candles lit for him, but she knew better. Those candles would do no more than burn.

Over the years, she had grown accustomed to being abandoned by those she loved. Her parents had been killed in the Pilgrim War, and the sisters who had raised her were little more than disciplinarians employed at an orphanage. Then, at sixteen, Mikhail had kissed her good-bye and had joined the Confederation Marines. Six months later she had learned of his death. The Kilrathi had torn him apart so thoroughly that only through dental work and dog tags could he be identified. Angel had fallen to her knees and had vowed never to love again.

But that vow had been too difficult to keep. True, she had successfully avoided romantic relationships until Christopher Blair had come along, but the love she harbored for friends had already taken its toll: Zigmaster, Throne, Rosie, and Bossman had all left behind their indelible marks. The shrinks had recently told her that her inability to become intimate was a natural defense mechanism against all of the loss she had suffered. She had become a textbook study in denial and insecurity, a psychiatrist's cliché, a self-destructive fighter pilot who allowed herself to experience only the most basic and necessary emotions, knowing too well that an entire universe of sensations continually passed her by.

"You don't know what I'm risking here."

"I think I do."

Maybe Blair *did* understand her. She had never met a young man more sensitive and as attuned to his surroundings.

But like the others, he had left.

Seething over the fact, she bolted from the desk, ripped the pillows off her rack, yanked the mattress from its frame, and threw it across the room. Panting through gritted teeth, she grabbed the small statue of the Brussels griffon sitting atop her desk and smashed it against her hatch. The little porcelain dog fell in a score of pieces that clattered across the deck. She lowered her head, eyes stinging with tears, then, on her periphery, she noticed her small computer terminal. Its thin screen showed the words ONE UNREAD TEXT MESSAGE in a beckoning flash. She went to the terminal, and with trembling fingers pulled up the mail:

IP PORT STATUS: UN**DOCKED**
OP PORT STATUS: UN**DOCKED**
CLEARANCE KEY STATUS: insertcard_verifying_denied_**accepted**
DATA SECURITY LEVEL: unclassified_**confidential**_secret_topsecret
ORIGINATION: Confederation Merchantman *Diligent*
RECEIVED: 2654.088 0448 Hours CST

Dear Angel,
Paladin and I are on our way to the planet.

He thinks Aristee's down there. I smooth-
talked him into letting me send you this. We
didn't get a chance to say good-bye, and I
don't know how long this is going to take.
To be honest with you, I don't even know
why I'm here except maybe as a witness for
him. He knows that most people don't trust
him now. I do. But I'm worried. Anyway,
take care, and if Maniac gives you any trouble while I'm gone, tell him he'll pay hell to
me with interest.

I want to sign off with love because that's
how I feel, but I won't. I'll wait for you,
Angel. I'll wait for as long as it takes . . .

Christopher

END TEXT TRANSMISSION
#89274UH9Y299
DUPLICATE COPY ROUTED OFFLINE MAIL-
BOX <<9802>>

She ran a finger over his name on the screen and whispered,
"Don't wait. I'm not worth it."

VEGA SECTOR,
DAY-DOUGLAS BORDER

CS OLYMPUS

EN ROUTE TO ALOY-
SIUS SYSTEM,
ROBERT'S QUADRANT

2654.088

2200 HOURS
CONFEDERATION
STANDARD TIME

After they had set down on the *Olympus*'s flight deck, Blair and Paladin had remained in their seats while the supercruiser made another jump. During that moment, Blair had once more experienced the indistinct figure that rose from the darkness, calling his name in a feminine voice, stroking his cheek, and reaching for him. However, the image had seemed brighter, the voice clearer—as though with each contact he drew closer to the person.

With the jump completed, Deck Boss Towers had given them permission to egress. When they had popped the hatch, they had been met by a pair of heavily-armed Pilgrim Marines. The Marines' dress had immediately struck Blair as odd: long, white robes tied at the waist by olive drab sashes and covered by breastplates of armor and conventional ammo belts. Combat boots had been replaced by loose-fitting sandals. Confederation Marines typically wore standard issue C–524 space armor, single piece units donned via an opening on the left side. Equipped with C–532 life support systems, the suits afforded them the ability to operate in a multitude of environments and struck a familiar image with all military personnel. These Pilgrim Marines looked like a pair of monks wielding C–47 ballistic assault rifles instead

of the holy books of Ivar Chu. Despite their dress, they did bran-
dish the same badass attitudes as non-Pilgrim Marines, and that
characteristic even Ivar Chu McDaniel could not educate or
"enlighten" away.

Hands raised, he and Paladin had shifted down the loading
ramp and into supercruiser's aft flight deck, once a meager hous-
ing for twenty or thirty fighters and bombers, now a spectacle of
recently added runways, aprons, and berths that extended nearly
two hundred meters longer than the *Tiger Claw*'s. Rapiers and
Broadswords stood in rows that stretched so far into the distance
that Blair had blinked to make sure he had not witnessed an illusion. Still, the rows were spread wide apart, and there probably
weren't more than sixty or seventy fighters. Even as Paladin continued to scrutinize their enemy's strike potential, Blair had taken
note of the dozens of techs who also wore robes and sandals similar to the Marines, though their jobs were identified by different
colored sashes rather than by the color-specific coveralls worn by
Confed personnel.

"What's with the costumes?" Blair had asked Paladin. "Looks
like a martial arts academy in here."

"Pilgrims are all about tradition, and this one was obviously
adopted from other cultures and religions. The robes are ceremonial reminders of oneness, of purity, of simplicity, and they're
made of *ko'a'ka*. Produces a calming effect similar to tobacco."

"They don't look calm. Just ridiculous."

That remark had caused one of the Marines to jam his muzzle between Blair's shoulders. Wincing from the pain, Blair had
wisely decided to remain silent for the rest of the trip to the brig.
Along the way, they had been met by the scowls and cutting
remarks of dozens of robed crew members, and though Blair
shared their ancestry, he felt alienated by these people; however,
they couldn't know his mother had been a Pilgrim.

The group had finally reached the brig, a narrow, utilitarian
chamber with six cells on each side of the passage. There, Blair
and Paladin had sat for hours, highly entertained by the durasteel walls and the buzz of sparse lighting. Blair's only visit to a

cap ship brig had been during the standard walking tour. Naval brigs hadn't changed much over the centuries. You had your walls, your bars, your sweet-smelling sink and toilet. You wouldn't find sophisticated energy barriers or hyperlined plumbing in Confederation brigs, just the cheap, effective, old-fashioned discomforts of imprisonment.

Surprisingly enough, Blair had discovered that the mattress on the cot was actually thicker and more comfortable than the one in his quarters back on the *Claw*—an illustration of military prioritizing at its finest, with thugs sleeping more comfortably than officers.

Paladin hadn't paid much attention to Blair's comments regarding the bunk. In fact, he had grown more restless, and the color had all but faded from his cheeks.

Noting that, Blair now mustered the courage to confront his mentor. "Are you all right, sir?"

"What?"

"Are you all right?"

Paladin blinked off the cobwebs of his introspection and faced Blair. "Yeah. It's just this wait."

"How long has it been since you've seen her?"

"I'm not sure. We bumped into each other a few times since she left. It's probably been five years. I guess I can wait another hour."

"With all due respect, sir, you look pretty nervous."

The commodore chuckled under his breath. "It shows that much?"

A sudden commotion at the far end of the brig drew Blair's attention.

"Watch it!" came a familiar voice. "You do that again, you'll be deep-throating that muzzle. Do we understand each other?"

"Shut up!" another man cried.

"Maniac?" Blair called, rushing to the bars. He glimpsed down the corridor and spotted his bunkmate being ushered toward them by their friendly neighborhood Pilgrim Marines.

"Hey, that you, Blair?" Maniac squinted to spot him.

"Yeah. I'm with the commodore. What are you doing here?"

"I'm on the free tour."

The Marines keyed open the cell beside Blair's and thrust Maniac inside. A solid wall stood between their cells, so Blair could only hear his wingman. "Thanks, guys," he told his escorts. "I'm looking at your hairy legs, and I gotta tell you, I'm feeling somewhat aroused."

"Close that hole, *human*," one of the guards retorted before he and his comrade beat a quick exit.

"You say it like a curse," Maniac cried after them. "At least I ain't a fanatic and a freak!" Suddenly aware of his company, he added, "No offense, guys."

Paladin arrived beside Blair, his once sallow face now aglow. "Lieutenant?" he called out to Maniac. "Explain your presence."

"You know it's actually good to see you two locked up. At least I know what side you're on."

"Lieutenant, answer my—"

"Sir, I took a hit, lost control, and came in close to the carrier as she was about to jump," Maniac began, sounding bored with having to relate the tale. "I drifted into some kind of neutral field that surrounded the ship. I fired a tow beam, just hung on, and figured I'd be wasted by the jump. On the other side, they sent out a couple Rapiers and tractored me back to the flight deck. Got interrogated by a few people. Don't know if they were officers, they wore those nutty robes with the symbols along the cuffs. One of them gave the order to have me executed."

Paladin snorted. "So why am I still talking to you?"

"Well, sir, I kind of dropped your name." Maniac's voice grew more tentative. "Told 'em I was a friend and that they should check with you first before they did anything. And son of a bitch, it worked. At least for now."

"That's pretty clever, Lieutenant."

"Why, thank you, sir."

"You idiot!" Paladin suddenly roared. "Aristee will bait me with your life."

"What was I supposed to do? Let 'em kill me? I don't think

so. And why can't she do the same thing with Blair?"

"She won't kill him—he's half Pilgrim. Your presence may have already compromised this mission."

"And what mission is that, *sir*?"

Paladin sighed disgustedly and shambled back toward the cot. He flipped back a stray lock of hair and sat, his expression returning to a tight mask of thought.

"Hey, I didn't ask to be here," Maniac added. "You guys did. Mind telling me why?"

Blair looked to Paladin, who shook his head.

"Hey, you guys eat yet?" Maniac continued. "The food any good? Or do these Pilgrims eat only holy rice or some other bull-shit?"

"Think you'd better sit down and find your own religion," Blair retorted. "You'll need it now."

Voices echoed faintly in the distance, then wore off into the sound of approaching footsteps.

"What now?" Paladin muttered.

Captain Amity Aristee emerged from the shadows like a dark-skinned archangel, cast out from the Confederation and ruling now in her own private hell. She did, indeed, possess that tor-turous beauty of which Paladin had so often spoke, and Blair found himself drawn to the forest in her eyes and the mysteries coiled through her black, shoulder-length hair. Aristee carried herself with a rhythm that seemed at once primordial and musi-cal, though in no way did it appear forced. Full, round breasts tented up her robe, with more than a hint of cleavage forming a warm home at her V-neck. She stood tall on firm legs, the calves smooth and well-defined, and her small feet with toenails painted white fit perfectly in her leather sandals. Blair amused himself by speculating on her undergarments—or lack thereof—before he noticed another man coming forward, a man he immediately rec-ognized, though he had first seen as part of the continuum, part of something universal, elemental, and baffling.

Frotur Johan McDaniel regarded Blair with warm recogni-tion. "Brotur Christopher." Then he eyed Paladin with a slight though detectable sneer. "And Brotur James. I never thought we'd meet again."

"For a Pilgrim with a perfect sense of direction, you seem to keep crossing my path," the commodore said coldly.

"Oh, but that's not my will. It's destiny tugging on your elbow. You've lived in denial long enough, haven't you?"

"All right, gentlemen," Aristee interjected. "We'll finish the debate later." With several rapid keystrokes on the cell's control panel, she opened the door. "Let's go."

Blair noticed how Aristee and Paladin would not look at each other. He had expected an awkward moment between them, a moment in which they painfully uttered each other's names followed by mawkish clichés like "It's been a long time."

"Whoa. Where are you going?" Maniac asked as they stepped into the corridor. "Hey, you leave me here, you're gonna have a major problem on your hands."

"Lieutenant," Paladin snapped, then added a glare to silence Maniac. The reprimand worked.

"I understand he's a friend," Aristee said, though she barely met Paladin's gaze.

"No, he's not."

"Sir?" Maniac cried.

"He's a good friend and one of most aggressive junior pilots in the fleet," the commodore added. "But he's still a human. I suggest you jettison him ASAP."

Blair turned to Paladin, mouth agape and eyes bulging.

"James, you know why I let him live," Aristee began. "Don't insult my intelligence again. You're not here to defect, and you don't want me to kill him. You're here to talk me into surrendering, but Ivar Chu himself couldn't do that now."

"At least hear me out," Paladin said.

"Oh, I will. We'll have plenty of time to talk. But first I want to show you something." She suddenly turned to Blair, scrutinized him for a second, then blurted out, "You look like your mother."

"Did you know her, ma'am?"

"I knew of her. I was pretty young back then and was only visiting Peron. I remember everyone being jealous of her good looks. Then when she married your father, that jealousy turned to hate." She moved away. "So it goes."

They followed her toward the hatch at the far end of the corridor, with Johan McDaniel bringing up the rear. "Broturs James and Christopher, many people scarified their lives for what you're about to witness. We shall honor them by remaining silent until we arrive," the frotur instructed.

Paladin looked askance at Blair and made a face. Blair nodded as the two Marines joined them at the hatch.

"Bring back some food," Maniac shouted.

Amity led them down several decks, toward the supercruiser's stern. They passed several torpedo launch bays, pilots' quarters, environmental controls, and a long storage area fenced off by polymeric bars. Crew members snapped to as they neared them, bowing instead of saluting.

It took all of fifteen minutes for them to reach the engineering deck. Two more Pilgrim Marines stood guard outside the oval-shaped hatch. As they drew near, one of the guards briskly keyed open the door. The drone of cooling units and air recyclers grew louder as they stepped onto a catwalk that encompassed a circular room. The catwalk permitted full view of the ship's drive system, a great metallic organ centered below. From a distance, the place resembled an amphitheater, with the drive at center stage and emitting a solid bass note so deep that Blair felt it pass through him as they crossed toward a staircase that dropped fifteen meters to the drive deck. He gripped the rail and descended, his gaze riveted to the hopper drive itself.

Mounted on a two-meter-high, rectangular durasteel base, the drive extended about fifteen meters, bearing the exotic curves of some black, incandescent melon. It tapered at the tail end to form a curving hose with the girth of two men. The hose arced back to the center of the drive, where it grew wider by a third and attached to a dome on the system's back. A conduit at least

five meters across jutted from the forward end and curved up
ninety degrees to reach the overhead. Blair assumed that the four
robed men who had risen from their control stations along the
perimeter were drive officers; they bowed as Aristee entered the
room.

"As you were," she said.

"Jesus," Paladin mumbled, gaping at the drive. "Must've
taken months to install this system."

"Nine-point-three," Aristee qualified. "The Confederation
could never maintain security as tight as mine or create a better
campaign of misinformation. Your friends at Intell thought they
had us figured out. I wonder what they think now. Even my own
command staff didn't know what was going on down here. Some
said it would be impossible." She sniggered. "Gentlemen, I present to you the impossible."

Paladin pointed at the tube extending to the ceiling. "Well
field integrator?"

"Very good. The matter-antimatter reactor is housed in the
dome. The reaction containment field is located below. Problems
with the old hopper drive occurred there. We used a Kilrathi
alloy inside the drive to foster containment, control the reaction,
and account for gravitic distortions from nearby objects. At least
the cats are good for something else besides killing."

"What's the range? If I recall, the old sloships were limited to
twenty or thirty percent of a light year."

"We're still experimenting with that, but our last jump took
us nearly halfway across Vega sector. You do the math."

"But isn't the field localized?"

"There's a relationship between the number of anti-gravitons
created by the field and the range. I don't pretend to understand
it, but the more we generate, the farther we go."

"Yeah, but as you generate more anti-gravitons, the well
becomes more unstable."

The commodore's fact left Aristee unmoved. "We're working
on that, too. But no matter how unstable the well becomes, we
can still navigate it, either through conventional NAVCOM AI or

a Pilgrim navigator. Frotur McDaniel is responsible for our success in that area."

"I'm just an old man," McDaniel said with a smile.

Paladin shook his head. "I wish you were."

"Ma'am, what you've done here is nothing short of remarkable," Blair said. "But for what? Why show us this? And how do you justify killing millions on Mylon? What do you want? Most terrorists have some sort of demands."

She stepped toward him, her fruity perfume beginning to sap away his anger. "I'm not a terrorist, Brotur Christopher. I'm a victim, same as you. We were chosen for the stars. The Confederation took them from us." She grinned wistfully. "I don't expect to get them back. But I will start a revolution the likes of which the Confederation has never seen. Even the Kilrathi will cower in our presence. I'm not some insane fanatic who's hijacked her own ship with the intention to kill as many humans as I can before I die a fiery death. You think I'm that reckless? I know what's right for my people. And I'm going to give it to them with the help of this drive. I show it to you because it's *yours*."

"No." Paladin's eyes narrowed in disgust.

"You can't strike and run forever," Blair said, his tone complementing the commodore's expression. "This is just one ship, and the fleet will eventually catch up with you."

"Of course it will, but not before I create a symbol of our renewed strength. Gentlemen, in approximately sixty days further modifications to this drive will be completed. They will allow us to generate a space-time well large enough to be placed near planetary bodies. At such time we will proceed to Earth and complete Brotur Wilson's mission. If we're not destroyed there, our next targets will include Sol system military installations." She focused her attention on Paladin. "You'll be supplying us with more specific data on bringing down their defense nets."

"Interesting the way you stand there and tell us you're not insane," Blair began. "Then you tell us your plans to take out Earth and the Confederation. Am I the only one who recognizes the irony? And if this is what being a Pilgrim is all about, then—"

"You're still naïve, Brotur. You'll come to understand," she assured him with a nod. "I don't like killing, but I will no longer tolerate the persecution of my people."

"I suppose you went to McDaniel for the protur's blessing," Paladin interjected. "You don't have it, and without it you can't succeed."

"On the contrary, James, I not only have the protur's blessing, but he's aboard this ship."

Paladin shifted his gaze to Johan McDaniel. "So you figured out where his retreat is. Did he come willingly?"

"Later on, I'll take you to see him," Aristee offered. "You can ask him yourself."

"I don't believe you've met the protur," McDaniel said, gripping Paladin's shoulder. "You must talk to him."

The commodore twisted out of McDaniel's hold, then scanned the drive room for effect. "All of this . . . what a waste."

"Oh, come down off your pulpit," Aristee shot back. "You wouldn't have said that ten years ago. We joined the Navy for the same reasons. You've just forgotten them."

As the commodore stood in silent consideration, McDaniel slid up behind Blair and whispered, "Haven't seen her yet, have you? Oh, you've heard her, but you haven't really seen her."

A bolt of chills impaled Blair's spine as he turned back to the old man. "No, I haven't. She knows my name."

"She knows more than that."

"Who is she?"

"It's not who but what she is," he said with a wink. "And that's not for me to answer, but for you to discover."

"Relayed drone message from the *Concordia* coming through now, sir," Comm Officer Zabrowsky reported.

Gerald nodded sharply. "Decrypt and route to OS station two."

"Aye, sir. Decryption in progress." The freckle-faced boy swiveled back to his instruments. "Routing to OS two."

As Gerald pulled his tired frame to the port-side observation station, he muttered, "It's about time."

The *Tiger Claw* had reached Netheranya three standard days ago and had assumed a high orbit of the mottled brown world whose oceans comprised only ten percent of her total area. Gerald had sent off a drone to Naval Station Gemini near the Enyo system to inform the admiral that they were at station. Gemini would in turn send off a jump-capable drone to the *Concordia*, now orbiting McDaniel's World.

Inter-ship, long-distance drone communications did little more than snail along, but the Hell's Kitchen system stood in an area of space known as the Vega cluster, with Enyo, McAuliffe, Dieno, Pephedro, Blackmane, and Cambria all within the grid and just a single jump away. With so many systems in the area,

Gerald had assumed there would be other fleet operations within direct communications range. They had detected and contacted
several Confed merchant and cargo vessels as well as several
civilian and commercial transports, but they had failed to find
any capital ships from the 14th Fleet. Gerald had grown a bit
unnerved by the prospect of the *Claw*, the *Mitchell Hammock*,
and the *Oregon* being the only capital ships within half of Day
Quadrant. He wondered why the admiral had spread the fleet so
thinly, and he hoped the communiqué would explain that.

Appearing to be his usual impeccable self, Tolwyn gave his
customary nod of acknowledgment and said, "Sorry for the
delay, Mr. Gerald. We'll get right to it. Interstellar probes detected
a Kilrathi battle group between Lafayette and Tamayo systems.
The cats are obviously after the *Olympus*. I've dispatched six
strike carriers with orders to find and destroy that battle group.
In the meantime, we're going to call Captain Aristee's bluff. At
this moment, nearly one hundred CF–20 ConCom ships are
deploying drones throughout Vega sector. Each drone will broadcast a long-range transmission for Captain Aristee. I've attached
a copy of the transmission for your review. In sum, she is ordered
to surrender her vessel—otherwise every Pilgrim system and
enclave within Confederation territory will be destroyed and all
surviving Pilgrims within our borders will be arrested and
imprisoned until she stands down. That last part won't be too
difficult since many of those Pilgrims have already sought shelter
in designated camps."

Gerald paused the message. Had the admiral lost his mind?
Yes, he might be calling Aristee's bluff, but if he actually ordered
the destruction, he would be personally responsible for the
deaths of billions. The senate would hang him. It took a moment
more for Gerald to realize what Tolwyn had done, and he smiled
inwardly. The senate probably had no idea of the admiral's plan.
However, if one of the drones were intercepted by the wrong
ship, and word leaked back to the senate—but by then it would
be too late to stop Tolwyn. On the other hand, the plan might
work. How could Aristee ever hope to build a force if the

Confederation wiped out the systems and enclaves? She might finally recognize the foolishness of her pursuits.

"Mr. Gerald, I want you to establish a no-fly zone around the Pilgrim enclave Triune on Netheranya. The strike bases at Tung and Sylee will provide atmospheric air support while your fighter wing will interdict all ships attempting to make orbit or planet-fall. I've already contacted the Pilgrim ambassador of Triune and declared a state of martial law. Now, Mr. Gerald, if we receive a refusal from Captain Aristee, know that I *will* give the order to destroy Triune and its four million inhabitants. In all, over two billion Pilgrims across three systems and five colonial enclaves will die. That's our worst case scenario, and I'm praying it doesn't come to that. But Aristee has been sending messages long enough. It's high time we replied. I'll keep you informed. Tolwyn out."

"You're really going to do it, old man," Gerald whispered to the blank screen. He glanced up at Netheryana, looming in the viewport. His mind traveled to the cities, the suburbs, the little farms, the wine fields, the hills that rolled on to the horizon. He thought of the children lining up behind their teachers, the old men and women gaming in the parks, the cool, dark waters of the many streams that ran through the simple land. He had had too much time to study the enclave, to drift through the holos that showed images as strikingly beautiful as they now were painful. He should feel glad that Tolwyn was taking extreme measures to bring in Aristee, but killing civilians just to make a point smacked of terrorism. *They're not civilians—they're Pilgrims. Hell, they don't even think of themselves as human.* The reminder hardly made him feel better. He craned his head to the comm station. "Mr. Z? Get me the COs at Tung and Sylee."

"Aye, sir. Establishing communications."

"Mr. Obutu? Recall security patrol and scramble First and Third squadrons."

Obutu repeated the command, then contacted the Rapier pilots presently flying patrol.

Gerald switched on the ship-wide intercom and hemmed. "All personnel, this is the captain. We have just received orders to establish a no-fly zone over Triune. I suspect we'll encounter a lot of resistance from commercial and civilian vessels. We'll remain secured from general quarters, but I'd like to maintain a heightened sense of readiness. Any one of those ships could take a potshot at us, and those skippers know we won't return fire and create an incident. I'd like to avoid becoming famous, but we *will* respond appropriately to significant threats. If you have any questions, consult with your department heads. That is all."

"Sir?" Comm Officer Zabrowsky called. "No response from the strike bases yet, but I have Lieutenant Commander Deveraux on a secure channel."

"I'll take it here."

Angel's bewildered expression lit the screen, with officers scrambling from the flight control room behind her. "Sir. We expecting Aristee?"

"I doubt it. The admiral's calling her bluff with this blockade, but my gut's telling me this isn't right. Exercise extreme caution out there. Divert civilian and commercial pilots to Enyo where possible. Notify any ships in need of refueling that we will accommodate that need as necessary."

"How long will this last?"

"Vega's a big place. And Aristee is a stubborn woman. I think we'll be anchoring here for a very long time."

"Have you received any word from Commodore Taggart?"

"I'm betting that when we hear from Aristee, we'll hear from him. Probably not before."

"Yes, sir." She ended the transmission.

"Sir? Contact bearing three-two-four by five-one-nine," Radar Officer Falk said. "Designate Bravo two-five, Wren-class commercial transport. Range: two-one-five Ks. Velocity: one-two-five KPS and slowing."

"And the party begins," Gerald said, then rose and skirted his way back to his command chair. "Hail them, Mr. Falk. Report perimeter violation of standard no-fly zone. If that captain gives you an argument, patch him through to me."

Blair shook his head as Maniac released an especially loud yawn. "I ever tell you about the time I took Casey up in my Rapier trainer? That was a date that blondie will never forget. Shit, even I remember it."

Maniac's words echoed hollowly through the brig, and for once in his life Blair truly wished he were alone. He had been sitting in his cell for seven days since first coming aboard. Paladin had been in his company for the first two days, then the Marine guards had fetched him, and Blair had not seen or heard from the commodore since.

He and Maniac spent most of their time talking. Blair told Maniac stories about his boyhood, stories of farming, of his first experience with his holographic assistant, Merlin, and of his first kiss in preschool. But this heart-warming, general audience stuff only inspired fits of yawning from his wingman. Living up to his reputation, Maniac related tales of his numerous and varied sexual encounters, he the virile hero whose presence struck down women with an overpowering desire to tear the clothes from their bodies and throw themselves at him. The stories grew more graphic, the women more beautiful, the truth lost in all of that heavy breathing. Marshall's call sign should have been *Nympho*Maniac.

By the third day, Blair's request for a shower and clean clothes had finally been honored. The guards had kept their weapons trained on them even while in the latrine and afterward had forced them to wear Pilgrim robes. Maniac had swapped a few insults with the guards, but for the most part they ignored his crude comments.

With the passage of each day, marked by a report from Merlin and the switching on or off of the lights, Blair grew more anxious and began to doubt that they would ever be released. Surely he had better things to do with his time than die in a miserable cell in the company of Todd Marshall. Even now, as Maniac launched into another of his tales, which somehow involved two people in the cramped confines of a Rapier cockpit, Blair rocked slowly on his cot and thought of his youth, of how much he had not seen, and of how his last image might be a sheet of scored gray steel.

And the questions, so many questions, continued to elude him. Where was Paladin? Why hadn't he come to visit? Why hadn't anyone come to see them? Why did Paladin bring him here in the first place? Where was the ship now? What was happening back on the *Claw*? What about Angel?

And the note. Had she received the note? The *Diligent*'s comm computer had reported a successful transmission. He wondered what she thought of it. He shouldn't have written the "L" word. He had probably frightened her. What a spectacularly foolish thing he had done. Well, it could have been worse. He could have listened to Merlin; then again, he would have someone else to blame if he lost her.

Why was he so afraid of losing her? What about her intrigued him so much? Her raw beauty and strong will had initially attracted him, but what now kept him rapt? Was it her pain? The emptiness he had already tried to fill? Did he want to save her from self-destruction? Or did he want to show her that chivalry still existed despite the years and distances? He should be with her for the right reasons, but what were they? He couldn't just be her savior. She would close up, resent him, because needing him would make her confront her own weaknesses, and while she could do that, the reminder would only bring her more pain.

". . . and you should have seen the look on my crew chief's face when the canopy opens and up pops Casey's head. I tell him that I caught her trespassing in my cockpit and that I'm turning her over to security immediately." Maniac chuckled over the memory, then his voice died off into the silence. "C'mon, Blair. You gotta admit that's funny."

"Uh-huh."

"What's the matter? Ain't you ever been locked up for a week aboard a supercruiser taken over by Pilgrims?" He snorted. "I know this sucks. It really sucks. I bet Taggart's up in the ward-room right now, eating like a king. Aristee's probably won him over already."

"No way. He's up there convincing her to stand down," Blair countered, wishing his words were fact.

"I ain't saying he's a traitor. She could've easily drugged him. He's Intell and privy to a lot of data that she'd love to have. Know what? I'm convinced she's done that. Otherwise, he would have already come down to see us. He's either drugged or sud-denly doesn't care. Or maybe *I am* saying he's a traitor."

"Paladin's no turncoat. He's more loyal to the Confederation than you."

"Then I hope his loyalty buys us a ticket out of this hole." A solid and familiar thump sounded from the wall that adjoined their cells. As he did at least once every day, Maniac had beat his fist on the steel. "Hey, guards?"

Someone approached, but the footsteps sounded a bit lighter than those of the guards, whose passage Blair had come to know well. He sprang from the bunk and gripped the bars of his cell, imagining for the nth time that he had the strength to bend durasteel. He jammed his head against the bars and squinted through the shadows vesturing the passage.

A figure came forward, his white robe extending to his shins and fluttering behind him with an almost underwater slowness. His face grew distinct, and Blair gasped. "Sir."

"Your ears must've been ringing," Maniac said.

Paladin arrived before Blair and gave a curt nod. "Lieutenant. How are you two doing?"

"We're all right," Blair answered. "They fed us well."

"If you call leftover rations a meal," Maniac qualified. "Prob-ably scooped them out of waste can. Hey, Commodore? Where you been? And when the hell are we getting out?"

"It's complicated. And I'm not sure if you'll be getting out anytime soon. Aristee doesn't have enough personnel to assign a guard to you. It's easier for her to keep you here."

"While you get to stroll around the ship unguarded?" Maniac quickly followed. "Excuse me, sir, but I have a slight problem with that."

"She's got a guard on me. He's waiting at the hatch."

"You talk to her yet?" Blair asked.

"I've had several opportunities, Mr. Blair. Suffice it to say, I need many more."

"Question is, do we have that time? Where is she headed? And how many more people do you think she'll kill?"

"She's arranged to purchase supplies and take on more personnel at Aloysius Prime. She's having some trouble with the hopper drive, so I expect it'll take us a while before we get there. I'm not happy with that destination. Aloysius is in Robert's Quadrant, right on the Kilrathi border."

"You're not happy with that destination?" Maniac snapped. "Why don't you do something about it? That bitch will never stand down. We need to take this ship by force."

"Excellent idea," Blair said, feigning his enthusiasm. "The three of us will take on the entire crew. Or maybe you'd like to do that single-handedly? At least you'd have something other than sex to talk about."

"I'm flipping you the bird right now."

Paladin shifted to Maniac's cell. "Mr. Marshall, we may very well have to take this ship by force. And if we do, I expect that you will follow my orders without question—no matter what I tell you to do."

"At this point, sir, I'm most concerned with getting my particular ass off this particular ship. If we can save the Confederation in the interim, more power to us."

"Sir?" Blair interrupted. "Why didn't you come to see us sooner?"

"She's been forcing me to attend her con-crit sessions and suffer through a series of songs and conversations, a kind of exorcism of old ideas through music and speech. Your basic brainwashing in the guise of spiritual pursuit. It takes nearly five days to go through the first sequence."

"Maybe they drugged you," Maniac said. "Maybe you're just feeding us bullshit."

"I haven't been drugged. Tampering with the body in that way is strictly forbidden. That's a covenant in our favor. They want to win over only cognizant individuals since cognizance is a prerequisite of ascension."

"These people don't hang out in shuttleports, chanting and handing out flyers, do they?" Maniac gibed.

"Don't underestimate them, Mr. Marshall. If you do, you'll wind up chanting and distributing flyers yourself."

"Sir, I've never been a POW," Blair confessed. "That Kilrathi tattoo on your neck helps you remember that you were. I don't want to pry, but tell me this: How did you get through it? What did you do to keep yourself sane? It's only been a week, but I feel more tortured by the monotony than if they came down here and beat me. I guess I have too much time on my hands. I'm getting wire happy. So's Maniac. Pretty soon we'll do anything to escape, even if it gets us killed."

"I think you get through it by reaching down into yourself and finding a real reason to live. Why are you here, Mr. Blair? What is your purpose in this universe? Big questions. They might even sound ridiculous. But if you can discover the answers, it won't matter what they throw at you. When the Kilrathi took me, it was like having a window to hell. They know exactly what can kill a human. Exactly. That's just what I said in my debriefing. I spent two long years in captivity, but I made it through because I'm here to affect as many lives as I can. My life was never mine. It took me a long time to reconcile with that."

"To be honest, sir, I have no idea why I'm here. But I'll try to figure that out. Thanks."

"Gentlemen, I'll visit again soon. Just hang tight. Do the Confederation proud."

"Oh, we're doing it real proud sittin' here," Maniac muttered.

Ignoring the remark, the commodore drifted off, into the shadows.

Blair remained at the bars for several minutes after Paladin left. He played over the commodore's advice, but his thoughts seemed as imprisoned as his body. *Maybe I'm just here to be a Confederation pilot. Maybe I don't have some higher purpose. Why do I even need one?*

Your purpose is with us.

The voice sent Blair recoiling from the bars to inspect his cell. She had spoken in his head. And it hadn't been during a jump. *Who are you?*

I'm not a ghost. I'm not reading your mind. I'm just letting you read the script of my thoughts. My script is here, in this ship. Would you like to know me?

Yeah, I guess so. What do you want?

I'll come for you when I can.

Who are you?

No response.

"Who are you?"

"What?" Maniac asked.

Blair drew in a long breath, rubbed his eyes, then dropped onto his cot. "Nothing."

"Know what's gonna happen, Ace? The Confed is going to pound this ship out of existence, and we'll be along for the ride. We're on death row."

"Hey, Maniac? What's your purpose in life?"

"Shit, that's easy. I'm here to strap on a starfighter and rack up as many kills as possible. I am a killing machine. I am population control. I am the final glimpse before eternity. Sivar loves me. I send him fresh Kilrathi souls."

"Seriously."

"*Seriously.* I am here to kill, kill, kill. And I'll give back to the universe by a making a few babies. But not any time soon. I need another decade or so of practice, with, of course, as many women as possible. You stand on your marble mountain and tell me I'm shallow. But I got no illusions about this. And if there is a supreme being, then I have to get credit for being exactly who I am. Love me. Hate me. But you have to respect that I know what I'm about. You? You keep turning back to this Pilgrim thing. So your mother was a Pilgrim. So what. Look at these people. Look at what they've done. You want to dial into this?"

Blair jerked himself off the cot and beat a fist into his palm. "Not all Pilgrims are like this. I wish somebody would teach me who they really are. Then maybe I'd know what I'm about. And so would you."

With a laugh, Maniac replied, "You're about fear. You're about confusion. You're about running. And it would make me feel a whole lot better if you were about kicking ass."

"Even if I were, what could we do about it? Try to pull off some pathetic diversion? You complain that you're sick, then the guard opens the door and you pound his ass? Then you open my cell, we take the guards' weapons, hightail it through the ship, and take Aristee at gunpoint? We're living this. It ain't some bad movie."

"We got nothing to lose. I say we try anyway."

Blair threw up his hands. "Go ahead. You can add stupidity to what you're about."

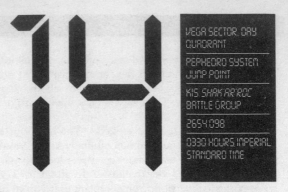

VEGA SECTOR, DAY
QUADRANT

PEPHEDRO SYSTEM
JUMP POINT

KIS SHAK'AR'ROC
BATTLE GROUP

2654.098

0330 HOURS IMPERIAL
STANDARD TIME

Admiral Vukar sat rigid in his command chair, his gaze traveling intently from station to station as the *Shak'Ar'Roc*'s bridge crew prepared to jump. His officers had just come off a five hour respite, and they appeared invigorated by the notion that they would once more pick up their quarry's scent.

Every heart was in the hunt. . . .

Tactical Officer Makorshk had predicted that the supercruiser would go to the Hell's Kitchen system, to a planet called Netheryana, to a Pilgrim enclave called Triune that stood directly in the supercruiser's last known trajectory. At tremendous risk, they had jumped back to Lafayette, moved on to Montrose, then on to Pephedro. Vukar felt certain that they had been spotted by Confederation reconnaissance probes, but he also felt certain that if they kept moving, they would remain relatively safe. He had already driven his battle group to its limit and had lost the Fralthi-class cruiser *Caxkolee* along the way. The ship's drive system had malfunctioned, and those warriors assigned to her had been transferred to the battle group's remaining six cap ships. As usual, they had set the cruiser to self-destruct to avoid its confiscation and study by the apes. Vukar wished they could hide the cruiser's debris from Confederation detection, but he lacked the time and resources for such a massive clean-up operation in enemy territory.

"Distance to jump point?" he asked Makorshk.

"Two-point-nine kilometers. Jump in three-point-zero-one standard minutes. All ships report positive lock on target. Final course corrections have been initiated. Jump commitment will occur in exactly three-point-one-one standard minutes, my Kalralahr."

Vukar flexed his fingers impatiently. He pictured himself seizing the supercruiser's captain by the neck and lifting him into the air. He would strangle the life out of the ape, demonstrating that their species had at least one tenet in common: justice through revenge. He stole another look at his tactical officer and considered the second fang's demise should the calculations prove wrong. For ten long days Vukar had placed his trust in the young warrior. On the other side of the jump point lay Makorshk's fate, and Vukar suspected that his subordinate knew that. Three days ago, the second fang had come to Vukar's ready room to assure him that their course was logical. Vukar had not wanted to hear about logic. He had asked Makorshk what his heart told him.

"My heart tells me nothing," Makorshk had replied.

"Listen more closely."

"As you wish."

"Fail to listen, fail to rely on your instincts, then you fail. This is the way of Sivar."

Since then, Vukar sensed that the second fang had reweighed his primitive beginnings and might draw on them now as a source of power. Makorshk had not come to Vukar with this revelation, but the glimmer in the young warrior's eyes seemed generated by an innate energy and not by thoughts of self-satisfaction. Makorshk had finally committed his heart to the hunt.

"Time?" Vukar asked the second fang.

"Thirty seconds to jump point."

"Mute the alarm before it sounds."

Makorshk threw a switch. "Alarm muted."

"All stations at pre-jump readiness," reported Comm Officer Ta'kar'ki. "Escorts confirm that Point of No Return velocity for Hell's Kitchen jump point has been achieved."

Syl'rkai, the present radar officer, suddenly lifted his voice. "Kalralahr? We have acquired a contact bearing one-one-two by three-three-seven at a range of nine-point-four-one kilometers. Velocity is two one four KPS. It is a Confederation communications drone broadcasting a holographic message on multiple long-range frequencies. Language: Terran standard."

"Helm is locked to autojump system," Second Fang Yil'schk cut in with his necessary report.

Vukar swiveled his chair to face Syl'rkai. "Translate that message and route to bridgecomm."

The communications officer grunted his acknowledgment and beat a near-steady rhythm on his touchpad to initiate the command.

"Twenty seconds to jump point," Makorshk said.

Vukar narrowed his gaze on Syl'rkai. "Do you have the message?"

"Message translated and stored," the officer said. "Routing to bridgecomm."

A meter-wide disk located on the deck in front of Vukar's command chair began to palpitate with light, then a shimmering white column coalesced into a tall, gray-haired ape standing on the bridge of a Confederation supercruiser. The ape folded his arms over his chest and stared angrily at Vukar. His lips moved, and after a nanosecond delay, the translator engaged. "Captain Amity Driftmadien Aristee, Confederation ID number 225X741, you are hereby ordered to surrender your vessel at the nearest Confederation world. Should you fail to comply by calendar date one-five-eight, we will destroy every Pilgrim system and enclave and imprison every known Pilgrim within Confederation territory."

"Ten seconds to jump point," Makorshk shouted over the message.

"By the time you receive this, we will have already established no-fly zones around each of those settlements, which are, as you know, dependent upon imports. Don't force your people into suffering, and don't be the cause of their deaths. You may have little regard for your own life, but think of them. Do what's right for them." The ape took a step forward, his face growing tighter, more intense. "I assure you, we're not bluffing. I invite you to initiate long-range reconnaissance to confirm our presence, and I look forward to your reply. Admiral Geoffrey Tolwyn, Chief of Fleet Operations, out."

"We're at the jump point," Makorshk cried, as the ship began to shudder. "We'll reach the gravity well's PNR in ten, nine, eight, seven, six—"

Vukar shot to his feet. "Abort the jump!"

Makorshk tilted his large head in confusion.

"Aborting jump," said Helmsman Yil'schk.

Comm Officer Ta'kar'ki's voice came in a wheeze. "Relaying abort order to battle group."

"PNR reached!" Makorshk said.

"Jump drive will not shut down," said Yil'schk. "Override clock exceeded. We are committed to the jump."

"Alert all ships to immediately set course for—" Vukar heard himself finish the command, but all activity on the bridge had already ceased. His vision lasted but another second before narrowing into a world of speckled darkness. The weight of his armor lifted from his shoulders, and the bindings on his boots no longer pinched. Even the sweet aroma of nutrient gas had been neutralized into a smell that was no smell. He pricked up his ears, straining to hear something. A distant rumble finally sounded, grew louder, then suddenly roared as he coughed, blinked off flashes of piercing light, then leaned onto his command chair.

"Jump completed," Makorshk said. "Drive systems nominal."

"Escorts report successful jump," added Comm officer Ta'kar'ki.

"Relay order for all ships to stalk. Low emissions. Run ultra quiet," Vukar ordered breathlessly. "Navigation? Helm? Set course for Hell's Kitchen jump point." He strode quickly toward the viewport to examine the shining dots of the system dead ahead. The jump point lay within that system, a gravity well about twenty thousand kilometers from the planet Netheryana.

"Jump point data is already in our system," Makorshk said. "Jump calculations will be available in approximately four minutes. We'll reach jump point in four-point-four minutes. Request permission to scan for ion emissions and gravitic residuum."

"Passive scans only," Vukar snarled. "You heard the ape. They've established no-fly zones around each of the Pilgrim enclaves and systems—including this one. We've just jumped head on into a Confederation battle group."

"No, Kalralahr. Passive imager has already detected three Confederation capital ships—only three," Makorshk said, bearing his fangs. "Largest contact identified as the CS *Tiger Claw*. Other two are Exeter-class destroyers CS *Oregon* and CS *Mitchell Hammock*."

"Navigation? Plot evasion course to jump point."

"We're not going to engage?" Makorshk asked, his tan eyes paling in surprise. "One strike carrier and two destroyers are an easy kill."

Heads turned toward the second fang who dared question his admiral's orders.

Vukar spun to First Fang Jatark. "Remove him."

"No," Makorshk cried. "The apes are there, helpless against us. You deny us the honor, Kalralahr? And you shame me with this order of removal?"

Drawing on his instincts, Jatark lunged over Makorshk's tactical console and collided with the younger warrior. Both Kilrathi roared as they rolled across the deck in a death clutch. Makorshk drew back a paw, serrated claws springing out as he slashed Jatark across the cheek. The parallel wounds spewed blood onto the first fang's skin. As the sting of his lacerations finally set in, Jatark emitted a terrific howl, released his grip, and extended the claws on both of his paws.

But Makorshk exploited that moment to reach into his thigh sheath and withdraw his *vorshaki* dueling blade, a curved knife with a sharp notch representing each of the noble clans of Kilrah. Makorshk's hand shot up with extraordinary speed. He jammed the blade into Jatork's neck, twisted the handle forty-five degrees, then drove the knife up with a horrible crunch.

A proximity alarm chirped from Makorshk's station, and Comm Officer Ta'kar'ki shifted toward it, his gaze never leaving Makorshk as the second fang continued working his *vorshaki* into Jatork's head. Meanwhile, Ta'kar'ki snapped his finger on a small bell, an ancient tocsin used to beckon the entire bridge crew. "Kalralahr! The strike carrier *Tiger Claw* and one of her destroyers have altered course to intercept."

Another alarm blared from Radar Officer Syl'rkai's station. "Six inbound contacts. Identifying." Syl'rkai took another look at his screen, then his voice dropped to ominous depths. "Kalralahr? Contacts identified as cap ship missiles launched from the *Tiger Claw*. Missiles will have lock in four seconds. Estimated impact in thirty-three seconds."

"We have to launch countermeasures," Makorshk said, wrenching his blade from Jatork's neck. The second fang shoved Jatork's body away and stood, his face and arm drenched in dark gore. He bolted to his station and began skimming data that scrolled across a trio of screens.

Vukar glimpsed Jatark, whose paws jerked spasmodically and whose body began heaving a stench. The admiral advanced toward Makorshk, reaching for his own *vorshaki* blade and feeling the frenzy claw into in his head.

"A blood duel, of course," Makorshk said. "I knew it could come to this the day we lost those destroyers. But is this the time, Kalralahr?" The steady beep of incoming missiles punctuated the second fang's question.

"*Kass'richak*," Vukar shouted, the ancient curse jarring his crew almost as much as Makorshk's attack on Jatark. "Launch countermeasures." He regarded the helmsman. "All ships to assume defense positions. Continue on evasion course." He cocked his head to Makorshk. "We will *not* engage. That is *not* our mission."

Makorshk lifted his chin high in disrespect. "Then we flee like lowborns, and your destiny lies alongside Bokoth's. Countermeasures away."

"Missiles have lock," interjected Radar Officer Syl'rkai. "Cruisers intervening."

Tearing himself free of Makorshk's bold stare, Vukar regarded the forward viewport, where the spectacle would play out before his eyes.

Missiles took form in the distance, etching their familiar and foreboding tracks across the void. Two of his Fralthi-class cruisers soared overhead and descended to provide a moderate shield for the superdreadnought's bow, while a third cruiser hugged the ship's belly and would interdict any missile fire to that region. His single Ralari-class destroyer would shift well ahead of the battle group and unleash torpedoes in salvos of eight. Turreted lasers would attempt to pick off the incoming cap ship missiles, as would the destroyer's pair of antimatter guns. The battle group's two Sivar-class dreadnoughts now lumbered into flanking positions. At over eight hundred meters and equipped with twelve torpedo tubes each, the dreadnoughts alone could take on the apes and emerge victorious. Never mind the dreadnoughts' fighter complements of over one hundred and fifty, and the tremendous meson shields that protected their streamlined, rectangular hulls. The torpedoes would be enough to gnaw away the strike carrier's shields and reduce her to a tumbling collection of gas-and-spark-laden rubbish. But as Vukar had reminded Makorshk, they should not waste time engaging. They would move as quickly as they could to the jump point.

As the dreadnoughts added their own antimatter fire to the growing defense wall, eight cone-shaped drones transmitting false electromagnetic signatures spiraled away from the *Shak'Ar'Roc* in an attempt to bait any missiles that might penetrate the escort defense. Vukar tracked the path of one such drone until it vanished behind a scintillating bulwark of laser fire that originated from one of his cruisers.

At the moment, the battle resembled a strange race, rounds

competing with each other as they blasted away from his ships and arrowed into the distance. With all of his senses, Vukar reached out into that distance, trying as his forefathers had to get a sense, a feel, for his enemy, but the vacuum barred him from satisfying that impulse.

"Kalralahr, two squadrons of fighters inbound," said Radar Officer Syl'rkai.

Vukar lowered his snout in expectation of the attack. "We'll let the dreadnoughts handle them."

"Shall I relay the order to launch fighters?" Comm Officer Ta'kar'ki asked.

"No."

"Kalralahr, some of those fighters will penetrate point-defense systems," Makorshk said, leaving his station and pounding his way toward Vukar. "We must launch a counter-assault."

"Return to your station," Vukar growled. "Ask Sivar for forgiveness *and* for a swift death."

Makorshk held his unflinching gaze for a moment, then spun and trudged back. Vukar could have easily summoned a replacement tactical officer, but despite everything Makorshk had done, the second fang had more experience than any of his other tactical officers. Now, in time of combat, he wanted Makorshk at his station. After the jump, dueling blades would settle their differences.

Like *szcaltal* flies that swarmed the skies during summer nights on Kilrah, the Confederation fighters skimmed and flitted and spun through the glistening tangles of fire, emerging unscathed and bound for the cruisers and dreadnoughts.

"Detecting Confederation Broadsword bombers now, my Kalralahr," came the still-ominous voice of Radar Officer Syl'rkai. "Two pairs with fighter escorts. They'll reach the dreadnoughts in three-point-two-zero minutes."

"Jump calculations nearly finished," Makorshk said, reading his screen.

"Drive crews report systems nominal," the comm officer relayed. "Escorts have established jump line and order."

"Can we jump before those bombers reach the dread-noughts?" Vukar asked Makorshk.

"We can increase thrust, overshoot them, and alter the jump line. The bombers will engage them as they attempt to jump. Or we can launch fighters to engage those bombers. Kalralahr, we may lose some of those fighters, but if we do not engage, we could lose the dreadnoughts. I believe we should have those dreadnoughts launch fighters and continue to maintain our position in the rear."

Vukar spared himself further consideration. He would cut his loses at the fighters and not sacrifice even one of his capital ships. He regarded Comm Officer Ta'kar'ki and said, "Contact our dreadnoughts. Give the order to launch counter-assault squadrons. Force should be equal in number."

Though he could easily fight off the pain of ordering loyal warriors to their certain deaths, Vukar welcomed the dark feeling as an immediate tribute to those brave souls who would die or be left behind. While in recent times the Kilrathi rarely took prisoners, the Terrans would attempt to bring in some of his pilots. Vukar trusted that they would not allow themselves to be shamed in that way.

It took no more than a few seconds for the first wave of Dralthi fighters to streak away from the dreadnoughts and festoon the heavens with the blue gleam of afterburners. Vukar suddenly held himself erect and mentally offered his pilots Sivar's blessing.

He could do no more.

"That battle group will reach the jump point in less than a minute," Angel cried, her cockpit instruments blinking and beeping in a rhythm as rapid as her pulse. "Bishop? Hunter? Maintain course. Draw that antimatter fire away from your bombers. Gangsta? Cheddarboy? Break off and target those guns on the portside dreadnought."

The terse replies came and went. Angel held fast to her own course, running escort for the pair of Broadswords targeting the dreadnought at her nine o'clock.

Sinatra flew at her wing, limiting his conversation to cool, curt reporting. "Bombers will be in range in nineteen seconds," he said, his chestnut brown eyes unblinking on Angel's display.

She looked away and confirmed his report on her own tactical screen. Incoming antimatter fire already wreaked havoc with her sensors, and the occasional glancing round struck the canopy shield and neutron gun with appreciable thunder. A ring of blips abruptly crawled onto her radar scope, and while she had seen the fighters launch, she had hoped they would get the Broadswords within bombing range before the Dralthis could engage. "Tick off the bombing range," she told Sinatra. "We break on one, they bomb on one. Are we ready?"

The bomber pilots, who had been monitoring the channel, uttered their assurances. Sinatra added his response then droned off the seconds with a remarkable stoicism as they plunged toward the expanse of Kilrathi plastisteel gathered into the toothy form of a dreadnought.

A vortex of fire erupted around Angel's canopy, and shield warnings darted and winked across her VDU. The Rapier could sustain three, possibly four more seconds of this intense bombardment before the shields surrendered and the incoming struck her fore armor. She would last another few seconds, perhaps even long enough for her to shift beam and run headlong into the cap ship's bridge.

Sinatra mumbled the last three seconds of the countdown and—

At once the bombers fell away and Angel lit burners. She jerked the stick sharply to starboard in a turn that made her stomach question her sanity but took her out of the incoming fire. Two Dralthis descended across her cone, and she slapped the HUD viewer over her eye.

"Torpedoes away!" announced one of the bomber pilots. "They've got a lock. Arming now."

"Got off the quad myself," the other bomber pilot said. "But I'm down to forty-five percent thrust. Port engine is offlining now. If I don't get some support in—"

A dim explosion met the corner of Angel's eye. She checked her radar scope. The Broadsword had vanished. Her heart sank, but as she always did during combat, she told herself that she had to stay with it, stay in it. She had already sighted one of the Dralthi, and the smart targeting reticle winked green and waved her on. White-knuckling her stick, she tracked the Dralthi and cut free her first salvo of neutron fire. Rounds struck sledge-hammering blows to the cat's shields as he rolled and broke.

Groaning against the Gs, Angel stayed with the Dralthi, deciding to take out her rage for the Broadsword's loss on this individual. He dove. She dove. He banked hard to port. She banked hard to port and fastened herself even tighter to the cat's shadow. He leveled off. She got missile lock. Took the shot. Tore off the bastard's port wing. Flew through the phantom of his ship. Looked back at the yawning mouth of debris. The cat's cockpit remained intact. Her VDU crackled with an image of the Kilrathi pilot, all coppery helmet and feline eyes. "This for the *hrai*!" With that rushed preamble, the Kilrathi got down to the business of killing itself. The cockpit burst into a thousand tiny fragments spanned by writhing but quickly-extinguished flames.

After wheeling around to face the incoming capital ships, Angel noted with grim fascination that the Broadswords' torpedoes had already impaled the dreadnought, detonated, and had quartered her unevenly, with the largest section belonging to the bow. As she had witnessed many times before, nutrient gas vented into space, along with thousands of other objects not pinned down when the bombs had struck. Kilrathi themselves spun head over heels through the devastation, serving as obscene flotsam and visceral reminders that this wasn't just about destroying ships and gaining tactical advantages on star maps; it was about killing. Killing. And killing some more.

While they had managed to take out one of the dreadnoughts, the cruisers, destroyer, and other dreadnought reached the jump point. Scoured by unremitting cap ship fire, they crunched out of existence amid ringlets of blue-white photons and neutrinos. The superdreadnought followed tightly on her escort's heels, her cannons recoiling and belting out fire to the last second. She dropped into gravity well, blurred and shrank for a moment, then threw up the blinding sheet of her exit.

Without ceremony or accompanying flourish, the battle simply ended with the jump and the successive self-destruction of the twenty or so Dralthi fighters left behind. Angel squinted as a Kilrathi at her two o'clock shook paws with Sivar.

"One cap ship for seven," Bishop grunted. "We suck."

"No, we're alive," Angel corrected. "Sucks for you, maybe." She checked her scope. With a sigh she noted that every member of the squadron had survived. "Regroup, ladies. Bishop's buying."

Angel switched off the comm and flipped back her HUD viewer. She figured that Gerald was already relaying their encounter with the Kilrathi battle group. Problem was, the task force Tolwyn had assigned to find the Kilrathi could not cut them off in time. That gravity well could take the Kilrathi to Enyo, to McAuliffe, or even out as far as Vega. Unless Tolwyn already had ships waiting in those systems, the cats would move through them, facing, perhaps, minimal resistance since the admiral had significantly tied up the fleet by establishing no-fly zones around the Pilgrim systems and enclaves.

Her VDU switched from a damage report to display an image of Gerald seated at an ob station. "Exceptional work, Commander. And now for the bad news. Two unarmed commercial transports from Nabco-Mills violated the zone during the attack. They made it past the *Mitchell Hammock* and into Netheryana's atmosphere."

"They made it past the *Hammock*?"

"I should have held back more patrols. In any event, the transport skippers refuse to turn back, and the strike base commanders on planet won't order their pilots to fire unless I take full responsibility."

"So take it."

"I have. Those transports are loaded with nothing more than foodstuffs, and each carry a crew of ten."

"Sir, why are you talking to me? You know the course."

"Yes, I do. And I shouldn't need reassurance, but I do. Thank you, Commander. And God forgive me. Captain out."

Unwelcome chills bridged Angel's shoulders as she imagined the two transports exploding into fiery bands across Neteryana's sky. The destruction would linger for hours and serve as a grim testimony to the inhabitants of Triune.

This can't go on. Even if Aristee doesn't stand down by Tolwyn's deadline, he can't possibly order the deaths of so many Pilgrims. Doing that will earn him a place in history next to Khan, Hitler, and Tralchar. It's enviable that he doesn't bargain with terrorists, but several billion innocent Pilgrims probably wish he would. If there's a way out of this, it lies with Paladin and Blair.

Damn it. Another day would pass and mark another failure. She played a game with herself now. She tried to go an entire day without thinking once of Christopher Blair. Ten days had passed since she had read his message. Ten failures. *You're weak. You're nothing. You're open, vulnerable, and you'll get hurt more than you ever have before. Besides, he's probably dead already.*

No, he's not. Paladin would not let that happen. The commodore needs him for something.

Okay, so maybe he is alive. Maybe he'll come back. Why does he care about you? The only thing not falling apart is your career.

He doesn't care about you. And you're burning those candles for nothing. There's no light.

Oh, God. She unbuckled her oxygen mask and touched her cheek. *Just to feel him again . . .*

Just to feel . . .

VEGA SECTOR,
ROBERT'S QUADRANT

15 HOURS FROM
ALOYSIUS SYSTEM,
KILRATHI BORDER

CS OLYMPUS

2654.112 (Z MINUS 46
DAYS TOLWYN CLOCK)

0730 HOURS
CONFEDERATION
STANDARD TIME

Sprawled out on his cot, head pillowed in his hands, Christopher Blair closed his eyes and transported himself back to Angel's quarters. His pulse quickened as he relived that precious time he had spent with her before coming aboard the *Olympus*. He could see her clearly, remember the fragrance of her hair and the way she breathed his name, but every time he reached out to touch her, he couldn't remember the texture of her skin, as though someone had stolen that sense.

Why can't I remember!

I'm sorry, Brotur, came a voice in his head. *It's my fault. I'm just jealous, I guess.*

An unseen hand stroked Blair's cheek. He sat up, shivering, fingers pressed to his cheek as though he could touch the someone who had touched him. "You said you would come," he whispered aloud. "It's been over two weeks." His shoulders slumped. He stared at the gray wool blanket covering his mattress.

I've been busy. Besides, you haven't been ready to receive me.

What does that mean?

It means what it means.

He ignored the impulse to roll his eyes. *Do you know any-*

thing about Commodore Taggart? Do you know what's going on up there?

Her reply did not come, and it dawned on Blair that maybe her voice, her touch, the glimpses he had caught of her were all products of stress or some virus he had contracted. His illness targeted his senses, caused him to hallucinate. She existed only in his head, and somehow Johan McDaniel had wormed his way into Blair's thoughts and learned of Blair's contact with her. Or maybe she had been created by McDaniel for some reason.

"I'll tell you who I am. I'll tell you all about me—if you'll let me."

The voice sounded different now, much more distinct, like the soft notes of a piano. He looked up from the blanket—

And locked gazes with a woman about his age whose large, azure eyes seemed, for a moment, to be the only source of light. A dozen shades of gold laced through long hair that spilled over her shoulders and partially veiled her small but firm breasts. Her Pilgrim robe fit her very well, or did she just seem more comfortable wearing it? She smiled tightly, her face bearing angles so delicate and precise that were it not for the blemish near her nose, Blair would have sworn she was an automaton. Unlike Amity Aristee, whose beauty seemed derived from the shadows and unseen energies of the night, this woman maintained an aura by remaining close to suns, to people who offered their own light. She would be perfectly at home on a sailboat, the wind fluttering through her hair, the sun baking her a deep, reflective brown. The mere act of recognizing her stunning beauty struck guilt in Blair. His heart belonged to Angel, but this woman's presence left him warm and trembling.

"I'm Karista Mullens," she said.

Though Blair now saw the woman and had heard her voice, he still had difficulty believing that she actually existed, even as she keyed open the cell door and moved slowly inside. The door thumped shut, giving way to Maniac's incessant snoring. Blair's wingman was probably dreaming up more ridiculous plans of escape. His feigned illness had inspired the guards to new heights of harassment.

Blair rubbed the sleep grit from his eyes, then climbed off the cot. He pulled his robe closer to his neck and held his grip as Karista took a seat on his bed. She surveyed the utilitarian splendor of his cell, and Blair thought he detected a trace of melancholy in her expression. He didn't know what to say, where to begin. "Why do you keep contacting me? Why are you here?"

She patted the mattress, gesturing that he take a seat beside her.

He shook his head. "Were you a Confederation officer?"

"No. I was a chanter and dancer in the protur's personal troupe. Now I perform for liberty, for a chance to regain what was ours."

Blair returned a weak sneer. "To be honest, ma'am, that speech is getting old."

"Have you forgotten Peron?"

"No, but I don't obsess on it, either. I'm not going to blame the Confederation or the Pilgrims for the death of my parents. It just happened. And I've had to deal with it all of my life."

"Have you ever seen holos of the atrocities committed by the Confederation?" She withdrew a small holoplayer from one of her robe's two deep pockets.

He waved her off. "You can save the show. And forget about any of your other techniques, like your, what do you call them, con-crit sessions? And your songs? Forget about them, too. I understand that Pilgrims were killed. I understand that during wartime atrocities are committed—by both sides. What I don't understand is what Aristee and the rest of you hope to gain. You're on a suicide mission, and the only message you'll send to your people is that if you defy the Confederation, you will be pounced and forgotten. She has one ship, and maybe the hopper drive is a powerful device, but she'll never get near Earth with it—not if the Confederation Navy still exists." He softened his expression. "You seem like an intelligent woman. What are you doing here?"

"Sometimes I ask myself that. Sometimes I have an answer. When I hear you talk, I remember my doubts." Her gaze lowered to her lap, and she returned the holoplayer to her pocket.

"What do want?"

She took in a deep breath and faced him, her expression growing more earnest. "The scripts of our lives are often naturally paired in the continuum. Some of us are lucky enough to recognize the pairing or have it pointed out to us by others. When you and I were just children, Frotur McDaniel discovered that your script and mine were a dyad. When I was old enough, he told me about it, but I didn't know what to do with that information. To be honest, I didn't really care. It's not an arranged marriage or anything."

"Then what is it?"

"We're always paired with our parents. And when we're close to the continuum, we can read their scripts, speak with them, with their energy, with the continuum itself. You've done that. Your mother keeps warning you not to learn too much about us. She says you'll fall like us."

Blair retreated a step. "How do you know that?"

"Because we're paired. You'll soon discover things about me that maybe I don't want you to know. But I have no choice."

"Why didn't you contact me years ago?"

"You're only half-Pilgrim. It's taken a long time for your skills to mature. You've been in touch with the continuum for only a few months now."

"How did you know I'd be here? Don't tell me you can see the future."

"I was on McDaniel when the *Tiger Claw* jumped into the system. I've known for a while that you were aboard that ship. I volunteered to come. I sensed you'd be here. Then I reached out for your script, and you told me to come."

"I don't remember that."

"You'd remember it as though remembering a dream. It may come. It may not." Once more, she caressed Blair's cheek without lifting a hand. He jerked back. "Would you stop that?"

"Okay. But wouldn't you like to get in touch with who you are? I can show you things, teach you things you never thought possible. Isn't that what you want, Brotur? Isn't that what you really want?"

"Maybe. But what's the price?"

"I said that pairing wasn't like an arranged marriage. And Pilgrims are free to seek whomever they choose for a lifemate. Those who obey the natural pairing are regarded as the most pure, the most powerful, and the most happy. Pilgrims who are naturally paired can combine their powers and travel through the continuum as a single entity. No union is more intimate. James Taggart and Amity Aristee are naturally paired."

"What?"

"Oh, yes, she's much more to him than an old flame. In the physical sense, paired Pilgrims are perfectly compatible with each other and experience greater sexual gratification than with any other partners. But I'm not here to seduce, Brotur. I just want you to learn the truth. And that's what you want. You can't deny that—at least not to me."

Blair realized that he still clutched his robe. He released his grip, and a pang of guilt hit him as his glance traced her curves. Her promise of unsurpassed sex sent a tremor through him.

Cunning. That was Karista Mullens. She knew exactly how to ruffle him. And her robe left little to the imagination. Their teacher-student relationship would break down within a week.

Then again, no one other than Paladin had volunteered to teach him about who he was. She did wield some power. She got into his head—or more precisely got in touch with his script—anytime she chose. Blair had done the same, but the act always felt clumsy. He wondered if his mother and Frotur McDaniel contacted him instead of vice versa. And the power to touch without touching, to manipulate a force like gravity, make it bow to your will without technology . . . yes, he would like to have that power. He would like to know why it existed and if it had a greater purpose than just surprising or taking advantage of individuals. What did it feel like to touch someone like that?

She patted the mattress once more. "I won't hurt you."

With a brief sigh of resignation, Blair padded over to the cot and sat at a distance that made her frown.

"I said I won't hurt you."

"I'm not worried about that. I just don't want this to—"

"You can't hurt me, Blair. I already know you too well. I know about Angel. But for now it's just us. And I want you to know everything."

"Not everything. Just teach me to touch the way you do."

"All right. Close your eyes . . ."

William Santyana double-timed down the corridor until he reached the intersecting passage. He raised his hand to halt the other three pilots who skulked along behind him. The intersection looked clear, and he signaled the rest to follow. They passed the environmental control bays, the engine room, then finally reached the main hatch leading to the brig. Two Pilgrim Marines stood guard outside, their rifles held tightly to their chests. One stepped forward. "State your business, brotur."

"We have orders to interrogate the prisoners," Santyana said, matching the Marine's forceful tone. He thrust forward his forged order card.

The Marine accepted the card, unclipped the rectangular datalink from his belt, then inserted the card. He paused a moment as the device's screen lit, turning his face a shimmering olive. Santyana glanced sidelong at Douglas Henrick, one of the three Pilgrim pilots who wanted off the *Olympus* as badly as he did. Henrick had spent the better part of his youth in a South Philly metroplex, where he had learned to forge datacards and create falsified confirmations on datanets that would immediately erase themselves after being accessed. In centuries past he would have been called a hacker or a chiphead or a zapper. Santyana just thought of him as an old-fashioned lifesaver. Of course, that label would change radically should the card fail to work . . .

"I don't know what the captain's thinking, but if you want to get something out of these guys, you'll have to beat it out of them," the Marine said, returning the card. "Especially Maniac. Give me five minutes with him. He'll be neutered. And cooperative."

"They won't respond to torture," Henrick jumped in. "The captain knows that. They might talk to other pilots. And they've been in there a while and had time to think. They might have grown a little soft."

The Marine turned back to the hatch and keyed in the appropriate code. "You're wasting your time."

Santyana crossed into the long corridor that divided the brig, his gaze sweeping both sides of the prison until it locked on a lanky, blond man dressed in a Pilgrim robe and curled into a fetal position on his cot. The guy communicated with his dreamworld through an atonal refrain of grunts and snorts. That would be Maniac. Santyana checked his watch, having forgotten how late it was: day 112, 2232 hours CST. He glanced to the cell next to Maniac's and found a dark-haired pilot lying on his belly, one hand draped over the side of his rack, the other placed firmly on his cheek. That would be Christopher Blair. "Gentlemen," Santyana stage-whispered.

No reaction.

"Gentlemen!"

Blair stirred a bit. Maniac pulled his knees deeper into his chest and buried his face in his pillow.

"Full flush scramble!" Henrick cried. "Out of your racks! Go! Go! Go!"

Per training and instincts, both young pilots practically exploded from their bunks and snapped to attention before the bars. They stood as sleeping statues, their eyes still tightened to slits.

"Good evening," Santyana said. "Sorry 'bout the wake-up, but we don't have much time."

"Well, you can have some of ours," Maniac said, licking his lips and grimacing over a bad taste in his mouth. "We got a lot."

"Who are you guys?" Blair asked.

"I'm Bill Santyana. This is Doug Henrick, Jadyk Charm, and

Joe Pazansky." Santyana gestured to the tall black man, the short, broad-shouldered Enyoian woman, and the curly-haired athlete respectively.

"Santyana. That name's familiar," Blair said. "You weren't a test pilot, were you?"

"For a little while."

"We read about you at the academy. Holy shit, man, it's a pleasure to meet you." Blair thrust his hand between the bars.

As Santyana went to take it, Blair suddenly withdrew.

Santyana proffered his own hand. "Hey, it's all right."

"I didn't know you were a Pilgrim," Blair said, then faced the bulkhead. "Seems like all of my role models are going to hell."

"That's not on my itinerary," Santyana said with a slight smile. "Getting off this ship is."

"You guys ain't Pilgrims?" Maniac asked, his eyes finally open.

"We are," Henrick said. "We were loyal to Aristee until the massacre at Mylon Three. She never told us we would torpedo the planet. I speak for us all when I say we don't mind taking on the Confed military—but leave the civvies out of it. She wanted to make a statement. We heard her, all right."

"Then skids up," Maniac said. "Key open the door. You guys armed?"

"Can't do that now," Santyana said. "We'll try to recruit a few more, then we'll make our break before we leave Aloysius. We'll be back for you."

"Yeah, I believe that," Maniac sniped. "When opportunity knocks, your asses will be airborne without a second thought. Why did you guys even waste your time coming down here? You don't give a shit about us."

Santyana nodded his understanding. "Truth is, Mr. Marshall, we need you. Sure, the more the merrier for our escape, but you've been in contact with Commodore Taggart. We could use his help to get off this ship, but we can't get close to him."

"So your whole plan is resting on us getting Taggart's help?" Maniac asked. "Guys, we've only seen him once since we've been down here. I'm sure that Aristee's already leading him around by the—"

"If we can get him down here, talk to him," Blair interrupted, "I'm sure he'd help. He probably can't get away. And I'm sure that he's been busy trying to get Aristee to stand down."

Maniac cursed under his breath. "Blair, you're so naïve."

"Taggart may still be with us," Santyana said. "But rumors have it that he and Aristee have become quite close. He's been seen on the bridge with her *and* seen leaving her quarters. But that's scuttlebutt. We need to know if we can count on him."

"Forget him," Maniac argued. "You guys want to get out of here? You get to a small arms locker, load up, and come back. We'll shoot our goddamned way out."

"But even if we make it to a ship, once we launch, they'll blow us out of the sky," said Henrick with a sobering nod.

Maniac shrugged. "I'd rather die trying."

"What if they can't get to Taggart?" Henrick asked Santyana. "Maybe we should leave him out of this and create a diversion of our own."

"I sayz we jet off onez we reach Aloysius," said Jadyk, her voice brushed by her Enyoian accent. "We go out on patrol and never come back. If we can get jump coordinatez, I think we can get out of range before they know what'z happening."

"That'll work for you three," Santyana said. "And if that's what you want, then I'll be your diversion. But I have a wife and child. I'm not leaving without them."

"We'll take the *Diligent*," Blair said. "I know the access code to her helm. But we still need cover after we launch."

"There has to be a way we can get to Taggart," Santyana said. "If only to get him down here. Look, no matter what happens, rest assured that we'll be back for you."

"I'm convinced," Maniac said, no mistaking his sarcasm.

Santyana opened his mouth to retort, but the general quarters alarm beat a loud rhythm that echoed through the brig.

"We're making orbit," Henrick said. "C'mon. They'll miss us on the flight line."

Santyana widened his eyes at Blair. "We will come back."
The young man nodded. "I believe you."

With an uneasiness fueled by their proximity to the Kilrathi
border and by his growing feelings for Amity Aristee, Paladin
stood on the *Olympus*'s bridge as the supercruiser shifted into
a low orbit of the planet Aloysius Prime. They would meet
their contacts on one of the northern continents, where lush,
tropical terrain stretched to escarpments overlooking a
turquoise sea that rivaled Earth's Caribbean in its beauty.
While the planet's gravity remained slightly higher than the
Earth standard reproduced on board the carrier, her atmosphere fully supported humans. Sure, the slightly denser air
would take some getting used to and oxygen masks might be
required for the first day or so on planet, but adjusting would
be far easier than some of the other places Paladin had visited.
Aloysius stood as one of those rare gems in the Confederation,
a world whose exotic species of flora and fauna flourished
under Confederation protection from colonization and
tourism. The fact that Aloysius stood on the Kilrathi border
only helped to dissuade poachers and other scum from plun-
dering the planet. An elaborate satellite defense system warded
off unauthorized vessels, but Amity had assured him that her
people on planet, one hundred or so Pilgrim mercenaries who
had been amassing foodstuffs and ordnance for nearly a year,
had taken care of that problem.

Sure enough, as they continued in their orbit, they encountered no resistance. However, Confederation cap ships assigned
to the quadrant frequented the system as part of their routine
patrols. Aristee could not protect against that threat. She gambled that she would have enough time to collect her personnel
and supplies before being spotted. Paladin had not even mentioned the Kilrathi threat; no doubt they were looking for her—
and no doubt she knew that.

In a few moments, Aristee would grace the bridge, offer him
one of her loving glances, then snap into the cold efficiency that

had become her trademark. He would stand by, as he had in days past, and simply observe.

I'm letting this go too far, he thought. *It's been twenty-four days. What am I waiting for? She won't stand down. I know what I have to do.*

But knowing doesn't help.

He should not have dined with her that first night. He should not have shared drinks. He should not have fallen back into her bed. But the bond of their pairing felt too strong to ignore. He knew he would succumb to its power, but even within that force he had thought he could still perform his duty. He had told himself that he would not be a Dante, guided by a lifelong idealized love. He would resume a relationship with Aristee, gain her trust, then sabotage her ship. He had already observed enough and had formulated several plans to do so. He had to act soon. Each day the responsibility of his position weighed heavier.

But an equally painful weight rested on his heart. He had to strike a balance somewhere. He had to dismiss his feelings and meet the expectations of the Confederation, of the intelligence community, of Admiral Tolwyn, and most importantly, of himself. *I'm not this weak. Or am I?*

"Thinking again?" Aristee asked.

Were they on the bridge of a Confederation supercruiser, her arrival would have been announced, but Paladin had noticed how her people embraced the practical side of military efficiency while dismissing or changing the more ceremonial aspects. No one saluted or snapped to; officers were sometimes addressed by rank, sometimes simply referred to as Brotur or Sostur. No one seemed entirely comfortable with the changes.

"Thinking again?" he repeated. "Yes. Bad habit."

"In your case, it is." She ran a finger along the collar of his robe, then let it travel over the Pilgrim cross she had given him on the day she had said good-bye. She traced the half-circle on the cross's top and added, "The sun has risen for us, James. I feel warm."

The ship's XO, a blonde, boyish-looking officer named Vyson, moved up beside Aristee. "Ma'am, our contacts on planet have transmitted landing coordinates. Escort fighters have launched and are in position. Troopship holds have been cleared out to make way for provisions and have been pre-flighted. They await your orders for launch."

"Give the order, Brotur Vyson."

"Aye, ma'am." He shifted back toward the communications station.

Aristee smiled over a thought. "I just came from Frotur McDaniel's quarters. He'll be supervising the cargo loading on planet."

Paladin frowned over the unlikely choice of supervisor.

"Yes, I know," she said, reading his expression. "I don't want him to go, but you know the way he is. Seems he's spent a lot of time researching this planet. Wanted to see it for himself. Of course, I'm sending along a Marine escort. Now then, are you ready? The captain's launch is waiting."

He glanced back to the planet and let his gaze wander on to the depths of Kilrathi-held space. "I think the frotur will adequately represent us, don't you? If we're attacked, well, let's just say you were lucky at Mylon and Lethe, even luckier at McDaniel. Don't push it."

"If I know Tolwyn, he's dispatched the fleet through the entire sector. Even if we do get company, we can handle them until we jump. Besides, we're running stealth mode, and my people on planet assure me that we can transport all ordnance and other supplies within forty-eight hours. And if it's the Kilrathi you're worried about, don't. Our mercenaries on planet have made a little deal with the battle group commander assigned to this border, cat named Dax'tri nar Ragitagha. He won't be giving us any trouble. His clan has been thoroughly compensated."

"With our technology, I assume. How much did your mercs hand over?"

She grinned, probably over his insight. "Not much. Most of the stuff's already outdated."

"I'm surprised the Kilrathi are still willing to deal—after what happened with Wilson."

"Oh, I think the emperor has definitely become shy, but individual warlords are still susceptible, especially those in clans that resist the emperor's plan to form a new alliance, like the Ragitagha. For centuries the noble clans remained separate but loyal to the imperial *hrai*. They maintained their own power, their own identities. Some Kilrathi feel that this new alliance will strip that away because it places more power in the hands of the emperor."

Paladin drew back his head. "I didn't realize you knew so much about Kilrathi politics."

"My mercs have kept me informed. I bet I know more than Confed Intelligence—no offense."

"None taken. Still, you're assuming we'll make it back in time and that the Kilrathi won't double-cross. You should be here in case that happens."

"Why James, you actually sound like you care." Her voice dropped to a whisper. "Has the sex gone to your head?"

"I haven't changed and neither has my argument. You know what I think of this. You know why I came. Call me demanding, but I'd like both of us to grow very old, whether we're together or not. Am I asking too much?"

"Maybe you are. And maybe you're forgetting that our lives . . . they're not ours. They never were. Didn't you tell me that?"

"Yes, but think about what you've done. Has it been for the people? You don't even have the protur's blessing."

"You spoke with him," she fired back. "You know I do. Go to him now if you've forgotten."

"Oh, I've spoken with him enough. He's Protur Carver Tsu the Third, not the second. I've known for a while now."

"He's the protur," she said, spacing her words for effect.

"A protur who assumed that position after Carver Tsu the Second died suddenly of natural causes during your visit to McDaniel. Remarkable timing, wouldn't you say? You didn't even let Frotur McDaniel in on your plan, and he disagrees with what you've done. You conspired with Carver Tsu the Third. Technically, you have the protur's blessing, but he is not a protur who represents the voice of our people. They don't want this war."

She seized his arm and pulled him toward the viewport, out of the crew's earshot. "How do you know what they want? You've been away for too long. Wake up, James. This is our time."

"Yes, it's our time to die. And for what?"

"For a chance to remind our people that the stars belong to the elect. I'd die for that."

"Who are we to claim the stars? Maybe they belong to no one. Or everyone. Why are we the elect? Because Ivar Chu says we are? What if he's wrong?"

She shook her head, unwilling to hear more. "We're going down to Aloysius. Once I take care of business, you and I will finish this. Let's go." She stomped off.

He stood there a moment, staring through fractured thoughts and suddenly realizing that there wasn't anything left to talk about, that he couldn't save her from herself. He had been living in denial for twenty-four days. The time had to come to act. And to grieve.

"Brotur Taggart?" she called from the lift.

With a perfunctory nod, he left the viewport to join her.

16

VEGA SECTOR,
ROBERT'S QUADRANT

FREYA SYSTEM,
KILRATHI BORDER

KIS *SHAK'AR'ROC*
BATTLE GROUP

2654.113

1100 HOURS IMPERIAL
STANDARD TIME

Admiral Vukar had tried for the past several days to ignite his darkened spirits, but the recent past held nothing but misery. Their jump into the Hell's Kitchen system had resulted in the loss of a dreadnought. First Fang Jatark had been killed by Makorshk, and Vukar had challenged his tactical officer. The duel should have already taken place, but Vukar had been agonizing over the date. He knew he should fight the second fang to the death, but he still recognized his need for the young warrior on his bridge. So he had decided that their blood duel would take place on Kilrah, before Satorshck and the rest of the clan elders. Makorshk had, of course, warmly accepted this idea as the rest of the crew grew more suspicious of Vukar's ever-growing tolerance. Though no one had voiced his objections, Vukar knew that his warriors did not understand his actions. Even warriors who unintentionally insulted their superiors were expected to commit *zu'kara*; Makorshk had done far more than that, yet Vukar allowed him to live.

For the past week, Vukar had emerged only a few times from his quarters to supervise jumps. He handled most of his inter-ship communications from there, which sparked even more rumors. He simply felt too broken, too dishonored to show his face. They had not detected the Confederation supercruiser. The ship could be anywhere. And jumping through Confederation space on a haphazard search would only result in the loss of more ships, even the loss of the entire battle group. Twice they had narrowly escaped Confederation cap ships that had jumped into systems even as they had jumped out. The apes' tenacious pursuit proved both enviable and unsettling. With little else left to do, Vukar had ordered their return to Kilrah.

Now, as he sat in his quarters, flooding his gut with the liquid warmth of *sckviska*, a celebratory drink he had been saving for the day they captured the supercruiser, he decided that the blood duel with Makorshk would not take place, that once on Kilrah, he would commit *zu'kara* to atone for his failure, for his disgrace.

"Kalralahr?"

Snapping out of his thoughts, Vukar regarded the comm unit atop his tusk-shaped desk. Comm Officer Ta'kar'ki's face contorted violently in a vision often produced by *sckviska*. "What is it?" Vukar hissed, then sat up and tried to collect himself.

"Dax'tri nar Ragitagha wishes to speak with you."

"Where is he now?"

"His battle group has just jumped into the system."

Vukar set down his ewer of *sckviska*. "He's here?"

"Yes, my Kalralahr."

"Establish a link."

Ta'kar'ki bowed his head, and the image switched to Admiral Dax'tri, an ancient warlord whose whiskers had thinned to just several pairs and whose eyes looked more gray than yellow. "Returning to the empire so soon, Vukar?" The old one's cutting tone reminded Vukar of the years of often violent rivalry between them.

Vukar dismissed the question with one of his own. "What do you want?"

"I thought I'd take a moment to bathe in your failure. This is typical of the Caxki *hrai*. You have always been the weakest of the noble clans. The emperor should have charged me with finding that supercruiser. We would have had it by now."

"My destroyers were lost. The honor was mine. And so now is the shame. But you shame yourself by reveling in my failure."

Dax'tri brightened as he leaned back in his chair. "You have failed. There is no doubt about that. But the leaders of our two clans have struck a bargain from which we will both profit."

"My days as Kalralahr are already over. No bargain can save them." Vukar closed his eyes, drew in a long breath of nutrient gas, savored it, then faced Dax'tri with a deeper look of despair.

"You plan to accept defeat without a fight? This I cannot believe."

"Had I the means to fight I would."

"Then I will give them to you. Your clan will secede from the emperor's new alliance if my clan gives you the location of the Confederation supercruiser and allows your battle group to recover it."

"Satorshck would not have bargained with your people," said Vukar, barely containing his roar. "You dishonor me and him by suggesting such a discussion took place."

"Oh, but it did, Kalralahr. And we *do* have the location of that supercruiser. I've had an arrangement with Pilgrim mercenaries for over a standard year now, and that's the reason why my clan has procured so much Confederation technology."

Vukar thought back to the many triumphs that the Ragitagha clan had claimed in the past year. Yes, they had confiscated more Confederation equipment and information than any other clan. Perhaps they did have an understanding with the Pilgrims, but Vukar had never known Dax'tri to be so forthcoming. "Why not take the honor yourself and bring back that supercruiser? It would not be the first time you strayed from an order."

"Breaking up the emperor's new alliance is far more important than the meager honor of recovering a single ship, whether it has a unique drive system or not. The alliance will destroy our clans. Our leaders recognize that. We should as well. Of course, Satorshck is taking full advantage of the situation. The Ragitagha and Caxki clans will work together to undermine this new alliance." Dax'tri raised his shoulders and leaned toward the camera. "Now, Vukar, listen closely. You will find the super-cruiser in the Aloysius system, in orbit of Aloysius Prime. She is there taking on personnel and supplies. You can reach her in twelve standard hours."

"Or I'll find a Confederation battle group waiting for me. This may be an elaborate scheme to bring down my entire clan. Why should I trust you?"

"You can verify all of this with Satorshck, but you will waste a lot of time. The Caxki clan will not secede until you confirm that the coordinates are correct. Nothing will happen until you report. But it is your duty to report as soon as you reach that system. If you choose to return home now, you do so with a *zu'kara* blade to your throat. As the apes say, you have nothing to lose."

"Except my entire *hrai*."

"I've done my part. Do yours. And once you gain control of that ship, you will return it to K'n'Rek, where our clans will assume joint possession."

"Or where your clan will be waiting to seize the ship. I think I *will* waste the time and contact Satorshck." Vukar drew back his lips, fangs jutting out.

"Yes, you could. But my reconnaissance informs me that it will only take two, perhaps three of their standard days to finish taking on supplies. If you travel to K'n'Rek to contact Satorshck, you won't make it back to Aloysius in time. You'd find nothing more than gravitic residuum and ion emissions that might yield a rough estimate of her next location—or yield nothing. The time to strike is now."

Exhaling loudly, Vukar turned away from the screen, his thoughts now caught in a crossfire. He could almost believe that Dax'tri would hand him the information so that the Caxki clan would join forces with Ragitagha and dissolve the emperor's alliance—but the threat of deception still loomed.

"Vukar, do not spend too much time contemplating this," Dax'tri warned. "What does your heart tell you?"

Yes, that is where I have gone awry, Vukar thought. *Fail to listen, fail to rely on your instincts, then you fail altogether. This is the way of Sivar.* He had reminded Makorshk of that teaching, now he should heed it himself. He reached into his heart, straining for even the barest whisper of truth.

Though Commodore Richard Bellegarde would never strike a perfect balance with his universe, he felt that in the past month he had come pretty close. He had been so busy analyzing the data from the Fourteenth Fleet's line captains that he had barely had time for self-pity and had only twice romanced his bottle since the admiral's visit to his quarters.

The no-fly zones they had established around the Pilgrim systems and enclaves and the task force they had deployed to capture the Kilrathi battle group within Vega sector kept everyone aboard the *Concordia*, especially Admiral Tolwyn, on the edge of their seats. Bellegarde especially enjoyed the reckless abandon, since he had been questioning his career with the Confederation Navy anyway. He and Tolwyn remained committed to their plan, whether it ruined their careers or not. If Aristee did not comply within the time allowed, Tolwyn would order the attack, an order that would send shock waves through the senate and the rest of the Confederation.

As Bellegarde sat in the wardroom with Tolwyn and Space Marshal Gregarov, he sensed that the precursors of those waves had already reached the space marshal and now bound her features in an unwavering grimace. She turned her hazel eyes on Tolwyn, took in a long breath, then, as always, measured each word as she spoke.

"Some members of the senate are already calling for my resignation, Geoff. They say I've employed one lunatic to find another. And the Pilgrim ambassadors have, to stay the least, been very vocal. You lied to the senate. You lied to me. What do you expect me to do?"

The admiral cocked a brow. "I wanted to keep you out of this. It's not your fault that I'm a . . . 'lunatic.' But let my clock run out. Forty-five days. That's all I'm asking. The senate will know that we gave Aristee ample time to recover one of our drones and consider our terms."

"What if she doesn't find a drone? You'll destroy those systems and enclaves without even hearing from her?"

"To do anything less would be bowing to terrorists."

"No, I can't allow you to do that."

"Ma'am, we would wipe out those systems in retaliation for Mylon Three," Bellegarde explained. "And while some members of the senate disagree with our tactics, others applaud our efforts. As usual, they're split along party lines. Our opponents know that you'll never resign, and it would take them months to indict you. By then, Aristee could have destroyed God knows how many systems. For centuries, governments have refused to bargain with terrorists. And for centuries, that policy has worked. But here we are, trying to make a deal. And in the dealing, civilians will die. You can blame Aristee for that. Not us. You might think the cure is worse than the disease, but we *need* a cure—not a bandage. We will cut off the enemy, demoralize her, then bring her to her knees. She'll die alone."

"As will you," Gregarov quickly amended. "To think that you can kill billions of people without consequence . . . Commodore, that's beyond my comprehension."

Bellegarde steeled himself. "She's an extremist. Do you know of a better way to combat her? We demand she comes to us. She doesn't, they die."

"And then what? We're back to nothing." Gregarov regarded Tolwyn. "I see you've stoked his fire with your own. Unfortunately, I'm here to extinguish both of you. Effective immediately, I want you to loosen up your no-fly zones and allow food and fuel to be delivered to those people. You'll get your forty-five days, but you will not, under any circumstances, attack those systems and enclaves."

"Aristee suspects, or will suspect, that we're making empty threats," Tolwyn said, his voice even, but a hairline away from becoming impassioned. "Impenetrable no-fly zones are the first statement. If we fail to maintain those, we'll be lowering our hand. She'll have confirmation that we won't attack. Richard and I agonized over destroying one of the enclaves to show her that we mean business, but we resigned ourselves to the zones. We need them as they are."

"Some of those people are beginning to starve," Gregarov shot back. "How will you account for their deaths?"

Tolwyn slowly shook his head. "I won't. They're Aristee's victims. Not ours."

The space marshal sighed and rubbed the bridge of her nose. "God, Geoff. What have we done? We're talking about genocide as though we're commenting on the financial markets."

"We didn't start the conversation, but we'll finish it."

She scrutinized him in an almost motherly fashion. "That kind of resolve *will* get you court martialed."

"Or promoted," Bellegarde said, wringing his hands as though her neck were between them.

"Have you gentlemen watched the Terran news channels?"

Bellegarde gave a half-shrug. "Just the local reports from McDaniel."

"Well, maybe you need some perspective." She reached into the attaché case on the deck beside her, withdrew a data disk, then slid it into the table's holoplayer.

A female reporter in trendy dress tunic shimmered above them. ". . . so the incident over Triune was just the first in this on-going series of challenges to the Confederation Navy's blockade of all systems and enclaves. Three more cargo vessels were lost over McDaniel's World just this week, shot down by fighters from the *Concordia* battle group, and massive rioting has begun in Spiritia, the Pilgrim enclave in the Ymir system."

The reporter dissolved into the image of a city street straight from one of the Pilgrim metroplexes on planet. A wall of fifty or so heavily-armed Marines pressed forward with their riot shock-shields, into a far larger wall of two or three hundred civilians throwing rocks, bottles, and whatever they could get their hands on. The image turned Bellegarde's stomach, and his jaw fell slack as the Marines fired sylago gas into the crowds. Emerald clouds billowed over the mob and descended, turning grimaces into vacant stares. For a few hours, the gas would make the mob quite agreeable. But far in the distance, another fifty, maybe sixty Pilgrims wearing gas masks and brandishing confiscated rifles ran a ragged pattern toward the frontline.

"Seen here in a Terran Six News exclusive, Marines try to quell the crowds, but their efforts are only marginally successful," the reporter said before her image returned. "The death toll in Spiritia stands at over three thousand. Nearly twenty million Pilgrims live there now, with just five hundred thousand Marines assigned to keep the peace. Reports of massive food shortages have already poured in from Spiritia and the other enclaves. Meanwhile, skirmishes continue to break out in and around the nearly ten thousand Pilgrim safe camps."

Bellegarde now studied the image of a university campus. Ancient brick buildings with signs identifying them as Library, Administration, Biological Sciences, Offworld Sciences, and Humanities and Fine Arts girdled an oval reflection pond about thirty meters across. The caption read: DESIGNATED PILGRIM SAFE ZONE: UNIVERSITY OF CENTRAL FLORIDA, EARTH. A half dozen rifle-toting young men sprinted along the pond's perimeter, with an equal number of Marines in pursuit. The men took up flanking positions near the library and unleashed a vicious spray of conventional fire into the building's glass doors as the reporter narrated the action. "Many Confederation citizens are using the current crisis as an excuse to take the law into their own hands. Some seek revenge for the Pilgrim war, and they intend to get it. Marines who have been assigned to protect camps like this one in Central Florida have been accused of doing a less than adequate job. One Marine, Private Jacko Fistalis, had this to say."

The chiseled young grunt held his combat helmet in the crook of his arm, and stared self-consciously at the camera. "Couple my buddies from boot were on Mylon Three when it was attacked. Yeah, we gotta protect these people, but if a few Pilgrims buy it, well, it won't be on my conscious. They got it coming. Hey, Mom! Hey, Pop! You [BEEP]ing believe this? I'm on the [BEEP]ing news!" The grunt's ridiculous grin dissolved, and the reporter returned.   "According to one insider, that apathetic attitude now permeates the military. And Terran Six News has also learned that Admiral Geoffrey Tolwyn, Commander of the Fourteenth Fleet, has given Captain Aristee until calendar date one-five-eight to surrender. After that, his forces will annihilate all Pilgrim systems and enclaves. We go now to military analyst Jobar Bouliano, author of the book *Why Your Military Hates You*." The holograph split into two vidboxes, one containing the reporter, the other a portly, middle-aged man wearing antique wire rims. As the reporter and Bouliano exchanged the requisite greetings, Tolwyn pushed himself up.

Space Marshal Gregarov scowled at the admiral. "We're not finished."

"I'm familiar with Mr. Bouliano's work," Tolwyn responded, remaining on his feet. "The man's assessment of our situation will be as biased and ill-informed as his book."

"Still, I'd like you to hear it."

"Ma'am, I'd rather not."

Gregarov switched off the holoplayer and stood to meet Tolwyn's gaze. "Geoff, you're the best I have. But I'll relieve you of command without hesitation. I've already sent for the rest of my staff. I'll be setting up a field office here."

"That won't be necessary."

Her gaze grew as heated as his. "I think it is."

"Lost your faith in the old rogue?"

"Not at all. I have complete faith that you'll eventually resolve this situation, despite broken promises. I'm here to make sure you do so without sacrificing your career." She shifted her attention to Bellegarde. "I'll try to save yours, too."

Unsure of whether to thank or curse her, Bellegarde opted for a weak nod.

"Gentlemen, we're off to the map room for my update." She fetched her attaché case and carried her solid frame toward the door.

Bellegarde shared a weary look with Tolwyn as they followed her out.

Who am I? Who am I? Really?

Paladin had not said a word to Amity Aristee during their trip down to Aloysius Prime. He had stared through one of the launch's portholes and had imagined himself as a numb, purely logical creature who knew what was best for the Confederation and for the Pilgrims. But he had kept returning to the notion that he should do what was best for himself, for his heart. Why couldn't that complement his duty? Why did they have to be at cross purposes?

The launch had set down in a wide clearing encompassed by a dense rainforest that reminded Paladin of the holos he had seen of South America during his secondary education. Dark green fronds the size of Rapier wings created a fettered canopy that split the sunlight into thousands of glimmering blades. Trees with trunks as thick as three meters soared upward, losing themselves in their own limbs and the limbs of neighbors. Brown, moss-like vegetation blanketed most of the forest floor, with the occasional splotch of rich, black soil seeping through. Surprisingly, it had only taken a few minutes to grow accustomed to the air, and a strange, almost familiar scent lingered, a blend of anise and cinnamon that seemed wholly out of place given the damp terrain. Paladin presumed the odor came from a particular species of flora, though he had yet to find it. He had cautiously moved through the bramble, avoiding thorns and stroking the leaves and stems of several plants his terrain scanner identified as nontoxic. He had marveled over velvety textures and the trilling some vegetation made when touched, one of the few sounds in an area that, were it on Earth, would bustle with the hoots and cackles of its denizens. Aloysius's indigenous forest dwellers, mammals ranging from the size of a fingernail to three meters tall when standing on hind legs, were some of the shyest creatures in the known galaxy; the fact that any of them had been recorded stood as a triumph of some remarkably patient researchers.

The slightly muffled roar of running water emanated about one hundred meters away from the clearing, and while Aristee had gone off to meet with Frotur McDaniel, Paladin had ventured down a steep, natural embankment to a spectacular waterfall that rose some ninety meters and thrust out its great chest for nearly twice that. The water fell partly in a large double drop and partly in a series of smaller cataracts that gave it a crescent shape at its apex. Clouds of mist surged up from the river below and wound their way through the verdant treetops guarding the falls. The soothing rush of water and the angelic vapor that glossed the scene had lifted Paladin out of the nightmare of Aristee's rebellion and had lowered him into a dream where he could be consoled, comforted, and loved without complications. After a few minutes of pure rapture, he had sat on a large rock whose face had been worn smooth. He had remained there for nearly an hour until Aristee had come down to find him. She had massaged his shoulders for a few minutes, then, like a giggling schoolgirl, had stripped out of her uniform and had jumped into the river. Paladin had shaken his head at her requests for him to join her. Then she had come ashore and had dragged him fully clothed into the water.

They had spent the rest of that first day at the falls, swimming, climbing the slick rocks to find purchase beneath some of the less turbulent falls, letting the water cascade over their naked bodies. They had even discovered a cave behind one of the cataracts, had speculated on the treasure that lay within, but visions of sharp-toothed predators had cured their curiosity. They had eaten fruit and bread that Aristee had stowed in her pack and were disturbed only once by a call from the XO, who had delivered a routine progress report. Paladin had wondered when Aristee would return to the conversation they had begun on the bridge, but she had seemed at peace with the moment and had not wanted to spoil it. He had tapped into a little of her peace and had avoided the issue as well. Given his surroundings, he could easily pretend that he had but one task: to draw pleasure from the environment and the woman.

After relishing in fourteen standard hours of sunlight, twilight had washed over the sapphire sky, and Paladin had suggested that they head back to the launch. Aristee had insisted that they camp near the falls. She had taken along a small, Marine Corps-issue survival tent, so they had sent up their bivouac on the shoreline. They had made love until they were breathless, then had remained in each other's arms, whispered to sleep by the falls.

Morning's light cut through the flaps of their tent and drew a blinding line across Paladin's face. He suddenly bolted awake, wondering how long they had slept. 1125 CST. Aristee lay on her stomach, head resting on an arm, hair curving across her smooth cheek. She breathed softly and looked frail, a young girl incapable of all she had wrought. Paladin shifted gingerly toward her pack and removed the palmlink. He slipped through the tent flaps and stood shivering in the cool, moist air as he opened a channel to the *Olympus*.

"Yes, Brotur Taggart?" came the comm officer's quick response, his face displayed on the link's tiny screen.

"Get me the XO."

"Aye, sir."

After waiting but a few seconds, the XO appeared, seated in the command chair. "What can I do for you, Brotur Taggart?"

"Status report on cargo and personnel loading."

"I'm sorry, sir, but I'm not sure whether I can—"

"Mr. Taggart has full security clearance, Brotur Vyson."

Paladin glimpsed over his shoulder at Aristee, her arms wrapped tightly around her chest. She shifted her weight from one leg to the other, struggling to keep warm.

"Yes, ma'am. Cargo and personnel loading proceeding behind schedule. Awaiting nineteen more troopship arrivals. Departure time now stands at 0200 hours on one-one-four."

Aristee tore the link from Paladin's hand. "What's the problem?"

"We've had a few delays on the flight deck, and we discovered minor hull breaches in two of the troopships. Repairs are nearly finished."

"Why wasn't I notified of this earlier?"

"To be honest, ma'am, I assumed you were . . . busy."

"Assume nothing. See if you can shave a few hours off that DT, you read me, Vyson?"

"Aye, ma'am. We're on it."

She thumbed off the palmlink, handed it to him, then puffed air. "Maybe you were right. Maybe we shouldn't have come down."

He shrugged and stepped away from her, conscious of his nudity. Back inside the tent, he retrieved his boxers. When he came out, she was already halfway to the shore line. She furrowed her brow at his underwear and beckoned him with an index finger. They did have the rest of the day to relax; why shouldn't he live the fantasy a bit longer?

The palmlink beeped for an incoming message. He accepted, and the XO's face reappeared. "Brotur Taggart? We've just intercepted a communications drone. Message has been decrypted. The captain needs to hear this."

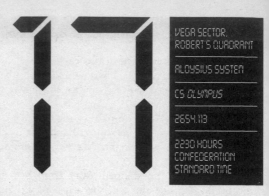

VEGA SECTOR,
ROBERT'S QUADRANT

ALOYSIUS SYSTEM

CS OLYMPUS

2654.113

2230 HOURS
CONFEDERATION
STANDARD TIME

"Try it again. Yes, that's perfect. I can feel it. Stronger now. Yes, stronger. What you see and what you feel—they should be much stronger, sometimes so strong that you can't bear them or distinguish between the two. But that's okay. That's normal, relatively speaking."

In his mind, Blair reached out to Karista Mullens. He touched her cheek and could hardly believe that what he felt wasn't actually happening. Yes, the senses seemed heightened and blended together in a sensation entirely new to him. He snapped open his eyes, breaking the link. "We're tapping into the quantum bond between particles. That's how it works. Your cheek is over there, my hand over here. But the particles in my hand and your cheek are already connected at the quantum level. We think we're separate entities, but we're not. On one side of the universe a particle's rotation stops. On the other side of the universe, a particle linked to that one stops as well. Distances don't matter. And I guess as Pilgrims we're just able to recognize the connection."

She rolled her eyes and fell back on his cot. "This is about *being*, about *emotion*, not physics."

"There's a reason why we can do this, a scientific reason."

"We could make love without laying a hand on each other. Why don't you consider that instead of trying to explain this away? Our ancestors suffered from Space Syndrome Mutation. So here we are. Isn't that enough?"

He muttered, "Oh, man," and went to the bars of his cell, leaning back to work out a kink in his shoulder. She had to mention sex again.

I'm not trying seduce you.

Uh-huh. . .

"Why won't you tell more about this ability?" he asked, steering them far and away from sexual speculation. "You've taught me how to focus my thoughts and tap into that quantum level, but what can we do with this? What kind of range does this power have? Can we use it as a weapon? Can I force someone's eyes closed, throw someone against a wall, squeeze someone's heart until it stops beating? What?"

"You've reached out into gravity wells and found your way through them. No one explained how to do that. I've pointed you in the right direction, but I can't do any more."

That drew his snort. "Where I come from we call that rhetoric. Why don't you just answer a simple question?"

She sat up, pulled her long, blond locks behind her head, then lifted a narrow brow. "Because I don't know the answers. It's different for everyone, stronger in some, weaker in others. Not every Pilgrim has this ability. It's pretty rare. Even Frotur Johan can't do it. Neither can Amity Aristee."

"How many are we talking about?"

"Out of two billion or so Pilgrims, there are a hundred of us, maybe more. It takes time to realize you can do it."

"It's like telekinesis or something. Maybe the mutation exploited this ability in our ancestors," Blair supposed.

"This isn't just telekinesis. We've compared what we do to a few Terrans confirmed with those abilities. They can't feel the weight, the texture, or sense the smell of the objects they move. They describe the feeling as a force against another force. Sure, that's extrasensory, but what we have is much more. Some call it hypersensory or extrakinetic." She pushed herself up and came uncomfortably close, her eyes presenting a dangerous invitation. "But you—you're even more remarkable, Christopher Blair. You're a half-breed who's retained the power. As far as I know, you're the only one who has. I sensed the first time I contacted you that it was there. What you do with it is up to you. I can tell you this, though. If the universe has a consciousness, then it also has an eye on us. Some Pilgrims tried to exploit the power during the first war. They were successful at first, but when the Confederation finally captured some of them, they were taken to hospitals and . . . well, studied, vivisected, you know the rest. They were punished for breaking the edicts."

"Are there more of us on board?"

"At least twenty-two more, but some of us can keep it out of our scripts, hide it from each other. The number's probably higher. If I were Captain Aristee, I would recruit as many of us as possible."

"Could we combine our power into a single force?"

She hesitated, then finally nodded. "It's complicated and has never been done with so many, but it's possible. I don't think Aristee could get everyone to do it, not unless the protur endorsed the order. Even then . . ."

"How much power are we talking about?"

"We could reach out and murder a capital ship crew. We could tear apart its ion engines. We could destroy the ship within a minute or two. But what we have is regarded as sacred, a gift from Ivar Chu himself, something to be used for knowledge and discovery. We know Aristee plans to use us to the contrary. We believe in the cause, but most of us will draw the line there."

He flashed a wry grin. "But some won't."

"They're free to join her."

"And they can cause a lot of damage. So how strong are they individually? How strong are you? Show me."

His head slammed against the bars as unseen hands throttled him. He grabbed at his neck, trying in vain to pull the hands away as his air supply thinned.

"You can't stop me with your hands, Brotur. What I do with

my mind is only as strong as what I can do with my body. You have to fight me on my terms."

Though still reflexively clutching his neck, Blair closed his eyes and concentrated on her image. He saw her standing beside him, eyes wide, arms extended, hands locked firmly around his neck. He seized her wrists and quite easily jerked himself free. Even as her hands left his neck, he gasped and opened his eyes.

"I hate that," she said with a shudder.

"I'm not exactly fond of it myself." He swallowed painfully. "What about objects? The cot? Move it across the room."

"No. There's a cold feeling that gets inside when you do that. It can take weeks to get out."

"Then maybe I can do it."

This time Blair kept his eyes open but focused on his thoughts. He envisioned himself walking over to the cot. He slid his palms under the durasteel frame and heaved. The cot would not budge. He looked up and saw Karista holding the opposite side of the rack. "You don't want to feel this," she said. "This coldness . . . it's not for us. Touch scripts. Touch people."

He strained against her and spoke through clenched teeth. "Let go."

She shattered like glass, fragments of her tumbling to the floor and on to the cot as he slid it across the cell—

And felt her promise of ice, of wind, of a winter colder than any he had known, a winter that coiled around his heart, gripped his head in a frosty vice, and sent chills dashing up his spine. He tore away from the rack and cried out, half surprised, half terrified. He focused on Karista, whose look of sympathy failed to warm him.

"W-why does . . . it feel like that?" he asked, shivering uncontrollably.

"The cot has no life force. You sense that. You sense one corridor of death. For the Terran, moving the cot is painless. But for us, well, you'll be cold for a long time. I'm sorry."

"Hey," Maniac called from his cell. "You guys still talking in there? Shit, if I had a conjugal visit, you can bet your ass we would get conjugal. Hey, Karista, any chance you fixin' me up with a friend? C'mon, honey. Think of me. Be nice to get laid before I buy it down here."

"W-we aren't m-married and this isn't . . . a conjugal visit Blair forced out. "Go b-back . . . to sleep."

"Can't. 'Cause I'm sick of this. Sick of these walls. Sick of your special privileges. Sick of just lying here. Why don't they brainwash us? Torture us? Something? It's worse to be ignored."

"Yeah, f-for once, you don't . . . have your . . . audience."

Karista started for the door. "I'd better go."

"Aren't you worried?" Blair asked, blocking her with his arm. "When you k-key open the door, I could tap into the quantum bond, rush you, and escape."

"You won't. It's not time yet. You're waiting for your friends to come for you. But you're worried because you haven't had time to talk to the commodore. You could probably make it down to the flight deck and launch in the *Diligent*, but you're still worried about being shot down."

The revelation that she had probed his script made him feel even colder than moving the cot. He battled against the shivers, keeping his voice hard and steady. "You didn't come here to teach me anything. This has just been an interrogation. You got me to sell out those pilots. And everything you've told me—was that a lie, too?"

She took his hands in her own. "I didn't come down here to interrogate you. I wanted to meet my pair. I want to teach you. I haven't told the captain about your plans. And I won't. But I don't want you to throw your life away. Christopher, you're meant for so much more."

"That does wonders for my ego, but it still doesn't convince me or get me out of this cell. You don't want me to throw away my life? Help me. Get a few of your friends. You could make this happen."

"I'll think about it."

"Think hard. Think fast."

Blair shifted away and collapsed onto his bunk. Anguish

seamed her face as she reached between the bars and keyed open the door. She gave him a final look, then fluttered off. He fell back on his pillow, lying in the cold clutches of himself.

Then, with a volume and abruptness that nearly made him fall out of the cot, the general quarters alarm sounded.

"Bet this ain't a drill," Maniac cried over the high-pitched tones.

Even as Blair opened his mouth to voice his own speculation, a powerful explosion ripped into the ship and sent massive tremors through the starboard side bulkheads. Every barred door in the brig rattled, and the deck heaved as it absorbed the potent force.

"Torpedo strike," shouted Maniac.

"Yeah, but whose?"

"Like it matters?" Maniac said through an ironic chuckle. "Our ride's about to end. I knew Aristee couldn't run for long. And now we pay for her mistake."

After listening to Admiral Tolwyn's message, Amity Aristee had turned to Paladin, her face lighting with the realization that her hopper drive modifications would be completed ten days before Tolwyn's purported attack. She had snickered as she speculated on whether Tolwyn would actually sacrifice so many innocent lives.

"Don't doubt him," Paladin had said. "I've known Tolwyn for a long time. He's a brilliant strategist with a touch of insanity thrown in for good measure. Makes for a deadly combination. He means what he says."

"I've known him for a long time, too," she had countered. "He won't toss away his career for this."

"Maybe not, but his blockade has been in place for awhile. And there's a witch hunt going on throughout the Confederation. Our people are already suffering and dying. By the time you're ready to make your statement, most of them won't be around to witness it."

She had considered that for a moment, then had nodded. "I

don't care what engineering has to do. We need that hopper drive modified much sooner. The second it's ready, we'll jump to Sol. But we have to finish loading cargo. I won't take us out under-staffed and unprepared. Since we have to wait anyway, let's put this aside. I know that might seem absurd, but I have to clear my head. I have to get balance somehow. Come for a swim. You look like you need one, too."

It had taken her several more minutes of coaxing before he had finally succumbed to her siren's song. And it had taken another few hours for Paladin to fully forget recent events that seemed to pull on his limbs as though he were strapped to some medieval instrument of torture. He had slipped even deeper into the fantasy than he had the day before, embracing Aristee with a love that had gone unanswered for too many years. He had felt the urgent desire to merge with her, become one, to live that way for the rest of his life.

Twilight had come on like a pallbearer, carrying the lost day on its back and leaving Paladin deeply troubled. Not long afterward the palmlink had beeped. The XO had nervously made his report to Aristee. "Captain. A Kilrathi battle group has just jumped into the system. Confirm a Snakeir-class superdreadnought and five escorts. No evidence that they've tagged us yet."

"Very well. Cease cargo loading. Recall all ships. Put the planet between us and that battle group."

"Aye, ma'am."

Paladin had given her a look.

"All right," she had said, rolling her eyes, "you told me so."

They had snatched up their clothes, had left behind their tent, and raced to the captain's launch. Within five minutes they had taken off, with Paladin at the helm.

Now, as they cleared Aloysius's atmosphere and spotted the shining speck of the *Olympus* dead ahead, Paladin pulled up a tactical report and noted the battle group's position. Although the *Olympus* had pulled around to the dark side of the planet, the battle group had shifted into a wide arc and had probably made visual confirmation before the *Olympus* could get into hiding. Yes, the *Olympus* presently operated in stealth mode, but that had failed to elude the Kilrathi and had proven that they knew the ship would be here and that Aristee had been double-crossed. The cats' first volley of torpedoes had already reconfirmed that assessment.

"Second salvo inbound," Paladin said as he tightened his grip on the launch's control stick. The sleek little shuttle with forward-swept wings responded well to even the slightest tap. He lit its twin afterburners and focused on the supercruiser.

Aristee faced the starboard Visual Display Unit, trading intent stares with the deck boss. "How many more troopships left, Mr. Towers?"

"Thirteen, Captain. I think we can get at least eight of them aboard before we're out of the system."

"Try to get them all." She tapped a touchpad below the VDU, bringing up the engineering station. "Brotur Hawthorne? Talk to me about my hopper drive."

The bedraggled man jerked toward the screen and tried to flatten his matted hair. "Still offline for modifications, ma'am."

"What?"

"You asked me to step up our schedule. I can't do that without taking the drive offline." He backhanded sweat from his brow and sighed.

"Well, I want it back online now. We have a Kilrathi battle group bearing down on us."

"I'm aware of that, ma'am, but the well field integrator has already been disassembled. I assumed you wanted me to make full modifications to the drive as we've discussed. I could have us ready to jump to Earth in fifteen, twenty days at the most, cutting our estimates in half. But the drive will have to remain offline."

"Forget about that," she said, on the cusp of swearing. "Just get it back online and get us out of here."

"We can reassemble within a day or two, but it'll take another eight to ten days to establish and moderate the reaction containment field. We'll have to add that time on to our estimates—and I know you want to get to Earth ASAP. If you want the drive to remain online during modifications *and* you want me to reassemble now, then we won't make it to Earth before one-five-eight. You told me we had to get there before then. I'm sorry, but this is the best I can do."

Aristee closed her eyes, her breath coming in ragged bursts. "Keep the drive offline. Carry on with modifications. I assume the helm will answer to full impulse?"

"It will."

She tapped in another code, and the XO turned to face her. "Captain, shields holding. I've launched countermeasures and shifted us into an evasion course."

"We can't jump, Mr. Vyson. Take the ship out of orbit. As soon as I'm aboard, we'll make way under full impulse."

"Aye, ma'am. But we'll be leaving behind some of the troopships."

"I know. Order those pilots back to Aloysius."

"Yes, ma'am. And I have one more report. Bad news."

"Of course it gets worse," she muttered.

"Three pilots from Eighth Squadron deserted their patrol sectors at the first sighting of the Kilrathi. They broke atmosphere and ejected in their pods."

"Eighth Squadron? Was Mr. Santyana with them?"

"He was out there, ma'am, but he remained in position. We lost Doug Henrick, Jadyk Charm, and Joe Pazansky. And ma'am, I'm sorry to report that four pilots from the One-Nine and six from the Two-Two also deserted their patrols and have gone planetside."

"Instruct cannon operators to fire upon any of our ships who make unauthorized breaks from their squadrons. Aristee out." She switched off the link and leaned toward him. "You believe that? Only a few of our people came unwillingly. I thought Santyana would be the first one to desert."

"Worry about your bruised ego later," Paladin said, consumed by the laser-lit chaos blooming ahead. "We're going to take a few hits. Hang on."

He jammed the stick forward and dove toward the fleeing supercruiser as it unfurled a long tail of fire back toward the Kilrathi battle group, roughly twenty-two hundred kilometers behind. Aloysius's lime-colored glow faded from the ship's hull as she continued her escape and Paladin raced to reach her. He wove his way through avenues of antimatter fire and lined up with the flight deck behind a pair of troopships that lumbered at a frustratingly slow velocity. The incoming fire tightened its grasp, with bolts now glancing off the launch's shields and tossing himself and Aristee against their harnesses.

Keeping an iron grip on the stick and screaming for the troopships to move their asses, Paladin concluded that if he waited for even a minute longer, the shields would bottom out and the launch's light armor would succumb to the torrential thrashing. The ship had been designed for diplomatic missions, for speed. Time to exploit that advantage. He lit the pipes and soared recklessly over the two troopships, then dove once more toward the aft flight deck's rectangular launch tunnel, sealed off by its glimmering environmental maintenance field.

"Captain's Launch Alpha One. You have not been cleared to land," said the flight boss, a cranky, thick-faced Pilgrim in her fifties with an unforgettable mug and a name so long it was barely pronounceable, let alone memorable. "What is the—"

"I have the captain aboard," Paladin barked. "We're landing."

But he had spoken too soon. A lone antimatter round tore into the launch's exhaust cones and divided into millions of creepers that burned into fuel and hydraulic lines. The ship's safety systems kicked in, saving them from the heat and radiation as it ejected the thrusters a mere second before they thundered apart and sent debris careening into the hull.

Now propelled by its own momentum, the launch plummeted through the energy curtain. "No response to course corrections," Paladin said, strangely intrigued by the moment of impending death. If he didn't get the nose up, they would strike the deck and be crushed into a neat, recyclable package fully appreciated by the deckdozer driver who would have little trouble clearing them from the runway. He ignored the tingle in his neck and the flashing indicator to lower the landing skids and just two-handed the stick, drawing it toward him in a last-ditch effort to belly flop. The launch remained on its collision course.

"I have attitude jets back online," Aristee suddenly announced. "Firing!"

"What's going on?"

The guards ignored Maniac, so, of course, he shouted the question again. And again.

"They don't know either," Blair finally said. "Just shut up. Listen."

"Oh, I am. Sounds like our funeral march."

The general quarters alarm had been switched off, replaced by the frequent rumble of shield impacts and the thrumming of the supercruiser's impulse engines. Seventy-three thousand tonnes of durasteel would soon reach a maximum velocity of one hundred kilometers per second. An engineering marvel, no doubt, but why hadn't they jumped yet? Had Confederation capital ships somehow managed to corner Aristee? That seemed unlikely. The drive's gravity well would prevent that. Wait. Paladin had mentioned that they had been having trouble with the drive. Blair's shoulders slumped. If they couldn't jump out, then maybe this was it. . . .

The brig's main hatch cycled open, and one of the guards spoke to someone with a voice too soft to discern. Blair hustled to the bars and spotted Paladin in a crimson flight suit, a nasty bruise purpling his forehead. "On your feet, Lieutenant," he said as he passed Maniac's cell.

With a swish and chink, the cell door slid aside, and in mild astonishment Blair stepped into the corridor. The ship suddenly listed, and he grabbed a bar for support. Maniac staggered into the corridor, behind Taggart, who turned wearily to face them.

"Sir? What's happening? Are you all right?" Blair asked, staring at the commodore's injury.

Paladin mustered a grin. "Rough landing. Are you all right? You're shivering."

"I'm okay."

"And I'm okay, too," Maniac said darkly. "And we're all just fine. Let's celebrate, goddamn it!"

"Gentlemen," Paladin began in a tone that forced even Maniac into silence. "We have a Kilrathi battle group on our tail, and the hopper drive is offline. We can maintain our gap with the dreadnought and the superdreadnought, maybe slip out of their cannon range or at least present a smaller target, but the three cruisers and destroyers can overtake us. Which is to say, we have a problem."

According to *Joan's Ships of Known Space*, an interactive database every Confed pilot worth his salt had memorized, Kilrathi cruisers routinely reached a maximum velocity of 150 KPS, while destroyers could reach 250. The numbers rarely lied. However, the cats would not be foolish enough to send out a lone destroyer; it would remain in the company of the cruisers.

"Yeah, we have problem," Maniac mimicked, "we're dead. But at least the cats will send us off instead of our own people."

Paladin lifted an index finger. "I said those cruisers and destroyer *can* overtake us. I didn't say they will."

"Sir, there aren't any asteroid fields or comet belts in this system," Blair said, recalling his cosmography. "Even the jump point's pretty far away. We have no cover."

"And no defense," Maniac added. "You think this ragtag bunch of fanatics can stop the Kilrathi? Shit." He rubbed his forehead. "We got a battle group out there? They got five, maybe six fighters to Aristee's one."

"Which is why you're suiting up. Mr. Marshall? You're Rapier came in redlined, but I'm told its been repaired and pre-flighted. Mr. Blair, we have a Rapier for you. Once we reach the flight deck, you'll launch and report to William Santyana, your squadron commander. He's a good man. Do what he says."

Maniac whirled toward his cell, walked back inside, then sat on his bunk. "It doesn't take much to get me in a cockpit, but if you think I'll fly for these people . . ."

"They die, we die," Blair said. "How do you *not* get that?"

"Six million killed at Mylon Three. And what about our own people? What about Second Squadron? You forgot about them already? I'd rather die than help these lunatics."

"You won't be helping them," Paladin corrected. "You'll be helping me. If we can evade this battle group, you'll buy me the time I need."

"Permission to speak candidly?" Maniac asked, throttling up the sarcasm.

"Say whatever you want, Mr. Marshall, but get off that bunk and join us."

"Sir, we've been on this ship for nearly a month. How much more time do you need?"

"Matters of diplomacy don't work on a timetable, Lieutenant."

"Well, I got a feeling the admiral won't let Aristee waltz around the sector for much longer. Maybe you can give your diplomatic efforts a boot in the ass, eh? And I have to wonder, what do you think you can accomplish? She knows you're here to stop her. She's waiting for you to make your move, and then you'll get the cell next to mine. Your strategy is a joke. Coming here was a joke. Unless you planned on joining her in the first place, which, given everything I've seen, makes more sense. I mean, you love her, right?"

Blair rushed by Paladin, stormed into Maniac's cell, and grabbed the wiry blonde's neck, fingers digging into Maniac's esophagus. "You're not just out of line, asshole. You've gone way beyond that. Unless you'd like me to tear you a new breathing hole, I suggest you come along."

Powerful hands clenched Blair's wrists and pulled him away from Maniac.

"We'll die before we settle this," Paladin said, releasing Blair. "Lieutenant Marshall, I can't force you to fly. But I can assure you that when the moment comes and you're staring at the ceiling and listening to the atmosphere whistle away through breeches in the hull, when you know in your gut that you have only a few seconds to live and you're thinking about your life and did you live it well and did it mean anything, when you realize that you're alone and helpless, that you can't fight back because you're locked behind these bars, I can assure you that you will, at that moment, wish that you had strapped yourself into a fighter, slammed on your helmet, and jammed down the trigger to fire in the face of death—because you're a Confederation fighter pilot and that's what you do. That's what's in your blood." Paladin swung toward the door. "Mr. Blair? Let's go."

VEGA SECTOR,
ROBERT'S QUADRANT

LEAVING ALOYSIUS
SYSTEM

CS OLYMPUS

2654.114

0022 HOURS
CONFEDERATION
STANDARD TIME

"Broturs and sosturs, I'm sure you know why I've asked you here." Aristee gazed intensely at the twenty-seven Pilgrims she had assembled in the *Olympus*'s wardroom. Some of the robed elect sat in chairs around the conference table while others stood shoulder-to-shoulder along the bulkhead. Each possessed the rare gift of being able to sense and manipulate gravitic fields with their minds—a gift Aristee desperately needed them to exploit.

But many of her people were already shaking their heads, and one in particular, Karista Mullens, left her seat at the table. "Sostur Aristee, when we realized that you had brought so many of us on board, we suspected this day would come. But we can't do as you ask. The edicts of Ivar Chu are clear on this. To reach out and kill contradicts everything we believe in. You know that. You know the pain it causes. The cold . . ."

"Of course she knows," came the baritone voice of Shutaree Zimbaka, a bearded black man who threaded his way toward the front of the room. "But the Kilrathi are back there. They won't stop. And we'll die unless we do something about that. The protur has spoken. Sostur Aristee has spoken. All of us should make the sacrifice."

Zimbaka had barely finished when an impact tremor came from the supercruiser's aft quarter and passed violently through the room. Another resounded just a second later, with still a third of equal force riding hard on its heels.

"I'm with you," came another voice. Aristee watched Mishalla Ti come forward on small, narrow legs, her stringy black hair swinging like a pendulum after the old woman.

Karista Mullens eyed the two defectors, her mouth agape. "You can't do it. You'll reach out to those Kilrathi and crush their eyes or stop their hearts, but have any of you done that before? Do you know what it feels like to rob a being of its life force? Do you know what it feels like to touch the dead?"

Four more Pilgrims elbowed their way to join Zimbaka and Ti. Three others slid up behind Mullens. Aristee's temper flared as her people continued choosing their camps. She spun away, swore, then spun back, directing her fury at Mullens. "I brought you on board with Frotur McDaniel's highest endorsement."

"An endorsement I deserve," Mullens said, her voice faltering. "I'll do anything for you. Anything but this."

"So you choose to defy me *and* the protur?"

"But haven't you and the new protur chosen to defy the edicts? The former protur would *not* have endorsed this order."

"Carver Tsu the Second is dead. Whether he would have endorsed the order or not is inconsequential." Aristee lifted her voice for all to hear. "We have a new protur. And as Brotur Zimbaka rightly pointed out, he has spoken. So have I. Anyone who chooses to disobey will be held in the brig and sentenced to the five penance."

"Is this how we'll shape our future?" Mullens asked. "By punishing people who refuse to break the edicts? We'll reward the sinners and damn the just?"

"We'll shape our future by changing our laws," Aristee countered as she began to count heads. Sixteen Pilgrims had gathered around Mullens, while only ten had complied with the order and stood near the starboard bulkhead. Aristee had failed to win over even half. She eyed the dissenters with disgust. "Be sure of your decision."

Mullens craned her head and studied the people behind her. Most stared on unflinchingly, their minds set. She faced forward and gave a solemn nod.

Aristee raised her chin at the Marine guards posted near the door and listened to the resignation in her own voice. "Take them to brig."

The Marines stepped back, allowing Mullens and the others to proceed to the hatch. Only a few gazes dared meet Aristee's. She felt sickened by the moment—but hadn't she known that some would not follow? She had, but not this many . . .

Once the last traitor had filed through the door, Aristee favored Zimbaka with widened eyes. "You're only ten. Can you still do any damage?"

Zimbaka scanned the others. Some shared his steady gaze of confidence while a few still looked uncertain. "We can do some damage."

"I'll take you up to the aft observation bubble," she said. "You'll have privacy and a direct line." She spun on her heel, strode to the hatch, then paused. "You're not breaking the edicts," she assured them, "because those edicts no longer exist. Yes, we're rewriting the law, all of us, and it'll be a law that establishes our rightful place among the stars. Our days of bowing to the Confederation and the Kilrathi are over."

Admiral Vukar swiveled his command chair and thrust out his jaw in the expression of demand.

Comm Officer Ta'kar'ki snapped his gaze toward his instruments. "Yes, Kalralahr, our cruisers and destroyer are jettisoning all non-essential equipment and personnel to increase thrust."

"How many warriors will give their lives?"

"Approximately eighty."

"Eighty . . ." The number gave Vukar pause. He closed his eyes and spent a moment in reflective silence, then said, "We send them into the void with Sivar's highest blessing. Their names will adorn the temples, their souls the heavens. If only *we* could be so fortunate . . ." His whiskers stood on end and salvia gathered in his mouth as he coursed with the renewed electricity of the hunt.

The moment they had jumped into the system and had detected the supercruiser, Vukar had cried out in relief and had launched a long-range communications drone back to K'n'Rek to confirm that Dax'tri nar Ragitagha had, indeed, provided the correct location of the supercruiser. The Ragitagha clan had behaved honorably, and now the Ragitagha would rejoice as the Caxki clan withdrew from the emperor's new alliance. Vukar would seize the supercruiser and take it back to K'n'Rek, where both clans would exploit its technology. Or, perhaps, he would take it somewhere else and send out scouts to K'n'Rek to make sure the Ragitagha had set a trap for him. That seemed a more intelligent plan.

"She is still traveling at full impulse," Tactical Officer Makorshk reported. "And still no trace of gravitic distortion." A wavering hiss rose from the second fang's gut. "Kalrahalr, something is wrong."

Since every bridge officer knew that a challenge existed between Vukar and Makorshk, any conversation between the two turned some of those officers into anxious, quavering fools who at any moment expected blood to spill. A few of the older warriors kept their composure and scrutinized Vukar, searching for a reason why he had permitted the second fang to live so long. Unlike them, Makorshk was not afraid to voice his opinion, to stray from blind obedience, to use his own initiative to solve problems. The young second fang represented a new generation of Kilrathi, one Vukar hoped would still embrace the old ways while developing a new and vital sense of individuality. Although he despised that aspect of human culture, he conceded that there lurked something very powerful within a thinking warrior who could also listen to his heart. Makorshk represented a blending of the old and new, and he would not be the last of the Caxki clan to challenge authority.

Without breaking his gaze on the glistening dot that he followed through the forward viewport, Vukar tilted his head in Makorshk's direction. "What is it?"

"We've been pursuing them for a few minutes now, my Kalralahr. Why haven't they engaged their hopper drive?"

Vukar had nearly forgotten about the supercruiser's capability. For too long he had fought against similar Confederation carriers equipped with the standard jump drive that required a natural gravity well or other anomaly to function. He had wrongly assumed that the supercruiser speeded toward the system's jump point, and relying on that assumption he had predicted that his battle group would cut it off before it could reach that destination. But if the ship could create its own gravity well at any time, then yes, why hadn't it jumped?

Vukar pushed his bulky frame up from the chair and pounded back to the tactical station. "Range of our cruisers and destroyer?"

"One-eight-five-six kilometers and closing," said Makorshk, tapping a long finger on his display. "All four ships continue the bombardment."

"Ta'kar'ki?" Vukar called to the comm officer. "Remind our captains that once her shields have been weakened, they will use only low-level lasers to disable her ion engines."

"Yes, Kalralahr."

"The supercruiser is sustaining heavy fire," Makorshk said, observing images coming in from the cruisers. "Perhaps they will draw our escorts closer, then engage their drive to destroy them. But in order to do that, they have to permit our ships to come within five hundred meters to be affected by their gravity well. We could easily disable her well before we came so close. Something is very wrong."

"I suggest you discover what that something is," Vukar said, making much more than a suggestion.

Makorshk slowly lifted his head from his screens and regarded Vukar with a near-frozen stare. "I think I already have. We should pull back our escorts and initiate long-range bombing. If you allow them to get any closer, we'll lose them."

"How? She lacks the firepower."

"Yes, she does, but she won't need her weapons. If her engineers have modified the hopper drive so that its gravity well can become larger than five hundred meters, then they *will* destroy our ships without launching a single torpedo. I've already presented this scenario to you, and it seems the only reason why they haven't jumped. They're baiting our ships. They could activate that drive at any moment." The second fang paused to pull in a long breath, seemingly overwhelmed by his own realizations. "Kalrahalr? You have a decision to make."

So Paladin lays on the guilt trip and me—the sucker—goes for it and here I am like one minute until launch and I'm about to fight for a bunch of fanatics and mass murderers and how's your day shaping up?

Maniac shifted his butt deeper into the seat, trying to buckle himself down for launch and adjust his poorly fitting Skivvies, issued by a farsighted Pilgrim supply officer. At least the Pilgrim repair crew had not screwed up; they'd done an outstanding job on his fighter. Most of the damaged thruster and reactor components had been replaced by new ones instead of the usual remanufactured parts; that fact alone deserved his admiration.

Okay, they fixed up my ride. It's not like I should thank them like this. Shit. I wish Zarya was here. I can't believe I miss her so much. Is it love? Or am I just horny? I need someone to talk to right now. Forget Blair. Can't talk to him. He's as big an idiot as me. The Pilgrims flash him some T&A and tell him some lies and they got him by the tiller. I can't trust him or the commodore anymore. I'm alone. It's up to me to take out this bitch. I do that, come out of this alive, they'll make me the goddamned space marshal . . .

"They say your call sign is Maniac," the flight boss said, her ghastly face a potent emetic that threatened to crack his Visual Display Unit. "Well, let me tell you something, Mr. Maniac, you try any bullshit out there, I got a friend up in fire control who will issue you an antimatter enema."

"Excuse me, ma'am, but I'm unfamiliar with the technical terms 'bullshit' and 'antimatter enema.'"

"But you *are* familiar with what a single round of antimatter fire can do to your day . . ."

"You seem uptight, ma'am. Sounds like you could use a little, I don't know, recreational spanking."

"Line up, mister!"

Maniac placed his gloved hand over the miniature camera mounted above the visual display, blocking her view. He nodded to the deck boss and followed the man's signals, positioning his Rapier between the hangar's bulkhead and the launch tube.

"Elect Five, you are cleared for launch," the old lady said, still boiling.

"Just call me Maniac, sweetheart. And have I ever told you about the time I got my tongue stuck in—"

He ignited his thrusters and lapsed into a howl that made the flight boss tear off her headset and possibly wonder exactly where his tongue had been. He didn't stop howling until he cleared the energy curtain and punched into the void.

That was ridiculous. Childish. I should grow up.

Why?

At about quarter klick off the *Olympus*'s stern, Maniac banked hard to join the fifteen Rapiers in William Santyana's squadron. They flew on the supercruiser's portside, in a loose wedge or, more precisely, an old-fashioned fluid four that resembled the fingers of an outstretched hand. The rest of the *Olympus*'s complement of seventy-one fighters and sixteen bombers had launched and divided into six and four squadrons, respectively. They encompassed the supercruiser and maintained the same heading. At the moment, Maniac appreciated Aristee's recruitment of equipment and personnel, and the modifications she had made to the flight deck to accommodate many more fighters and bombers than the usual twenty or so Rapiers and half dozen Broadswords assigned to Concordia-class supercruisers.

But they were still outnumbered. Each of the Kilrathi cruisers carried at least fifty Dralthi; the dreadnought boasted one-hundred and fifty herself; and the superdreadnought, well, Intell reported its fighter complement at over two hundred.

Hey, man. Take it easy. The more cats, the more kills . . .

The VDU snapped on. "Santi to Maniac. Welcome aboard, Lieutenant." Santyana flipped back his HUD viewer. "Good to be flying together again. At least this time we're on the same side, if not the wrong one. You kept up with me pretty well over McDaniel. For a moment there, I wasn't sure I could lose you."

Maniac thought back to that furball. He had been chasing a Pilgrim fighter and had narrowed its lead to twenty meters. The Pilgrim had leveled off, cutting through a gauntlet of fighters and bombers crisscrossing about a quarter kilometer away from the moon. Maniac had had trouble believing that the enemy pilot could navigate through coordinates so densely packed with other starcraft. That feat resulted in the jock's escape and Maniac's unfulfilled promise to find and smoke him. "That was you?" he asked incredulously. "I owe you a missile, Commander."

"Consider us even." Static cut across the display, then Santyana's dark features returned as he transmitted now on the squadron's general frequency. "All right, listen up, cowboys. We're point squadron. For those of you who missed or slept through the briefing, they'll be a bombing squadron with fighter escort targeting each of those cap ships. All *we* have to do is draw fire away from them. The captain assures us that the lead cruiser will cease fire in a minute or two. The others will follow."

"What's she going to do?" Maniac began amusedly. "Get that skipper on the comm and say, 'Uh, excuse me Mr. Cat, sir, but would you mind like ceasing fire for a little while so we can barbecue your god-ugly asses?'"

"Trust me, Lieutenant. Those guns will cease."

"Sir, is she using Pilgrims to do that?" Blair asked. "I mean Pilgrims who can—"

"I'm afraid she is, Lieutenant. Can't say I agree with her methods, but I don't have any particular love for the Kilrathi either. Politics and edicts aside, this is about saving our butts. And we're all pretty good at that. Stand by. Ready now? Break and attack!"

Still confused, Maniac shrugged and obeyed the order, looping back to fly inverted relative to the oncoming cruisers. He rolled upright and tensed as he surveyed the scene. The Fralthi-class cruisers had spread themselves into a wide, flat arrowhead, with the destroyer lining up behind like the arrow's shaft. The radar scope showed the dreadnought and superdreadnought positioned well behind them, spearing their way forward on full impulse. Strangely enough, they held their fire, letting the cruisers and destroyer communicate for them. And given their position, maybe they wouldn't launch fighters. One hundred and fifty from the cruisers still gave the cats a roughly two-to-one advantage.

Okay. What do we got? The battle group's flagship and an escort are hanging back. This tells me they want the Olympus *intact. Of course they want the ship. They want the drive. And they'll use that destroyer to deploy boarding details. Subtle the cats ain't. Then again, that pack hunter mentality might come into play. Maybe they're driving us forward, toward another battle group that'll spring and attack. No way, man. Don't get that paranoid.*

A proximity alarm squawked. Maniac frantically scanned the HUD, then rolled onto his side as a pair of torpedoes streaked by with a salvo of antimatter fire running shadow.

"Oh my god," somebody said over the general channel. "Look."

Maniac leveled off, and as he dived toward the lead Fralthi, he suddenly realized that her trio of antimatter guns had fallen silent, that her tube doors had closed, and that her bow began pitching down a few degrees. Despite that, wave after wave of Dralthi fighters fled like hungry bats from her cavernous flight tubes, as they did from the other two cruisers.

"Okay, our first bombing squadron is clear," Santyana shouted. "Let's bait those fighters."

Scanning the comm channel list, Maniac found Blair's private frequency and tapped for the link. "You mind telling me what's going on? Does Aristee have spies aboard that cruiser or what?"

"Why are you sweating the details? Just do the job. You got my wing." Blair cut the channel.

Whatever. Maniac kept Blair's Rapier in his field of view as it jerked into a high-G climb that beckoned a trio of Dralthi pulling away from the cruiser. "Got three taking a sniff," he told Blair. "Maintain that heading. I'm coming in behind to skin 'em."

"Do me a favor?" Blair asked. "Don't miss."

"Me? You've lost your memory, Ace."

An old girlfriend had once asked Maniac if he had ever grown tired of dogfights. Wasn't it the same old thing, time and again? You fly into the furball, try to get a bead on the enemy, fire, and blow him away. So what? That wasn't profound or artistic. And didn't he suffer from the cookie factory syndrome and have an aversion to flying unless it pertained to his job? And hadn't he grown tired of bragging about the missions, describing the same types of situations, using the same old words? *I came in from his eleven o'clock, swooped to line up on his six, got the lock, thumbed off the safety, and wham, I'll take mine extra-crispy. Hey, can I buy you another one of those, sweetheart?*

Even if he kept a journal of his exploits, it would hardly amount to a reflection of literary depth or afford him a meaningful look at his psyche.

So what kept him going?

"It's the juice, honey. The feeling it gives you. You can't duplicate that anywhere else. And it's different every time. Yeah, the words get old, and sometimes the kill is the same. But the feeling . . . it's always different. Keeps me coming back."

And the juice did, indeed, course through Maniac as he studied the three Dralthis closing in on Blair and issued a voice command to the Tempest targeting computer. "Missile select? Guided. I want two. Multiple launch on my mark."

"Ordnance ready," came the AI's breathy, female voice that had once roused Maniac into a fit of dirty talk.

"All right. Let's take a look." He swiped the HUD viewer over his eye and waited until the smart targeting reticle appeared and locked on. "Mark!"

Two guided missiles ignited on their upper port and starboard mounts—

And Maniac jammed down the primary weapons trigger, express-delivering synchronous neutron fire to the center Dralthi, no signature required.

The Rapier's wings shook as the missiles thundered off, adding to the potent vibration generated by the fighter's rotary barrel cannon.

Fountains of diaphanous blue energy clouded the center Dralthi's shields. Maniac kept the fire coming and kept hard on the cat's tail until the pilot rolled to port and suddenly dove.

Even as Maniac slammed the stick forward to pursue, his missiles struck the other two Dralthis. The feline fireworks showered overhead as he stayed with the last cat.

"Only two?" Blair teased. "You got rusty lying in that cell."

With a quick snort in reply, Maniac dedicated himself to the last Dralthi's destruction—just to shut up his wingman. The enemy's shields finally dropped for the count, and Maniac let his neutron gun play connect the rivets on virgin plastisteel as the alien transmitted a taunt.

"No honor is greater!" the Kilrathi cried in a poor attempt at standard speech. The thing stared at Maniac with those pissyellow softballs it called eyes. "You apes will never know such glory! Ahhhhhhh!"

"Got news for you, pal. I'm feeling pretty glorious right now." Maniac grinned as he corkscrewed a path through the fiery garbage. "And that's three, Blair. You were saying something about being rusty?" He turned on a wing, slashing back to regroup.

Meanwhile, the four Broadsword bombers below had come within torpedo range of the lead Fralthi, and while their fighter escorts warded off attacking Dralthi and a few Salthi light fighters that had joined the fray, the bombers each launched a pair of torpedoes at the foundering cruiser. Maniac could not help but watch for a second as the eight projectiles struck in succession, blasting apart the cap ship's port bow, her superstructure, and tearing gaping breeches amidships. Four hundred and seventy-five meters of Kilrathi engineering began to break apart, illumined by the flickering light of her explosions. Nutrient gas streamed from at least a dozen ruptures in her hull and formed long, emerald pennons that trailed the devastation. Tattered pieces of plastisteel tumbled and glimmered, and a few of the Rapiers nearby narrowly avoided colliding with some of the larger rubble.

"Maniac? Blair? Get back to the destroyer and lend those escorts a hand," Santyana ordered. "The rest of you stay with the two cruisers. The one to port has ceased fire."

"Jesus," Maniac gasped. "I don't know how Aristee's doing this, but if she can take out a Kilrathi battle group this easily, then how does Confed brass expect to stop her?"

"We haven't taken out this group yet," Santyana reminded. "Move it."

Complying with a burst of thrust, Maniac soared up beside Blair's Rapier. They darted over the two remaining cruisers and dove forty-five degrees toward the Ralari-class destroyer in the rear. The ship's two turreted lasers wreaked equal opportunity destruction and had already crippled three of the seventeen Rapiers escorting the bombers. Another three Rapiers had broken off to tractor in those pilots who had ejected.

Still, the destroyer's lasers weren't the most serious threat.

Her twin-barrel antimatter gun swiveled and tracked the bombers, then belched out a humbling and steady flow that had the entire group suddenly dispersing as salvos ripped through the phantoms of those crafts.

A flash from the radar scope now showed a band of red blips that represented a full squadron of Dralthis coming in from Maniac's six o'clock low. "Multiple hostiles bearing four two-four by six-one-three. Range: one point five Ks. They'll reach us first, Blair. My little sweetheart AI counts nineteen."

"Reverse course on my mark," Blair said, his masked face abruptly lighting the VDU. "Let's tie 'em up for a while."

"You want to play chicken with nineteen Dralthi? Look, I've noticed that you can't use your 'Pilgrim' call sign here. Makes for a little confusion. But now I'm thinking you deserve mine. No way in hell am I going to play chicken with nineteen Dralthi."

"We'll kill thrusters and hit the brakes about a hundred meters out for a little over and under S and S."

"Now you're talking. But we haven't pulled that one since training. What the hell. I get top, clockwise rotation."

"And I got control. Steady now. Mark!"

They peeled away, with Blair banking to port, Maniac to starboard, and came around to reassume their formation flying abreast. The Dralthi hurtled toward them like a heated braid of silver and tarnished copper that would for a few seconds wholly deceive the casual observer.

"Range: six hundred meters."

"Oh, God," Blair said through an audible shiver. "Back there this seemed like a good idea."

"Hey, I say that myself—usually when I'm climbing out of her bed the next morning and can't remember her name. Range: four hundred meters."

Hungry for their first kill, the cats opened up with wing-mounted laser cannons. Bolts perforated the vacuum around Maniac's Rapier, and a trio spattered across his forward shield and sent shock waves ripping through the ship. He thought better of adjusting course, though. Any change would ruin their ploy.

"About ten seconds now," Blair cried. "Merlin says that the odds of us taking out all nineteen are—"

"Unless he's taking bets, tell the old geezer to shut up."

Maniac fastened his gaze to the nav clock and its pretty green numbers that blithely ticked off the final seconds.

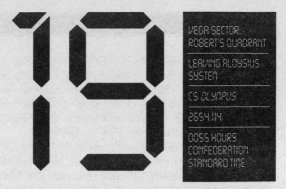

VEGA SECTOR,
ROBERT'S QUADRANT

LEAVING ALOYSIUS
SYSTEM

CS OLYMPUS

2654.114

0055 HOURS
CONFEDERATION
STANDARD TIME

Hard brake. Cramp in shoulders. Damned harness. Velocity zero. Holy . . . They're right on top of us! Maneuvering thrusters: fire. Commence rotation. Neutron cannon engaged . . .

Maniac had positioned himself about ten meters directly over Blair. They held their coordinates and broke into clockwise and counter-clockwise flat spins, creating deadly girandoles of fire. The tactic, dubbed a "sit-'n'-spin," worked well if you were alone and well away from your comrades since whatever entered your cone of fire would wind up dead meat, whether you wanted it dead meat or not. Not many pilots would attempt a duel spin since one misfire of manuerving jets could result in point-blank friendly fire—certainly no way to get friendly.

But Maniac and Blair had perfected the maneuver. With the tap of a switch, he had turned over maneuvering to Blair as the Dralthi fanned out and climbed, seconds away from swooping down and attacking them from above. Blair rolled both Rapiers onto their sides so that they fired vertically relative to the Dralthi. He continued the roll, adjusting course as necessary and producing gyroscopic inertia and precession, forces that, despite the dampeners, they could not sustain for long without blacking out.

As Maniac tightened his stomach and forced bile back down his throat, he caught the barest glimpse of a Dralthi breaking apart under Blair's fire, then he spotted another disassembling under his own wrath. Red blips on the scope broke off and knifed back toward the bombers and escorts. Just as well. Shadows crept into Maniac's peripheral vision. Time to call it.

"Stalled them as long as we could," Blair said, probably feeling the same effect. "Slowing to break link. Five seconds."

After a slight thump, control returned, and Maniac eased on the throttle, pulling forward and away from Blair's Rapier. He savored the few seconds he had to compose himself, then rolled back to glide over his wingman.

About a quarter klick ahead, the destroyer turned hard to starboard, retreating from the bombers and fighters. A beep from Maniac's radar scope alerted him to the presence of a vessel much larger than a fighter: one of the Fralthi-class cruisers; it too retreated from the *Olympus,* with a squadron of Pilgrim bombers diving toward its six. Behind it, a portico of sparking rubble forged a gateway back to the *Olympus.*

So Aristee's people had somehow taken out two of the Fralthi-class cruisers and now had the third cruiser and the destroyer on the run. The dreadnought and superdreadnought kept their distance but continued to follow the *Olympus*, and Maniac figured that the cruiser and destroyer would regroup with them. He guessed that Aristee didn't have spies aboard the surviving Kilrathi ships since they continued to rattle off anti-starcraft fire or retain their present headings.

The bombers hunting down the cruiser found their locks and unloaded their ordnance in an exhibition of well-choreographed firepower. Like the fingers of some enormous hand, the torpedoes descended upon the cruiser.

But the ship's antimatter guns found three of those fingers off its aft quarter and detonated them harmlessly over the hull. The explosions tossed a fourth torpedo into a fifth, driving both well off course and into a concentrated burst of laser fire that turned their destructive capacities inward. The sixth projectile locked onto a cloud of chaff twinkling and expanding in the cruiser's wash and lifted a white-hot explosion that swallowed the last two torpedoes. Eight shots. Eight misses. The bombers pulled out of their run in sixty-degree climbs, then, as though with their tails between their legs, beat a full-throttle retreat back toward the *Olympus*.

Meanwhile, the bombers targeting the destroyer fared no better. Maniac drew closer to the scene as antimatter fire, superheated countermeasure cones, and what he deemed lucky guided missile strikes by Dralthi pilots lashed at or lured away the ordnance. The last torpedo met its fate by cannon fire as he and Blair buzzed over the destroyer, all but ignored by squadrons of Dralthi and Salthi fighters hightailing it back to the flagship.

"Looks like they're cutting their losses," Santyana said. "Eighth Squadron? Let's cut our own. Return to base."

Nearly in unison, Maniac and Blair pulled away from the destroyer and aimed for a loose blue wreath of thrusters. Maniac flicked back his HUD viewer, massaged weary eyes, then pulled up Blair's channel. "Nice little spin back there, Ace. Next time I got the stick."

"Fair enough," Blair answered, blinking clear his vision and looking about as spent as Maniac.

"So I'm still sweating the details. How did Aristee get those cruisers to cease fire?"

"Like this."

Maniac's head snapped up as an unseen fist struck a mild blow to his chin. "Hey, what the—"

"Some of us, not many, have this thing, an extrakinetic power they call it. Kind of like telekinesis, telepathy, and extrasensory perception, only different is the way we experience it. And it's pretty deadly if we want it to be."

"How'd you get it? You're only half Pilgrim?"

"Guess I got lucky," Blair answered, sounding anything but. "And you know what? I thought about using it to bring down a few of those fighters. But to kill someone like that . . . I don't know . . . it's supposed to make you feel kind of dead yourself.

When you touch inanimate objects, it gives you the shakes like you wouldn't believe."

"Does that mean you can read minds like your girlfriend? Like maybe you can read Zarya's mind and let me know what's up with her? And poker! Holy shit, man. We can make a killing."

"Some of us can access scripts and read thoughts. But I'm not sure if I have or not. It's like I can talk to other people in my head, but that's it."

Maniac rubbed his chin. "Punching me from over there . . . that still ain't bad. Can you squeeze a woman's breasts like that? And what did you say? Access the script? You lost me there."

"I'm not squeezing any breasts with this, you idiot. Look, I'll tell you the rest when we get back. We'll have plenty of time."

"You mean when we get back to our cells? I'm not going."

"Wasn't too long ago when you wouldn't leave."

"We're out here now. We got the firepower. Let's take the shot, disable the ship. Some properly placed missiles to her ion engines will take 'em offline. Hopper drive's down, so she can't skip out. A comm drone carrying our mayday would only take about a week or two to reach the trade routes. It's not like we'd be stranded out here for long."

"Uh, excuse me, but that battle group, or at least what's left of it, is still pursuing. That ship's our only ride. And even if we move in to attack, her cannon operators—or even pilots from this squadron—will be on us before we get off a shot. Besides, can you imagine what would happen if the Kilrathi got their hands on the hopper drive?"

"Yeah, I can. They would, like Aristee, use it to destroy Earth. And your point?"

"Tell you what. We lose this battle group, then *maybe* I'll consider your plan."

"Chris, we swore an oath. We have to do this. We won't get another chance."

"You don't know that. And like I said, if we disable the *Olympus*, then the cats get her. Hell, they get us. They're carnivores. I heard they eat live prey."

"Wait a minute. You said Aristee took out the other cruisers by using Pilgrims with that, what was it, extrakinetic thing? Those Pilgrims are on board the *Olympus*, right?"

"Yeah, so what?"

The idea unfolded a little more and drove Maniac to straighten in his seat. "Then that battle group is no problem. We disable the *Olympus*, draw in the Kilrathi, then Aristee unleashes her people. We kill two birds. You with me?"

"I don't know."

Admiral Vukar beat a fist on the control panel beside Tactical Officer Makorshk. "I said why?"

"And I'll repeat, my Kalralahr. I'm not sure." Makorshk clenched his own fist but kept it resting steadily on the panel. "After we lost contact, her defense systems came down. She did launch fighters, but they also lost contact with her. It seems both cruisers suffered the same fate, which, my Kalralahr, I'm at a loss to explain."

"Interesting. For once you don't have all the answers."

Vukar tore himself away from the tactical station and tramped to the viewport. Out there in the void, beyond the wash of infrared radiation that appeared like a bloodred foam to his eyes, the supercruiser streaked off unabated, carrying with it a drive of enormous power and another weapon arguably even more powerful. And maybe the destruction of two cruisers represented but a mere glance at its potential.

"Kalralahr?" He spun toward Comm Officer Ta'kar'ki's station. "I've been scanning the recordings of intership communications. You must see this."

Vukar took several hurried strides and arrived behind Ta'kar'ki. A holograph of a communications officer making a routine report flickered above the station. Sans forewarning, the warrior's head shook violently and his eyes snapped close. He shrieked, extended his claws, and began gouging out his own eyes as static filtered into and washed clean the transmission. Vukar held himself a moment, considering the horrific image. He felt hot breath pass across his neck and cocked his head to find Makorshk seething behind him. "Comment?"

"Interesting. Now I *do* have an answer." The tactical officer returned to his station and quickly buried himself in his displays.

Expecting that in a moment Makorshk would share his findings, Vukar paused at the comm station and waited.

The moment passed, but the second fang ignored Vukar and the other officers, everything save for his data.

With his blood frenzy reawakened and thoughts of initiating the challenge here and now, Vukar crossed to Makorshk's station and once more beat his fist on the control panel, jarring the tactical officer. "If you have an answer, let's hear it!"

"I've just scanned data that we recovered during the Terran-Pilgrim War. What we just saw? It's nothing new. Some Pilgrims, not many, possess a form of telekinesis that they can use as a weapon. However, their precepts rule against such use. The Confederation hunted down as many of these Pilgrims as they could, but it seems a few got away. I'm certain that's what we're dealing with now."

"We're not *dealing* with them. We're being *slaughtered* by them. But why this method now? Why not use their hopper drive? Can they still engage it?"

"I don't believe they can. I ran a multi-emission scan of the ship, searching for evidence of a reaction containment field or other controlled matter-antimatter reactions. I found none, which may mean their drive is offline, possibly for repairs. If it were not, then yes, why would they turn to their brethren for help and break their own precepts? The gravity well would kill us far more efficiently. And there's another interesting fact. The Confederation was able to capture many of these Pilgrims because once they reach out and kill a life form, they need time to recover, sometimes as long as several standard days."

"What if those Pilgrims expended most of their energy on our cruisers? That would mean . . . ."

"Yes, Kalrahalr. Now *you* are the one with the answers."

Vukar repressed his reaction. No sense in letting the bridge crew see his amusement over Makorshk's compliment, perhaps the first he had ever given. Vukar shifted to the comm station and gave the order: "Dispatch our cruiser and destroyer. Launch all fighters from the dreadnought to escort. This time the Caxki clan will take her."

The command chair felt too small, and the bulkheads seemed to inch a little closer toward Amity Aristee. She bolted from her seat, her breath coming in an uneven burst. The XO, seated at the port observation station to study a tactical report, glanced back and registered his concern.

"Captain?" That from Sostur Charity, the radar officer on duty. "The Kilrathi cruiser and destroyer are breaking ahead of the battle group. Count one-eight-seven bandits in escort."

"How many?"

"One-eight-seven, ma'am. A combined force from the cruiser and dreadnought."

Aristee nearly lunged back to her command chair, slid over the comm screen mounted on a swivel arm, and dialed up the aft observation bubble. "Brotur Zimbaka?"

No response. She hit the override to engage the comm unit's camera and remote operate it from the bridge. She panned across the wide, circular room crowned by a hemisphere of Plexi, spotted the narrow columns of telescopic imaging components, then something told her to pan down.

Zimbaka and the nine others who had agreed to help lay on the floor, some shivering violently, some staring off at a cold tomb of horrors. Zimbaka himself sat up with his knees pulled into his chest. His head jittered, his eyes looked red and clouded, and his mouth hung open. Drool dripped from his chin.

"Brotur Zimbaka?"

He tilted his head a fraction to the left, as though recognizing her voice, but continued to shake, to drool, to remain lost in a labyrinth of pain.

She called again. No reaction.

Aristee banged off the comm unit and regarded Sostur Charity. "How long until the Kilrathi are in cannon range?"

"They're accelerating to one-five-zero. ETA to cannon range, three-point-three-one minutes."

At least the cats would only launch a limited torpedo barrage and not call upon their new Skipper missile. They clearly intended to take the ship intact. They would, as they just had, direct their fire toward the ion engines to disable the ship. And without the help of Karista Mullens and the others, the cruiser might get in close enough to deliver the crippling blow. The seventy or so Rapiers left in Aristee's complement would surely be overrun by the Dralthi, even with James's help out there. She clutched the arm of her command chair, closed her eyes, and groped for a solution. Groped again. Something now . . . something . . .

Eyes open.

Fingers tapped hard on the comm touchpad.

"Yes, Captain," Karista Mullens said, staring nervously at the camera.

"Sostur. You and I need to talk. I'm coming down."

Maniac shifted course three degrees to starboard. The targeting reticle rested squarely over the *Olympus*'s portside ion engine. Range: four-zero-nine meters. The computer continued to flash warnings along the perimeter of his HUD, which he translated as, Hey, you're targeting your own ship. *Sorry, honey, but this isn't my ship at all.* "Maniac is locked on," he told Blair.

"Locked myself, but I'm picking up something right on the fringe. Can't get an ID yet. Looks big, though. Maybe we should—"

"No way. This is it. I'm making the run, with or without you. And like you said, at any second the cannon operators or other pilots will get wise."

Blair sighed in resignation. "All right. This is the right thing. This is what we have to do."

"That's right. Keep convincing yourself. I'm telling you, it's all going to work out. Let's get in just a little—"

"Whoa, whoa, whoa," Blair cried. "Something moving into

her wash. Searching . . . Aw, shit. It's a Rapier, alternating course between exhaust nodules."

"It'll be the memory of a Rapier in two seconds," Maniac promised.

"Break off," Paladin ordered, assuming an expression of unflappable calm as he piloted the fighter shielding the *Olympus*'s engines.

Maniac scowled at the display. "No, sir. *You* break off. Otherwise I'll wax your ass. *Sir*."

"Lieutenant, you won't get that chance. The big guns'll shovel enough antimatter fire into your face to make you burst into flames before you get off a shot. Every nerve in your body will register the sensation of being burned alive. Don't believe me? Scan the ship. You're dancing in their sights."

"Like I care, *Pilgrim*. I'll go out doing the right thing, not selling out to the goddamned enemy. How do you live with yourself? You're supposed to be a commodore, for God's sake. All it takes is one whiff of Pilgrim poontang?"

"Sir?" Blair cut in. "I know you've done everything you can to get Aristee to stand down. But she obviously won't. It's time to act. And if we die now, well, we knew that could happen going in."

"Mr. Blair, this won't solve anything, and you'll lose your lives for nothing."

"But we can do this now," Blair implored him. "Why don't you help us? We can disable the ship and put an end to all of this."

"Yes, we'll end everything. The cats will get the ship. We'll die. Wrong ending, Lieutenant."

"What about Aristee's people, the ones with the extrakinetic thing?" Maniac asked. "Why doesn't she just let 'em loose on the cats?"

"She did. They're incapacitated now. Could be days before they recover. And gentlemen? It gets more interesting. Seems that the Kilrathi have done their homework. They've realized what we threw at them, figured out that our Pilgrims need down time, so they've launched another assault. The cruiser and the destroyer are inbound, along with nearly two hundred fighters. We have about seventy or so Rapiers to throw at them. The bombers have headed in to reload." He paused to take a long breath. "Still want to disable the ship?"

"Maybe I do," Maniac answered. "Maybe when Aristee knows the cats are going to take possession, she'll blow it up. We die, yeah. But the Confederation wins."

Blair stifled a laugh. "You're so full of shit, Maniac. You love yourself too much. You want to win *and* live."

"I'm not going back to that cell. I'm not going to sit around while this ass-kisser undermines the Confederation and everything we believe in. Mr. Taggart? You have five seconds to break off."

"You do this, and maybe I'll come in behind you and wax *your* ass," Blair said.

Maniac gritted his teeth and snorted. "You've got the aim but not the balls. Hey, Taggart? You're out of time."

As Maniac throttled up and brought the burners on line, his skin crawled as he thought about being burned alive.

"Todd! Don't do it!" Blair unbuckled his oxygen mask and vigorously shook his head.

Disregarding the display, Maniac forged on, two guided missiles ready to drop away from his wings and alter the *Olympus*'s destiny. He eyed the supercruiser's aftmost antimatter cannon. The second he saw it flash, he would thumb off the missiles.

"Listen to me, Todd. We might just die anyway. All we can do is try to outrun the Kilrathi and tie up as many of their fighters as we can. Didn't you say that you'd rather be killed by the Kilrathi?"

Clever trick, Blair. Twisting my words. I said I'd rather get killed by the cats than by our own people, but when I said our own people, I wasn't talking about Pilgrims. They might as well be the Kilrathi.

"Lieutenant Marshall, I'm locked on to your fighter, as is the cannon above me," the commodore said. "Even if you get off your missiles before we smoke you, we'll still have time to take them out. Young man, I want you to take a deep breath and *think*."

"That's all I've been doing. Now I'm going to take a deep breath and act."

Like a pair of yellow eyes fringed in blue, the *Olympus*'s massive ion engines swelled into view, with the shimmering dot of the commodore's Rapier swerving like a pendulum between them.

"I am right on your six," Blair suddenly said. "Locked on to your stubborn butt. Let's call this and fight the real enemy."

"Like I thought," Maniac muttered. "I'm alone."

The antimatter cannon flashed.

Maniac flicked his thumb twice on the secondary weapons trigger while using his free hand to flick aside the safety and punch the ejection button. Half-muffled explosions ringed the cockpit, and Maniac felt his shoulders slam toward his chest as the pod's thrusters swept him up and away from the Rapier—

Just a few breaths before a gleaming net of antimatter fire devoured the stubby-winged fighter.

To the stern, a phosphorescent thorn of debris nearly caught Blair's Rapier before he banked to dodge it.

Maniac fixed his gaze on the antimatter cannon as it swiveled to track him. A pair of flashes to his four o'clock revealed that the commodore had, in fact, intercepted the guided missiles.

"I'm wheeling around to get you," Blair said. "I'll tow you back in."

But the commodore apparently had something else in mind. "Stay where you are, Mr. Blair."

As Maniac stared down the barrels of the antimatter cannon and pried as much thrust as he could out of the pod's meager engines, putting more distance between himself and that cannon, he decided what he would do if another flash came. He armed the self-destruct system, routing control to his stick. One tap on the primary weapons trigger would end his life—and at least *he* would be the one to do that, a pilot to the end, not wasted by traitors, his death the ultimate act of defiance. He jerked away the HUD viewer, unbuckled his mask. The VDU remained dark. Instruments ticked, beeped, and hummed, and the pod's thrusters issued their rhythmic bursts. It took but another second for the moment to unravel the remnants of his nerves. "C'mon? What are you waiting for? Fire!"

"Brotur Syllian?" Paladin called, using the general frequency for Maniac's benefit. "Is your cannon locked on to the pod?"

"It is, Brotur. Awaiting your order."

"Release lock. New target: incoming cruiser. Compute firing solution now," Paladin said tersely. "Mr. Blair? Take Lieutenant Marshall to the *Olympus*. Reload and refuel, then get back in the fight."

"Aye-aye, sir."

"Hey, Blair," Maniac called, having switched to the private channel. "Now that they've let down their guard, you can make your own run."

"Are you drunk, dense, or deaf? The plan won't work."

"I've revised the plan. It's now about getting Aristee to destroy the ship."

"I know the commodore's working on a better way out of this. I just know it."

Maniac fell back hard against his seat as Blair's retrieval beam clutched the pod, shifted it behind Blair's fighter, then began towing it toward the aft flight deck's launch and landing tunnel. "Blair, when are you going to realize that we can't trust Taggart anymore?"

"Don't write him off yet. Just give him more time."

"We've been there. How much more? A year? Two? A lifetime? This 'more time' bullshit is just that."

"Well, this is interesting. The commodore just told me that they have another Rapier for you. It's an old F44-A but still functional. He wants you in it and out here ASAP."

"Proves my point what an idiot he is. Now he's going to put me back in another Rapier? Hell, I'll just make another run at the engines."

"You're going to be a little too busy for that. Check your scope. Here they come now."

A dense band of blips crept up from the bottom of Maniac's radar display. The commodore had said that nearly two hundred Kilrathi fighters were inbound, but the words hadn't seemed real.

Now the radar image provided one hell of a reality check.

"I'm sorry, Sostur, but there is no way you can make us do this. We've already seen what it's done to Brotur Zimbaka and the rest. We won't help under any circumstances."

Aristee stepped farther into Karista Mullens's meager quarters. Dozens of oil paintings of scantily-clad Pilgrim dancers leaned against the bulkheads, along with a sundry of homemade musical instruments, including the Pilgrim *soultom* and *soultar*, variations on the ancient drum and guitar. Aristee nearly tripped over a stack of smaller, unframed artwork piled beside a standard issue desk chair. "I won't explain it again. I won't ask you again. You say you and the others won't help under any circumstances? Then I'll gather you up, take you to an airlock, and jettison you one by one. No, strike that. That's too clumsy and slow. I'll take you down to the flight deck and have you stroll through an energy curtain. That's quicker, and we'll have a little audience."

Mullens, her back pressed against a hatch leading into the latrine, seemed to expect such a threat and gave a microscopic nod. "We're prepared to die."

"Maybe *you* are because you've met your pair and he's not, well, he's not all that you've dreamed of. But the others? I don't think they're ready to die—especially the younger ones—and none of you are ready to watch your broturs and sosturs lose their lives."

"You won't kill us. You need us."

"But if you won't help me, then you're worthless. Most of you lack military training. Not one of you is a pilot—except Blair— and he's out there. You consume resources and return nothing save for your artistic diversions. We can live without them."

"But you won't live. None of us will. Maybe that is Ivar Chu's will. Maybe we shouldn't fight it."

"It's not his will that we die," Aristee said, nearly tasting the bitterness and futility of the notion. "If you want to know his will, then speak with the protur."

"We *don't* recognize that man as the protur."

Aristee held back her snicker; no sense in wasting any more emotion on the woman. "We're finished here. You and the others will be taken to the flight deck." She went for the exit, then halted under a thought. "You've assumed a position of leadership among them. It's not easy to watch your people die. I'll be sure to kill you last, so you'll understand exactly what I mean."

20

VEGA SECTOR,
ROBERT'S QUADRANT

PERIMETER ALOYSIUS
SYSTEM

CS OLYMPUS

2654.114

0122 HOURS
CONFEDERATION
STANDARD TIME

Blair carefully shifted the miniature joystick on the tractor retrieval system's panel, setting down Maniac's pod on one of the aft flight deck's circular orange pads designated for such emergency landings. With Maniac safely grounded, Blair cut the beam and glided forward, following the deck boss's cues until he slipped into a repair bay.

Under the shadows of two colossal durasteel braces, he kept his Rapier in a hover as a Pilgrim crew of three performed the hazardous operation of refueling and rearming a hot fighter. He exchanged a few words with the crew chief regarding the Rapier's status, then gave a final admonishment to Maniac before the pilot left his ejection pod. Aristee did not have a Pilgrim Marine waiting for Maniac; instead, the flight boss herself had elected to leave control and come down to personally welcome back the ship's now most infamous pilot. The woman's Pilgrim robe failed to disguise her considerable girth, and despite being a full head shorter than Maniac, she stared up at him, seeming to curl into the folds of her body like a rattlesnake before the strike. Blair grinned broadly as he watched Maniac flinch under the old lady's oration.

Behind them, a ragged line of people under the scrutiny of four Pilgrim Marines walked along the catwalk. The Pilgrims forged on toward the twenty-meter-high maintenance curtain, descended the staircase to the runway level, then paused at the red line marking the field's four-meter safety zone. A blur of white from the catwalk signaled the entrance of Amity Aristee. She beat a quick two-four rhythm down the stairs, paced as though inspecting the group, then spoke.

"What's up with them?" Blair asked his chief.

"Don't know."

One of the women in the group turned her head, and goose-flesh ran a marathon across Blair's shoulders and arms. Karista Mullens. His pair. But why was she here? Hadn't Aristee convinced her and the rest to bring down the two cruisers? Shouldn't they all be recovering? Blair swore over the fact that he couldn't get out and ask. Maybe they had already recovered and were getting ready for the next battle? That would be good news to the poor souls sitting in Rapiers who probably stared slack-jawed at the angry horde of Kilrathi fighters barreling toward them.

A wave of something passed through the group. Was is it shock? Fear? Some of the Pilgrims clutched each other. A chubby blond boy no more than ten or twelve gripped Karista's waist and began to cry.

The flight deck trembled a second as a Broadsword passed through the energy curtain like a finger through gelatin. Once the ship roared clear, a short, gray-haired man with slightly hunched shoulders detached himself from the group. Under the vigilance of the nearest Marine guard, the old man crossed the red line and shambled toward the fluctuating field. Blair's pulse raced as the man lifted his arms, giving himself to the unthinking, unfeeling wall of energy.

"What's he—" The crew chief broke off.

Blair engaged the external microphone, even as the old man shrieked and stepped into the curtain.

One voice in Blair's head implored him to turn away. But

another, more powerful voice appealed to his dark fascination for things horrific. The old man's head melted into shoulders as they melted into his chest in a swirling, hissing mixture of pale white, blue, and wine-dark red. His arms flailed a moment before they peeled back like a pair of lit matches. He shrank into a lumpy puddle that swelled across the flight deck and into the vacuum on the other side of the curtain. Out there, steaming goo stretched and broke apart like taffy and began floating away.

The man's death, or, more precisely, his execution, made Blair realize what was happening. Some Pilgrims had obviously helped Aristee—but not these. Those who had helped were now recovering. Those who had refused would now be sent into the curtain.

One of the Marines near the rear came forward, seized the boy by the back of the neck, tugged him off of Karista, and drove him toward the red line.

Blair hit the canopy release.

The crew chief's voice buzzed loudly in his headset. "Hey! What are you doing? You have to stay in the pit and monitor the flow."

"What's it look like I'm doing?" Blair tore off his mask and helmet, unbuckled only one side of his harness, then wrenched himself free. The canopy chinked into place behind him, and the overpowering din of his thrusters pressed on him like thick pillows. He stood on his seat, levered himself out of the cockpit, then dropped two meters to the deck.

"Come back here, Brotur!"

But Blair had already bounded away from the fighter. It would take much more than a command from a Pilgrim crew chief to stop him. He sprinted onto the runway, inspiring a chorus of shouting from the rest of his crew and the techs working the area. A hollow drumming resonated from the energy curtain to his left, and he cocked his head as another Broadsword bomber injected itself into the bay, sweeping just a meter above the deck. The bomber's blunt, durasteel nose came headlong at him—

Even as the reflex to duck sent him belly-flopping to the deck.

The bomber rumbled over as he slapped palms over his ears and pressed his cheek to the cold metal. Out of the corner of his eye, he saw the aft, portside landing skid cleaving toward him with just a quarter meter gap between it and the deck. With palms still glued to his ears, he rolled left, onto his elbow, as the skid scraped along his chest and finally moved clear.

The bellow of thrusters faded behind him, and he removed his hands from his ears—but another sound even more painful erupted ahead.

"No! I can't!" shrieked the boy. "I'm sorry! I don't want to die!"

Heavy boots thudded on the catwalk above. Blair didn't bother to look. That would be deck security, out to apprehend him. He sprang to his feet and charged toward the Marine strong-arming the boy. Others in the group shouted and bawled as the boy swung wildly at the Marine's chest plate.

"Let him go!" Blair ordered, reaching reflexively to his hip for his C–244 pistol. Of course, the Pilgrims had not issued him a sidearm or utility knife.

"Blair?" That shout from Karista.

As he came within a few meters of the Marine, the guy craned his head, swung up his rifle. "Right there, mister."

Blair whirled to face Aristee. "What is this?"

"None of your concern, Brotur. Get back to your fighter"—she tipped her head toward the Marine—"or he'll shoot you where you stand."

"You're killing them because they won't help? That it? Pilgrim fascism at its finest, eh?"

"*Get back to your fighter! Now!*"

"No." He gave her a moment to let that sink in, then added, "I won't let you do it. You'll have to shoot."

Karista scuffled toward him, her eyes ringed in shadows and doused pink. "Don't get involved in this."

"You're going to let her kill all of you?"

"We won't help. We won't break the edict. And if this is our fate, then—"

"Break the goddamned edict!"

"We can't. Don't you understand? We just can't."

"I don't understand. How could you stand by and watch that old man die? How can you watch this kid die? How can you do that?"

"Because she's stubborn. And foolish," said Aristee. "And mostly because she's selfish. All of them are selfish. For centuries parents have let their sick children die because their religious convictions would not allow them to seek medical treatment. As Pilgrims, I thought we were beyond that kind of irrational devotion. I thought we were rewriting the laws here, establishing a stronger bond, a stronger community than we've ever had before. But some of us refuse to let go of the old ways. Some of us would rather die than do so." She gave an exaggerated nod as her gaze passed over the group and finally settled on Blair. "Last warning. Get back to your fighter."

A howl from above split the air. Blair jerked to spot Maniac launching himself from atop the catwalk railing to plunge four meters down, colliding with the Marine guard holding the boy. All three slammed to the deck.

Maniac got his hands on the Marine's rifle, tore it free, then rolled up, alternating his aim between the guard and Aristee.

The boy whimpered and crawled a few meters away, then rose and scampered to Karista.

With a groan, the Marine sat up and slowly raised his palms. A black grin curled his lips as a trio of beeps resounded from the rear.

The three other guards had armed their rifles and now trained them on Maniac, who eyed the jarheads and said, "Guess we're all pretty good shots here. I'll take out the captain, you take me. You get your kill. But so do I."

A chill in Blair's neck announced the approach of something else, something that panned out as the flight deck shook under the first strike of Kilrathi cannons belting out rounds from long range.

"We don't have time for this little standoff," Aristee said.

"Mister, what is it, Marshall? You have a habit of getting your-self into no-win situations. Bravo. You've done it again."

"Captain," Blair called, stepping in front of Maniac. "I'll help you. I'm not that good at manipulating the fields yet, but I'll help."

"You bastard," Maniac shouted. "You Pilgrim bastard. I knew you'd sell out—just like your goddamned buddy. Now that I think about it, you've had the power to kill her all along."

"I'm not selling out," Blair snapped. "And killing her isn't going to stop this. The XO, the protur, McDaniel, or someone else would carry on."

"Then kill them all."

"Right. And have no one left to monitor the ship's systems or direct this battle. Forget it. The priority right now is staying alive." He softened his expression as he addressed the group. "Listen to me. All of you. What good are your laws if all they get you is dead? Aren't they supposed to enhance and give order to your lives? Your laws obviously don't apply here. Anybody who wants to live can join me. Pretty simple."

Wiping away his tears, the boy stepped cautiously toward Blair, then took up a position beside him. A middle-aged woman found a place beside the boy. Then a young man with shoulder-length black hair circled around and set a palm on the boy's shoulder.

"Blair, you can't do this," Karista said.

It hurt to face her. "I'm sorry."

Two more of the sixteen Pilgrims defected to his side.

"Hey, Karista? Maybe we should start our own team," Mani-ac said. "Looks like you, me, and the captain are the only ones loyal to our beliefs"—he turned a malicious gaze on Blair—"which *are* worth dying for."

Blair mirrored the look but clung to his silence.

Aristee brightened and turned to the group assembling behind Blair. "I'll have you escorted to the aft observation bubble. And if you want to believe in something right now, believe in your right to live."

"I'm going with them," Blair told Maniac. "My fighter's almost ready. Take it."

"No, I think Mr. Marshall will be heading to the brig," Aristee corrected.

"You think wrong." Maniac adjusted his grip on the rifle. "You need pilots."

She nodded. "Pilots who don't point weapons at their superiors. Pilots without plans for sabotage."

"Tried that. Failed. But I'll eventually bring you down. In the meantime, I need to be out there. I can't stay in that cell and wait to die. Can't do it. Won't." Maniac could not wait for her reply, either. He threw the rifle back to the Marine, then pounded off toward the runway.

The Marines trained their weapons on him and waited for Aristee's signal.

She stared at Maniac for a few seconds, wearing the inkling of a smile. "Let him go."

Blair crossed to Karista and grabbed her wrist. "Come with us," he whispered. "You don't have to help. Just come."

"I can't."

"Forget about her. Do this for me."

"I just . . ." She lowered her chin.

"Please."

As Blair stepped into the aft observation bubble, he felt a strong sense of déjà vu. He knew he had never been to this part of the ship, and he slowly realized that the brilliant night sky seen through the Plexi reminded him of the sky over his uncle's farm on Nephele. The farm stood four hundred kilometers away from the nearest metroplex, thus the light pollution that too often robbed the stars of their luster had never been a problem there. He could easily pick our stars like Mylon, Tyr, Kurasawa, Gimle, and even K'n'Rek, part of the Kilrathi empire. Though the stars were somewhat different here, their clarity and brilliance suggested something innocent and untainted by humans. Sadly, they had come to shed blood across the heavens, and Karista's face registered that grim fact.

She had lied to the captain, had saved her life, but she wouldn't
help. Of course Aristee could never be certain whether or not
Karista actually engaged in the killing unless one of the others
revealed that fact. Blair figured that if they survived the Kilrathi
attack, Aristee would have Karista killed anyway. Every other
Pilgrim in the group had agreed to help, and if they, too, decided
to back out at the last minute, then the Kilrathi would surely take
the ship. Blair considered reminding them of the consequences,
but they knew the facts and had watched the old man die. He
had to believe that they wouldn't change their minds.

They joined hands to form a circle that wasn't necessary or
traditional but seemed to ease everyone's nerves. Karista's hand
felt cold and clammy. He glanced at her a second, then at the
middle-aged woman to his right who squeezed his hand tightly
as their eyes met. "Thank you," she said softly. "I feel terrible
about this, but you're right. We deserve to live."

He smiled tightly, then stared beyond the faces of those in
front of him to the commencing battle. Laser bolts from the far-
off destroyer and cruiser collected into twin conduits that riddled
the supercruiser's aft shields. Like low-lying nimbus clouds
auguring a storm, the Kilrathi fighters sprang ahead of the cap
ships, following the bolts' fiery lanes. The eight squadrons of
Rapiers that vectored toward them looked like a diminutive force
of foolhardy or suicidal pilots. And only now did the first
squadron of Broadsword bombers launch from the aft flight
deck, their torpedoes hastily loaded, their damage inspections
even more hastily completed. Blair tried to comfort himself with
the reminder that although the Pilgrims were outnumbered, they
were superior navigators. During the battle over McDaniel, Blair
had witnessed some of the sharpest, most reactionary piloting he
had ever seen. Maybe sheer numbers would actually work
against the cats. Maybe.

Blair looked again to Karista. She stood there, biting her lower
lip, eyes brimming with tears. He urged her on with his gaze, fig-
uring she would at least tell the others what to do. She opened her
mouth, and the words finally came out with sober resignation.

"People. This may hurt some of you as much as it hurts them. All I can say is try to remember that you're not alone. And you won't die. We'll come together as one and move swiftly, a thief in the night robbing of them their lives. It'll hurt a little more with each one. You'll feel the need to let go and wander off. Don't. Stay with your broturs and sosturs. Try to keep them warm. You'll know when it's over. Trust me. You'll know. Close your eyes."

Night turned into the familiar, mottled darkness within himself. The woman beside Blair released an involuntary whimper that sent a shudder through him. Others gasped or murmured their trepidation.

Yes, they were afraid—despite their experience with delving into the quantum level, with manipulating the fields, with thrusting themselves into the continuum, the universe. Blair's experience had been limited. Any more consideration of that would buckle his knees. No, he wasn't completely green. The others had never killed like this, either.

He imagined himself standing with the group, holding hands, then soaring up and leading them through the Plexi bubble and out into space. They glided with ease and grace, a flock of angels casting not a single shadow over the Rapiers and Broadswords below them. Their scripts were now joined in a quilt of thought through which any one of them could converse, learn, enlighten, even love. He felt everything they felt, thought everything they did, and doubted that he was capable of so much sensation. He found himself suddenly preoccupied with the link itself. He wound his way through the dark, braided corridors of the quilt, asking others if they had seen Karista Mullens.

The boy Maniac had saved rounded a black column that Blair sensed had been woven of pure fear. The boy picked his nose a second, gazed sheepishly as he spotted Blair, then touched the material as though it were hot. "They said you're looking for Karista. She won't come here."

"How can we convince her?"

"She loves you. She's your pair. That's your job." He winked and got stitched back into the fabric.

"My job?"

Suddenly, a terrific wind knocked over the black column and pierced Blair with a trillion icy blades. He spun away from the wind to lock gazes with a Kilrathi pilot who banged his melon-like head repeatedly on his cockpit seat. The cat's eyes bulged a moment before he reached up, extended his claws, and tore out those eyes amid torrents of blood.

Blair turned his head a fraction to the left, where the captain of the Kilrathi cruiser sat in a command chair. Five bridge officers behind him lay on the deck, writhing spasmodically in pools of blood ornamented by massive eyeballs. Blair felt himself linked to the others as they coiled through the gravitic fields surrounding the captain's arms and drove them against the man's flesh. Unable to resist, the captain brought thick paws to his face, and the serrated claws went to work.

Though Blair had focused on those two particular deaths, he knew that he and the others had already caused many more, but something prevented him from experiencing all of them simultaneously. He could select each moment, one at time, sift through them as though they resided in memory files, but he felt denied of the true experience. He needed to know just how cold it would get.

He turned again, saw the captain of the destroyer bring himself up to a full three meters, raise his long arms toward the overhead, then shriek as blood gushed through the seams in his armor. Blair and the others had shifted the gravitic field within his body and were squeezing his internal organs as though they were citrus. Blair craned his head a few inches more and now watched from about a half kilometer out as the destroyer tacked to starboard, putting it on an intercept course with the cruiser.

I can see this. But let me see it all. Feel it all. I want to know who I am . . .

Breaking into a sprint, he threaded his way farther through the quilt, stumbling over Kilrathi corpses and ducking as rubble fell like flaming hail. A tingling sensation rose up through his legs as he neared what he thought was the center of the quilt. Maybe there he could experience all of it at once and shake off this force on his back.

Out of breath, he staggered into a zone that resembled billions of illuminated fibers, a bizarre kind of interchange that spun into and formed a glistening white cone stretching up to touch the stars. He crossed to the base of the cone, which now throbbed and seemed to enlarge by the second.

An old man whispered in his ear, "You'll get your answer at the top."

He gripped the first fibrous tube, no wider than a meter, and began his ascent. The air grew colder as he climbed, and the images of Kilrathi steering their fighters into each other or exploding or imploding at their stations aboard the cap ships grew more frequent, more vivid, the stench of them voiding themselves now even tighter in his nostrils. The higher he got, the more exaggerated his progress became. He would reach up to the next tube, and suddenly find himself a thousand meters higher, find himself staring into the pale, wrinkled, bewhiskered face of another dying abomination. He shivered uncontrollably and held his jaw tight to prevent his teeth from chattering. He forged on, driven by much more than curiosity. The answer to who he really was lay just ahead. One hundred meters. Fifty. Twenty. His hand struck a smooth, frigid surface. He pulled himself a little higher and tried to remove the hand. His flesh remained locked. He yanked again, and the pain snaked up his arm. He swore aloud, having come so far only to be stopped by something so ridiculous as—

"Don't go any farther, Blair." Karista stood beside him, shifting in and out of the illuminated mountain as though it were her dress, a dress made of rushing water. She held his hand in her own, their fingers interlaced.

"You've decided to help us," he said excitedly.

"No. I've been here. Hiding. Waiting. Knowing you would do something like this. You can't experience it all."

"I can! It's my choice!"

"Then you'll fall. Like the others."

He ripped his hand away. "Sorry. I have to know."

She cried out for him to stop, but he thought her away. She darkened into dust quickly dispersed by the gale. He hauled himself to the top and stood on a plain of black that reflected the stars.

Images of the battle struck successive blows, knocking him back like a boxer whose glory days had slipped by. Kilrathi wailed. Kilrathi died. The destroyer's bow caught the cruiser amidships in a glittering string of detonations that abruptly congealed into a single, debris-strewn globe. The explosion struck Blair's ankles, surged up his legs, then swallowed him in light for a blink before vanishing. Transparent thunderheads grumbled above, and he lifted his gaze to the traceries of lightning that joined the stars and discharged around him. He lifted his arms and surrendered to the knowledge—the history—delivered on bolts from the vacuum.

He saw Pilgrims living aboard ring stations, felt their fear and anxiety, lived their lives with and for them; he saw embryos with horrible mutations and sensed the warmth of their mothers' wombs; he saw Ivar Chu speaking in thunderous words to a crowd of millions, then spoke the words for Chu himself and heard cries of ecstatic joy in return; he gasped for acrid-smelling air as he died with hundreds of thousands aboard sloships attacked by Confederation destroyers. He saw it all at once, and it kept coming, faster and colder—

"I *can* change your path!" a woman cried. "I *can*."

His body shook, and the collar of his flight suit dug into his neck. A single countenance seeped through the trillions of images and sensations: the face of his mother, her cheeks red and tear-stained, her eyes brightening into twin novae. She took form, gripped his flight suit, tried to shake him to attention.

He looked at her uncomprehendingly for a second, then uttered, "Don't."

"Christopher. I can't let you do this."

His hands found her wrists, pulled them off—

And the effort forced him back. He lost his footing, felt the summit's edge drag across his boots.

Then he fell, the wind fluttering through his flight suit, the mountain of radiant thought wiping by below, the tangled surface of the quilt hurtling mercilessly toward him. He remembered his mother's warning when he had first encountered her in the continuum. He thought of how Karista had spoken the same words: *Then you'll fall. Like the others.* He thrust out his palms and tried to scream, but nothing would come. Now a feeling from the core of his being told him he could not save himself. He had tapped too deeply into the continuum, into the scripts, into a quantum level that was the blood of the universe.

He struck the quilt, felt his body spread across its surface and slough off a cloak of darkness. Then he froze into a solid, flat mass cupped by something warm. The quilt felt different, harder, smoother, with the trace of a vibration moving steadily over its surface. Seconds ticked by, with only a dark drape of nothingness before him. Then a light appeared, enlarged, focused into a glassy sheen of stars half-eclipsed by a familiar face. "Blair?"

His lips and tongue felt numb. But his eyes, yes, his eyes took Karista in with gratitude, with a softness that said he was sorry, but one she did not recognize.

"I'm getting you to sick bay. But don't worry. It's over. It's over now."

21

VEGA SECTOR, DAY
QUADRANT

MCDANIEL'S WORLD

CS CONCORDIA

2654.128

0900 HOURS
CONFEDERATION
STANDARD TIME

"Message forwarded from the *Barnicket Light*, sir. The destroyer *Windmar* intercepted a distress signal from Aloysius Prime during standard patrol. They now have thirteen Pilgrim pilots in custody, along with twenty-one mercenaries and five troopships registered to the CS *Olympus*. They've interrogated the prisoners and forward the recordings."

Commodore Richard Bellegarde shook a fist. "Yes! We have a trail."

Comm Officer Wilks went on, picking up on Bellegarde's excitement and pouring some into his own youthful voice. "The *Windmar* tracked ion emissions and found the remains of three Fralthi-class cruisers and a Ralari-class destroyer. The emissions continue on past the battle's coordinates, and the *Windmar*'s skipper believes that at least two Kilrathi capital ships are in pursuit of the *Olympus*."

"Contact Admiral Tolwyn," Bellegarde said, then hurried across the bridge toward the lift. "Tell him to meet me in the map room."

"Should I alert Space Marshal Gregarov as well?"

"Not yet."

"But sir, she instructed that—"

"I'm aware of her instructions. And I wouldn't want you to disobey orders. Just give me and the admiral about ten minutes."

Wilks grinned his understanding. "Aye-aye, sir."

Bellegarde had already pulled up the holographic map of Robert's Quadrant by the time Tolwyn arrived. The systems of Baird's Star, Tartarus, Dakota, K'rissth, and Freya glinted in three dimensions within a rectangular box comprised of hundreds of green cubes. The portal system of Port Hedland stood just outside the box, and a solid red line marking Aristee's last known trajectory curved from a point between Tartarus and Freya and headed on toward Port Hedland, where the line became dotted to indicate Bellegarde's projection.

"What do we have, Richard?"

He spoke rapidly, realizing that he should calm down—but the news represented their first real break in fifteen days. After he finished relaying the data to Tolwyn, he turned to a communications monitor and activated an audio-video recording. A muscular black man appeared, his face sweaty, his eyes like heavy gray sacks. Bellegarde thumbed down the volume and said, "I just glanced at a few of these interrogations before you arrived, and this one seemed particularly interesting. Man's name is Doug Henrick. Says he was taken by force and ordered to fly. Says the others were as well—that's why they sent off a distress signal instead of trying to hide from the *Windmar*."

"Or they were just disabled, knew they couldn't make it back to the ship, and figured they'd lie so we wouldn't execute them for treason," Tolwyn said. "No, they willingly joined Aristee's force. They were either left behind or had second thoughts and went AWOL."

"I agree. Anyway, this guy thinks Aristee intercepted one of our comm drones near Aloysius. He also says that she plans on modifying her hopper drive so that it'll create a much larger gravity well. He says that by one-four-eight, maybe sooner, she'll have it ready. Her next stop? Earth."

"Convenient timing. Ten days shy of our deadline. But what if Mr. Henrick allowed himself to be captured to feed us misinformation? I'm sure he hasn't submitted to a cerebral scan—and even those can be fooled with the right training. I'm dubious because he knows too much for a pilot."

"I thought the same, until I learned that he's had contact with Christopher Blair. They went to Blair for help in getting close to Paladin. He says the situation got too complicated and he and a few others decided to make a run when the cats attacked. They left behind William Santyana. Name ring a bell?"

"Brilliant test pilot. Retired too young. I see Aristee's conscripted only the best."

"Santyana wants out as well—but Aristee has his family on board. He's working with Blair and Paladin." Bellegarde paused to consider the tone he would use to deliver his next bit of news. He simply had to say it. "Sir, Henrick also says that there's some doubt as to Paladin's loyalty."

"I'm not surprised."

"I guess you were worried about him. Why?"

"We'll leave it there. For now, we'll have to trust him. Paladin has rarely let me down."

Bellegarde shut off the recording, then eyed the holograph. "Sir, I know that last week we sent the *Tiger Claw* and *Fosubius* battle group to Earth, but I respectfully suggest that we join them to strengthen our presence, whether Henrick is lying or not. We can't afford to ignore this. Aristee can jump to Vega and follow the Ulysses corridor right back to Sol."

"That would be the long route, Richard. With her hopper drive, she might be able to jump directly from Port Hedland. In fact, she doesn't even need to reach that jump point. If our information is true, then right now she's remaining within interstellar space and buying herself time until her drive is ready. Trouble is, she's got the Kilrathi on her tail."

"But she managed to take out three cruisers and a destroyer—with no evidence that she used the hopper drive to do so. Considering that she has only one ship, I find that unbelievable. Or has she formed a battle group? But where would she get the ships and the resources? All of our vessels are accounted for."

"She has another weapon, Richard. Access the datanet when you get a chance. Search for Pilgrims, extrakinesis or hypersensory perception. You'll find it interesting."

"I found it interesting when I studied it as a cadet. But there were only a few Pilgrims with that power, and using it to kill was against their edicts, so most of them stayed out of the war. I thought we wiped out the ones who fought."

"A lot more fought than history records. And we didn't kill them all. The escapees have had children by now. If we look at the *Windmar*'s analysis of the debris, we'll find Kilrathi bodies with crushed organs, missing eyes, and other evidence of gravitic manipulation."

"And they're powerful enough to destroy four Kilrathi capital ships? My God. . . ."

"During the war, they were even stronger. But the power drains them. That's when we struck."

"So if Aristee arrives in Earth orbit with her hopper drive online, she can use her people to stall us long enough to engage the drive and draw Earth into the well."

"Clever woman. Her plan would've been even more effective if Bill Wilson's timing had been better. He should have delayed his deal with the Kilrathi. They shouldn't have attacked Pegasus until Aristee's hopper drive was modified. That way if Wilson failed, Aristee could move in quickly and take out Earth. I'm speculating here, but I think the cats wouldn't wait, and Wilson got cocky enough to take on the whole mission himself. He failed, and Aristee was left ill-prepared to accept the baton. But she's running with it now."

"The *Halstov* battle group is at Port Hedland right now," Bellegarde said, pointing to a cluster of blue orbs on the holograph. "Let's move it to intercept. Between us and the cats, we'll take her out."

"You're forgetting our order to recover that ship intact." He took a deep breath. "Now Richard, what I'm about to tell you is highly confidential and could get me court martialed, but the time has come for you to know. Just after Aristee attacked Mylon Three, the space marshal persuaded the joint chiefs to recover the hopper drive at all costs. I mean at all costs. Aristee's targets were considered expendable. I viewed the holo of Gregarov's meeting with the joint chefs, and her fervor was, in a word, unsettling. So I've been doing a little digging since this all began. Called in a favor at Confed Intelligence, and my source just came through." Tolwyn took a step closer and lowered his voice. "For the past three years Ms. Gregarov has been receiving her-eyes-only intelligence reports regarding the Pilgrims' construction of the hopper drive. The system's components were assembled on all five of the enclaves and on McDaniel. Pilgrim engineers worked in isolation, and only one group knew how to assemble the drive. That group is on board the *Olympus*. Most of the other Pilgrims who worked on the components have been taken into custody."

"So Gregarov stood by and did nothing while the Pilgrims assembled the drive?"

"She wanted them to build it. Pilgrims were the original engineers, and the unit often requires a Pilgrim to assist in the operation. She figured she'd take possession before they could use it. Trouble is, the Pilgrims realized there was a leak and fed misinformation to Intell. Aristee got the drive online before Gregarov could react."

The magnitude of what the space marshal had done sent Bellegarde toward the bulkhead. He raised his fist, thought better of slamming it on the durasteel. "She sat there in the wardroom and tried to blame us for civilian deaths. The blood's on her hands. Did she know about Bill Wilson as well?"

"I'm not sure. In any event, you and I have new orders for which I take full responsibility. If we can't confiscate that drive, then no one else can have it." Tolwyn looked sadly to the deck. "And if that means destroying the ship and losing two of our own, then so be it."

The hatch suddenly opened, and Space Marshal Gregarov carried her glare into the map room. "Lieutenant Wilks just summoned me here. When I asked him to report, he provided me with a lengthy description of a message forwarded from the *Barnicket Light*. Why wasn't I informed sooner?"

She had directed her question to Tolwyn, but Bellegarde jumped all over it. "Why weren't we informed of your decision to allow the Pilgrims to build a hopper drive?"

"Richard, this is neither the time nor the—"

"I think it is," Bellegarde boldly corrected. "I think the space marshal owes us an explanation—and an apology."

Gregarov lifted a derisive grin. "I heard you weren't much of a diplomat, Mr. Bellegarde. I got a taste of that in the wardroom, but now I really see what they mean. Guess the bottle can do that."

He opened his mouth to launch a retort.

"You can't blame this crisis on me," she went on. "But you have no conception of the forces at work here."

"Then educate me."

"I'm sorry, but I'm not at liberty to divulge that information."

"Ma'am?" Tolwyn said, slipping between them. "It's highly likely that Aristee will get that drive modified and head back to Earth to create a gravity well that will consume planet. The *Tiger Claw* and the *Fosubius* battle group are already standing by there. I've left the *Oregon* and *Mitchell Hammock* at Netheranya. We'll join the *Claw* and post our battle group here to maintain the no-fly zone."

Gregarov swung her head toward the holograph gleaming above them. "When you look at the stars like this, they seem . . . I don't know . . . deceptive. You don't realize that billions of people are out there living on those dots." She faced Tolwyn, her eyes welling up. "geoff, you have to believe me when I say I didn't know so many would die. None of us did."

"You gambled. You lost. Now the bill's come due." Tolwyn raised a brow, then hustled toward the hatch.

"Next time gamble with your own life." Bellegarde didn't

wait for her reply. He double-timed into Tolwyn's shadow, leaving Gregarov alone with her remorse.

Which wouldn't change a damned thing now.

Never before had Admiral Vukar watched so many brave warriors plummet to their deaths. The Pilgrims had squeezed their organs or had forced them to gouge out their eyes or even their hearts. The mutated apes had dishonored him and his clan on a scale once unimaginable. A single dreadnought escorted his flagship now, a single dreadnought depleted of its fighters.

They continued pursuing the supercruiser, and Tactical Officer Makorshk had twice during the past fourteen standard days led a team charged with lightening their load and increasing their velocity. Perhaps they could narrow the gap enough to make one last assault on the supercruiser. Still, during their last strike, they had thought that the Pilgrims with telekinetic-like powers would be recovering from destroying the cruisers; he and Makorshk had not figured that more Pilgrims waited in reserve, and those fanatical apes had effortlessly plucked his last cruiser and the destroyer from the sky.

At the moment, more Pilgrims could be standing by, waiting for them to make a move. No, Vukar would not recklessly throw away his warriors' lives, despite the honor of dying in battle and the heat of the blood frenzy that left him tense and sweating at the end of each day. There had to be a way to disable that lone ship and take possession without springing the enemy's trap.

"Kalralahr?"

Vukar stirred in his meditation chair, then reached to the comm display's control panel. Makorshk stared back at him, the folds of his face loose and forming an expression of despair. "We've jettisoned the last from engineering and crew's quarters, but we've only brought velocity up to one-two-nine KPS. The drive's beginning to superheat. The *Kot'Akri* reports the same. Our prey continues to lead by nearly one hundred and eighty thousand kilometers. Ion emissions remain stable. We have a distinct trail."

"But we won't get close enough to launch another ship-to-ship assault. It is a physical impossibility."

"Yes, but we do have two weapons left. Our fighters and our Skipper missiles. We've given the Pilgrims too much time already. They'll jump soon. We're at maximum velocity and as close as we'll get. The time has come."

Vukar drew nutrient gas through his broad nostrils and exhaled in a burst. "If we send fighters, they'll simply kill our pilots with their minds. And if we launch Skipper missiles, we won't disable the ship—we'll destroy it. Perhaps no one is meant to have that drive."

"It may take a few hours, but we can replace the warheads in our Skippers with low-level explosives and program them to lock on to ion engines. The photon cloaks should help to get them close enough. Fighter interdiction will be the Pilgrims' only way to stop them."

"What makes you believe our Skippers can evade their counter-assault?"

"We can launch our fighters to keep theirs busy. We outnumber them nearly three-to-one. But most of our pilots won't make it back. They'll either run out of fuel or exceed the ten-hour life support limit."

"Or have their hearts crushed, their eyes torn out."

"We have no defense against that, but we cannot shame ourselves and our clan. If we die, we die with honor. Perhaps you believe that you've already sent too many of the *hrai* to their deaths. But Kalralahr, not a single life was wasted—all fought with honor until the end. So should we."

"You sound more like an elder than a tactical officer," Vukar mused. "It seems you've found your way in a changing universe. And you remind me of my own."

"Kalralahr, I knew that one day we would embrace in death. Whether it be here or on the challenge ground hardly matters. Know that I've despised you to the core. But you have done something no other officer would: you let me speak, and you listened. For that, I owe you my life, and there is no one else more worthy to receive it."

Vukar scrutinized the young warrior, probing for insincerity but discovering only a stalwart commitment to the words. Makorshk had come a long way, and Vukar felt even more justified in delaying the challenge. "Give the order. Modify our Skipper missiles. Prepare our fighters for launch. I'll be here or in my quarters. Alert me when the time comes."

Makorshk bowed and reached to end the link.

Leaning back in his meditation chair, Vukar considered what he would do if this final assault failed. Any other kalralahr would not entertain the possibility of life after such a disgrace. Vukar's duty would be to return home and commit *zu'kara* before the clan elders. But Makorshk's sense of independence had become infectious, and Vukar suddenly believed that failure should not cost him his life . . .

"After all of this, after all that's happened, we've changed nothing."

Blair sat on the edge of the cot and glanced idly around the sick bay. He had spent the past two weeks recovering with the others in the long room lined with too many bunks and filled with too many nasty smells. His body temperature had dropped five degrees and hadn't risen for nearly ten days. A non-Pilgrim might have died from such a long period at hypothermic levels, but Blair's physiology had kept him alive. Barely. He finally turned to Karista, who sat next to him and stared blankly across the room. "Did you hear what I said?"

She nodded. "Sounds like you've given up."

"What else can we do? She's getting her hopper drive ready as we speak. How are we supposed to stop that while we're under guard?" He raised his head toward the two Marines posted just outside the open hatch.

"I don't know." She stood with a sigh of frustration. "Today they're moving you back to the brig. Our esteemed captain gave me the honor of escorting you. I almost wish she had killed me. Maybe she already has. The guilt . . . it's a slow poison. I tossed away everything I believed in."

"No, you didn't."

"The others needed me during the attack. While I was helping you, I was also back in. Some of them were like you—they wanted to feel too much. They would've died."

"Why did you wait so long to tell me?"

"It's my problem, not yours. But I'm weak. I guess I need your help now."

"You don't need me, and you didn't do anything wrong."

"I did exactly what she wanted. I sold out." Karista crossed to the opposite cot and sat with a huff. "I don't even know who I am anymore."

Blair closed his eyes, and, reaching out with his mind, he moved beside her, slid an arm of gravity over her shoulders, and held her close. "You're someone amazing. And I am honored to have you as my pair."

Murmurs came from near the hatch, followed quickly by two distinct rounds of conventional gunfire that echoed violently through the bay. Blair opened his eyes as the two Marine guards slumped to the deck, wearing bloody jewels on their foreheads. William Santyana stepped over them, turning his pistol on a medic seated at a bank of monitors near the hatch.

"Please," the medic said, raising her hands.

"Get back," Santyana ordered, waving his pistol toward the rear of the bay.

The medic had no trouble complying.

"What are you doing?" Blair asked Santyana. "This isn't going to work. We already played this out. We get to the flight deck, launch, and they shoot us down."

"We're not going to the flight deck, Mr. Blair. The hopper drive is almost ready. We'll be jumping to Sol within the hour. Look, I never wanted this job in the first place. And I'm supposed to be retired. But I'll be damned if I sit around and let this bitch kill more people. We're going down to engineering. I want you and Karista to keep those engineers busy—give them a mental itch they can't scratch. I'll take care of the drive."

Blair looked for Karista's reaction. She looked impassive but did get to her feet.

"What are you waiting for?" Santyana asked him. "Should have your sea legs back by now."

"Yeah," Blair moaned, then tightened the sash on his Pilgrim robe, slid into his sandals, and started for the hatch to retrieve one of the Marines' rifles. He scooped up the weapon and turned to encounter a familiar, cocky grin.

"Long time, no see, Ace. Looks like push has come to shove, and we'll really see where your loyalty's at." Maniac jabbed the muzzle of his rifle into Blair's chest. "Don't let me influence you in any way."

"I won't," Blair said, then slapped the barrel away. "You look like shit."

Maniac rubbed the blond stubble on his chin. "It's called being locked in a supply room for two weeks—my reward for racking up a dozen kills. They let me out to shit and shower. That's it. Believe it or not, I asked about you. They wouldn't tell me jack. I should have went back to my cell." He crossed to pick up the second Marine's rifle. He thrust it toward Karista, who kept her arms at her sides. "C'mon, sweetheart. You need some firepower. Or are you going to use that . . ." He fluttered his fingers near his temple.

She sneered and pushed past him.

"What'd I say?"

Blair shook his head in disgust. "She's not some carnival freak."

"With an ass like that? Of course not."

Santyana, who had skulked along the corridor to reach the first intersection, waved them forward. Maniac shouldered the second rifle and charged ahead of Blair.

"We have to get by the torpedo launch bays, pilots' quarters, environmental controls, and the aft storage area," Santyana said. "We'll drop anyone who gets in the way. Do not hesitate. Understood?"

Blair glanced back to Karista. "You don't have to—"

"It's all right," she said firmly, perhaps more for her own benefit than his.

"Coffee break's over," Maniac said. "It's not like no one else heard those shots or that medic's not going to call for help. Let's haul butt."

Santyana took point, with Blair and Maniac two meters back in flanking positions. Karista kept tightly behind Blair, and he felt the necessity of protecting her tighten his muscles. They reached a stairwell without incident and ventured down into the torpedo launch bays. Massive conduits stretched overhead, with the multicolored tubes and the loaders themselves off to their right. A young specialist lifted his head from a loader's display panel.

His last act.

The poor boy took a 2.3mm caseless projectile the hard way, and Santyana did not bat an eye. Four other specialists raised their hands from touchpads as the quartet jogged by. Maniac fired a round into one of the control units, which reacted with a sizzle and a brief puff of smoke. The specialist near it shrieked and shined the deck with her rump.

They forged on through the bay, nearly slipping on a freshly scrubbed floor and winding through narrow passages made even narrower by the intestine-like rubber ducts mounted to the bulkheads. Somewhere behind them, a klaxon rang out and wound Blair's nerves a little tighter. Another hatch leading to a stairwell came up quickly. They filed into it, beat a chaotic rhythm on the durasteel, then finally emerged into a corridor lined on both sides with hatches: the pilots' quarters.

"Here's where we catch a break," Maniac said. "This shouldn't be a secured area."

But he had spoken too soon.

Three Pilgrim Marines rounded the corner of an intersecting passage, their movements tight, deliberate.

Santyana and Maniac dove for the bulkhead to their left, while Blair dropped to one knee. "Down," he instructed Karista.

"Hold your fire!" Maniac shouted. "We surrender."

The three Marines spread out and cautiously advanced, their knees slightly bent, their rifles held high and fixed on Santyana,

Maniac, and Blair. "Weapons to the deck. Now," the lead
Marine instructed, her face growing more flush by the second.

Barely moving his lips, Blair whispered, "Karista, we have
to—"

"Shhh. I know. Close your eyes."

He left himself crouching on the floor, and in his thoughts
glided up to the Marines with Karista at his side. She glanced at
him, the pain and resignation renewed in her eyes. "We don't
have to kill them. Watch." She shifted up to the lead Marine and
placed a hand on the woman's chest plate. The Marine gasped,
dropped her weapon, and reached for her throat even as Karista
shifted to the next and repeated.

Blair went to the third Marine and touched the armor, imagining a force that would partially constrict the Pilgrim's airway.
The guy's breath came in a weird crackle, he tugged at his collar,
then fell back toward the bulkhead.

"C'mon, asshole."

Who said that? Blair blinked hard and focused on Maniac,
who had grabbed his wrist and now yanked him to his feet. The
three Marines lay on the floor, contorted and barely able to
breathe. Karista stood staring at them in a trance that sent Blair
toward her. He touched her shoulder. "You all right?"

She shivered. "I guess so."

"Hey, lovers," Maniac called out. "This is great. You got 'em
flapping like fish, so let's go. Blair, you can give her that tongue
bath later." He hustled off toward Santyana, who had hunkered
down at the intersection.

"Sorry about him," Blair said. "He has a few psych problems.
Can't help himself. It's all in his profile. You can read it yourself."

She didn't buy that and began to say something, but the sudden pounding of boots from the stairwell sent them dashing
toward Santyana, who suddenly sprang into the intersection and
pumped automatic fire into the passage to their right. He reached
the other side, took up a position behind the corner, then sent off
another salvo of suppressing fire. "Five comin' at us," he cried.

"And more back here," Blair relayed, hazarding a look over his shoulder at the Marines bounding from the stairwell.

Santyana ducked back and turned his weapon on the nearest hatch control. A triplet of fire rendered the panel a smoking piece of tattered metal, but the hatch did not open. "Only works in the movies," he said with a snort, then waved them over. "Come on!"

Maniac bolted across the intersection, opening up on the Marines advancing from the right. He reached the other side and jogged on toward Santyana.

"Take my hand," Karista told Blair. "Drag me over there. I'll slow them down." She lifted her head toward the Marines Maniac had evaded.

"But what about them?" Blair asked, gesturing to the group coming up hard to the rear.

"There's just too many. We'll try to outrun them."

With a nod, he seized her wrist and pulled her toward the intersection. As they crossed into the open, he spotted twin lines of Marines lying on their stomachs along the passage. The first two soldiers in each row rolled onto their backs and clutched their throats.

"We're across," he told Karista, then tightened his grip on her wrist. Her eyes refocused, and it took but a few seconds more for them to break into a sprint.

They jogged straight for about fifty meters, the Marines behind them thankfully holding their fire. Conventional rounds fired within the ship could cause serious damage—not that Maniac and Santyana cared about that. It also seemed likely that the jarheads had been ordered to take them alive.

The corridor dead-ended at a sealed hatch whose control panel flashed the usual authorized personnel only warning.

"Hey, you can't pick locks with that little power, can you?" Maniac asked Karista.

"No, but I can shut mouths."

Maniac's lips sealed, his eyes bugged out, and he began to groan under Karista's gravitic gag. She let him suffer a few seconds more, then freed him. "Hey, honey," he said, his lips and tongue moving spastically. "Take it easy."

"Everybody back," Santyana cried, the status light on his rifle's underslung grenade launcher flashing red.

"Let's make this a quick bang," Maniac warned. "Hunting party's just down the hall."

They retreated about eight meters from the hatch, and even before Blair could find a spot against the bulkhead, Santyana rang the doorbell with his concussion grenade. A terrific thunderclap reverberated through the corridor, succeeded by a muffled burst as the hatch blew inward.

"I always like to make an entrance," Maniac mumbled as he followed Santyana into the rising smoke.

Blair put his hand on Karista's shoulder and ushered her in behind Maniac. Shouts to halt echoed from behind them, and Blair smiled over a sudden idea. He thought himself in front of them and moved swiftly through the ranks, tripping one, two, three, a fourth Marine. The five or six others behind them collided into the heap of tangled limbs. *Too easy. Too funny.*

Then he took himself back, his eyes now watering from the smoke. They passed onto the first catwalk of the environmental control bay. Scores of monitors walled in the rectangular room, and at its center lay the fifteen massive, drum-shaped air recyclers that rose five meters to the overhead.

Wasting only the few seconds it took to appraise the surroundings, they darted across the catwalk and took a stairway down to the operations level. The five techs assigned to the station had already gathered near the first drum to regard them with curiosity and a healthy measure of respect.

"You're not authorized to be in this area," a gray-haired tech, probably the department head, shouted.

"Very good," Maniac returned. "You got any more keen observations before I pick your nose with a round?"

The Marines in pursuit reached the catwalk, and a trio made it to the stairs much sooner than Blair would have liked. He spotted the next hatch that would take them into the aft storage area.

Once again, they would have to stall the Marines so they could blast themselves a course.

Damn it, if we only had access to the security network, we could open the hatch before we even get to it.

Wait a minute. Maybe we do. "Merlin. Activate."

Blair had to grin as the old holographic assistant jogged next to him on a course of air about shoulder height. "You realize you're killing me, don't you, Christopher?"

Why Merlin had chosen to jog was beyond Blair, and he hardly had the time for an explanation. "Get into the security network and open that hatch."

"You make it sound so simple."

"Just do it!"

"What is that?" Karista asked.

"My holographic assistant. I would've introduced you to him earlier, but he tends to embarrass me."

"He lies, Ms. Mullens. Oh, how he lies."

Santyana reached the hatch, and as he glanced at the control panel, a string of lights switched from white to green. He faced them, confused.

Blair winked at the holograph. "Very smooth, Merlin."

"You kidding? I didn't do anything. I'm still trying to break into the net."

"Then who opened the hatch?"

"I'll trace the command. Well, I can't. I'm blocked."

"Who cares who opened it," Maniac called back. "We'll thank them later." He followed Santyana into the next passage.

Karista slowed as she reached the hatchway. "Are you thinking what I'm thinking?"

"I thought you didn't need to ask. But yeah, I am. Just be ready."

22

VEGA SECTOR, DAY
QUADRANT

EN ROUTE TO
PORT HEDLAND

CS OLYMPUS

2654.128

1000 HOURS
CONFEDERATION
STANDARD TIME

Blair remembered the aft storage area from the first time he had passed through it, on his way to view the hopper drive. The polymeric bars that fenced in literally thousands of storage containers reminded him of the brig: one of two possible homes for him if they failed. The second lay out there, somewhere, in the continuum. He guessed his script would live on, as his mother's did, but to die, to end in the physical sense . . . better not to think about it.

Ahead and behind the bars, a crew of three ran a small loader with a hydraulic claw secured to its tapered nose. They shifted a column of containers toward the starboard bulkhead. Consumed in their work and deafened by the whine of the loader's engine, the techs failed to notice Santyana and Maniac as the two hauled by. Even as the tech nearest Blair and Karista turned his head and spotted them, a voice boomed loudly from the shipwide intercom:

"This is the captain. Broturs and sosturs? The time has come. Report to jump stations. We'll reach interphase point in six minutes. Captain out."

"There's the hatch," Santyana said, pointing ahead to the oval-shaped barrier.

"Where are the guards?" Blair asked. "Supposed to be a couple of guards."

"And the door's unlocked," Maniac said, eyeing the control panel.

Santyana broke out of his jog and stood at the door, panting. "They're waiting for us in there."

"So we go in shooting." Maniac grimaced and shook his rifle, demonstrating how he would punch holes in the next contingent of Marines.

"Blair? Karista? When I open the hatch, you reach in there first," Santyana said. "See what you can do." He thumbed the touchpad.

And Blair surrendered to that other place inside him. He and Karista stepped gingerly onto the circular catwalk overlooking the coliseum-like drive chamber. A score of Marines had strung themselves along the walk at three-meter intervals and leaned over the rail, sweeping the room with their rifles. The two jarheads nearest the hatch rushed forward, though everyone kept hidden in the corridor outside—a position good for only another few seconds.

Moving with the fluid grace of a breaker, Karista reached the first Marine, raised her hand—and froze. She looked at Blair, shocked. "I can't."

A tall black man materialized next to her. He had already seized one of her wrists and now grabbed the other and forced her back. "No, Sostur. There's nothing you can do here."

Blair dove toward the man, but a palm of force held him in midair. He fought against the gravitic barrier, against an impossibly strong mind, then suddenly dropped to the deck.

Gunfire reverberated nearby. He tried to stand but couldn't against the riptide.

Then he opened his eyes to find himself back in the corridor with the others, rifles pointed at their heads. Santyana and Maniac had shot three more Marines before being overrun. The Marines confiscated their rifles and eyed them with a vengeance clearly restrained by an order from Aristee.

"Inside," one jarhead said, shifting his position to drive them back toward the hatch.

"Well, what a supreme waste of time this has been," Maniac said. "Like we had a chance—"

"If you don't shut your hole, you're going to suddenly hate me even more," said the Marine guarding Maniac.

"What happens now?" Blair asked.

"Guess we're in time for the show," Santyana answered. "Look."

Paladin, Aristee, and Frotur McDaniel stood on the lower deck, at a U-shaped control panel positioned near the foot of the hopper drive. Four drive officers sat at their stations near the bulkhead behind Aristee, and three other Pilgrims now gathered near the control panel, one of whom Blair recognized as the black man who had seized Karista. A rhythmic churning sound came from the drive itself, as though the thing were some curving beast consuming shadows and whipping itself up into a frenzy.

"There he is," Maniac muttered. "Our goddamned hero. Pin a medal on his ass." He cocked his head to Blair. "What do you think now, Ace? Look to you like the commodore's trying to stop her?"

Blair swallowed back his reply as he gripped the staircase's railing. They descended to the lower deck as Aristee left the control panel, probably on her way to gloat over their capture.

But as she came forward, her face tightened in a curious expression of grief. "You think I like doing this? You think I don't realize how many people are going to die? We didn't ask for any of this. We were first. We were meant for the stars. No war will ever murder that truth." She regarded the Marines. "Return to your posts. Keep them in your sights."

As the Marines dispersed, Maniac slipped a few steps away and swung his glare on Paladin. "You goddamned traitor!"

The accusation hardly struck a blow as Paladin continued watching the monitor before him.

"Sir?" Blair cried.

Paladin would not look up.

"Sir? Is it true?"

Aristee closed in, blocking Blair's view. "Commodore Taggart was a Pilgrim first, Mr. Blair. He can't change that. No one can. Follow his example. You've assimilated your Pilgrim side even more than I thought you would, and you're not finished. And you," she began, twisting her lip at Karista. "Maybe you'll come to see the truth in our new order. Change is always difficult. I'll give you time."

"Trying to keep your enemies close?" Karista said with canines fully exposed.

"We're the same—determined, stubborn, in touch with what burns inside us. That's why we're so powerful. That's why I want you close."

"Captain," Paladin said, raising his voice. "Brotur Vyson reports multiple bogies inbound. Had them on the scope for a moment, then lost them."

Aristee stormed to the control panel and worked the touch-pad. "Give me the XO."

Blair moved in with others, ever wary of the Marines above. He spotted the grim-looking XO on a comm monitor, with bridge officers darting behind him.

"Ma'am," the XO began curtly. "First contact bearing three-two-four by five-one-nine. Designate Alpha three-one, Kilrathi Skipper missile. Range: two-zero-one-five-two Ks. Velocity: three-seven-nine KPS and holding. Five similar contacts, designated Alpha three-two through six inbound, with headings and velocities marked. We've lost them again."

"How much time?"

"Missiles will impact in forty-nine second . . . mark."

"Brotur Hawthorne?" Aristee cried, spinning toward one of the drive control officers. "We need to jump in thirty seconds."

"Captain," the XO called. "Count one-eight-seven bandits closing. Range: two-one-two-seven three Ks. Velocity: three-eight-nineKPS. Dralthi fighters. ETA: fifty-four seconds . . . mark."

"They've sent in their fighters to tie up ours, so we can't interdict the missiles," Paladin said. "We couldn't scramble enough fighters in time anyway."

"And there's no way we can jump in thirty seconds," Drive Officer Hawthorne said, tearing fingers through his shaggy hair. "The containment field is only operating at ninety percent. If we jump now, we run the risk of an antimatter leak that would destroy the ship."

"Brotur Zimbaka?" Aristee said to the black man who had stopped Karista. "Can you reinforce the containment field?"

"We can."

"Very well. Do so." Aristee rushed over to McDaniel and placed an affectionate hand on the old man's shoulder. "Frotur, are you ready to input jump coordinates?"

McDaniel regarded the panel. "Computer, ready to receive NAVCOM coordinates for hopper drive jump?"

"Ready," came the NAVCOM's even voice. "Jump interphase point reached."

"Brotur Hawthorne?" Aristee said. "Engage the drive."

As the system's whirring turned into a riot of booms and bellows, Blair turned burning eyes on Paladin. How could a man whom he admired so much resort to something as heinous as this? What had happened to him?

Frotur McDaniel gesticulated wildly as he recited strings of coordinates as though they were songs, holding his vibrato on the last number in each set.

"Report on the field?" Aristee said to Hawthorne.

"Up to ninety-six percent, with no signs of leakage."

Blair looked to Zimbaka and the other two pilgrims. All winced and leaned back on the bulkhead, using their extrakinetic ability on an inanimate object. They would pay the price for their actions. Blair shivered as he remembered moving his cot and the sensation that effort had produced.

"Hey, Ace," Maniac said, edging closer to Blair. "Get ready to shield the jewels."

"Don't try—"

But Maniac was already halfway to the control panel, with

fire from above tracking his steps and ricocheting off the deck. Blair dropped to his stomach but continued to watch as Maniac sprinted up behind Aristee, slid his arm around her neck, then turned to face the Marines as he slapped a palm on the side of the woman's head. "I'll break her neck," he shouted. "I learned the same way as you." Then Maniac cocked his head to Drive Officer Hawthorne. "Shut it down."

The man lifted shaking hands.

"Lieutenant, do I need to point out the obvious?" Paladin asked.

"It ends here," Maniac said.

"Frotur?" Aristee gasped. "Frotur!"

McDaniel touched a thin line of blood that trickled down from a dark, gaping hole near his temple. He turned his head a bit, an expression of helplessness and horror beginning to form before he suddenly slumped to the deck.

"Not him," Karista wailed. Oblivious of the Marines above, she bolted to the frotur's side and rolled him onto his back. She shut her eyes, placed a hand on his wound, then wrenched away as though shocked. "It's too late. I can't help him."

"The well is open," Hawthorne cut in. "Jump in eight seconds."

"Brotur Taggart," the XO beckoned from the comm monitor. "Second bearing on the missiles. They're moving into our gravitic field. Lead missile has already increased velocity by twenty percent."

"Launch countermeasures," Paladin ordered. "Rig the ship for impact."

"Belay that," Maniac said. "And abort the jump. Or she dies." He tightened his grip on Aristee's neck and dragged her toward Paladin.

The commodore nodded coolly. "You'll have to kill her, Mr. Marshall."

"I got a clean shot on him," one of the Marines exclaimed from the catwalk. "Just give me the word, Captain."

Shudders muscled through the bulkheads as the ship neared the gravity well. One of the monitors mirrored an image from the radar officer's station and showed the inverted V formation of red blips closing in, with a throng of smaller dots in tow. Blair felt the desire to act surge through him. But what to do? Stop Paladin? Maniac?

"Point of No Return velocity in five, four, three, two—"

A shot drowned out the drive officer's countdown.

And a curious look came over Maniac's face. He grasped his neck, then released Aristee and fell onto his rump. "Ah, shit."

Blair closed his eyes and took himself up to the catwalk. He glided behind the first Marine and shoved the woman over the rail. She hollered and fell headfirst onto the deck. As he threw himself onto the next jarhead, Santyana dove for the first Marine's rifle and rolled up with it. Under heavy fire from the remaining Marines, he scurried behind the main control panel, then popped up a second later to send a flurry of rounds streaming across the catwalk.

As Blair lifted the next Marine, a massive explosion wrenched him away from the catwalk and back into himself. Even as he opened his eyes, the deck dropped nearly a meter, and he crashed onto his side. The impact continued to reverberate as he struggled to sit up.

"We've been hit!" the XO said from the comm monitor. "Port ion engine offline! Hang on. Here comes the—"

Bulkheads thundered so loudly that they overpowered the XO, the drive, and the gunfire traded between Santyana and the Marines.

Then every sensation got locked inside that trillion-year second of the jump:

Karista hovered over Frotur McDaniel, her face like a plate of shattered glass.

The flash from Santyana's muzzle hung like a silk blossom, and a round floated just a meter away from the gun. With ruddy cheeks and bulging eyes, he had begun to shout something.

Maniac gaped at the blood on his fingers. More blood had streamed down from his neck and onto the collar of his Pilgrim robe.

Although Aristee had been freed, she had only made it halfway to the control panel, had felt the oncoming jump, and had reached out in vain before the drive rooted her to the deck.

Zimbaka and the other two Pilgrims had sought cover behind the curving back of the panel. They huddled together, eyes closed, heads tucked tightly into their shoulders.

While the drive officers had remained at their stations, all four had attempted to lift their legs and squeeze themselves into the padded confines of their chairs.

Then there was Paladin, who had assumed McDaniel's place at the drive's control panel and wore his mask of quiet intensity as he gripped his Pilgrim cross.

A key suddenly turned, the chest of the moment yawned open, and chaos escaped as though held under pressure.

"We've taken another hit to the port engine," the XO said over the comm monitor. "But the jump was successful, Brotur Taggart."

As Santyana cut loose another volley at the Marines above, Blair crawled on his elbows toward him.

Karista darted to Maniac, slung his arm over her shoulder, then hauled him to the relative cover of the hopper drive's massive pedestal.

"Hold your fire," Aristee roared. "Hold your fire!"

Rounds beat in triplets off the catwalk's railing as Santyana drove the Marines back toward the corridor. That accomplished, he straightened and swung his rifle at Aristee.

In the meantime, Blair glanced at the Marine he had tossed over the railing. While Santyana had confiscated her rifle, her pistol remained holstered at her side. Blair kept hunched over and stole his way to the unconscious soldier, withdrew her sidearm, then, two-handing the weapon, he slinked back behind the panel and stood beside Santyana.

"Brotur Vyson," Aristee said, directing her voice to the monitor and ignoring the weapons trained on her. "Report."

"We're five minutes from Earth orbit. Picking up massive electromagnetic signatures. Hold a minute. Contacts identified as the strike carrier *Tiger Claw* and the supercruiser *Fosubius* with her standard two-by-one escort."

"I was hoping for a smaller reception," Aristee muttered.

"Those pilots on Aloysius must've been picked up and tipped off Tolwyn," Paladin said. "But it doesn't matter. We can open the well now and take them all out. Computer. Initiate pre-jump sequence."

"Initiated."

"Don't do it, sir," Blair said, following Santyana around the control panel. Santyana broke right to close in on Aristee, while Blair continued on toward Paladin.

"Look up," Aristee said. "We have you covered again. You shoot. They shoot. So we're back to our standoff."

She hadn't lied. The Marines had once more fanned out along the catwalk, though Blair counted only seven now.

"Shoot her, for God's sake," Maniac cried. "And cap him, too, the scumbag traitor."

Blair closed his eyes and took himself toward Paladin—

But Zimbaka suddenly appeared and bent his knees in a battle stance. Blair didn't know which form of martial arts the man practiced, but he did know he was about to find out. "I don't think so, Brotur."

A hand fell on Blair's shoulder. "The containment field is operating at one hundred percent," Karista said. "Brotur Zimbaka and his friends are free to stop us. And they can. Forget it, Blair."

"But we have to do something."

After word had reached Captain Gerald of the *Olympus*'s jump into Sol, he had decided that Angel's squadron would be designated Alert One and held in reserve to escort the *Tiger Claw*. Before the launch, Angel had gone to his ready room to dispute that decision.

"Don't question my judgment," Gerald had warned.

"You think my prejudice will falter out there?"

"Of course it will."

"We don't even know if Taggart and Blair are still on board that ship. I've been at this too long to let emotions get in the way. You know that."

"The admiral has ordered us to take the ship intact. If that's not possible, we *will* destroy it. To be honest, Commander, I don't think you're up to the task. You weren't particularly aggressive over Triune, and one of your people lost a Rapier because of that."

"But as I recall, I wasn't the one with doubts, *sir*."

"You have your orders."

"We're point squadron. Keep us in the rear and you're wasting resources."

"Thank you for that unsolicited opinion, Commander. You're dismissed."

She had considered pounding out of Gerald's ready room; instead, she had lifted a crisp salute, spun on her heel, and exited. Any display of anger at that point would have revealed that her emotions did get in the way.

But it hurt so badly to bury her feelings for Blair. She felt guilty, felt as though she were betraying herself.

Now, as she hovered with the rest of the squadron off the *Claw*'s portside, she wondered if she could muster enough control to stand by and watch nearly five hundred Rapiers and a hundred Broadsword bombers—a combined force from the *Claw* and the *Fosubius* battle group—attack that lone supercruiser. Then again, maybe Gerald had done her squadron a favor. If the cruiser opened a gravity well, the battle over Lethe would repeat itself but on a much more devastating scale.

Dozens of thrusters speckled the night like sapphires and joined into necklaces that twisted back to the *Fosubius* and her escorts.

"Well, mates, there they go," Hunter said, transmitting on the squadron's general frequency. "And here we stay."

"Yeah," Bishop groaned. "Our first real shot at payback, and we're benched. Typical."

"At least we got good seats for the show," Gangsta said, her spirits only slightly higher than theirs.

"Hey, don't want to sound, well, scared, but I kinda like it where we are," Cheddarboy confessed. "Beats being flushed. You just know they'll open a well."

"Commander?" Hunter called. "Any idea why the captain held us back?"

Angel hesitated. "Ladies, it's my fault."

"Your fault?" Hunter asked. "You piss him off or what?"

"That's nice of you, Captain, but you know damned well why we're back here. You can't tell me you haven't heard the rumors about me and Lieutenant Blair."

"I, uh, didn't want to bring that up, ma'am."

"Well, there it is," Angel said.

"Maybe Gerald thinks we won't fight aggressively either, since one of our own might be on that ship," Bishop added.

"You people tolerate Mr. Blair, but you wouldn't disobey orders to save his life. Gerald knows that. But me? Maybe I would." Angel pressed her head into her seat and shut her eyes. "Maybe I would."

"What are you talking about?" Gangsta cried. "He pulled us out of that well over Lethe. We owe him. And if we get a chance to save him now, then we should."

"Hey, I need this job," Bishop said. "And holy shit, people! They're opening a well!"

The voice of the *Olympus*'s NAVCOM AI resounded over the ship-wide intercom: "Attention. Attention. Jump interphase complete. Jump sequence engaged. Ship will reach Point of No Return Velocity in nine-point-zero-three minutes. All systems locked out. Ship is committed to the jump."

"Oh my god," Blair rasped, holding shaky aim on the commodore. "What have you done!"

"He's created the well," Maniac shouted from his seat on the deck. "You should've killed him!" With a shriek, Maniac jerked himself up and started for Paladin.

But a shot from the Marines glanced off the deck in front of Maniac, and he turned into a mannequin of himself, shifting just once to catch his balance.

Santyana swung his rifle toward the catwalk and sprayed the Marine who had fired. The jarhead staggered back as several rounds blasted off his armor. He dropped his rifle and collapsed.

Aristec's gaze swept across a bank of monitors, then something she saw there drained the confidence from her expression. She stared accusingly at Paladin. "A standard well? Five hundred meters? This won't . . ." She yanked the Pilgrim cross from her chain and fingered the center button. With a swish, the cross's long blade telescoped from its bottom. She drew back the cross, knife-end sticking from the bottom of her fist, and went for him. "You bastard!"

As Paladin raised an arm, the NAVCOM boomed again over a sudden squawking of alarms: "Warning. Error in second set jump coordinates. Suggest course correction immediately."

Aristee's blade came down on Paladin, but he deftly blocked her forearm with his own and seized the cross. "I've just opened a well that'll consume this ship."

"But I love you. We're paired. You told me you understood. You told me it was time to create a home."

"Warning. Error in second set jump coordinates," the NAVCOM droned on.

Aristee glanced to the drive control panel. "Input the coordinates. At least let us jump."

"I'm sorry." He threw her cross to the deck, shoved her back, then touched a comm control. "All hands, this is Brotur Taggart. I've just sent off an automatic message relaying our surrender. I suggest that all of you immediately abandon ship. We won't reach the gravity well's PNR for another eight minutes. That's all the time you have. I'll direct the NAVCOM to issue automatic clock reports." He paused, never looking more grim. "Save yourselves."

"They won't do it," Aristee said. "Not unless they hear it from me."

His hand shot out, locking her neck in the vice of his grip. "Then give the order."

"I won't. They pledged their lives to this rebellion. Now they'll make the sacrifice. And maybe that's our statement." He held her a moment more, then twisted away.

"Blair? Maniac? Mr. Santyana? Round up as many as you can and abandon ship."

"Finally an order that makes sense," Maniac grumbled, his palm still pressed firmly on his neck.

Aristee went to the main drive panel and stood there, once a woman who had gathered power and strength from the night, now a woman whose night had turned against her. For a second, Blair left himself and tried to touch her thoughts. Towers of fire and ice stood in his way. He did sense that she had no intention of leaving the ship, not only because she was its captain but because the well would embrace her in martyrdom.

Blair returned to himself and rushed up behind Paladin. "Sir?"

The commodore would not turn. "What is it?"

"Let's go."

"I'll meet you on the flight deck," he answered a little too quickly. "But here . . ." He removed his Pilgrim cross, then turned and proffered it to Blair. "In case I don't make it back."

"I can't."

Paladin tossed the cross, and Blair could not help but catch it. "You're my anchor, Mr. Blair."

"That why you took me along?"

"You've been pressing me about Pilgrim culture and history. So you got a look." He glanced to Karista, who had once more moved to brace Maniac. "And you met your pair. Now evacuate this area. That's an order." The commodore suddenly looked very old, very lost, sure of nothing.

Blair hoisted a painful salute and mumbled, "Aye-aye, sir."

"Looks like our Marine buddies know what's good for them," Santyana said, scanning the empty catwalk. "Maniac, can you move?"

"It's just a little hickey. Hurts like a mother, though. Let's throttle up."

After slipping Paladin's cross over his neck, Blair joined Santyana, Karista, and Maniac as they mounted the stairs. He glanced over his shoulder and saw Brotur Zimbaka scrutinizing them as he spoke with Aristee. Her gaze found Blair's for a second, then she regarded Zimbaka and shook her head.

"Our fighters are breaking off," Bishop noticed. "Can you say: *What?*"

If Angel had not heard the order herself, she would have had as much trouble believing it as the rest of her squadron. But Gerald had spoken the words himself, and Angel assumed that the *Fosubius*'s skipper had done likewise. "Commodore Taggart just relayed a message of the Pilgrims' unconditional surrender. It's over, ladies." Angel muted her headset's mike and breathed a tremendous sigh of relief. At least Paladin had survived, and if he was looking out for Blair, then maybe, just maybe . . .

But did he wait for me? Probably not.

But you didn't want him to wait.

You lied.

It had been a long time since Angel had seen so many starfighters operating in a single Area of Operations, and it had been even longer since she had seen so many engage in a synchronous withdrawal. Rapiers by the dozens banked or wheeled or looped back, away from the undulating target of darkness off the supercruiser's bow. Bombing groups broke into lazy turns to streak across the moon's pale white brilliance. The cap ships themselves framed this spectacle; the *Fosubius* stood a kilometer off to starboard, with its escorts spread out like the buoys of a fishing net, and the *Tiger Claw* lay to port, her tubes ready to open for a little cap-to-cap combat.

"Hey, mates, if they're surrendering, then why are they launching fighters?" Hunter asked.

"Maybe they're abandoning ship," suggested Gangsta.

"But what about that gravity well?" Cheddarboy asked. "That ship's going to jump."

Pilgrim Rapiers continued rocketing from the *Olympus*'s aft flight deck and forming into squadrons. They slowed as they grouped up, making it clear that they would not pursue the retreating Confederation fighters and bombers.

Then an unprovoked squadron of Confed Rapiers near the rear and closest to the Pilgrims turned tail, broke box formation, and vectored toward the enemy.

"Hello," Angel muttered. She quickly dialed up the *Claw* and had Gerald within seconds. "Got a squadron from the *Fosubius*—"

"We see them, Commander. They have no authorization to attack. That squadron commander is operating on his own."

"Sir?" Radar Officer Falk called in the background. "Second squadron joining in the attack."

"What's going on?" Angel demanded. "Those people have surrendered."

Neutron fire glittered in the distance, then two Rapiers, either Confederation or Pilgrim, exploded in a one-two punch, signaling the start of the battle.

A half dozen more Confederation squadrons took their cue and swung around toward their comrades. Angel scanned her communications menu, then touched to monitor the point squadrons' general frequency. Masked faces flashed on her VDU:

"They smoked Sly Honey!"

"Ladies and gentlemen, this is payback one-oh-one. Today we're going to teach you eight silent ways to toast a Pilgrim."

"Order to recall coming in."

"We've been provoked. You will ignore that order and defend yourselves at all costs."

Angel selected the squadron commander's private channel. The guy went by the moniker of "Tyrant," and if he had half a brain, he would listen. "Angel to Tyrant, copy?"

A web of scars lay over the man's cheeks and brow. He had been badly burned and probably couldn't afford a new face. At least his oxygen mask covered most of it. "Tyrant here. What do you want, Commander?"

"Break off your attack."

"Attack? We're on the defensive."

"Break off your attack!"

"You know the rules of engagement."

"I know 'em, and you broke 'em. They've surrendered."

"They had us locked on. We were targets."

"Of course they had you locked. Standard precaution. They didn't—"

"Look, lady, I don't have to justify this to you. Tyrant out."

"Son of a bitch," she whispered, then threw back her head.

"Ma'am?" Sinatra sounded over her private channel. "Gettin' hairy out there. What say we drift over and pop us a few Pilgrims?"

"Shut up," she yelled. "Just shut the hell up!"

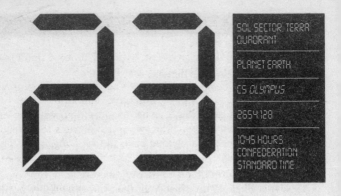

SOL SECTOR, TERRA
QUADRANT

PLANET EARTH

CS OLYMPUS

2654.128

1045 HOURS
CONFEDERATION
STANDARD TIME

"It'll take a couple of minutes to get everything online," Blair said as he tapped in a code on the *Diligent*'s ramp control panel. "But we can make it."

"In this bucket?" Maniac asked as he watched the ramp lower into place. "Where's my Rapier?" He pulled away from Karista and had retreated not more than a few steps when a half dozen Pilgrims whose sashes identified them as ordnance specialists shoved their way around him. They ignored Maniac's cursing, focusing intently on the troopships across the bay.

Blair looked past Maniac to a surreal image of blistering panic. Though many of the Pilgrims on board remained at their stations, there had to be two, maybe three hundred people screaming and crowding the ramps of those eight troopships, and Blair imagined a similar riot on the *Olympus*'s forward flight deck. The frenetic atmosphere left Blair feeling as panicked as the others. Somewhere across the bay, gunfire tore holes of silence in the commotion. More screams. And the chaos returned, mounting steadily toward a crescendo.

Just clear your head. Do the job. Fly them out.

"Most of them won't make it," Karista shouted, blinking to hold back the tears. "How many can we take?"

"Ten, fifteen at the most," Blair said. "But we have to save room for Santyana, his family, and the commodore."

"If they don't get their asses here soon, I'd go without 'em," Maniac said as he surveyed the swarm of Pilgrims for a second, then shook his head and headed back for the *Diligent*.

"Hey!" a young woman cried, clutching a boy of two or three. "Are you getting out? Can you take us?"

"Attention," came the NAVCOM AI's disembodied voice. "Ship will reach PNR velocity in four minutes."

Blair tensed as he studied the woman. "Get in."

"Thank you, Brotur. Thank you." She hustled past him.

"What're you gonna do, Blair? Make us too heavy to escape the well?" Maniac snarled. "Give me this!" He ripped the pistol from Blair's hand, then cocked his head toward the hold. "Get this bitch pre-flighted. I'm guarding the hatch."

Realizing that an argument would only waste time, Blair staved off his anger and shifted inside. "Karista?" he called back. "I need your help."

After making sure that the woman and child had found the crew cabin jump seats, Blair nervously tripped and banged his way to the bridge, where his trembling fingers drummed on touchpads at the helm and navigation stations. He swiveled a pair of screens closer and watched data bars flood and scroll with ship's status reports. Emergency warm-up and pre-flight in progress.

"What do want me to do?" Karista said, staring at the foreign landscape of flashing displays.

"Just get in that seat," Blair said, gesturing to the copilot's chair to starboard. "Panel there marked life support. Activate, select diagnostic, vital systems only."

She sat, lifted a hand. "Uh, okay."

"Hey, Merlin. I need you, too."

The old man coalesced from the flash of his activation and paced along the top of the navigation console. "*Now* I know how it is, Christopher. You only call when you want me to pick locks or when you're about to be atomized. You wouldn't just like to hang out some time and, as they say, shoot the breeze? No. I'm just a tool, a holographic helot."

"A what? Forget it. We'll talk about this later. Right now I need you to link to ship's systems. Monitor diagnostics and give the commands for emergency repairs as needed."

"Why do you need me for that? You can—"

Blair sprang from his seat.

"Where are you going?" Karista asked.

"This means a lot to him," Blair said, holding up Paladin's cross. "He's not coming back."

"And neither will you if you go after him."

"I owe him."

He ducked and wound his way toward the hold, feeling a definite rumble pass through all one hundred tonnes of the old errant.

"Attention. Ship will reach PNR velocity in three minutes."

An almost deafening discord filtered in from the open hatch. Troopship turbines warbled over the cursing, the shouting, the moans. As Blair drew closer, he saw that Maniac had backed himself up to the hatchway and now waved his pistol at a wall of fifty, sixty, maybe seventy-five Pilgrims, their faces burnished an angry red. "Let me out," Blair said.

Maniac ignored him, his attention commanded by the mob. "*I will shoot!*"

"Let us on, you bastard!" someone clamored. "You've got more room on this errant! The troopships are full! Don't let us die here!"

A round ricocheted off the hull, missing Maniac's shoulder by a finger's length.

"That's it," Maniac said, then ducked back into the hold and slapped his hand on the interior ramp control.

Seven or eight Pilgrims jumped onto the gangway as it angled up, hydraulics groaning under the added weight.

"Get off," Blair shouted. "It'll crush you."

A teenage boy and a heavyset woman of forty or so managed to pull their arms and legs completely onto the ramp and came sliding into the ship. Three more rioters slipped off and fell back into the crowd. Another two met the same fate, but the last man, a muscular blonde of about twenty, got his hands caught in the ramp as it began to seal into the hull. Blair looked away as the Pilgrim shrieked, bones crunched, and the severed appendages thumped to the deck.

Maniac jammed his pistol into the teenage boy's head. "You're going back out." Then he aimed at the lady. "So are you."

"Captain's quarters are back there," Blair told the two Pilgrims. "Get in and strap down."

"We got no reason to save them," Maniac said, so enraged that he nearly foamed at the mouth. He turned the pistol on Blair.

And for a moment, Blair felt the same. Here they were, saving four strangers, when Santyana and his family and the commodore were still out there. But how would those two get past the mob? Maybe Paladin could escape on the captain's launch. Maybe Santyana could catch a lift on one of the troopships in the forward deck.

That won't happen. You know that. You just want to make yourself feel better about abandoning them. You are abandoning them. And maybe it was fate that these four strangers got on board. Don't question it. Just go. Do the job.

More gunfire pinged off the sealed hatch. Footsteps rattled from the overhead.

"Christopher?" Merlin called, perched on the ramp's control. "Pre-flight is complete. Diagnostics complete. Impulse engines answering to commands. We're good to go, but I count nineteen Pilgrims on our hull. Two are trying to destroy our communications array. I should also point out that there is no response from the flight control officer; therefore, there is no flight order, and I've failed to locate the deck boss."

"Attention. Ship will reach PNR velocity in two minutes."

"So what about these two?" Maniac asked, leering at the boy and woman.

"We don't have time to lose them."

"You bastards are lucky. That's all I can say." Maniac spun back toward the corridor and small hatchway leading to the bridge. "Two minutes. Shit. Blair? You coming or what?"

"Go strap in," Blair repeated to their new passengers, then bounded after Maniac.

Save yourself.

Maybe I don't even want to anymore.

Santyana . . . Paladin . . . they're going to lose their lives. And for what? Does Aristee really know what she's done here? So many people have died . . . will die. It doesn't seem real.

Back on the bridge, Blair settled in at the helm and engaged the engines. Maniac had replaced Karista in the copilot's chair, and Blair motioned that she strap in at the navigator's seat behind them.

After the usual jolt, the *Diligent* rose off her landing skids, and Blair brought her around. The flight deck's environmental maintenance field panned into view.

"Most of the Pilgrims on our hull are jumping off," said Merlin, now standing atop Blair's console and facing the forward viewport. "But the two near the comm array are still up there."

"Let 'em stay there," Maniac said. "The energy field will waste 'em."

Two Broadsword bombers nearly collided as they flew abreast and blasted through the curtain. Three Rapiers bucked wildly from their berths and chopped their way through the bombers' turbulence. Two of those fighters swept through the field, but the third dipped too low and crashed nose-on into the angle where curtain met deck. Fuel ignited. Orange flames balled and erupted toward the overhead, flanked by steles of swirling black smoke— even as another pair of fighters plunged through the fire and escaped.

Resigned to the fact that no other ship would yield, Blair increased thrust, steered them onto the runway, then punched the bank of afterburners for launch.

Twin streaks of durasteel stole into view as two more Rapiers fled the deck, their pilots giving Maniac some competition for reckless flying.

Fifty meters. Twenty. Ten. The energy curtain abruptly wrapped the merchantman in an opaque blanket that as rapidly yielded to the gray, rectangular launch tunnel.

"Christopher?"

"Wait, Merlin!"

They cleared the tunnel, and never in his life had Blair been more glad to see an unremarkable field of stars. He felt suddenly cradled in their light—

Until the well extended one of its gravitic tentacles and slapped it on the merchantman. The engines quaked against the force, the bulkheads broke into their creaks of protest, and the velocity gauge began racing backward.

"C'mon, honey, you've done this before," Blair muttered. He glanced at an aft camera display showing the *Olympus* encompassed by the black pool. Small explosions blotted her port ion engine, and still more fighters fled from her bowels.

"If we can't escape the well, can you jump it?" Maniac asked. "Can you do your Pilgrim thing?"

"I don't know."

"Christopher?" Merlin cried, this time sounding more urgent.

"For God's sake, what is it?"

"I think we're going to—"

Everyone fell forward.

"—break free of the well."

Maniac howled in triumph.

"Did we make it?" Karista asked.

"Not yet," answered Merlin. "First we have to—"

"Take down the six bandits on our ass," Maniac finished. "Bearing four-four-one by three-three-five. Didn't the old man tell 'em we surrendered?" He rechecked the radar scope. "Great. Six more riding the rear."

"Get up to the ion gun," Blair said. "Merlin? See if you can get them on the comm. And try to hail Commodore Taggart. Maybe he got out."

Even as Maniac threw off his straps and stood, neutron fire raked its way from amidships to the bow, and Blair watched the shield level indicators drop into the red.

"Well, I've hailed those Rapiers three times," Merlin reported. "No response. And it's clear that every vessel that leaves the *Olympus* is a target. Our registration and Confederation ID code lack validity since this ship might have been captured by Pilgrims."

"Then contact the *Tiger Claw*. Get us an assist."

"Christopher, you're assuming these fighters aren't from the *Claw*."

"Well, are they?"

"As a matter of fact they're from the *Fosubius* battle group. But I don't think that makes a difference now."

"Just contact the *Claw*."

With that, Blair seized the control wheel and drove it toward the console, diving twenty, thirty, forty-five degrees as Maniac, up in the gunner's nest, hurled back the first of their retaliatory volleys. Four of the Rapiers buzzed overhead, their thrusters flickering as they looped back to begin another strafe.

Blair knew the math, and the math sucked. The *Diligent*'s maximum velocity peaked out at one hundred and fifty KPS, while the Rapier pilots could propel themselves up to three times as fast, and the fighters were, of course, more maneuverable and better armed.

He suddenly remembered a line Paladin was fond of, a line from a story called "The Open Boat," written six centuries ago by a fellow named Stephen Crane: "When it occurs to a man that nature does not regard him as important, and that she feels she would not maim the universe by disposing of him, he at first wishes to throw bricks at the temple, and he hates deeply the fact that there are no bricks and no temples."

"Request denied, Commander. Your squadron will maintain position. You will not engage. Gerald out."

It's all about politics now, Angel thought.

Gerald couldn't order her to attack other Confederation fighters. Never mind the fact that those pilots were killing Pilgrims trying to surrender. Never mind the fact that those pilots had provoked the Pilgrims into battle. Never mind the fact that Paladin and Blair could be on any one of those fleeing ships . . .

"Got a Proxima Errant on my scope," Bishop reported. "Looks like the *Diligent*, Commander. She's under attack."

Sorry, Mr. Gerald. Court-martial me later. "We're out of here, ladies. Fluid four to the *Diligent*. Break and attack on my mark, clearing zone and falling in to escort positions."

"Uh, ma'am, are you asking us to fire upon Confederation pilots?" Cheddarboy asked.

Bishop guffawed. "No, boy, she's askin' us out to lunch."

"Commodore Taggart may very well be aboard that merchantman," Angel told Cheddarboy. "Those pilots don't seem to care about that."

"Yes, ma'am."

"Burn on my mark," she instructed. "Three, two, one. Burn!"

Hurled forward by full afterburners, Angel braced herself and skimmed each of her displays. Gerald's wonderful mug snapped on the left VDU, which she summarily snapped off, imagining his you're-abandoning-your-post-and-if-you-do-not-return-blah-blah-blah rant that meant absolutely nothing to her at the moment.

She led the other five pilots toward that merchantman, opening her mouth a little as she saw it dive and fall under the relentless cannon fire of a dozen trailing fighters. Someone manned the ion gun, swiveling in an abortive effort to track the attackers. The operator finally got off a shot that sheered off a Rapier's wing and punched it into a spiraling climb.

"Here we go, ladies," she began, then kissed her career goodbye. "Break and attack!"

Bishop and Hunter responded immediately, peeling away and booting off guided missiles.

Although Cheddarboy and Gangsta hesitated a second, they pledged themselves to Angel by showering two of the Rapiers with concentrated blasts of neutron fire.

The veteran Sinatra banked hard and came around on the *Diligent*'s six o'clock to simultaneously launch two dumbfire missiles at nearly point-blank range. No, he hadn't directed his fire at the merchantman, but at two Rapiers whose pilots were obviously too intent on their strafe. They flew in a tight pair, just a couple of meters off each other's wings.

"Ouch," Sinatra said dryly as the two fighters vaporized in a rolling carpet of contiguous explosions.

Another Rapier sliced across Angel's cone of fire, and she banked on a wall of vacuum to follow. A guided missile veered after the Rapier, accelerated at the last second, then jammed itself up the fighter's port exhaust cone. She grimaced as sophisticated machinery became scorched scrap metal. Then the strange absence of blips on her radar scope drew her attention. Six blue dots appeared on the display, with a quartet of enemy contacts shifting off to port.

"The rest are buggin'," Gangsta said. "Descending to escort position."

"All of you shift to escort." Angel turned on a wing and thundered off to catch up with the merchantman. She opened a comm channel, general frequency. "Angel to *Diligent*, copy."

Blair appeared on her Visual Display Unit, and suddenly his absence felt more like years than weeks. He looked somewhat leaner, his face more haggard, more lined, his hair a little longer than she preferred. What was with that robe? And hadn't he lost his Pilgrim cross? "Commander," he said stiffly. "Lieutenant Marshall and I have five civilians on board."

"Marshall's alive?"

The blond jock shoved Blair away from the camera. "Lieutenant Todd 'Maniac' Marshall back from the dead, *ma'am!*"

"You would've liked your memorial service, Maniac. Lot of women were there. What did you do? Score with half the crew?"

"Those days are behind me."

"Really."

"Is Zarya with you? I can't find her private channel."

"Commander?" Bishop said, breaking into the link. "Check out the supercruiser."

Angel looked to starboard, where nearly a kilometer away the grand capital ship seemed to cower before the faceless black head of the well.

"Hey, Commander? I asked you a question," Maniac said. "Is Zarya with you?"

Blair pulled up a telescopic image of the supercruiser. He held his breath as she soared at Point of No Return velocity toward a gravitic winter storm consuming thousands of metallic leaves. Its power ghastly, breathtaking, even beautiful, the gravity well marked an ebony dimple in a sheet of space otherwise illumined by Earth's pale blue glow.

"She cut the transmission," Maniac cried, scowling from the copilot's chair. "You believe that? I think something's happened to Zarya."

"The *Olympus* has reached the jump point," Merlin said. "In about five seconds it'll tear apart just like that Snakeir we baited into Scylla. And still no word from Commodore Taggart. I'm continuing to hail on all frequencies." He cocked a thumb back at the viewport. "Our capital ships are opening tubes. If the well doesn't get the *Olympus*, the torpedoes will."

Scores of white lines stretched from the string of Confederation ships and crossed each other's trajectories in a patchwork of residue that needled on toward the supercruiser. So startling was the image of the well, the fleeing ship, and the horde of pursuing torpedoes that Blair had trouble watching.

Paladin's not on board. He's not.

The *Olympus* began pulsating with light, as though waves of gravity lapped at her bending and coruscating hull. Her wedge-shaped bow seemed to tuck itself in, and her mountainous super-structure began to flatten toward her antimatter guns, as though she shied from the enormity of her fate.

And then . . .

. . . with a blinding flare that enveloped her from bow to stern . . .

She jumped the well and vanished.

Blair stared dumbstruck at his display. "They jumped."

"They what?" Maniac asked.

"They jumped. They weren't torn apart. They jumped the goddamned well."

"Son of a bitch! Taggart lied to us! The bastard lied!"

SOL SECTOR, TERRA
QUADRANT

PLANET EARTH

CS CONCORDIA

2654.130

0800 HOURS
CONFEDERATION
STANDARD TIME

Blair and Maniac stood at parade rest in the *Concordia*'s wardroom. They had been debriefed by Captain Gerald back on the *Tiger Claw*, had submitted their After Action Reports to Admiral Tolwyn only a few hours prior, and had just completed a verbal defense of those reports to the admiral, to Commodore Bellegarde, and to Space Marshal Gregarov. The questions had been probing, and many had concerned Paladin. Blair had repeatedly felt the need to qualify his answers, but Bellegarde or Gregarov would lean forward in their chairs and cut him off before he could fully explain. It seemed that at least two of his inquisitors had already condemned the commodore.

As had Maniac.

Blair had insisted that his wingman remain as unbiased as possible and only report the facts—which Maniac had done until the concluding paragraph of his report, wherein he offered his own scathing critique of Paladin's actions. Worse still, Maniac had refused to show Blair the report before submitting it, and only during the meeting had Blair learned of the incendiary notes. Blair decided that once they were outside in the corridor, he would throttle Maniac to within a heartbeat of his life, then tear him that new breathing hole he had promised while back on the *Olympus*.

"Well, then, lieutenants. Do you have anything to add?" Tolwyn's gray eyes wore a noticeable sheen, and while the admiral had carefully guarded his tone during most of the meeting, his words now rang sullenly.

"No, sir," Maniac replied.

Blair cleared his throat. "Sir, since you have accepted Lieutenant Marshall's report, which contains his opinion of Commodore Taggart's character, I respectfully request a moment to offer my own observations."

"We're concerned with the facts, Mr. Blair. Nothing more."

"I know that, sir. And I understand that you might consider my opinion biased because I'm half Pilgrim, but I deserve an opportunity to speak."

Gregarov raised a hand at Tolwyn. "Go ahead, Lieutenant."

"I haven't known the commodore for very long, but I've never met a man more loyal or one with a clearer sense of mission. Whatever happened out there, I'm certain that it's in the best interests of the Confederation. You can't ignore the commodore's reputation for reliability—and loyalty. Don't condemn him before you really know what happened. That's all."

The admiral fixed Blair with a hard gaze. "Lieutenant, according to your own report, Commodore Taggart was the only one who could've programmed that hopper drive. He had locked everyone else out of the system. His orders were to seize control of that vessel and return it to the Confederation. By feeding in those jump coordinates, the commodore committed an act of treason—one for which he will be executed."

"Sir, you don't know if that was an act of treason."

"He had the opportunity to deliver the ship to us," Gregarov said with a raised finger. "He could have shut down the drive. He did not. We have no choice but to regard him as a traitor and fugitive."

"But you don't know the whole story."

Tolwyn stood. "Thank you for those thoughts, Mr. Blair. We'll need to meet with you again in the next few days. You'll be taken off your roster until our inquiry is complete. Dismissed."

◆   ◆   ◆

Blair waited until he and Maniac were about twenty meters from the wardroom hatch, then he whirled, took Maniac's neck in his grip, dug a thumb into the bandage covering Maniac's flesh wound, then drove the skinny jock into the bulkhead. "Do you know what you just did?"

"Let . . . go!" Even with both hands locked around Blair's wrist, Maniac could not break free

"When they find him, they're going to execute him."

"Good," Maniac wheezed.

Tearing his hand away, Blair swore then pounded down the corridor.

"Hey, Chris? He chose the Pilgrims. Deal with it."

"We don't know that."

"You mean you don't have any doubts? Come on . . ."

Blair rounded a corner—and nearly ran into Angel. "I got tired of waiting around that hatch, so I went and got something to eat," she explained.

"It's your time. You didn't have to come." He leaned on the bulkhead and lowered his head. "They've made up their minds."

"They're doing what they have to do, but I know. I know." She reached to touch his chin but suddenly withdrew. "We should get back, otherwise you'll miss saying good-bye to Karista."

"Nothing happened between us."

"Why do you keep saying that?"

"I just want you to know."

"It's all right. I didn't want you to wait for me."

"But I did."

She shifted away and tossed her hair back. "They're going to interrogate Karista like you wouldn't believe. Then they'll ship her off to an interment camp. You okay with that?"

"We're talking about us."

"You two are paired."

"Whoa," he said, recoiling, then backhanding sweat from his brow. "You two comparing notes or what?"

"I could sense there was a connection between you two, so I asked her. She didn't want to tell me, but she did."

"It doesn't matter."

"Yes, it does."

Blair closed his eyes and touched Angel's cheek with his thoughts. He moved down to her neck, feeling her bow into his touch. Then in one eager motion, he took her into his arms and kissed her deeply, fully, gently. He finally pulled back, let their lips linger a moment, then opened his eyes. "You don't know me. Not really. Give me a chance to show you."

When he opened his eyes he found her pale and astonished. "How did you—"

"The spaces between us mean nothing," he said, closing her lips with a finger. "We're fighters. Let's fight for this."

"Oh, God," Maniac said, suddenly behind them. "Why don't you two get a room?"

Angel glared. "How long have you been standing there, Lieutenant?"

He tapped his chest: *Me?* "Enough lollygagging. I gotta get back to see Tibby in the quartermaster's office. He's picked up a little something for Zarya that might cheer her up. She's still bummed out. It's not like no one's ever lost a fighter before. So she lost one on her first tour. So what. She's alive, right?"

"She got lucky over Triune. But her luck won't hold. It never does," Angel said. "She'll be off the duty roster for another week. And she won't be back in a Rapier until she proves herself on the simulator."

"With me as her instructor? No problemo."

Blair snickered. "I got a feeling your lessons won't involve flying."

Maniac winked. "She's a quick study. Just like you."

Amity Aristee forced herself up, out of her command chair. "Brotur Vyson?"

He read her expression. "Aye, Captain. I have the con."

She left the *Olympus*'s bridge with a deep sense of dread that slowed her pace. She barely acknowledged others in the lift and corridors as she steered herself toward her quarters. There, she regarded the hatch control as though it were a warning sign and lazily keyed in the code. The door hissed aside, and she felt her way through the shadows toward a flickering light that outlined her bedroom hatch. She took a deep breath, braced herself, then pushed in the door.

James Taggart sat up in her bed and leaned back on an ornate trioak headboard. Were it not for his scowl, he would appear almost angelic, framed by the leafy designs carved into the rare wood. A lone blue candle as thick as his wrist sat on an equally ornate nightstand, and in that poor light he had been reading hard copies of ancient star charts which now littered the deck and sheets. He acknowledged her presence with a meager glance.

"James, you've been in this bed for two days. You have to get up. You have to eat something."

"No."

"You're brooding like a child. You made your choice. You chose blood. Just like your father did. Now it's time to move on." She stepped toward the bed, then toed off her sandals.

"Move on? To what? We've lost nearly half the crew and we're operating on one ion engine. It's only a matter time before we make a wrong jump."

"If you're so certain that we're going to get caught, then why did you change your mind?"

He just looked at her, as though he didn't know himself.

She shook her head, undid her sash, and let her robe slink to the floor. She slid naked into bed and rested her head on his chest. "We can't get caught," she whispered, tracing his navel with a pearly fingernail. "And we can't die . . . because there's too much war left to fight."

PETER TELEP came wet and screaming into the world over three decades ago. He received a large portion of his education in New York, spent a number of years in Los Angeles, then returned east to Florida, where he finally earned his undergraduate and graduate degrees and now teaches composition and creative writing courses at the University of Central Florida.

While out west, he tricked people into believing he was a talented screenwriter and actually worked for such television shows as *In the Heat of the Night* and *The Legend of Prince Valiant*. Once producers discovered that Telep was a novelist, they booted him and his desire for creative control out of there.

Mr. Telep's novels include the *Squire Trilogy*, two books based on Fox's *Space: Above and Beyond* television show, a trilogy of novels based on the best-selling computer game *Descent*, and this, the third of four books in the film-based *Wing Commander* series. You may e-mail him at PTelep@aol.com. But be warned. He *will* sucker you into writing reviews of this novel at various online bookstores.

BE
MATURE

An expository study of
The Epistle of James

Warren W. Wiersbe

This book is designed for your personal
reading pleasure and profit. It is also designed for group study. A leader's guide
with helps and hints for teachers and
visual aids (Victor Multiuse Transparency
Masters) is available from your local book-
store or from the publisher.

VICTOR BOOKS
a division of SP Publications, Inc.
WHEATON. ILLINOIS 60187

Offices also in Fullerton, California • Whitby, Ontario, Canada • Amersham-on-the-Hill, Bucks, England

Other books by Dr. Wiersbe are:
Be Complete (Colossians)
Be Faithful (1, 2, Timothy, Titus)
Be Free (Galatians)
Be Joyful (Philippians)
Be Mature (James)
Be Real (1 John)
Be Ready (1 and 2 Thessalonians)
Be Rich (Ephesians)
Be Right (Romans)
Meet Yourself in the Parables
Meet Your King (Matthew)

Eighth printing, 1981

Scripture quotations in this book are from the Authorized (King James) Version unless otherwise noted. Other quotations are from *The New American Standard Bible* (NASB), © 1960, 1962, 1963, 1968, 1971, 1973 by The Lockman Foundation, La Habra, Calif.; *The New International Version: New Testament* (NIV), © 1973 by The New York Bible Society; *The New Scofield Reference Bible* (SCO), © 1967 by The Delegates of the Oxford University Press, Inc., New York; *The New Testament in Modern English* (PH), © 1958, by J. B. Phillips, The Macmillan Company; *The New Testament in the Language of the People* by Charles B. Williams (WMS), © 1966, Moody Press, Chicago, Ill.

Library of Congress Catalog Card Number: 78-52558
ISBN: 0-88207-771-6

VICTOR BOOKS
A division of SP Publications, Inc.
P. O. Box 1825 • Wheaton, Illinois 60187